THE WATER

NANCY JACKSON

As always I must dedicate my work to my family. Being a wife and mother has been the greater pleasure of my life.

I want to dedicate this book as well to my greater cheerleader and publicist, Mickey Bunal. Here enduring energy and excitement has blown me through some doubtful clouds as a new author. There are not enough words to thank you for what you constantly do for me.

To Angela Westerman who creates my original book covers and graphics. Thank you for 'getting me'! Look her up and hire her for yourself at AKOrganicAbstracts.com

CONTENTS

Chapter 1	1
Chapter 2	3
Chapter 3	26
Chapter 4	40
Chapter 5	52
Chapter 6	69
Chapter 7	95
Chapter 8	117
Chapter 9	134
Chapter 10	154
Chapter 11	172
Chapter 12	194
Chapter 13	216
Chapter 14	238
Chapter 15	254
Chapter 16	274
Chapter 17	293
Chapter 18	318
Chapter 19	337
Chapter 20	358
Chapter 21	380
Chapter 22	386
Authors Note	393
About the Author	395

CHAPTER 1

The water was cold. It had slapped her face and had taken her breath away when he'd plunged her head underneath. The hands gripped her hair tightly and she could not resist the force he used to hold her head underwater.

Her arms and legs flailed about in an effort to land on the object of her resistance. The need to breathe fresh air deep into her lungs mounted a fire inside them. She could feel the hands firm against her skull, but their lack of confidence was unveiled by the slight tremor which she felt vibrating through her body.

Odd how she could notice such things at this moment which she knew to be her last. It had to be the adrenaline that surged through her body making her acutely aware of all things, such as his smell. It was a strong body odor masked by cheap big box store after shave.

Finally, her body could fight no more and it relaxed, taking in the water that it had fought so hard to refuse. Peace came at last as her body slumped and her limbs went limp. He no longer had to fight to hold her head underwater.

It was done now. He released her hair, letting her head fall. Stepping back, the realization that he had once again failed, hit him hard. She was not clean; she was dead.

CHAPTER 2

It had been three months since Randy Jeffries and Carrie Border turned the Senna Carter murder case over to the district attorney. The broken ribs that Carrie had received from a bar night out gone wrong were healed and she could even complete her workout regime faithfully each day now, when she had the desire to do so.

But the internal trauma remained and taunted her every day. As she sat at her desk, she once again remembered that at her lowest point it was easy to resolve that her life must change, but somehow in the light of a new day, it seemed much harder to do.

On the day of her parents' death eight and a half years earlier her life had changed in an instant. The news had sucked the life out of her. And without the slightest effort on her part her life, personality, and priorities had all changed.

Now that she wanted her life to change for the better, she seemed powerless to make it happen. She thought of the shame that surrounded her when she was forced to tell others how she had wound up beaten and broken. Self-hatred was her constant friend and had dampened her spunky spirit.

The bruises of the beating and sharp pain of the broken bones had been replaced for a few weeks by the abusive workout routine she had instituted on her own. She herself wasn't even sure if it was a form of self-punishment or merely an attempt to distract herself from the mental anguish she couldn't escape.

But her strenuous workout routine had not lasted, and she was feeling the overwhelming pull of her old life. She knew if she would just relax her resolve even the slightest, she would be completely back where she had been months ago.

"Good morning," said Randy as he walked up to their adjoining desks.

"Good morning," Carrie replied.

Randy smiled at her. It had been a hard year so far, but their working relationship had not only survived, but grown stronger. The bond was tighter and even though they both felt it, they never spoke of it.

"Did you have a good weekend?" Carrie asked Randy.

A carousel of emotions flickered across Randy's face.

He was thinking the entire weekend over in a flash, to determine an appropriate response before answering.

Carrie smiled. Randy was a thinker, and the play of various emotions his face displayed was the external indicator that his mind was not only thinking of how he had felt now about different stages of the weekend's events, but how he felt during them. Not until he had weighed all events, would he determine the overall outcome of the weekend.

With a slight outward puff of air he replied, "Overall, I would say it was good."

"Anything better with you and Sandy?"

Randy nodded. The thought of his and Sandy's separation was still sharp. "We're talking. She's been going to church and wants me to go with her to a marriage group."

Carrie was considering how to respond. She didn't know what the best thing for them was and had no basis in her own life to give relationship advice. She certainly had no advice about church, as she hadn't gone to church since she was very young.

When she didn't respond, Randy continued, "I love her and want our marriage to work, but I have never enjoyed going to church, and I'm not sure I want them meddling in my life."

"Is there any other option? Like maybe just a licensed counselor?" Carrie thought that sounded safer than airing one's dirty laundry to a group of judgmental church people.

"I've asked her, but she is convinced that this is the best way."

"Oh. Well, what are you going to do?" Carrie asked.

"Not sure yet. Still thinking," said Randy.

The sharp ringing of Carrie's cell phone startled her back to the office and the work surrounding her.

"Hello," answered Carrie.

"Hey there gorgeous." It was Mike Brown's smooth voice coming over her phone line. He was a detective with the Oklahoma City Police Department. A year or so earlier, while working a case together, they had gotten close. But when the case ended, so had their little tryst.

"Hmm, it's you." Carrie was grinning. She loved flirting with Mike, but somehow the fun of it all seemed tainted since her attack. Her chair groaned as she leaned back to listen. *Would he get to the point or continue to flirt,* she wondered.

Randy could tell who it was just by Carrie's body language and the sound of her voice. He was in total opposition to their breaking protocol during a case. When it had ended, he was glad it had not come back to damage both her career and the case.

"Well, we have a case they have asked us to bring the Oklahoma State Bureau of Investigation in. Are you where you can come to a crime scene now?" said Mike.

All business, Carrie leaned forward now on guard and said, "Yes. Text me the address." She was already standing and reaching for her keys when she heard the phone go silent. Looking at Randy she motioned in a nod towards the door.

"That was Mike. They want us at a crime scene."

IF THEY HAD NOT HAD to fight the reconfiguration of the Centennial Parkway and I-44 crossing, they would have made it to the scene in only ten minutes.

As they approached the crime scene, the rectangular spires of the Chesapeake Boat House rose before them. Carrie remembered that just a few short years ago this area was a neglected and almost unliveable area.

The small houses were so ramshackle and decrepit that it was hard to believe they were in the middle of a prosperous city. This part of town had always felt creepy to Carrie, too.

She didn't get scared, she would be any good at her job if she did, but there had been something that had just felt evil to her in this part of town. Of course that was long before those in charge had decided to make it a shining facet in this jewel of a city.

Tucked underneath the eastbound I-40 overpass just west of I-35 was a crew of Oklahoma City police offers, crime investigators, a medical examiner, and a few other necessary individuals.

At the end of a manmade canal feeding from the Oklahoma River there was a body. Carrie could see Rick

Morris, a detective with the Oklahoma City Police Department, gesturing with his blue gloved hands, to Mike.

"It's not an easy place to get to," said Randy as they walked the long distance from where they had to park. The noise was almost deafening underneath the busiest highway intersection in Oklahoma. Carrie just nodded to avoid having to yell a comment back to her partner.

Rick turned towards them as they walked up and without thinking, used his shirtsleeve to wipe his sweaty brow, still keeping the blue gloves away from contamination.

"What were you two discussing so animatedly?" asked Carrie.

Rick shook his head and snapped off his blue gloves apparently finished with them. He looked at the two OSBI agents with a concerned look, two quick beats before speaking.

"I hate to say it, but this looks and feels like another bad one. I don't think this will be a one-off murder. I just have that feeling in my gut. Mike disagrees," said Rick.

"We can't know that for sure yet. I just don't want to jump to conclusions until we know more," said Mike.

"We were wondering why a single murder in your jurisdiction would warrant calling us," said Randy. "What have we got?"

"White female, mid-twenties. Appears to have been drowned, but we won't know for sure until the medical examiner is done. She is wet from the shoulders up where she was apparently submerged in the water over there near the end of the canal." Rick was reading from his notes and stopped to gesture to where the body had been found.

"She is blonde and approximately 115 pounds. She is dressed as if she was out clubbing, but honestly her clothes don't look like some rich girl out on the town. Her clothes are very worn and shabby. Her high heels are old and scuffed." Rick took a breath and looked at Randy and Carrie.

"Could she have tripped and fell in and maybe it was an accident?" asked Carrie.

"Nah. I don't think so. What would she be doing down here? No, no reason I can think of. This is just drainage and overflow for the river," Mike responded.

"My opinion is that she is a working girl, and it all went bad. He either brought her here for privacy or brought her here on purpose to kill her," said Rick.

Carrie stepped aside as the gurney approached with the covered body. They slowed as she motioned for them to stop. She took a breath and held it to prepare herself to see this young girl, once vibrant with life, now cold and void.

As she gently and respectfully pulled back the sheet, the matted and wet blonde hair sat haphazardly around her pretty face. Even in death it was easy to see that she had been beautiful.

Carrie replaced the sheet and motioned for them to continue on. Sadness over the ending of this precious life settled in. It was that sadness that would drive her to find who did this. Soon it would be replaced with die hard anger and determination, and she would use it to find the killer.

As the body continued on to the transport vehicle, the four of them went to where the body had been found. Tall weeds, dry now from the hot August heat and lack of rain, lay strewn and windblown. Trash was everywhere.

Carrie looked from where she stood and carefully did a 360-degree turn looking for something, anything that might help lead her to the perpetrator. Nothing, she could determine from there.

The water's edge was concrete at this point. This was a manmade canal that fed from the river. The ground was now dry, but it was easy to see where it had become wet and where the ground had been disrupted in a struggle.

"I don't think she went willingly," said Carrie. "The ground over here is a horrible mess." She motioned for the guys to come closer.

"I would bet this is where her feet were digging into the ground as she tried to gain a foothold. And here," she walked closer to the edge and slightly to the side. "He could have been here, and these indentions were where he was digging in with his knees or feet to press her hard into the water."

Mike squatted down by her and gently moved the flattened grass aside with his gloved hand looking, hoping. Finally he stood and snapped off his gloves too.

His brow was deeply furrowed as he looked around. "Hopefully forensics will turn up something. Let's see if we can find out who this girl is and find out more about her."

The four of them walked up the slope towards where they had parked. They were solemn, and each one was looking around as they walked, hoping to find even the smallest of clues. But the debris of countless passerby's was everywhere, so who could know what was relevant? It would take more time than one might want to take to sift through all of this, but they would.

Once back at their cars Carrie began, "Well, what is the plan?" She was shielding her eyes from the sun. She needed her cap to keep the sun from coming in through the tops of her sunglasses, but had forgotten to bring it.

"We'll have Sylvia gather missing persons as usual," began Rick. "Then get with the coroner."

"Let us know when they do the autopsy and we'll be there," said Randy.

"Will do," replied Rick.

They all turned to make their way out from under the overpass and loaded up in their respective vehicles.

Carrie was deep in thought. Her mind raced through a variety of reasons why this girl would have been murdered. Of course, she quickly realized that the list was virtually endless, and until they knew more about this girl, there was no way to narrow that list down.

"Are you up for a little detour?" asked Randy.

Carrie looked over at her partner wondering what he was up to. "Sure."

Randy pulled the car onto Reno Ave. and headed east

a few blocks. At a rundown shanty of a place with an old neon sign out front that said Lulus, he pulled in and parked.

Carrie snorted a laugh. "Where have you brought me?" She leaned forward to get a better view of the front of the building through the windshield.

Randy opened his car door, so Carrie did likewise. Just once, Carrie wished her job would take her to somewhere really nice like the Petroleum Club for an elegant evening out, rather than one more below the belly bar. *But then I feel right at home in a bar, don't I*, she thought.

The parking lot had been graveled, but over time the gravel had been pushed deep into the mud and huge holes and dips had formed. The building looked as though it might fall down at any moment. There were literally patches of random wood boards and sheets of tin nailed all along the front in what appeared to be an attempt at repairs.

Carrie wrinkled her nose and put her wrist up to block the stench. "What is that awful smell?" Her head was swiveling from right to left to locate the violator.

Randy's nose was wrinkled up too even though little got to him. She followed him as he walked to the side of the building where the odor grew stronger. As they turned the corner, a hoard of flies assaulted them.

"Whoa!" Carrie stepped back quicker than she had stepped in and was flinging her hands and arms wildly to fight off her attackers. She turned and ran back to the car where only a few dedicated flies followed.

She stood by the car still swatting when she saw Randy come around the corner. "What on earth was back there?" Carrie asked.

"A dead dog."

Carrie's mouth fell open. "Are you kidding me? Who wouldn't know it was there and not move it? I can't believe it's good for business." She looked up and around. "If there is any business."

"There is," said Randy as he headed for the front door. He tugged on the knob but it was locked, so he pounded.

"Hey Lenny, you in there?" Randy stopped to listen, but heard nothing, so he pounded and called again.

"What are we here for?" asked Carrie.

"I have a hunch."

"A hunch," mumbled Carrie. The smell of the dead dog was still strong and making her feel sick to her stomach.

The squeak of the rusty hinge brought both Randy and Carrie to life as the door came open an inch or two. "What you want?" It was an old voice, a man's voice.

"Hey Lenny, it's Randy."

"Randy?" The voice asked.

"Yes Randy Jeffries, with the OSBI."

The door inched open a little further and a fluff of gray hair peeked through, then a wrinkled face with wise eyes. The eyes frowned at Randy, then recognition surfaced and a smile crossed the old face.

"Randy. I remember. Come on in." The door opened wide and Randy and Carrie followed the old guy into an almost pitch dark room. The only lights were a few neon beer signs. The old man led them to a round table after flipping on a light over the bar.

"Lenny did you know you had a dead dog over on the east side of your building?" asked Randy.

The man stopped before sitting and shook his head at Randy. "Nope. Could be my old Jonas. I ain't seen him in a day or two. I called and put out food, but I don't get around so good anymore, so I didn't go out looking for him." The old man's eyes grew sad, and he pulled out the chair to sit. He was studying the edge of the table lost in thought somewhere else.

Carrie thought he could have just woken up. His feathery gray hair was tousled on his balding head. He had on a pair of faded overalls with only one strap up on his shoulder over a thin white undershirt, and no shoes.

Lenny sat for a moment staring at his clasped hands laying on the table before him. Both Randy and Carrie wondered about the dog. *Was it a long-time companion or a stray? Should they offer to help dispose of the remains?* Then Lenny seemed to recover and looked up at Randy.

Almost as if he was reading their minds he spoke, "He was an old stray that came by several months ago. I didn't want to take him in, but he kept hanging around. After a few days I noticed how thin he was, so I put out scraps for him. That's all. I'd put out scraps and water each evening and he would eat and go lay back in the back of the lot under the tree."

"Do you want us to help you dispose of him?" Randy asked half hoping Lenny would say no.

Lenny shook his head, "No. I got an old boy that helps me out around here. I'll have him do it." Then as if realizing for the first time he had two OSBI agents sitting in his bar, he looked up at Randy and asked, "What brings you by here?"

"We found a young girl, think she may be a working girl, under the overpass by the river. I thought she may have passed by here." Randy pulled out his phone and pulled up the picture of the dead girl's face. He put the phone over where Lenny could look.

For the second time in less than ten minutes, Carrie saw the old man's face grow sad. He nodded. "That's Cami."

Randy pulled the phone back and got out his pad to take notes. He wrote the name Cami and then looked up at Lenny. "How do you know her?"

"Well, you know that a lot of the girls who work this area come by here from time to time. I used to do what I could to help them out if they needed something, or were scared.

"I'm older now and the ones who really knew me have mostly died or gone from the life. But they have passed my name down. If you need help, go to Lenny."

"What can you tell us about her?" asked Carrie.

Lenny's face was far away as he pulled thoughts of Cami to the forefront of his memory. "She was a pretty one. Most are, but she was a real beauty. She could have been a model or a movie star. Young too. I don't think she had been around here more than a year, maybe two." Lenny looked up at Randy.

"Do you know who she hung out with? Was she under someone's protection?"

"Yeah, she came by here with another girl named Jenny. I think they are both with Gus." The disgust on Lenny's face was palpable. He rubbed his hands together as his mouth twisted.

"Do you know where we might find Jenny?" asked Carrie.

Lenny took a minute to think then nodded, "I think they are staying over with a lady called Pride."

"Pride?" asked Carrie. She thought she had surely heard him wrong.

"Yeah, Pride. Long story on that one. She's had that nickname since she started walking. Rumor is that even doing what she had to do, she still kept her pride. She's too old to be out now, but likes to help the girls when she can. Gus is okay with it as long as she doesn't try to pull 'em out."

"Where can we find Pride?" asked Randy.

Lenny gave him an address close to his bar and Randy jotted it down in his pad. "Anything else Lenny that you can tell us? Do you know of anyone who would want to kill Cami? Anyone who would want to hurt her?"

As Lenny shook his head he said, "Nah. No one I can think of. If I do, I'll call ya."

Randy scooted his card across the table to Lenny and

stood up. The chair screeched and skittered across the woodend floor, and in the room's quiet the noise seemed to put an edge to the air.

Carrie's eyes had adjusted to the dark and as she stood she took in the surroundings. An old window unit worked hard on one wall to push cold air into the room. Old metal signs and posters completely covered the walls, some so old and faded it was difficult to tell what they had once said.

Wood booths lined two walls with round tables in the middle. The bar spanned the back wall and was like almost any old bar in any old joint in town. She personally knew this for a fact.

They shook Lenny's hand and walked out into the light. The smell reminded them that the dog was still around the corner and was still dead. They both hurried to get in the car.

As a matter of habit Carrie cranked up the AC as soon as the engine turned over and Randy just shook his head. He could remind her yet again that until the engine cooled a bit, the AC air would be hot, doing no good to turn it up, but he didn't. She always did that, and he always said that. It was time for a change.

"So how do you know Lenny?" asked Carrie.

"When I was at the OKCPD, we became very familiar. He was younger and his place was much more active back then. He kept his nose clean, but the bar attracted a lot of people up to no good. Lenny always had a heart to help them out. He didn't condone what they did, but he cared about them. Rare if you ask me."

"The bar looks like it is about to fall down," said Carrie.

"Yeah, it never was a place to go because of its looks. The people who've always gone there are those who are up to no good. They go there knowing they are so far out of the way that they are safe. There are a few neighborhood people too, that stop in after work for a drink, or ten.

"Through the years though, as Lenny has aged, he doesn't have the strength, energy, or money, I would assume, to keep the place going. Also, the younger crowd have other places they frequent. I wasn't sure he would know this girl, but I thought I'd take a chance."

"He seems like a sweet old man," said Carrie. "They all need someone to care."

JENNY SAT on the back porch step of Pride's old run-down house and fiddled with a thread of tobacco. It had stuck to her lip from her cigarette and rather than toss it; she had rolled it between her fingers. She was on edge and fidgety.

Dropping the bit of tobacco, she lifted the cigarette to her mouth and took another long draw. A tear ran down her cheek. She knew something bad had happened to Cami, and she was terrified.

The back door creaked as Pride's large frame stepped through and onto the porch. She lumbered over to the rickety chair and squeezed herself in.

Once Pride had had a natural reason to feel pride. She had once been a stunning beauty, but that was a long time ago. Age had not treated her well, or maybe it had been her lifestyle, or maybe both.

The woman who looked back at her in the mirror now had a face lined with wrinkles and hair that was so thin it was almost non-existent.

Someone had told her once that pride comes before a fall. She had only laughed then, thinking them a religious fanatic, or just crazy. Well, if that saying was ever true, it was true now. Not one thread of her former beauty remained.

"Have you heard from Cami yet?" Pride asked Jenny.

Jenny looked up at Pride, winced, then looked away. "Nah."

There was a sensation down in Pride's gut that told her something bad was afoot and that Cami had stepped right into it.

"Have you talked to Gus?" asked Pride.

Jenny just shook her head.

"He won't like it that she hasn't come home. He'll think she ran away." Pride looked into the ragged backyard and wished it were pretty and tranquil.

"I know something bad happened to her," said Jenny. "I know it sounds crazy, but I feel it."

"Me too," agreed Pride.

"Should we go to the cops?" asked Jenny.

"No. They'll come to us. If we call them to hunt for her, they won't. They never go looking for people like us. If she turns up, we will know when they show up at our doorstep."

Jenny nodded and stamped out the butt of her cigarette on the porch step, then tossed it into the backyard. She thought about going back in. It was August and even though it was before noon it was almost 95 degrees. No doubt it would be well over 100 again today.

Pride stood. "I'm going in. Too hot out here for me."

The door once again creaked and Jenny stood as well. The little house felt too confining most of the time, but it was too hot to be outside.

As she stepped onto the cracked and yellowed linoleum of the tiny kitchen, Jenny heard Pride at the front door talking with someone.

She hung back just enough to stay hidden, but still hear. She could hear Pride's heavy footsteps walking toward her favorite chair. Jenny could hear other footsteps following her and then growing quiet.

"Jenny, you might as well come on in here, girl. I know you are listening, but you need to talk to these people too."

Jenny didn't want to talk to cops, and who else would it be? Maybe if she stood super still, then Pride would think she wasn't there after all.

"Come on now. Git on in here."

With resignation Jenny smoothed down her wrinkled

denim skirt. The cops would know what she did as soon as they saw her. The skirt was way too short, and she still had on her fancy hose from last night. In fact, she hadn't changed at all from the night before.

Jenny quietly slid around the edge of the doorframe and stood right on the other side. She could slip back around when no one was looking.

"Come on in here and sit down," said Pride. She knew what the girl was thinking, everything she was thinking.

Jenny ducked her head, walked to the sofa, and sat on the end farthest away from the cops. She hadn't looked at them yet. Would they haul her off to jail? The knot in her stomach said yes.

"Hi Jenny, I'm Carrie Border and this is Randy Jeffries with the OSBI." Carrie's voice was gentle. She could see the fear in this girl's demeanor.

Jenny nodded her head, still looking down.

Pride leaned over and rested her hand on Jenny's knee. "It's ok. They're not here to get you in any trouble. They want to talk to us about Cami."

Jenny looked up at Pride with tears in her eyes and Pride nodded her head. "Yes, they found her."

Huge sobs sucked the air from Jenny's lungs and puddles of tears blurred her vision. "No!" She screamed. "No. No. No!" She shook her head hard from side to side, her limp hair with it. Her hands flew to cover her face. *She couldn't be gone.*

As the sickness rose up, she ran from the room. Once done retching, she continued to hold on to the toilet seat, sitting with her eyes clamped shut. Cami was gone, really gone. What would she do now without her?

She jumped as a hand touched her shoulder. "Are you ok?" It was the lady cop. Her voice was nice, and Jenny thought she might be okay, but she knew she couldn't trust a cop no matter how nice.

Jenny nodded her head and moved to get up. The water from the faucet she splashed on her face was cold and it felt good. But something had broken inside her that the cool water could never fix.

Her steps were robotic as she walked back into the living room. The lady cop was following her and sat down on the sofa with her, but thankfully a safe distance away.

Silence dominated the room for a short time before Jenny had the courage to ask, "Where did you find her?"

Carrie looked over at Randy. Should they tell her or let Pride tell her later? She seemed so fragile, but then living in this world, just how fragile could she be?

"We found her under the overpass over by the Chesapeake Boat House." Carrie watched as Jenny pressed her eyes tight together, a tear spilling out.

"You and Cami were close, weren't you?" Carrie asked. She kept her voice soft. She didn't want to add any more pain to Jenny's ordeal than she had to.

Jenny nodded her head, eyes still shut tight. "I loved her. She was my friend." Carrie thought her heart would break. "What will I do without her?"

Carrie looked up at Pride. Grief covered her face as

well as sympathy for young Jenny. How many times had this old woman seen this, or something like this, happen to these young girls?

Randy sat back taking notes. He could see that with Jenny, Carrie would have a greater success. He did not want to scare her or cause her to feel intimidated.

He had noticed that the room where they sat was small, but clean. The carpet was old and worn and the walls needed paint. But there were pictures of young girls placed about the room from better times. Wide smiles crossed their faces as they laughed for the cameras.

"Jenny, I know this is hard, but you know that we have to ask some very hard questions of you so we can find out who hurt Cami." Carrie wanted to be respectful of Jenny's pain while coaxing her to talk to them.

First a slight nod came, then open and clear eyes. "What do you need to know?" Jenny was ready.

"When was the last time you saw Cami?"

"Last night at about eight." Sobs threatened her voice, but Jenny held firm.

"And where was that?" asked Carrie. She knew Randy was taking notes, so she didn't bother.

"We were downtown. There was some kind of event at the arena and we were outside the Renaissance Hotel hanging out." Jenny had never talked to the cops before, so she didn't know just what she could say, or should say. She wanted to help them find out who hurt Cami, but she didn't want to get herself in a mess either.

Pride took Jenny's chin in her hand and turned the

young girls face to look at her. "It's okay Jenny. Tell them everything. They're not here for you. Tell them the truth." The look on Pride's face told Jenny she could trust these cops, so she nodded at Pride.

"We were working. We hung back because the cops would haul us in if we got too close to the arena where the event was. They are extra thick when they are having something there.

"So we always hang back up Broadway in the dark. There are a few trees along the street where we hang at until afterwards. Then we come out."

"What time was the event over?" asked Carrie.

"Well, I don't know exactly. We had walked over to the Cox garage about eight. We knew the guy working the gate that night, and we went over to talk to him. Sometimes he let us in and we would hang out in there. So we were standing around talking to him, and this guy in the garage motions to us to come to him.

"Cami said she would go see what he wanted." Jenny squirmed in her seat; of course they knew what he wanted. "Then she looked back at me and nodded. I knew she was going with him."

"When the event ended I hung out just inside the garage and then went with a guy coming out from the arena. When I left him, it was about eleven. I didn't see Cami the rest of the night.

"I finished working about two-thirty and came home. Cami wasn't here and Pride was asleep." Her last words were soft as if she ran out of steam.

Randy had gone to the kitchen and came back with a glass of water for Jenny. She thanked him and took the glass. The sour taste lingered in her mouth from being sick, and the water washed that away.

Heaviness hung in the air. Jenny's grief was strong, and they all felt it, but Carrie and Randy were here to do a job, and they could not let that stop them.

They got the best description they felt Jenny could offer of the guy that Cami had gone with. It would be a long shot that he'd been her killer. He'd made himself too visible too early in the evening, but they had to check. It would hopefully lead them to Cami's next move, if they could even find him.

"Pride we need to talk to Gus," Randy said.

Both Jenny and Pride's heads went up and over to look at Randy. Pride took a deep breath. He was right; they needed to talk to Gus, she just hated to be the one to direct them his way.

"I don't know where he lives, but he will come by here about five to see Jenny." He always makes his rounds to get the previous nights proceeds at about five each evening.

They asked both Pride and Jenny several more questions about Cami, then about Gus. Where does he hang out? Who does he hang out with? How did he treat Jenny and Cami? Who were his other girls?

Both Jenny and Pride answered all they could think of as honestly as they dared.

CHAPTER 3

The days right before school started were always strange. Summer was over and that was always sad, but there was excitement too. The hope of things to come in the new school year always reminded Sandy of why she kept on teaching.

"Dang it!" Sandy exclaimed as she looked at the broken fingernail. She'd just ripped it to the quick trying to pick up the heavy box of classroom decorations.

She shoved it in her mouth to stop the trickle of blood and went to locate her nail clippers. Nothing was where it should be yet. Over the summer, the rooms had all been repainted, so she had had to box up everything. Her nail clippers were in the box that held her desk supplies and she hadn't located it yet.

Seeing a pair of scissors, she grabbed them up and used them the best she could to clip the nail close to the skin. She hated that she'd lost the nail, but she wasn't prissy like a few of the teachers she worked with. They would call to make an emergency trip to the nail salon.

Standing behind her desk, she looked around the kindergarten room. Soon, this room would be filled with twenty tiny little faces with a variety of emotions. Some would be terrified, while some would be so excited that they wouldn't even be able to sit in their chairs.

There were no desks in the room, only tables and work areas. Everything was arranged, mostly, the way Sandy wanted it. She was trying to work on getting the walls done with cute decor and a host of visual learning opportunities.

The desk chair let out a puff of dust when she plopped into it. She was pooped already, and it was only noon. After ten years of teaching, she thought she might be loosing steam. She hated that because these kids deserved someone who was firing on all cylinders. Maybe she was just tired because of all the drama over the summer between her and Randy.

She shivered. The air conditioning chilled the air with only a few bodies in the building to challenge the temperature. Digging in her tote bag for her sweater, she noticed the glow of her cell phone. It was on silent out of habit, so she hadn't heard it ring.

A spark of adrenaline shot through her when she saw who had called. It was Beth. She had recently recruited Sandy to help her with the Safe At Last program she was in charge of.

Oklahoma City, because of its position, was the actual crossroads of human trafficking in the U.S. Two major highway systems, I-40 which ran east to west across the entire country and I-35 which did the same but from north to south, crossed in the dead center of the state.

Safe At Last was an international ministry that helped rescue those individuals kidnapped and trapped by human traffickers, and sometimes prostitutes and club dancers too. It used to be just young girls, but now young boys were also falling victim to this heinous crime.

As much as Sandy loved her little kindergartners, she felt a strong passion for these victims, and in her heart of hearts she wished she could stop teaching and devote herself to this program full time.

"Beth? It's Sandy. I saw you had called," Sandy replied to Beth's hello.

"Oh Sandy. I didn't know for sure if you would be available since you are setting up for school. But, if you have any time at all this week, I could sure use your help," said Beth.

Sandy was quickly thinking of all that she had to do and how quickly she could get it done. "I would love to help, but I'm slogging through unpacking my classroom. When do you need me?"

"I will take any help you can provide. We have rescued three new girls and are trying to get them settled in the safe house. We are short on volunteers to help here," said Beth.

"Let me hurry through here, and then I can come

spend the evening. Randy can pick the kids up from my mom's and then I can stay as long as you need." It was hard for Sandy to hide the excitement in her voice. She found such purpose in this, and she felt equally bad she no longer felt that same kind of purpose in teaching.

"Wonderful! Call me as soon as you are done there, and I'll get you situated on where to go and what to do."

Sandy bounced up from the desk chair while simultaneously clicking the red dot on her phone. Excitement fueled her, and she unpacked and arranging her room like a madwoman.

At around four she remembered she hadn't asked Randy to pick up the kids or even told him of her plans.

While she listened to the ringing of the phone, she hoped that this would not start yet another fight. Randy felt as strongly against her being involved in the Safe At Last program as she felt for being involved.

"Hello," greeted Randy.

"Hi," responded Sandy a little tentative.

"How's your day going? About to get your room situated?"

"I've made a lot of progress. Only a little left to do."

"That's great!" Randy's voice carried the surprise he felt.

"Can you pick the kids up from my mom's after you get off work?" She held her breath.

Randy's voice came across the phone slowly, "I can. Why?"

"Well, Beth called and asked if I could help her this

evening." She was nibbling on a remaining sliver of a nail she'd not been able to cut off earlier with the nail clippers she'd finally found. She could not control her nervousness.

There was silence on the other end of the phone, then… "What are you going to help her with?" She could hear the forced control in Randy's voice.

"I'm not exactly sure," said Sandy. Then her excitement took over, and she gushed. "They rescued three more girls and they need my help at the safe house getting them settled for the night."

Randy was furious. He did not want Sandy involved in that. All summer he'd tried to tell her how dangerous that world was. He had enough on his plate as it was and didn't want to have to worry about her as well.

"You're set on going no matter what I say, aren't you?" asked Randy. His face was flushed, and he had to fight the urge to throw down the phone.

What should she say? She was, but if she said that, it would only start another fight. She wanted Randy to support her choice to help.

"This is really important to me Randy. I can't tell you how much I want to help those girls."

"You have your kindergarten kids to help. School starts soon and I seriously doubt you are as ready as you're letting on." Randy's gut wrenched into a knot.

"Fine. Go ahead. I'll pick up the kids." Randy was grinding his teeth, but he knew that she would only become more determined the more he pushed back.

Sandy literally bounced up and down. "Thank you. I'll call you later to let you know that I'm okay," she said. "I never asked how your day was going."

"We found a dead prostitute down under the I-35 overpass. She was only twenty-one. And you want to go be in the middle of those people."

"I will not be in the big middle of *those* people! I will only be at the safe house helping three scared girls!"

"What if someone comes after them to take them back? What will you do then? Do you have any idea just how much danger you are putting yourself into?" Randy could feel his blood pressure rising as he spoke.

"What if I were a cop like you? I would be in the *big middle* of it every single day. Do you worry about Carrie and what will happen to her?" There, she'd said it.

She wasn't really jealous in the traditional sense of Carrie, but there was no doubt in her mind that Carrie and Randy were much closer in many respects than she and Randy were.

Randy wiped his hand over his face. He was so tired of their fighting. His job was stressful and then he had to deal with this at home. The silence between them over the phone was deafening.

"As a matter of fact sometimes I do worry about Carrie. But I love you! I made a vow to protect you and I can't do that when you insist on inserting yourself into this type of situation."

Sandy felt ashamed that she'd thrown accusations at

him. She knew he loved her, but he had to love her enough to let her follow her heart.

"I know you love me. I love you too," she said. "But love me enough to let me be and do what I feel I have to do. I love my kids here at school, but I feel a different tug on my heart to help these girls. Please understand and support me in this." Her voice had grown softer, and the anger had drained from her words.

"I know. Someone has to help them. I only wish it wasn't you. I'll pick the kids up after work. Do you have any idea what time you will be home?" Randy was hoping she would just be there a short time. That would reduce her vulnerability and he could get to bed early.

"No. But I should know by the time I call you back," said Sandy. "Once I get with Beth, she can give me some idea of what I'm to do and how long it will take."

"Sandy… Never mind."

"What?"

"Please be careful. I know you think you are, but you can never be too careful where you're going."

"So we know her name is Cami, but neither Pride nor Jenny knew if that was her real name or a work name. They also weren't sure what her last name really was even though she told them it was Anderson." Carrie was talking half to herself and halfway to Randy.

Having their desks facing each other with only a low

partition between, left little privacy. But she might as well have been talking to herself because Randy seemed a million miles away.

Carrie looked up to see Randy's face once again showing a revolving door of emotion. He was focused on something on his monitor which was turned away from her.

She got up and stood just watching him. The phone call with Sandy had been a tense one. Unfortunately, this had become commonplace lately. It seemed every time he talked to Sandy there was residual tension in the air.

Only four short months ago Randy had told both her and their Special Agent in Charge John Bracket that Sandy had asked for a divorce. Carrie knew they were trying to work through things, but she couldn't decide if things were getting better or worse.

"Is everything okay?" asked Carrie. Her voice was quiet, not sure if she should even ask. Sometimes he didn't care and then sometimes he would explode all over the place.

"Yeah," then rethinking his comment he said, "No, it isn't."

Carrie sat back down in her chair which put her eye to eye with him over the divider. "Want to talk about it?"

"Have I told you about this thing that Sandy has decided she wants to do? There is this lady she met at church who works with a program that helps rescue victims of human trafficking, and then keeps them in a safe house and works to get them home to their families or rehabilitates them back into society."

Carrie shook her head. "No, I don't think you ever mentioned that. It sounds like a great program."

"Of course it is, but it's dangerous. Just today we saw what happened to that poor girl. I don't want Sandy putting herself into a situation where she could run crosswise with someone dangerous. They do tend to take their property back by force. She could get hurt."

Carrie sat and thought about what Randy had said. Yes, it was dangerous but she could see the great need. "Are the people who work in that program trained to defend themselves?"

"I have no idea." The frustration was clear on Randy's face.

"Have you asked her? Maybe if you knew more about the program and learned what they actually do, then you would feel better about it."

"When I married Sandy she was so sweet and innocent. She wanted nothing more than to teach cute little kindergarteners. Things aren't the same with her."

"We all change Randy. We grow and learn. You aren't the same," Carrie gauged her words. "You love her, right? Then you want to give her emotional support to be the person she needs to be."

"I know. I just wish who she wanted to be wasn't someone who wanted to put her life on the line."

"Like you?"

Randy just ducked his head and once again became engrossed in what was on his monitor.

"What has you so transfixed over there?" asked Carrie.

She got up and walked around the desks to see what he was looking at.

"This is the little I can find out about that program. Not much online and no details as to location, etc. There are task forces in place just for this type of thing. There are professionals to do this. Why does she need to get involved?"

"Rescuing them is only the first step in helping these people. Once law enforcement's role is over, others have to step in and help them get back on their feet.

"This program looks like it has many trained volunteers, but I'm sure that there are many needs that Sandy can fill which won't put her in danger. I would think once they have been rescued and the perpetrators are in jail, there is nothing for Sandy to fear."

"You know better than that. Just because someone is rescued doesn't mean that everyone who was responsible was arrested and convicted. We see this constantly. I know you're just trying to make me feel better."

Randy was tired of talking about it. He knew Sandy would do what she wanted, regardless of what he said or how he felt. She would ask, they would fight, and then she would go off and do whatever.

He wasn't sure what made him feel worse. The fact that she would disregard his wishes or that she was willfully putting herself in danger.

∼

Gustavo Alejandro Hernandez stood in the shade of the towering oak tree in front of the run-down vacant house across the street from Pride's. He'd gotten word earlier that the cops had been by and was suspicious that they would be waiting for his five p.m. pickup from the girls.

He felt nothing for that dirty Cami who had gotten what she deserved last night. He felt nothing but disdain for her, spitting on the ground as he thought of her.

This street and the surrounding ones were void of cops. He had taken his girlfriend's car and driven through the neighborhood for an hour prior to coming here.

Parking three blocks over, he had walked here through alleyways and backyards to spy on Pride's house. Had there been grass underfoot, he would have trampled it bare by now with his pacing. He had Cami's money in his pocket from last night but he still needed to get Jenny's.

He grimaced and spat as he bit down on the bitter peanut he'd mindlessly tossed in his mouth. As he paced, he scattered the empty peanut hulls. Waiting like this caused him anxiety, so he shelled and ate peanuts while he waited.

He could delay and get her money another time, somewhere else. Walking to the shelter of the vacant house, he pulled out his phone and called Jenny.

"Hello," Jenny's timid voice came through the line.

"It's Gus."

"Hi Gus," she replied.

"You got my money?"

"Yes."

"Cops been there? They know I'm coming back at five?" asked Gus.

Jenny hesitated just long enough to confirm what Gus already suspected. "You bitch!" Gus bellowed.

"No Gus, I didn't do anything," Jenny was bawling into the phone.

"You told them I would be there at five. Don't lie to me!" Gus was seething. But what did he expect from these dirty whores?

"First stop tonight I'll be there and I'll get my money," Gus' voice was sharper than a steel blade.

"Yes Gus. I'll be at my first stop."

The line went dead and Jenny felt sick again. She needed something to help her through this, but if she took something now, she might be late to her first stop.

Hovering just outside Jenny's door, Pride had heard the phone, and she knew Jenny was aware she was out there. Her current girth made it impossible to travel across the old wood floors quietly.

The tapping on Jenny's door confirmed that Pride was indeed out there. "Yes," Jenny's voice was weak, but not as weak as she felt. Curled up on the bed midst dirty wrinkled sheets she felt used up.

The creaking of Jenny's door revealed Pride and her concerned look. "You okay, honey?" Memories of her life on the streets came thundering back painfully each time she looked at these young girls. But she was at a loss when it came to a solution to help them, really help them, out of this life.

Pride noticed a slight nod coming from the heap of a girl in the covers. She noticed how rail thin Jenny was.

"You using again Jenny?" Again, a slight nod.

A sigh escaped Pride's mouth, and she lowered herself onto the edge of Jenny's bed which threatened to topple in Pride's direction. "Come here, girl."

Pride motioned for Jenny to scoot her way so she could envelope her in her beefy arms. Lacking strength, Jenny only reached out to Pride and laid her hand on Pride's knee.

"That was Gus on the phone, wasn't it?" asked Pride.

Again, a slight nod was all Jenny could do.

Silence engulfed the room except for the drip of the faucet in the bathroom. Finally, Jenny garnered enough strength to pull herself up on one elbow, tucking her dingy pillow underneath herself.

"Pride I don't want to live like this anymore. I'm afraid and I just want to die!" Jenny's faded green eyes pleaded up at Pride and her heart shattered into a thousand tiny shards.

Pride had opened her home years ago to these girls to help in what small way she could, but she wasn't a wealthy woman and she distrusted most people who said they wanted to help. In her experience, very few people wanted to help do anything for anyone without getting something in return.

So, she had tried to help them on her own, but there

was little she could do. What life did she know other than this? Her government disability check barely kept her alive and only provided meager accommodations for a couple of girls.

Jenny needed real help. Help that Pride didn't have. After Cami's death she'd made a firm resolve to do whatever she could for Jenny.

Gathering strength from deep inside, Pride steeled herself to reach out beyond her comfort zone. She patted Jenny's thin hand and kissed the top of her head while reassuring her it would be okay. She got up and ambled to the kitchen.

Terrified that her world was about to change, possibly for the worse, Pride opened her kitchen junk drawer and dug for an old flyer someone had passed to her one day years ago. She really didn't know why she had kept it, but maybe somehow she had known this day was coming.

It was folded into quarters and the edges were worn and dirty from being shuffled around in the drawer for so long.

Pride had learned the hard way to never trust outsiders, so this was new territory for her. *Would these people truly do what they said they would? Would they be able to make Jenny's life better? Could they be trusted or would the cops come lock, not only Jenny up, but Pride too?* Pride wondered.

The broken heart she'd carried since hearing of Cami's death propelled her to pick up the phone for Jenny's sake.

"Hello, this is Safe At Last. How may I help you?"

CHAPTER 4

The mornings were the worst. By the end of a long day, Carrie was too tired to care what she did, her resolve having worn thin. Justifications for why it was okay to drink were plentiful.

But with morning, came a fresh realization she once again did not do what she had set out to do, get sober and stay sober.

Moderation. Wasn't moderation the key? She could do that couldn't she? The true answer was no, she could not.

She lay on her back in the rumpled bed and stared at the ceiling. Each morning she had to face the fact that she had failed once again.

Last night she had come home from work with firm resolve. Then after thirty minutes on the sofa watching some silly sitcom, she had convinced herself she could go play one game of pool at Hudson's. Just one game. She wouldn't even have to drink at all.

But once inside, the smells, the sights, and the sounds prompted her to do more. Just one drink. She could do that, she was a strong, willful woman. So she would order just one drink. And then with each subsequent drink came further justification.

Trauma remained from her ordeal last spring, but each week that went by, her resolve weakened. She'd almost convinced herself that she didn't need to quit drinking; that her assault was not a direct result of her drinking and carousing.

But in the light of day, she was always faced with the truth. Sadness overwhelmed her. She missed her parents still after all these years. They had been good parents, no — great parents, and there was a huge hole in her life where they had been.

The pain had been so intense after losing them she had walled herself off in order to feel nothing at all. And that is what pushed away the most wonderful man she had ever known. She had been engaged to be married when she received the news of her parents' accident.

The relationship had only lasted two months after that. No one was equipped to suffer the abuse she had dished out. She had finally convinced him she didn't love him anymore. And she was right, she had hardened herself to the point where she felt nothing, not even love.

So why did she drink if she felt nothing? Because the truth was she did feel and each day it was getting increasingly difficult to avoid the reality of old emotions begging for reconciliation.

Buzzzz. Buzzzz. She looked over at her phone buzzing on the nightstand and limply retrieved it. Laying back against her headboard, she looked at the name of the caller. It was Mike.

"Hey there," Carrie greeted Mike.

"Hey yourself. You okay? You don't sound like yourself."

Carrie was tired of the flirtatious banter she and Mike constantly engaged in. "I'm fine. Just woke up."

She flung her legs over the side of the bed and sat with her arms on her thighs; the knobby points of her elbows wobbled to find purchase.

Suddenly all business, Mike began, "Sylvia found dozens of missing persons that could be Cami. None of them had a name even close. Honestly, she may not even be from here."

"True. Facial recognition might help, but I doubt she's in the system, and even if she is, it will take time. I don't want this poor girl's murder to be another one that goes unsolved."

"I know." And Mike did know. They had too little to go on and so little time to get everything done that they needed to do.

"What's on the agenda for today?" asked Carrie.

"One reason I called is that the autopsy is scheduled for two today."

"Ok, I'll be there," said Carrie. "Were you guys able to

find that Gus guy? Did he come to Pride's to get Jenny's money last night?"

"No. We hung back and tried to not give ourselves away, but he's on to us. My guess is he made plans to pick it up somewhere else."

"I want to coral this guy and interview him. I want to know if he is the one who did this," said Carrie. "We need to find him."

"We have to be careful though so that Jenny and Pride don't feel backlash from it," said Mike.

"True, but they are much stronger than you realize from living in that world each day." Carrie knew that the life of a prostitute was not an easy one and that those girls grew up quick in order to survive.

"I'll see you at the autopsy then?" asked Mike.

"Yep, I'll be there," replied Carrie. Her voice was tired and weak for so early in the morning.

"Are you sure you are okay?"

Carrie sat on the edge of the bed staring at the floor. The high whine of a rogue mosquito next to her ear didn't even cause her move to swat at it. "I'm fine. Just tired."

"Well okay," Mike responded, then almost as an afterthought, "You know Carrie, we've been more than colleagues; we've been friends. Yes, a little more than friends with all the flirting and all, but I'm here for you. I do care for you and I want you to know you can come to me with no strings attached whenever you need to talk." Mike finally stopped talking as though he'd hit a wall, not knowing what else to say. He wasn't good at this sort of thing, but hoped that Carrie could sense his sincerity.

"I know Mike and I appreciate it." And she truly did. Mike was comfortable, like an old familiar part of your life you knew was there should you ever need it. But she was tired of the shallow flirtatious game they'd been playing over the years, and yet, she knew she didn't want more from Mike.

These last four months since the attack had caused personal reflection on her life, and she didn't like what she saw. For the first time in a very long time she was forced to take a long hard look at herself, and with that came the awareness of just how desperately damaged she was.

Pain swallowed her and sucked her strength. But even so, she pulled the energy from somewhere deep inside to get up from the bed and shuffle to the shower.

The hot water felt like tiny hot needles on her face and the steam enveloped her completely. She let the pain from the hot water consume her and she held her face firmly towards it.

Where had her resolve gone? Soon after the attack she had such firm resolve to change, to turn her life around. She had wanted to and knew she could.

Her workout routines had not only resumed with a vengeance once her wounds had healed, but she had approached them with a fervor unlike anything she had ever done before. She was soon working out at least two hours, sometimes more a day, every day.

But that didn't help what was still inside, and soon the struggle to keep from sliding back into her old life overwhelmed her. It was easy at first to resist. She had felt so good physically that her confidence was high.

But work locked her into an old familiar routine: long hours, poor eating habits, anger towards perpetrators, and the resignation that nothing ever really changes. So, hope slowly faded a little more each day.

The buzzing of her phone once again brought her back to the present day, so she shut the shower off and grabbed a towel.

"Yep," she greeted Randy.

"G'morning," said Randy.

"You sound perky."

"I am. And I'm not sure why. Just feel good this morning," said Randy.

Carrie wondered what was up with him. He'd been in a perpetual bad mood for months.

"Things going better with you and Sandy?" asked Carrie as she slid on her bra and buckled it. She'd long since learned she could multi-task with the phone on speaker.

"Well...," Randy hedged. "We talked when she got home last night. She went to that place, but was only gone for a couple of hours, so I was relieved."

"So you are okay with her doing that now?"

"I wouldn't say that, but when we sat there talking, and I saw her eyes light up, I felt so guilty for not wanting her to be involved. I realized I was trying to take away something she loved doing, something that gave her purpose.

"I still don't like it and I'm still aware that she is inserting herself into a dangerous situation, but I have to let her do it because I love her. It felt good to let some anger go."

Grabbing her gun and badge, Carrie looked around the room to double-check she had everything. A smell caused her nose to wrinkle. She had to clean up her house and take out the trash soon. Life didn't stop because she was in a funk.

"That's good. I'm headed out the door now. Mike called and said autopsy is at two this afternoon. Also, that Gus didn't show at Pride's last night."

"Hmmm. That's interesting. He's either avoiding Pride's because he knows her place is being watched, or he's gone. Or something," mused Randy. "I'll see you at the office in a bit."

"Ok." The phone went silent and Carrie cranked up the radio. She tried to sing along to the old 80s tunes, but she just didn't feel it.

"Did you see Gus last night?" Pride asked Jenny. Jenny's face showed little improvement from the day before. The girl had just shuffled into the kitchen where Pride was making coffee.

"Yeah. He met me at my first stop." Jenny fell into the

wobbly kitchen chair. The torn vinyl pinched her thigh, so she shifted to avoid it.

Pride poured a cup of coffee and sat it down in front of Jenny, then turned to pour herself one. "Are those new bruises on your arm?" Pride asked.

Jenny squirmed and pulled her thin robe up to cover herself better.

"He hurt you didn't he?"

Jenny nodded. "He's crazy mad about Cami. He didn't like her, but he's mad she's dead. He thinks, well knows, we talked to the police." Jenny raised the steaming cup of black coffee to her mouth and gently blew the black brew.

They sat quietly sipping their coffee. Pride sat wondering who killed Cami and what to do. "I made a phone call yesterday." Pride was hedging her words. She didn't want Jenny to panic and not hear her out.

Jenny looked up over her cup and waited for Pride to continue. "There's a place that tries to help girls, well boys too, to get them out of prostitution and trafficking."

Jenny slowly sat her cup back on the table. Her mind was suddenly flooded with so many conflicting thoughts and emotions that she couldn't sort them out. It was true she'd told Pride yesterday she'd wanted out. But how did she dare hope she could be free from all of this?

When Jenny didn't respond, Pride continued, "You know that I don't normally trust those who haven't lived in our world, cops and such, but I have to believe that there are good people out there. Sometimes you just have to take a chance."

Pride reached across the table and laid her hand on Jenny's. Finally, Jenny looked up from her cup to Pride's face and slowly nodded. "I don't have the strength to fight Gus. He'll kill me. He may have been the one who killed Cami."

A frown creased Pride's brow. "Why would you say that?"

"Pride, he's crazy. I know I said he's crazy mad about Cami, but that was for more reasons than one. She kept bucking him and going against him. Knowing Gus, he killed her and now is blaming her for making him do it!"

Jenny looked back down at her chipped cup. Her focus blurred and she no longer saw the cup at all, but the night before when Gus had grabbed her and shook her arm with such fury that she thought he would break it.

She had given him the money, which was never enough, and then he had started in about them talking to the cops. "He's convinced that we had the cops waiting for him last night when he should've come here to get his money. I told him they came by, and yes they may have been around, but that it wasn't our fault."

Jenny reached in her robe pocket for her cigarette pack, shook out a cigarette, and searched for her lighter. *Where had she laid it now,* she wondered? She didn't feel like she had the energy to search for it, but her need for nicotine was greater.

While Jenny was on the hunt for her lighter, Pride rose to cook breakfast for the two of them. She knew Jenny would try and refuse to eat, but she had to get her to, somehow.

The smell of bacon sizzling in the pan reached Jenny's nose in the bedroom. It smelled good, maybe she would eat. She wasn't sure when the last time she ate was.

Finding her lighter on the floor next to her bed, she bent over and picked it up. Waves of dizziness washed over her and she thought she might be sick again. When she shut her eyes, pinpricks of light shot behind her eyelids.

She sat on the edge of her bed to attempt to regain her bearings. Tears slid down her face once again as she thought of Cami, then Pride's voice rang through the house. "Jenny come eat breakfast. I insist."

Jenny took a deep breath and stood. She knew she needed to find some resolve deep within herself not only to survive, but to overcome. She had no idea how to do that, but for Cami's sake, she would try.

"The bacon smells good." Jenny looked at Pride with gratitude from her downcast eyes. Then she smiled a weak smile and Pride pulled her in to a tight embrace.

"I love ya girl. We'll get through this somehow, some way." Then patting her back, she released Jenny. "Here. The first step is to eat and try to gain some of your strength back. Then, we'll talk and come up with a plan." Pride loved Jenny as if she were her own daughter and her smile revealed it.

Jenny laid her lighter on the table and picked up her fork.

Sandy was back at work in her kindergarten classroom, but all she could think about was the night before at Safe At Last.

The three girls were so young, and it gripped her heart. One was only twelve! That was just four years older than her own daughter.

Her lack of training had relegated her to menial tasks such as showing the girls where everything was, helping with dinner, and just being there with them for company. But she didn't care. In fact, she had loved it.

Fear had only gripped her stomach afterwards when she pulled into her own driveway, concerned about what Randy would say. She didn't want another fight.

But when she walked in at nine, he looked surprised and relieved. He must have expected her to have been home much later.

It put him in a good mood and she had felt safe to talk to him more about her desire to get trained and to continue volunteering there.

He was skeptical, but agreed to help more with the kids when he could.

Last spring they had separated. She had been convinced she wanted a divorce. The constant fighting was more than she could take and she had made him move out.

There was only one drawback. She loved him. Since he

was home so little, the kids missed him; and she wanted to make it work somehow.

A friend from school had invited her to go to church with them. She was entirely resistant to it. The little denominational church she had attended from time to time while growing up, held no appeal to her, and she was still trying to shake guilt that had wormed its way into her soul.

Finally though, she had reluctantly given in. It had been nice, and the kids liked it. But she still just had not bought into it all. She continued to go because the kids begged her to each week.

But then she had met Beth and heard about Safe At Last. Her heart came alive as she listened to Beth talk about the horror of human trafficking and how prevalent it was.

Then she had expressed an interest to Beth in helping. Beth had just looked at her for a moment and then simply said, "Well, just pray about it."

Pray about it? That had taken Sandy back. Why, she wasn't sure. Maybe it was because she didn't know how to pray, but maybe more so, why to pray. Either you wanted to do something and did it or you didn't. *What did prayer have to do with it*, she wondered.

She had only nodded in agreement to Beth. If she were honest with herself, she felt like an imposter at church, but she kept going for the kids' sake. And if she admitted it to herself, it was growing on her too, just a bit.

CHAPTER 5

"Can we narrow down the missing persons' list that Sylvia gave us?" asked Carrie.

Randy was shaking his head at the large number of girls they had to sift through. "Maybe if we tighten the description down. Did she have any distinguishing marks on her like moles or tattoos?"

Carrie looked through the thin file they had so far. "Nothing yet. We need to talk to Pride and Jenny again to get more specifics on her. Hopefully, they are over the shock and can think of things they hadn't before."

"We have the autopsy at two this afternoon, that may give us something there. If we can identify this girl, then we may find this was personal," said Randy.

"It was personal even if it was just directed at her personally as a prostitute," said Carrie.

"Has forensics turned up anything at all from the crime scene?" asked Randy.

"There was so much to sift through that it will take a while."

"We've got time to go back to Pride's before we head on over to the coroner's office," said Randy glancing at his watch.

Carrie nodded and gathered together the file she'd been reviewing.

The hot August sun assaulted them as they stepped from the shadow of the OSBI building. Carrie had remembered not only her sunglasses this time but also her cap.

The fabric seats seared the backs of her arms as they hit the seat. When Randy cranked the engine, she pressed the down button on her window. She was trying to break her old habit of fiddling with the temp control as soon as he started the vehicle. Thinking of all their banter back and forth regarding that very thing, she chuckled.

Randy looked over at her as he was pulling out of the parking lot. "What's so funny?" He asked.

"I'm trying to break some old habits, so instead of cranking the AC when you started the car I rolled the window down. I just thought of all the fighting we've done over those controls all these years." She continued to look out the front window, but had a huge grin on her face. "You didn't even notice."

Randy's eyebrow rose as he thought about what she had said. "I would have said something. You need to roll that window up now though, the AC is cooling off."

"Never content, are we?" Carrie asked. She was joking and Randy knew it. She was incredibly comfortable around Randy. He truly was her best friend. But there was still a hole in her heart she thought may never be filled.

As they drove through the congested city streets towards Pride's house, Carrie looked out at all the people and wondered where they were going and what their lives were like. *Were they happy,* she wondered, *or numb and just going through the motions like she was?*

Fifteen minutes later, they were pulling up to Pride's house. The neighborhood appeared quiet. The front door opened soon after Randy knocked. It was Jenny who'd answered.

Jenny's stomach knotted immediately when she saw the cops standing on her front porch. Pride had gone to the grocery store and Jenny was home alone.

"Can we come in and talk to you Jenny?" asked Carrie.

Jenny was wringing her hands unsure of what to do. "Pride's not home."

"That's okay. We need to talk to you," said Carrie.

Jenny looked out into the neighborhood before stepping back into the small living room, allowing Carrie and Randy to enter. As soon as they did, she took one more look out, then closed the door. There were always eyes on her and on everything she did.

"May we sit?" asked Randy.

Jenny nodded then gestured toward a chair. She wasn't sure whether to sit or to stand. If she sat, they might stay longer. Indecision led her to look for her cigarettes and lighter.

Two deep puffs in she felt calm enough to sit down. When she did, she said, "Gus is furious. He knows you were watching for him last night."

"Not us, but some uniformed officers," said Randy.

Jenny's irritation escalated. "I told you he would take it out on us, on me."

"Is that what that bruise is on your arm?" asked Carrie.

Jenny glanced down at the bruise and then back up. "Yes."

"Jenny, do you think Gus was the one who killed Cami?" asked Carrie.

Randy was jotting notes down in his notebook. Carrie had removed her sunglasses in order to see Jenny clearly in the dim room. When Jenny didn't answer immediately she let the silence draw her out.

Finally, Jenny said, "I don't know. He could have." She looked down at the hem of the shirt she was wearing and worked the threads back and forth with her free hand.

"Tell us about your relationship with Gus. What are his rules for you and his other girls and what makes him mad?"

Jenny looked back up at Carrie and took another puff. There wasn't enough nicotine on this earth to calm her nerves and she craved something stronger.

With an exhaled breath of resignation Jenny began, "We get an 80/20 cut. He gets 80 percent and we get 20 percent. He always has eyes on us, so he knows how much we should be making. He gives the eyes twenty percent. So obviously he doesn't trust us.

"We have to work every night. If we are sick, he makes sure we are sick and then he'll decide if we are too sick to work." Jenny stopped and rested her chin on the upturned palm of the hand holding her cigarette. She gazed off somewhere that Carrie couldn't see.

"I've worked nights so sick I could barely move. If we look too sick, no one will go with us so we have to try hard to look okay all the time."

"Does he beat you?" asked Carrie.

Jenny shrugged. "He knocks us around some, but I don't know if they would be considered beatings. I had beatings when I lived at home. Gus is nothing like that."

Carrie wondered about this girl whose life was gauged good or bad on the depth of the beatings she was having to endure. She suddenly felt ashamed for complaining about her own life.

Jenny stamped out the butt of her smoked cigarette and searched for another, then thought better of it. Looking up at Carrie she asked, "What else do you need to know?"

"Did Cami have any tattoos or moles or other things that would distinguish her from someone else?" asked Carrie.

"She has a tattoo of a hummingbird on her shoulder blade. Left side." Jenny motioned with her right hand to her left shoulder blade.

"You told us the other night you didn't know where Cami was from, where she had grown up. We thought maybe you might have thought of something since then." Carrie had wanted to say, *after the shock of her death had worn off*, but she wasn't sure it ever would.

Jenny shook her head, but Carrie could tell there was something. "Are you sure? We're trying to help find her killer. What if Gus did it? Don't you want to see him pay, and to keep him from doing it to someone else, even you?" Carrie's words were emphatic.

Jenny looked up at Carrie through a lock of brown hair that had fallen across her face, then back down.

"I do. I just don't know what to tell you."

"Can we look through Cami's things to see if there is anything that would tell us where she came from or where her home was?"

Jenny shrugged. She didn't know what it would hurt. She stood up and pulled her arms around her midsection as if she was cold even though the room was far from it.

"We shared a room. Pride gets one room and we have the other." Jenny led them to her room and stepped inside. Her eyes were darting around wondering if she had anything that the cops shouldn't find, which she could have forgotten about.

She gestured to the twin bed opposite hers. "That was Cami's bed, and that's her stuff there. We shared that closet."

Jenny went to her bed and sat on the edge while Randy and Carrie looked through Cami's things. On the wall over Cami's bed were photos that had been thumb tacked to the wall. Carrie stood for a long time studying them.

After a few moments, Carrie reached up and pulled one down off of the wall, walked over to Jenny, and sat on the edge of the bed beside her.

"This photo here," Carrie held over to Jenny, "is this Cami?"

"Yes."

"Who is with her?"

Jenny took the picture from Carrie's hand and sat looking at it. In the picture Cami was younger than when she had come to Pride's. Jenny was trying to remember what, if anything, Cami had said to her about the picture.

"I think those are her sisters," said Jenny looking up at Carrie.

"Did she ever talk about them to you?" asked Carrie.

Jenny looked back at the picture in her hand and was trying hard to think. Then she pointed to the one on the right side. "I think that one left before Cami came here."

"Left home? Before Cami came here to Pride's?" Carrie was trying not to force this forward, but she could feel momentum and was growing eager.

Jenny looked up at Carrie. "I think I remember when I first met Cami, that she talked about her. She said someone had taken her right before she'd left home. A man I think. Her sister never came here to Pride's, and I never met her."

"A man took her?"

"I'm not sure what happened. Cami never really talked about it." Jenny's face was sad. "I really don't remember anything else," and she handed the photo back to Carrie.

"Can we keep this photo?" Carrie asked.

Jenny shrugged then nodded. "I guess so. Take whatever you want that will help."

Randy had finished searching through the couple of drawers that had been hers, her pockets, and under the bed. He'd found nothing he thought would be of any use.

"Jenny, here's my card. I know we gave you one the other day, but I want you to keep this one. If you need us, if Gus or anyone else tries to hurt you, promise me please, that you will call me." Carrie was holding Jenny's gaze.

As Jenny looked into her eyes, she thought she could maybe trust this lady cop. She didn't know why, but she would try. What did she have to lose?

BACK IN THE HOT CAR, Carrie cranked the AC as soon as the motor roared to life. Randy just looked at her and said nothing.

Carrie buckled her seat belt and studied the photo. "I know where this photo was taken."

"Where?" asked Randy surprised.

"There's an old abandoned amusement park outside of town. I'm guessing that it was abandoned in this photo but not yet dismantled."

The photo was faded and had a pale yellowish tint from being in the light, but Carrie could see what looked like old bumper cars in the background behind the short wall the girls were leaning on. She tilted the photo and thought, yes, there was a Ferris wheel in the background as well.

"Not much to go on," said Randy. He wondered just how many people had taken pictures at that park.

"True," Carrie said looking out her side window. Her mind was engineering a strategy to find out who Cami really was.

"The sister. Wasn't that odd what Jenny said? A man took her. But she didn't indicate that Cami had been alarmed about it." Carrie was looking at Randy to gauge his reaction.

"Just because Jenny hadn't said she was, doesn't mean that she wasn't."

Carrie took a deep breath and sighed. It was time for the autopsy and she hoped that would reveal something for them.

Cami lay on the cold steel table in the autopsy room with Henry Bloom standing next to her. His six foot three inch frame, rotund in the middle, seemed to fill the room.

Carrie and Randy had arrived about ten minutes early, coming straight from speaking with Jenny. Henry didn't like to start until all parties were present so he wouldn't have to repeat himself, but Carrie thought it would be okay to ask a couple of questions.

"Henry, we're having trouble locating her family. Does

she have any distinguishing marks, moles, or tattoos?" Carrie knew that she should have a hummingbird on her shoulder, but her position on the table hid it from view. She hoped Hendry would confirm.

"She did. A hummingbird on her left shoulder." He produced a photo he'd taken earlier. "As for moles or other marks, none I could find, and you know I try to be thorough."

Henry was thorough. He was a great medical examiner. Carrie had the highest respect for the man.

The swinging stainless steel doors whooshed open and in walked Mike and Rick. "Sorry we're late," said Rick. His face was red and flushed and he was wiping sweat from his forehead with a man's handkerchief. Carrie didn't realize they still made those, or that anyone still bought them. A pang of sadness swept through her.

Her father had always carried one of those with him, and she remembered the feel of the soft cotton on her cheeks when he would wipe ice cream from her face. Shaking herself out of the memory she smiled at them both and nodded to Henry to begin.

"She was drowned. It appears to me that the perpetrator held her head under water by holding her hair close to her scalp. If you push the hair aside, you can see bruising as if knuckles pressed into the back of her scull."

Henry presented photos showing the bruising. "They were perimortem, so they occurred prior to death. Also, if you notice here and here, there are small spots where it looks as though tiny clumps of her hair were pulled out, presumably in the struggle while gripping her hair tightly." Henry was demonstrating with his hand as though he were grabbing someone by the hair tightly and then pushing down.

He then moved around to where Cami's left hand lay and picked it up. "If you notice here, her fingernails are chipped and broken to the quick. I scraped underneath and found dirt and other small bits of debris. I'm hoping she scratched her killer in the struggle."

He laid her hand back down and raised the sheet to reveal her feet. "She lost both shoes in the struggle and there was considerable dirt underneath her toenails as well. The tops of her feet were caked with mud too." He produced yet more photos of her toenails and feet.

"This goes along with the indentions in the mud at the crime scene where it appeared she had dug into the ground with her feet trying to escape," said Carrie as much to herself as to the others.

They all envisioned this tiny petite young girl struggling against someone who was strong enough to grab the back of her head with her hair and simply hold her head underwater until she drowned. They could see in their minds, her hands and feet flailing seeking a way to break free from her assailant.

"Were there any additional injuries?" Randy asked.

"There was considerable bruising to her upper arms." Henry produced yet more photos, but with her laying before them they could see for themselves the imprints of fingers laying in dark blue stripes across her thin upper arms.

Carrie thought of Jenny and what her arm had looked like earlier. "Can you get us some measurements so we could compare that hand print to another one?" Carrie hoped that Jenny's bruises would yield the same type of print, but then realized that Jenny's bruises were already too faded for a distinguishable print.

Henry thoughtfully nodded and said he would do his best. The photos he had handed them though, were taken with his ruler in place. Carrie was hoping for a full hand print in exact measurement, size, and scale. She wanted to be able to take Gus' hand and lay it on the photo and see an exact match.

"There were no cuts or other abrasions on her body." Henry concluded.

They all four left deep in thought. Once in the hallway Randy and Carrie discussed with Mike and Rick what they knew about Gus. Carrie had taken a picture of the photo they had taken from Cami's bedroom wall with her phone and sent it to both Mike and Rick.

"I remember that place. When I was a kid, we used to go out there," said Rick. "I don't think that place has been running in years."

"I don't think it was running in this picture," said Carrie. "I have a feeling these girls were just out exploring. Sometimes places are more fun to explore in their graveyard state than they are when fully operational."

She saw both Mike and Randy nod their heads. Who

hadn't loved exploring crazy places like this when they were kids?

"If that's the case, then these girls probably lived close to the park," said Mike.

"I know it's a long shot, but we can try. I want to get this to forensics to see if there is anything they can get from the photo that isn't readily obvious to us. Who knows, maybe we will get lucky and find they lived right next door," Carrie smiled at the group. The clues were slow to come and hard to pull out, but they were still coming.

"Beth, I want to volunteer more," Sandy was saying to Beth over the phone. She felt a nervous excitement as she spoke.

"That would be wonderful. Things seemed to go well last night. The girls warmed to you, and I believe you were a comfort to them."

"I start back teaching in a few days so I can only do nights and weekends then, but whatever you need," said Sandy.

"I'll put together a schedule and email it to you. I will also send a list of meetings I would like you to attend. It's important that you gain as much knowledge as we can provide you. Many on our staff are licensed counselors volunteering their time. We also have many other professionals who are well acquainted with the needs of these victims.

"You being a teacher is a great asset, but the trauma we need to help them deal with is in a whole other realm. If we don't approach them appropriately, then we can do more harm than good. The more training you can get, the better you'll be able to help them," said Beth.

Sandy was listening intently to all that Beth was saying and growing more excited with every word.

Sandy's phone beeped to notify her of a call coming through. "I hear you have a call and I have to go, anyway. I'll email you soon," said Beth.

Sandy saw it was Randy calling, so she answered. They'd had a good talk the night before when she came home. It was good to have him back in her life.

"Are you busy?" asked Randy.

"Not too much. I just got off the phone with Beth. I called her to tell her I want to do more volunteer work," said Sandy. She was sitting on the edge of her desk at school and was nervously flopping her sandal off and on again. She still held her breath every time she talked to Randy about volunteering at Safe At Last.

"You'll do great. I admire your compassion and love for others," said Randy. His response surprised Sandy.

"Thank you."

"I can't say I won't worry about you, but you have a good head on your shoulders and I hope you won't put yourself in any unnecessary risk."

Sandy was now chewing on a cuticle. "It'll take time

away from you and the kids. I'm only available to volunteer in the evenings and weekends."

"Can you find a balance? A night or two a week would be enough I would think, and then certainly only an occasional weekend," Randy was trying not to get frustrated again. He really wanted to understand, but he was genuinely opposed to this. He was trying to be the husband she needed him to be.

"True. I want to start out slow, but there are also meetings I will need to attend to get additional training."

"Ok. Well, I'm doing my best to be supportive. I'll help with the kids when your mom isn't available." Randy was rubbing the bridge of his nose.

"Will you be home for dinner tonight?" asked Sandy. She hoped so. They hadn't had dinner together as a family for several days now.

"I plan on it, but you never know. I'll call you later," said Randy.

"I love you," said Sandy.

"I love you too."

CARRIE WALKED into her empty home with thoughts of Cami and Jenny on her mind. She looked around her simple home, the home she'd made for herself alone, and realized she was doing okay. It wasn't a mansion, but she wasn't forced to live on the street and sell her body the way those poor girls were having to do.

Then the thought raced through her mind, *No you simply give yourself away for free.* Shame overwhelmed her. Since Billy, she hadn't dared take a chance on a relationship, only an eight-year run of one-night stands. Well, except for Mike that was. But that wasn't a relationship either. They'd both known what it was when it started, a fling while they were working on a case together. It had ended when the case had ended.

She was sick of it all, but didn't know what to do. Self control, which had always been her modus operandi, wasn't working for her now. Growing up, if she wanted something, sheer force of will and determination had made it happen for her. Now it seemed that she had no control over her toxic emotions and behavior.

It had been suggested to her by Randy and SAC Bracket that she talk with someone. But what would talking do?

She locked her gun away in her bedside safe and laid her badge on the nightstand. Sitting on the edge of her bed she could already feel the pull of old habits drawing her to the bar. She shut her eyes and attempted to will herself to shun the desire, but that only made it intensify.

For eight years she had walked through life as a zombie. This had to change. She didn't want to live like this anymore. The joy of her life was her job. It had been her dream for so long, and she had seen that dream come true. But even the love of her life, her job, couldn't fill the huge hole in her soul.

She stood up and walked over to her dresser and dug

in the top drawer she used for a catch-all. Half hoping she wouldn't find what she was searching for, she almost gave up, but then there it was. The card that SAC Bracket had given her four months ago.

The card contained the name Irene Lee, LPCC, her address and contact info. As she stood looking at the card she wondered how could she share the dirty things she'd done in her life with another person? And she felt just that, dirty to the core.

She tapped the card on her other hand as she turned from the dresser. Taking a deep breath, she reached for her phone and dialed the number on the card. Soon a voice-mail recording came over the line. Of course, it was after hours. She hung up, not sure what to say. She would call back tomorrow — maybe.

Out of desperation she grabbed her swimsuit and decided she would go to her neighborhood pool. She could feel the desperate pull inside herself to stop trying to deny the old habits and urges. She hoped that actively doing something else would fix it.

She dressed quickly, almost in a panic to force the old behaviors aside. She found herself shoving random things in her old canvas tote, a book, sunscreen, a towel, headphones, and what else? Her old straw hat.

Just as she was rushing out the door she thought she had a six-pack of tall boys in the fridge. The debate on whether to grab it or not didn't last long. It was only beer, right? What could it hurt?

CHAPTER 6

"We have another body," said Randy first thing the next morning.

How many times in this job were those words the first thing I've heard in the morning, thought Carrie. And this was a second body which always changed things. It shifted the focus of the investigation away from a purely personal motive to a broader one.

"I hate to ask, but is it Jenny?" Carrie didn't want to know but had to.

"No, it isn't Jenny," said Randy.

A wave of relief washed over Carrie. Relief, not so much for Jenny, but that Carrie didn't have to feel the pain of losing this girl she had come to know and feel compassion for. She was rooting for Jenny somewhere down deep inside.

"Where at?" Carrie asked.

"Eagle Lake," replied Randy.

Carrie searched in her mind for recognition. Eagle Lake, she muttered to herself. "I don't know where that is," said Carrie.

"It's a little man-made lake between Reno Ave. and NE 4th Street in Del City."

"Oh wow, that's close to where the other one was found."

On the drive out to Eagle Lake, Carrie spent the time searching the internet for information on the lake.

"It says here that lake used to be called Thompson Lake, but they changed the name over to Eagle Lake when the city of Oklahoma City bought it. The city cleaned it up, and it is a back-up water supply for OKC should Lake Thunderbird go dry. Lot's of fishing, crappie, and some bass, catfish too," said Carrie.

Can't be too big. Probably like a big pond," replied Randy.

As they pulled into the park area, they could see the usual cluster of law enforcement on the far edge of the peninsula in a small cove. The pavement ended about midway, so Randy had to park and walk the rest of the way.

"So once again we have to walk quite a little distance from where a person could park, to where the body was found," said Carrie.

"Are they lured to this spot, or carried, or drug out here against their will?" asked Randy.

"I don't see any drag marks. Cami was petite. She could have been carried."

Mike and Rick stood next to the body of another young girl. Her hair was black and lay disheveled and muddy around her head. Both high heels were off and scattered to the side as if lost in a struggle.

Quick nods were exchanged between them. "I'm assuming this is not where she was found," said Carrie.

"No. She was half in the water. The coroner's crew pulled her out. She was face down again. This time we found a small purse over to the side." Mike pointed back about twenty feet from where they'd come.

"ID?" asked Carrie.

Mike shook his head. "Condoms, lipstick, and a compact mirror."

"No money?" asked Randy. Again Mike shook his head.

"Two girls, petite and drowned," said Rick.

The forensic team bagged the shoes and added them to the tub of other bits of debris and samples they had found, including the girls purse. Carrie reached into the tub and brought out the clear bag with the purse inside.

It was a small hard shelled evening bag with sequins in various colors. Many were gone and the black satin fabric underneath was worn and frayed. *Her little bit of glamor*, thought Carrie as she laid the purse back down.

The body was loaded onto the gurney and into the body bag. Carrie reached down with a gloved hand and brushed the girls wet soppy hair gently away from her face.

She'd been pretty, very pretty. Long dark lashes rested on her pale ghostly white cheeks. Her red lipstick was smeared from her mouth across her face, and there was a little dark mole on the side of her face just under her left ear.

Randy stood beside Carrie taking notes as usual. Mike and Rick walked around and stood on the other side of the gurney. Rick and Randy had daughters, and even though this affected Carrie and Mike, the concern the other two felt was more acute.

"So," Carrie began, "now there are two. Do we push to follow a personal lead on Cami?"

"Mike and I will follow up on the park and the surrounding area to see if we can find her family. We need to find them for notification reasons if nothing else."

The bag was zipped and the dark-haired petite girl rolled away toward the van. *She's leaving in peace, but how did she arrive, and who brought her here*, wondered Carrie?

"I want to talk to Gus, now," fumed Carrie. She didn't know if this was one of his girls, but it was possible.

Back in the car, Randy suggested they go back yet again to Pride's. "Let's see if she or Jenny know this girl too."

Jenny was still in bed when Randy pulled their SUV up to the curb in front of Pride's. However, Pride was up and watching Wheel of Fortune when she heard the knock on the door.

"Good morning Pride," said Carrie.

"Is it?" asked Pride. Cops coming to her door were never good.

"No, not really. Can we come inside?" asked Rick.

They were once again led into the small dim living room. As Pride made her way back to her chair, the one with the large dip in the center where the cushion had long since given way to years of pressure, sat down, and flipped off the tv.

"Jenny said you came by yesterday asking more questions," said Pride.

"We did. She was very helpful," said Randy.

Carrie pulled out her phone and opened the picture of the girl they had found this morning. "We have another girl," said Carrie. She was respectful of the fact that this could again be a very painful moment for Pride. "We're hoping you might help us identify her."

Pride shut her eyes and attempted to prepare herself for what she was about to see. She hoped with everything in her she would not know this girl. She then looked at Carrie and nodded reaching out for the phone.

The face in the picture would not look like what Pride would remember. It lacked vibrance and animation. Pride stared at the photo for what seemed to Carrie, an eternity. Her face did not reveal recognition.

Pride handed the phone back to Carrie. "I'm not sure. It's possible I may have seen her, but she hasn't come around here that I remember. Jenny may know."

Carrie nodded. "Where is Jenny?" Carrie asked.

"She's in bed. I'll go get her." Pride pushed hard on the arms of the chair to help push herself up. Once standing, it took her a minute to move forward. Carrie wondered about her health and the difficulty it seemed she had moving. Maybe she should have gotten Jenny instead of bothering Pride.

There were muffled voices from the other room and soon Pride came back with Jenny in tow. She was wrapping herself in a thin threadbare robe and her hair was a matted mess.

Jenny sat on the edge of the sofa that seemed to be her spot, and looked at Randy and Carrie with sad eyes, but said nothing.

"Jenny, we have another picture for you to look at." Carrie hated this. This girl's prints were not in the system either. If there was any other way to get a quick ID, she would.

Jenny nodded and reached out for the phone. She held her breath until the phone was in front of her. The look on her face told Carrie she knew her, but gave her time to comment.

Jenny just stared at the phone. Finally Carrie asked, "Do you know her?"

Jenny once again nodded and then handed the phone back to Carrie. "Her name is Amanda. We called her Mandy."

"Was she one of Gus's girls?"

"Yes." Jenny's voice was barely above a whisper.

THE FIRST THING Carrie did when they arrived back at the office was to run a search in their system for Gus. It didn't take long. He had a long list of priors. She printed out his sheet and motioned for Randy as she stormed towards the door. She was on a mission.

Back in the car, Randy said, "You need to calm down."

"I'm calm," said Carrie, but she was grinding her teeth. "Two bodies in three days and they were both Gus' girls."

"Doesn't mean he had anything at all to do with it. They make him money so why kill them?"

Randy was right, but the coincidence just seemed too great to Carrie.

Gus lived on the south side of Oklahoma City. The neighborhood was run down and unkept. Carrie assumed they were primarily rental homes, whose tenants didn't care whether someone kept them up or not.

The home that was listed on Gus' sheet was sandwiched in between two other homes that looked just like his, the only difference was color. His was green. On the front porch sat two men with scowls on their faces.

"This should be fun," said Carrie, as Randy put their SUV in park.

The two men stood as they approached and crossed their arms across their chests. *Were these sentries who guarded the entrance to Gus,* Carrie wondered?

Randy flashed his badge and introduced themselves to

the men. The expressions on their faces didn't change, and they didn't move. "We're here to see Gus," said Randy.

One sentry tilted his head. They were big men and Carrie didn't relish a tussle with either of them.

"Gus ain't here," said the one on the right.

Carrie knew they would have said that whether he was or not. They were here for the sheer purpose of guarding Gus.

"We don't want any trouble, but we have to speak to Gus," said Randy. He was firm and had no plans to let these two prevent them entrance.

Randy stepped forward and the two men stepped together closing the gap between them. "Gus ain't here."

"Then there should be no problem letting us knock on the door," said Carrie.

The two men looked at her as if noticing her for the first time. They were totally unconcerned about her presence. But they should have been, she was determined to see Gus, and was full of grit.

She stepped forward and shoved herself between them, with Randy following. Once at the front door, she banged hard. "Gus, this is Carrie Border with the OSBI. You need to come out and speak with us."

They stood on the porch for several silent minutes. Then just when Carrie was about to bang on the door again, it cracked open. An eye peaked out through the crack.

Carrie had her badge up in a second so the eye could

see. "I'm Carrie Border with the OSBI and this is Randy Jeffries also with the OSBI. We need to speak with Gus."

The crack in the door widened and a Hispanic man of about thirty-five opened the door and led them into the front room. It was a ramshackle room with little to no furnishings. The scent of frying chorizo filled the air, and they heard crackles coming from the other room.

"Did you leave something on the fire?" asked Randy.

"No. I pulled it off." But the man casually turned and walked back to the kitchen. Carrie and Randy followed.

"Are you Gustavo Hernandez?" asked Randy.

"I am." The man appeared unconcerned that two OSBI agents were standing in his kitchen. He moved the skillet back to the flame of the stove and was stirring the chorizo in the skillet. He reached over and whipped three eggs sitting in a bowl, then added the eggs to the chorizo.

"Do you know this girl?" Carrie shoved the picture of Mandy in front of Gus. She saw surprise brush across his face, but in an instant it was gone. He turned to look at her suddenly very serious.

"Where did you take that picture?" Gus asked.

"Where we found her body," said Carrie.

Was that sadness she saw on Gus' face? It was hard to tell. She assumed he was practiced at hiding such emotions in his line of work.

He finished stirring the mixture in the skillet until the eggs were done, then once again removed the skillet from the stove turning off the burner. "Let's go in here and talk. He motioned for them to walk back into the living room."

He gestured to an old sofa and said, "Please sit." He himself sat in a recliner that looked fairly new. Carrie and Randy sat on the edge of the sofa.

"Did Mandy work for you?" Carrie asked as Randy pulled out his notepad.

"What do you mean work for me?" Gus asked in return.

"Gus we know the arrangement you have with certain working girls. This is no time to play coy with us. We need to find her killer," said Carrie.

The expression on Gus' face was blank, but his black eyes were piercing. Carrie thought he might be trying to decide just what he should and shouldn't say.

"I knew her."

"The medical examiner estimated her time of death between two and three this morning. Where were you?" asked Carrie.

Gus turned his palms up and said, "Right here in my bed asleep."

"Can anyone corroborate that?"

Gus grinned. "No mujer hermosa. You come be mi amante you can corroborate."

Carrie's blood boiled. Usually when a man called you a beautiful woman it was a complement, but from Gus, it made her skin crawl. And she certainly couldn't stand the thought of being his lover.

Randy cleared his throat and glanced over at Carrie, prepared to hold her back, but she was still planted firmly on the edge of the sofa.

Carrie was trying to calm herself down. She hated slime like Gus. After seeing both of those dead women and Jenny's bruises, she was convinced Gus had killed them.

"Gus stop playing games. If you don't want to help us here, we will load you up and take you in for interrogation." Randy wasn't playing around. Gus' black eyes swiveled to Randy and his smile faded.

"What time did you get home last night?" asked Randy.

"I got home about midnight. Ask my boys out front," said Gus.

"You can bet we will," said Randy.

"When was the last time you saw Mandy?" asked Carrie.

"About three yesterday afternoon."

"When was the last time you saw Cami?" asked Randy.

Gus' lip snarled and he spat. "La perra."

Randy stopped taking notes and Carrie sat watching Gus with keen interest. Calling her a bitch in front of them must mean Gus hated Cami to the core.

"What did you have against Cami?" asked Carrie.

"She was una puta sucia," growled Gus.

"Unlike your other sucia's?" asked Carrie. "What was so dirty about Cami?"

Gus looked away. Carrie was trying to read the emotion she saw on his face, then suddenly she knew.

Carrie snorted a laugh. "You loved her!"

Gus' head shot back around. "You loved her and she turned you down. And you couldn't bear to watch her go with all those other men." Carrie was guessing, but could tell by the look on Gus' face she'd hit the nail on the head.

Gus quickly recovered and sat stone faced. Carrie continued, "Did you kill her because she turned you down?"

Gus did not respond, his eyes boring holes into Carrie.

Randy suddenly flopped his notebook shut and stood. "Okay, Gus. Let's go. I'm tired of playing your games and you are looking more and more like our guy. Stand up." Randy was done with this sorry excuse for a human.

Fear briefly flashed across Gus' face and then was just as quickly gone again. "No, no, amigo. I'll cooperate." Gus was motioning for Randy to sit back down. Randy and Carrie knew the last thing Gus wanted was to be hauled in.

"Then start talking," Randy demanded.

SANDY SURVEYED HER ROOM. She was finally done and excited to be so. Now she had the entire afternoon open to go help Beth at Safe At Last. She hadn't felt this much excitement in a very long time.

Driving to the safe house, it was hard to contain her anticipation. It was located in a part of town she was not familiar with, but remembered the way from having gone there before.

She exited off of I-35 onto I-40 east and took the first exit which said Scott St/Reno exit. She then went north on Scott Street, then east again, before winding through the neighborhood searching for the nondescript two-story house which was Safe At Last.

After back tracking a few times, Sandy finally turned into the driveway that led to the back of the house. She locked her door and walked to the house. *Why does this neighborhood make me feel so uncomfortable*, she wondered?

She had to be admitted into the house by someone on duty. They had state-of-the-art security and surveillance cameras. Once in, she stored her belongings in a locker she could, and did lock.

Beth led her to the kitchen where preparations were well under way for lunch. Sandy noticed that Beth seemed distracted. "Are you ok?" asked Sandy.

"We'll talk after lunch," Beth whispered to Sandy.

They currently had five girls living on the premises and the resident supervisor which was Beth. Lunch was simple, grilled chicken on beds of salad greens.

Two of the girls had been here awhile and had begun to feel safe and comfortable. The other three were new and still lived in constant fear. During lunch, those three picked at their salads and barely touched the chicken.

Sandy was welcomed to eat with them, and she did. She didn't talk much, merely observed. Her desire was for the girls to get comfortable with her presence and not feel as though she was intruding.

Once lunch was over, the girls were charged with cleanup. Beth led Sandy to her office and shut the door.

Sandy frowned. "What's going on Beth?"

"We're on tighter than usual security right now. There have been two murders of prostitutes in the last three days. Both were within a couple of miles of here."

A tingle of fear erupted inside of Sandy. "Do you know why they were killed?" Sandy asked. She wondered if this was what Randy had told her about and the reason for his concern.

"No we don't. We have to assume that none of our girls are safe, and we must take extra precautions for all our sakes. This may also mean two things. Some additional girls may want to come to us for safety, others may want to run away from here, out of fear."

"What should I do?" asked Sandy.

"Be vigilant when coming and going. We have security and won't allow anyone to enter that we don't absolutely know and trust, however we cannot keep the girls prisoner. I will allow them to go to their jobs and other necessary places. I've arranged male volunteers to go with them escorting them to and from work."

Sandy sat with concern on her face and fear in her heart. She nodded in response to Beth. "How much do the girls know?"

"They know enough. They've heard gossip, the news on the TV, and what I felt was necessary to tell them. It wasn't right to keep it from them, this is their lives. I had to explain to them why there would be volunteers taking them to and from work."

A knock on the door interrupted Sandy's thoughts. It was one of the girls asking a question. Beth rose to go with the girl and at the same time, telling Sandy that was about all she knew and would keep her posted.

Sandy rose to leave Beth's office, her mind raced with random thoughts. She felt totally out of her depth. This was the type of thing Randy and Carrie dealt with on a daily basis, but not Sandy. She wondered if she'd made a mistake volunteering here at Safe At Last.

"We're having a group session where the girls can talk about their situations and also their goals. This is not a therapy session, but provides a sense of healing. Please join us. I think it will help you get to understand them better and in turn help them," said Beth.

In the living room sat the five residents, Beth and Sandy, and one other volunteer. Beth opened in prayer, asking God to give the girls peace and comfort. Sandy hoped for that as well.

"Let's talk about the elephant in the room. You've heard about the two murders. Whoever wants to talk about that, please do," Beth began.

Sandy could see fear and concern on the faces of the girls, and her heart felt compassion for them, but she still didn't know them and their world.

"I knew Mandy," one girl named Lisa began. Tears fell from her eyes.

"I'm so sorry Lisa," said Beth. Sandy could see deep

compassion on Beth's face. She loved these girls as her own sisters. "Do you want to talk about that?"

Lisa nodded and used a tissue that someone handed her, to wipe her cheeks. "I'm from south Texas, El Paso actually. I ran away from home when I was fourteen because my mom's boyfriend beat me. My mom was on drugs. I left. I was staying at Mandy's home for a while, but things were only a little better there.

"We spent a lot of time out at night and before long, met up with some guys who said they would take care of us. We were young and stupid." Lisa crossed and then uncrossed her legs, uncomfortable.

"One night we were out and hanging in an old house. I don't know whose it was, it was pretty shabby, but we were away from home so it was okay by us. I think those guys drugged us, because the next thing I knew, Mandy and I both woke up in the back of a semi-truck with a bunch of other girls from Mexico.

"The truck smelled. I think those girls had been in there for days traveling in the heat. I was terrified and so was Mandy. Our purses were gone and our cell phones too.

"It seemed like we rode forever. It was so hot in the truck that I kept feeling like I was passing out, but then it would bounce and shake me awake."

Lisa sat staring at nothing in the middle of the floor for a few minutes. Everyone in the room gave her time to gather her thoughts.

"We stopped here in Oklahoma City. A man I didn't

know pulled four of us off of the truck in the middle of the night and shut the door on the others. Mandy and I were shoved into the back of a car and were driven to a house where we were told to bathe and change clothes.

"We did. It felt good," Lisa's face remembered the pleasure of the bath after so many days in the heat. But then the smile faded.

"The house was divided into several rooms upstairs. Like where there had been one bedroom it was maybe divided into two or three. There was only enough room for a small twin mattress in each." Tears rolled down Lisa's face again.

"I thought they had abused me when I lived at home, and I guess I was, but nothing like that." A huge sob wracked her body, but she quickly recovered, needing to talk.

"They separated Mandy and me, but in between men, we could go to each other's rooms and talk. We tried to plan a way out, but there were big men guarding us and the rooms. There was always someone there.

"They offered us drugs. We resisted everything at first, but after a while we felt so hopeless that we gave in. The days were often a blur.

"Then one day there was a huge commotion downstairs. People were running and shouting. A man I didn't know came and grabbed both Mandy and me and took us out.

"I'm pretty sure I heard cops and cop cars somewhere in all the ruckus, but I was still pretty high, so I'm not sure. The man took us in his car to another house. His name was Gus, and he was nice to us, at first.

"We still had to work, but he let us out to work the street rather than being stuck in a little room all day. We got to eat good food, and he eased us off of the hard drugs. We felt like we had been liberated. We were so thankful to him.

"But then as time went on, we saw that he was strict in his own way. But it was still better than the house, so we were loyal to him. We were afraid if we weren't that he would send us to another house just like the other one."

Lisa stopped for a time, and when it seemed like she was done talking Beth said, "It left you with two bad choices, two painful choices and you chose the less painful of the two. There is no shame in that."

Lisa looked at Beth and asked, "Do you think Mandy would still be alive if we had stayed in that house?" Lisa's face was wracked with pain. *Could it be that she blames herself for Mandy's death*, Sandy wondered?

"Lisa, do you want to tell us how you came to be here and not Mandy?" Beth asked.

Lisa nodded, once again being pulled from her faraway thoughts. "Word had gotten around about Safe At Last. Mandy and I had talked about it, but it terrified us. Gus was good to us, but then he used that to put fear in us. The thought of leaving him terrified us."

Lisa ducked her head as if she were ashamed. "And honestly we didn't know how anyone could really help us. We were young and stupid and used up. If someone said they would get us out, then what? We didn't even graduate out of high school. We had no place to live and didn't know how to work anywhere else."

"But then one day when I was working, a lady gave me a sheet of paper, and that sheet talked about Safe At Last and that they would help us get our GED, get a job, and help us get a new life.

"I took the paper home that night and talked to Mandy about it. She wanted to believe it, we both did. But she was so scared of Gus.

"The night I left I had called the number on the paper and they planned to meet us and bring us here. We didn't know where 'here' was and that's good. Mandy and I were set to meet at the right time, but Mandy never showed."

A deep sigh escaped Lisa's lips. "I wanted to wait for her, and we waited for a while, but the lady said someone could catch us the longer we waited. Finally, we left. Then this morning we heard that Mandy was dead."

Lisa looked up at Beth. "I think Gus killed her because I left. I think he tried to make her tell him where I'd gone. He bought and paid for us and we were his property. I've seen Gus' temper and I have no doubt that he killed Mandy, and it's my fault." Lisa finally stopped. Tears were running in sheets over her cheeks as she sat and tore her tissue to shreds out of sheer anxiety.

"Lisa, it's not your fault. Gus, no one, has the right to buy and sell human beings. You were not his property. I know you believe that Gus killed Mandy and that it is because of you. We don't know that Gus killed her and if he did, that is a choice he made. The fault lies with him, not you."

Sandy felt the deep sadness that blanketed the room. Inadequacy flooded her. Randy was right, she had nothing to offer these girls. She was so ill equipped to help them.

Then Sandy felt a tiny thin hand slip into hers. She looked down to see that the little girl beside her had reached out to hold her hand. Sandy looked up from their hands to her face, and the girl, not yet thirteen, smiled a timid smile back at her. "I like your pretty blonde hair," the girl said.

Sandy thought her heart would break in two. She squeezed the girl's hand and gave her the biggest smile she could offer. Then she reached out and gave the girl a hug.

Maybe, just maybe, she did have something to offer them.

"Jenny, I spoke with that place Safe At Last," Pride said. It had taken her a day or so to mention it to Jenny and even now she held her breath. The last thing Pride wanted was for Jenny to think Pride no longer wanted her there. But with two girls dead, the most important thing was Jenny's safety. Jenny looked up from the magazine she was looking at.

"You did?" A cocktail of emotions flooded her. She had been terrified since Cami's death, then another kind of fear came when Pride had talked about her going to that place.

"I'm so afraid that you are going to wind up dead like Cami and Mandy." The look on Pride's face was pure agony. "I can hardly bare the thought of you leaving me. I love you like my own daughter, but would sooner die as see you harmed."

Jenny looked back down at the magazine. Beautiful ladies wearing expensive clothes looked back at her from the page. Did people really live like this, Jenny wondered. The pretty blue top one lady wore said it was $125.00, and the pants were $165.00. This was a magazine of fairytales, but Jenny didn't live in a fairytale. She pushed the magazine away and looked up at Pride.

"What did they say when you called them?"

"They're primarily for rescuing victims from human trafficking, but they also take in prostitutes and dancers if they feel they are at a place where they truly want to make a change. They don't want to take someone in who isn't serious about leaving the life and doing what it takes to do so." Pride was at the sink washing dishes and now had her back to Jenny. Jenny wanted to see her face so she could read it.

Jenny didn't say anything for the longest time. She'd known this life for so long and didn't know what it was like to have any other life. Gus would never let her go. He would find her and maybe kill her. She glanced back at the open page of the magazine. The smiling ladies beckoned to her. "Come join us."

"Pride come sit with me," said Jenny. She wanted to talk more, but wanted Pride's honest opinion and she didn't know if she was getting it if she couldn't see her face.

Pride glanced over her shoulder, then dried the dish she was working on and sat it in the drainer. With a practiced swoop she flicked the towel over her shoulder and pulled out the chair across from Jenny.

"What would you do Pride?" asked Jenny.

Pride was awash with her own regrets. What would she do? She knew what she would have done at Jenny's age. She would have made the wrong choice for the wrong reasons. But now, older and wiser, she knew what choice she would make.

"I would get out of this life once and for all." Pride reached across the table and shut the magazine, then motioned for Jenny's hands. When Jenny complied, she squeezed them tight and looked her in the eyes with sincerity.

"I've made too many mistakes and lived a life of regrets. I can't change a one of them now, but I can tell you that now is the opportunity for you to get out. To get out and not make the same mistakes I made.

"Gus will find me and kill me," said Jenny.

"This life will kill you if you don't go," Pride was matter-of-fact.

Jenny pulled her hands away and nodded. Pride

didn't want to push Jenny. If she wasn't ready, then it wouldn't stick.

"What do I have to do?" Jenny asked. Her face was pinched with worry.

"I don't know. I think the best thing is to just talk with them first. Before you decide, you need to know as much as you can about them and the program."

"Do you think Gus killed Cami?" asked Jenny switching gears on their conversation, but in her mind the decision to go into the program was linked.

"I don't know," said Pride, and she didn't know. But someone was killing those girls and even if it wasn't Gus, Jenny could be the next one.

"If I'm not doing this — what I do now, what will I do? I didn't finish high school. No one will hire me."

"I think the program will help you with that."

Jenny got up and walked to the coffeepot and filled her cup, both she and Pride let their conversation rest for a moment.

"When can I talk to them?" asked Jenny.

Pride turned around in her chair to face Jenny. "I'll give them a call."

THE MAN USED his left hand, the one with the diamond ring, to smooth back his greased hair. It was in order as usual, so he lowered his hand slowly back down to the arm of the black leather chair where he was seated.

"Gus, we've been patient with you," the man, Alexander, said.

Gus was sitting in the chair opposite of Alex, the man who had snared him and his life over twenty years ago. His blood pressure was high and pressing against the top of his skull. This meeting with Alex would not end well.

Alex uncrossed and recrossed his legs in the opposite direction. He looked down and ran his fingers along the sharp crease of his expensive gray trousers.

He spoke again without looking at Gus. "Why are my girls dying? Are you not in charge of protecting them?" His voice was eerily calm and smooth. It made shivers ripple up Gus' spine.

Gus willed himself to remain calm. Panic would only prove that Alex had something to worry about with Gus. "You've known me for a long time. I've never failed to do anything you asked me. I have men watching these girls. I don't know who's killing them."

Alex looked up at Gus. His black eyes were as cold and lifeless as Gus' were, but unlike Gus, pure evil radiated from them like tractor beams sucking you into the hell they came from. Gus had to look away for fear of losing his soul.

The man used his thumb to rotate the diamond ring on his finger; its facets catching the light. Gus watched the dance of light and wished he was anywhere but here.

"Gus you are failing me. What? We now have two girls dead and I suspect that one is missing and maybe dead.

Two of them lived right underneath your roof. You will die if you do not tell me the truth."

The man tilted his head back and looked at Gus downward as if looking down his nose at him. His eyes had narrowed into slits and Gus could not look at them.

"Why would I kill them? They did their jobs. They made us money. I had no reason to kill them." Gus was clenching his jaw. He tried to reconcile his fate. Today he knew he was going to die.

"What am I to do with you Gus?" Alex grinned and stood. He walked over to Gus and patted his cheek full on with his palm. The pats felt like slaps to Gus.

With a nod of Alex's head the two goons who stood in the corner, dressed in suits that cost more than Gus made in a year, walked over to Alex. With unspoken understanding the two men easily pulled Gus up from the chair with their bulky arms.

Gus hung in the air suspended between the two brutes, face to face with Alex. "You will die. Not today, but you will die and it will be at my hand if this does not stop. Find the missing girl and bring her back."

Gus nodded. He did not want to appear weak, but for all of his hardened demeanor, he was terrified.

The two men carried Gus to the front door of the dimly lit restaurant, each holding one of his arms up under the armpit. Then without ceremony, they literally threw him out the front door.

Gus landed on his feet after a stumble, then looked up and down the street to see who had seen. He took a deep breath and then stood tall as if he had not just had a meeting with the devil himself.

His two men had stayed in his black SUV as instructed. It was parked on a gravel lot to the side of the building, so they hadn't seen Gus' humiliating exit. A cauldron of terror and anger danced throughout his body as he opened the passenger door, sat down, and slammed the door closed.

They sat with the engine running, waiting for Gus to give them instructions. Then suddenly, Gus began beating the dash with both fists, screaming and cursing. Once his tirade had ended, he commanded the driver Vince, to take him to Pride's. He was going to get to the bottom of this.

CHAPTER 7

Beth's Safe At Last dedicated cell phone rang. She was walking down the hall to her office after their group time.

"This is Safe At Last. How may I help you?" She unlocked the door to her office and tucked the key in her pocket.

"My name's Pride, and I have a friend here who wants to talk to you about your program." Pride's words sounded stilted and awkward. She was nervous and not sure what to say to this lady.

"Ok, can you put her on the phone?"

"Would it be ok if I put you on speaker so I can hear too? She trusts me to help her and I need to hear what you have to say as well."

"That would be fine," said Beth. "What's your friend's name?"

She could hear the girl ask the lady named Pride if she should tell her her real name. Pride confirmed that it would be okay. Beth wondered if this was her mother. No, she had said she was a friend. But Beth knew she must be an older friend, a mother figure to this girl.

"My name is Jenny."

"Hi Jenny," Beth's voice was calm and soothing. "What can I do for you?"

"I - I...," Jenny began.

"Go ahead," encouraged Pride.

"I'm a prostitute." Tears slide down Jenny's cheeks. Saying the words brought shame and humiliation. What would this lady think of her? Would she think she was the dirty trash she felt?

Beth could hear the pain in Jenny's words. "Jenny it's ok. That's what we are here for. How can I help you?"

Jenny let out a sigh. Could it be possible that this lady really could help her? Fear surged through her once again, and she had the impulse to hang up, but Pride held the phone.

"I'm afraid. I don't want to live like this anymore," said Jenny.

"Do you have a family?" asked Beth.

Jenny shook her head, then realize Beth needed to hear an answer. "No. Well, I have Pride. She's my family." She looked up at Pride and Pride's warm smile gave her courage.

"How long have you been a prostitute?"

"A few years now. But I'm scared and I don't want to do this anymore."

"Why are you so scared now?" asked Beth.

A sob caught in Jenny's throat as she answered. "Someone killed my friend Cami. She was a prostitute too. Gus is real mad and I'm so scared." It all came out in a ramble.

Beth felt this girls fear. It was genuine if her friend was one of the murdered girls. "Okay, Jenny. Are you ready to come here to Safe At Last?"

Jenny's stomach gripped her. "Right now you mean?"

"When were you thinking? Are you in immediate danger? If you are, don't you think it best we move quickly?"

"What do you mean immediate danger?" Jenny asked.

"Are you concerned that someone will harm you soon?"

"Yes — No. I don't know." Jenny began full out bawling.

Pride took the phone from between her and Jenny and spoke to Beth. "Can we meet somewhere and sit and talk with you? She may be in immediate danger, but it terrifies her to take this move too. Maybe if we meet somewhere, we can talk and make a plan." Pride had pulled Jenny in close with her free arm, patting her thin back.

Beth was thinking hard. They could meet in an out of the way place. But she had to be sure that this wasn't a ruse to draw her out and then follow her back to the safe house.

"We have to be careful. If you are in danger, then you could lead them to me and therefore to the girls I'm trying to protect.

Do you have a pen and paper handy? I'll give you a series of instructions to follow. If you see anyone suspicious following you, text abort to this number immediately, wherever you are. Do you understand?"

"Yes ma'am. I do. I'm ready." Pride let go of Jenny and listened intently to Beth's instructions, writing each one down then confirming she had them correct.

"I will meet you there," said Beth as she closed the phone.

THE WHITE BOARDS held photos of two girls, Cami and Mandy. Details written in wipe off ink surrounded their faces. Also on the board was a photo of Gus.

"So both Mandy and Cami were Gus' girls," Carrie said out loud. She was deep in her own thoughts, but often saying it out loud helped. She drew a red line from both Mandy and Cami to Gus.

"Gus had the opportunity and the means," said Randy. "But did he have the motive?"

"He loved Cami." Carrie turned to look at Randy for confirmation. After a few seconds Randy nodded still looking at the whiteboard. "Maybe when she kept denying him, his temper got the best of him and he killed her." Carrie paused again thinking.

"But what about Mandy?" Randy asked. "I can see what you are saying about Cami, but that wouldn't fit for both girls."

"But he could have gotten angry at Mandy for some other reason," said Carrie. She dropped her crossed arms in a huff and sat down in front of the computer. She felt like she was trying to shove a square peg in a round hole.

"Have we heard from Mike and Rick yet about canvassing the old amusement park?" Carrie asked. *Maybe looking in another direction will give me some perspective*, she thought.

"No," replied Randy.

"We have Mandy's name, but we have no idea where she's from. Gus was no help on that. Either he really didn't know where she was from or he is still lying to us."

Carrie was typing furiously on the keyboard. She was searching the criminal database to see if there were other similar crimes in other states or areas. Maybe this was bigger than she thought. But after searching with several parameters, she found nothing exactly like their cases.

Carrie turned her chair and leaned back looking at Randy. "So Jenny and Cami worked together, and they both lived at Pride's. I am wondering if Mandy worked with someone who also lived with Gus. We need to find that girl and talk to her."

"Gus won't give us a name," said Randy.

"I hate to bother Jenny again," said Carrie. "Maybe we could call her instead of going back down there."

Randy nodded and looked for Pride's phone number.

The phone rang for the longest time, but then on what had to be the last ring Pride answered. "Hello," said Pride.

"Hi Pride, this is Randy Jefferies with the OSBI. I hate to bother you and Jenny again, but we talked to Gus and we know that Mandy lived with him." Pride said nothing, only listened.

"Both Cami and Jenny lived and worked together. Did someone, another girl work with Mandy and live with Gus'?" asked Randy.

"I don't know. Let me get Jenny."

Randy could tell that Pride had either covered the receiver or muffled it into her bosom in order to talk to Jenny.

"Jenny says she thinks a girl named Lisa lived with Mandy and Gus. She said she hasn't seen Lisa around for a while."

"Is there anything else that Jenny can tell us about Mandy and Lisa?" asked Randy.

Once again muffled voices was all Randy heard.

"Not that she can think of," said Pride.

"Thanks Pride. We appreciate you and Jenny's help."

Once off the phone, Randy relayed to Carrie what Pride had said. "She hasn't seen Lisa for a while. Could we have another body and just haven't found it yet?" Carrie asked.

"Could be," replied Randy.

Carrie walked to the whiteboard and drew a square next to the photos of Cami and Mandy, then drew a question mark above and the name Lisa inside. She then drew a red line straight to Gus.

"We should probably go back and talk to Gus about Lisa," said Carrie. He made her skin crawl, and she hated being in the same room with him, but if that's what it would take to help her find these girls' killer then she would.

Just then Randy's phone rang. It was Rick. "Hi Rick I'm putting you on speaker so Carrie can hear too. Whatcha got?"

"Well, we did a canvas around the old amusement park and we found the girl's family. Her name was Camelia, Camelia Anderson. Both the other girls in the picture were her sisters. The one to her left that Jenny pointed out is Samantha, they call her Sam. She and Cami went missing at about the same time. They're both in the missing persons database. We were looking for her under her nickname Cami and not her actual name Camelia."

"So what happened?" Carrie asked.

"They just disappeared. The parents both work all the time and my guess is they aren't real attentive to the girls. Looks like they kind of raised themselves."

"Did you talk to the other sisters?" Randy asked.

"I did, but they didn't know anything. There are two more. One is in the photo and the other one was taking the pic. They are Adelaide and Bridgette. They are fourteen and fifteen now. They were twelve and thirteen when the other two went missing."

"We are meeting the parents at the morgue to id the body," said Rick.

They said their goodbye's and hung up. Carrie's mind was racing. She went back to the whiteboard and drew another box next to Lisa's and put in Samantha's name with a question mark.

"Have we searched for any Jane Doe's at the morgue? Of course we have," said Carrie answering her own question.

"I am so frustrated with this case. Why can't we find any clues?"

"Well, they are still sorting through the debris at both sites. Neither one was kept clean. The lake more so than under the bridge, but they are still going through each little piece of paper and trash," said Randy.

"I want a rush on the scrapings under their fingernails," said Carrie. She called the crime lab and sweetly demanded they put their case and the fingernail scrapings at the top of the list. The tech sweetly told her to get in line.

Randy sat thinking about Sandy. "You know Sandy has started volunteering at the program Safe At Last. I wonder if they know anything that could help us," said Randy.

"I would imagine that they are pretty tight-lipped. Too much attention could get those girls hurt," said Carrie, but she was already concocting an angle to see if they could talk to them, without getting them caught in the crossfire.

"Has Sandy said anything about the girls there? What their names or ages are? What they look like?" Carrie was doing that rapid fire thing she always did. After eight years Randy had grown quite comfortable with it. He'd learned to just let it all settle, then respond.

"No, I don't think she knows any of them well enough yet to say anything. They may have cautioned her to not talk about them. I do remember her saying there were about five girls there, but that number goes up and down," replied Randy.

"We could call and make a stern request to come to their location, but even if they complied, I don't want to draw attention to them and in turn hurt the girls or the program," said Carrie as she paced the floor.

"Let me call Sandy and see if she can connect me to the director and we'll pick her brain about what to do."

"We can't wait for another body to turn up before we do something," said Carrie.

"Beth," began Sandy, hesitant to bother Beth, "My husband Randy is on the phone and was wondering if he could talk with you." Sandy was new here and felt as though she were on a trial basis. The last thing she wanted was to violate some code of privacy.

A second or two passed by before Beth answered, curious about what he wanted. Did he want to talk about

Sandy, she wondered. She didn't have time for another concerned husband.

"Okay," said Beth as she reached out for the phone. She walked into her office and shut the door.

"This is Beth."

"This is Randy Jeffries, Sandy's husband, as you know. I'm not sure if you also know that I am an OSBI agent and am working on the two recent prostitute murders."

Beth, suddenly interested, leaned forward in her chair placing her arms on her desk. "I remember Sandy mentioning you were and OSBI agent, but I didn't know that you were working on the murders."

"I wanted to reach out to you because we are hitting a hard wall. My partner and I understand and respect the work you're doing and don't want to do anything that would put you or your victims at risk…

"But," said Beth.

"But we were wondering if we could speak with you. Off site where there would be no danger of revealing the location of the girls."

"Are you going to want to speak with the girls?" Beth had to draw the line there. They were too fragile.

"Not now. If we feel that any of them have something that could help us, we can discuss how to approach that when we meet."

Beth twirled her pen as she thought. "When and where did you want to meet?"

"We want to meet as soon as you are available. You name the place so you will feel comfortable."

"Do you know the old cafe off of NW 35th and May? They call it Penny's Place, a small out of the way place that few people know about. I can meet you there for breakfast in the morning. I have another meeting today that will take a while and then I have things I have to finish up here this evening."

"That will work. And just so you know, I haven't discussed this case with Sandy and don't intend to," said Randy. He was hoping she would read his underlying meaning that he hoped to keep this as private as possible.

"I understand," answered Beth.

GUS WAS BANGING on Pride's front door so hard that the little house was in danger of altogether collapsing.

"Pride I know you or Jenny are in there! Open this door right now." Gus couldn't remember when he had been so angry. He motioned for his guys to go around to the back.

He stepped to the edge of the porch and looked out into the street and surrounding neighborhood. It was quiet. He then whirled around and gave the front door one powerful kick.

The wood snapped and the door jamb hung in splinters. "Pride, Jenny!" Gus yelled through the house. His men, having heard the crash of the front door came running back around to the front and into the house. They were on hyper-alert and ready for battle.

When they realized, along with Gus, that the house was empty, they relaxed. Gus strode through the house with his hands on his hips, looking, thinking, contemplating what to do next.

Finally, he turned to head out the front door. "We have to find them," he said.

"Where do we look boss?" One of the men asked.

Then suddenly Gus thought of something he'd seen in the house and turned around and trotted back in. Yes, there it was on the small kitchen table, a tablet with indentions where someone had been writing on the sheet that had been on top.

He carried the tablet over to the kitchen window for more light. He could tell it was a list of instructions, but couldn't read them. He glanced around and found a stub of a pencil in a drawer. Then lightly, as he had seen done on tv, he brushed the pencil lead across the paper.

The indentions revealed words. It confused him at first, but then he realized that the first few lines were instructions for metro bus lines. He ripped off the page and headed back out the door.

Once in the car, he snickered with an evil laugh. "I've got 'em." He then gave Vince the first instruction on the list.

By the time Gus arrived at the first bus stop, no one was there. He had missed them. Pulling out his phone he searched for metro bus lines and their stops and times. If he was reading this list right, then this bus would head to Bricktown, the renovated district just east of downtown.

Vince sped away at Gus' instruction and he looked back at the note. He saw that from there; they were to exit the bus and take the trolley to the Transit Center at 4th and Hudson.

He looked at the time and realized that they had probably already been and gone at Bricktown and were likely at the Transit Center by now. Rather than have Vince stop in Bricktown, they raced on through.

As the Transit Center came into site, he saw the bus pull away that he knew they had to be on. *Where are they going*, he wondered? He decided rather than haul them both into his SUV when he caught up with them, he would follow them and see where they were going.

There was no name on the paper that he could see, only instructions of various bus lines to follow. *So who are they going to meet and why take such a convoluted method of getting there*, he wondered?

The bus Pride and Jenny were on drove on a route leading to NW OKC. Gus followed for almost an hour until the bus arrived at the Warr Acres Metropolitan Library. He saw both of them get off of the bus and go into the library.

Gus was getting itchy to get at them, but he knew according to the list of instructions that this was not their final destination. If they wanted to read a book or check one out, there were tons of libraries they had passed on the way here.

After about thirty minutes, Pride and Jenny came out of the library and walked back east until they came to a bus stop about one quarter of a mile away. They were going back the way they had come. Maybe this had been their destination.

Gus sat in the parking lot of a shopping center diagonally across from the bus stop. But before he could decide what to do, the bus stopped, and they got on.

He referred to the note. From there they were to take the bus to Deaconess Hospital. They did as someone had instructed them with Gus right behind them.

Once at the hospital they walked in. After ten minutes Gus was getting worried. It was a big place and the next note was not as clear as the others.

He once again referred to the map of routes he had pulled up on his phone. There was another route that picked up passengers on the other side of the hospital. That is where they were!

He had Vince hurry to the other side of the hospital and saw the bus pull away from the curb. He had not seen Pride and Jenny get on. But the notes had instructed them to, so he assumed they had done that just, as they had followed all the other instructions.

After three hours of playing this cat-and-mouse game of busses and trolleys, they were back at Bricktown and on a trolley. Gus was fuming. He didn't have time to waste playing this charade. But if they were going to so much trouble to avoid someone following them, then that someone was probably him. Wouldn't they be surprised when they saw him, he thought.

Back in Bricktown, at the corner of Mickey Mantle Dr.

and Sheridan Ave., they got off the trolley and walked north on Mickey Mantle. He instructed Vince to hang way back, knowing they could easily be spotted here.

When they got to Main Street, they turned east. "Damn," exclaimed Gus. They were almost to the Bricktown police precinct. Gus had Vince park in an alley with heavy tree cover and waited.

Instead of going into the police precinct they went into the bail bondsman across the street. Looking at the sheet there were no instructions after arriving at Bricktown. Apparently whoever had been giving her instructions, told her to remember their last destination or Pride just thought she would, and saw no need to write it down.

That's okay, Gus thought. They will come out eventually and then he would have them.

ONCE INSIDE THE Presto Bail Bond building, Pride and Jenny just stood there unsure of what to do. It had worn them out traveling for over three hours in this hundred degree heat. Arriving here was their last instruction, so they waited.

"Are you Pride?" A lady came up and asked them?

"I am," said Pride. Her face was red, and she felt as though she would faint.

"Here sit down. You look like you might pass out. Are you okay?" The lady asked.

Pride gladly fell into a chair. The whooshing was loud

as the air exited the pleather cushion. Her heart was pounding. The exertion of their afternoon travels was threatening to kill her. It had been hard on Jenny, but at Pride's weight, it could prove fatal.

The lady left and returned with two bottles of water and gave one each to Pride and Jenny. They both thanked the lady, and Pride gulped hers down even knowing that drinking too fast wasn't good.

Her thin cotton house dress was wet with perspiration and her thin hair was damp and limp against her face. She knew she must look a fright, but all she wanted right then was to catch her breath and breathe.

Jenny's concerned face looked at Pride. "Are you ok?" Jenny asked.

Pride patted Jenny's hands that laid in her lap and smiled. "I will be. I just need to catch my breath."

About fifteen minutes after they arrived, a nice-looking lady with short brown hair came from the back. She looked to be just a little younger than Pride, but maybe she had just lead an easier life, Pride thought.

The lady squatted down in front of where Pride and Jenny sat. "My name is Beth. We spoke on the phone." Her voice was low so prying ears couldn't hear.

Let's slip out the back to my car and we can go to a better place to talk. Pride had had time to catch her breath, so she and Jenny stood and followed the lady out the back door.

There to the right off of the back door sat a silver Toyota Highlander, fairly new. Beth motioned for them to quickly get inside and as soon as they shut both doors, Beth had the vehicle moving.

"Are you sure no one followed you?" Beth asked.

"We looked and we couldn't tell. I really don't think so," said Jenny. She was scared to death. This traveling and skulking around had set her nerves on edge. Then there was Pride. Jenny had thought more than once she would pass out on her. She couldn't lose Pride, she just couldn't.

They rode with Beth until they reached Penn Square Mall. Beth pulled into the garage parking and traveled to the top of the garage. She parked close to the bridge which led to the mall. She then led them across the bridge and into the mall itself.

It was late afternoon in the middle of the week and the mall was subdued. Pride immediately felt self conscious. She knew she looked atrocious.

Pride stopped once inside the mall and said, "Beth I don't belong here. I look terrible. I'm hot and sweaty from being out in the heat this afternoon and honestly I can't walk another step."

Beth gave Pride a genuine smile and put her arm as far around Pride's shoulders as she could. "Pride you are fine and you are beautiful in God's eyes. We aren't going far."

She led them to a little eatery that was just a few feet inside the door they had entered from. Jenny's mouth was agape at the sites and sounds around her. Across the way, she could see mannequins of beautiful new clothes like the ones she'd seen in the magazine. Clothes she would never own.

Beth sat them at a table. "Shall I get you something to eat or drink? Have you eaten today?"

"I would love some water," said Pride. Jenny asked, "Can I have a Dr. Pepper?" She was almost too afraid to ask, but was willing to pay for it if she needed to.

Beth laid her hand on Jenny's as she was reaching to pull money out of her little purse. "No Jenny. I want to treat you." Then she smiled at Jenny.

"I think I would like a snack," said Beth hoping that if she ate something, then they would not feel timid about also eating. "What would you like?"

"Come on now, it's my treat," Beth encouraged them.

Jenny perked up and said, "I would like to have some of those fries with chili and cheese on them." She pointed at the picture meant to entice customers.

"Pride, what about you?"

Pride was not used to allowing people to give to her. It usually meant they would want something in return. But his lady made her feel different. She felt genuine.

"I'll have whatever you're having ma'am. I'm not picky," said Pride.

Both Jenny and Pride felt out-of-place even though this wasn't a fancy place. They well knew of their station in life and that it was well below anyone that would be at this mall, or any other mall for that matter.

Beth returned with a red tray full of fresh hot french fries topped with chili and cheese. Three orders, one for each. Normally Beth would have ordered something else, but she wanted more than anything for these ladies to not feel out of place, so she followed Jenny's lead and ordered chili-cheese fries for them all.

Beth allowed the ladies to rest, eat, and settle into her company before attempting any more conversation. Once they'd made a considerable dent in their food, Beth began, "How did you ladies come to know about our program?"

Jenny and Pride looked at each other then Pride said, "Well a few years ago someone gave me a paper with your info on it. I don't normally keep stuff like that, but this time I did. I folded it up and shoved it in the back of my junk drawer. I'd forgotten all about it until lately."

"I would like to hear more about you ladies. Can you tell me a little about yourselves?"

Jenny ducked her head and kept nibbling on her fries, so Pride began, "Well, years ago I was a prostitute," Pride swallowed and continued. "Finally, I couldn't do it no more. I get a disability check each month and that keeps me alive. I have… had two girls live with me. I kind of watch out for them." Then the reality of what Pride had just said overwhelmed her. She had not taken good enough care of Cami though, had she?

She choked up and looked away from Beth as tears slid down her cheeks. Beth reached out and covered Pride's hand with her own. "Pride what is wrong? I'm here to help." Beth's face was compassionate and her voice sounded sincere.

Pride took a long look at Beth, then told her of Cami's

death and all about Gus and Jenny. Jenny let Pride tell the tale, she wasn't sure if she would have the words.

Once Pride had told Beth everything she could think of, Beth turned to Jenny. "Jenny our goal at Safe At Last is primarily for rescuing those who have been victims of human trafficking. We want to rescue them and then get them home to their families. Sometimes they have no one to go back home to.

"They have no skills or knowledge of how to live in the world. We provide an initial place to stay, we have counselors that come by and help them to get past the pain, shame, and guilt of that life. We have other volunteers that help prepare them for the GED so they will at least have a high school equivalency.

"Then we work on job placement. We know that just getting one out of the life is no good if we can't provide them with the skills to live life differently.

"I will tell you that if you are serious about this, you will have to be willing to do the work. You will have to stay focused on learning and doing what is necessary. You must leave that life and all those that are tied to it. You must, absolutely must, break all contact with anyone you are currently associated with now." Beth stopped to let that soak in.

Jenny wasn't sure she comprehended everything Beth had just said. She had no one to leave behind. She had lost Cami and part of the whole point of this was getting away from Gus. Surely she didn't mean Pride too.

Her concerned expression looked from Beth to Pride and back again. "Surely you don't mean Pride too."

"Jenny I know that is hard to comprehend. Pride has done right by you. She has loved you and taken good care of you, but those that are in that world, Gus and the others will use her to get to you if they know you are still in contact with her. For Pride's safety and your own, it is best to cut all ties."

Jenny thought her heart would break. She began shaking her head. "I can't. I just can't." Jenny thought she would be sick.

"Jenny, don't worry. I am not here to force you to do anything you do not, cannot do. But I want to be honest with you. We go to great lengths to keep the whereabouts of the safe house private so that the residents can feel safe."

"But," Jenny turned to look at Pride. "Pride won't be safe if I leave her. Gus will come looking for me whether I break ties with her or not and he will kill her!"

Panic set in and Jenny felt dizzy. "We're dead. We're both dead Pride. He'll kill us both no matter what we do." Jenny turned in her chair and bent over resting her head on her hands.

Beth got out of her chair and squatted down by Jenny putting her arm around her. The girl, riddled with panic and grief, was resistant to her comfort. "Jenny we'll try to help Pride too." Beth's heart was breaking. There had to be something they could do for Pride too. She knew Pride loved these girls.

"No ma'am. I'm okay. Jenny I'm okay. You hear me now, girl? You can do this. You have to do this. Do it for me, please." Pride's eyes were pleading with Jenny. She knew Beth was right, Jenny had to break all ties with everyone from her past. Gus didn't scare her. She had dealt with men like him all her life.

She would miss Jenny, but there would be other girls come along that she could help. Girls that didn't want to leave the life. It would break her heart though. She had gotten so attached to Jenny. Had Pride ever had a daughter, it would have been Jenny.

"You don't have to decide right now Jenny. But with a killer on the loose and killing girls you know, the sooner you decide, the better."

Beth stood up and sat back down in her chair. She began cleaning the trash from the table piling it back on the red tray. Jenny sat numbly looking at Beth's actions.

Pride couldn't look at either of them.

CHAPTER 8

*P*enny's Place was an old traditional diner. Randy liked it. It was filled with early morning workers stopping to eat before heading on their way. The waitress Alice, her nametag read, seated the three in a booth by the front windows.

"Thank you for agreeing to a meeting with us Beth," said Randy.

"I want to do whatever I can to help, but please remember I have to walk a fine line to keep my girls safe," said Beth.

"We understand," said Carrie.

They ordered breakfast and Randy and Carrie talked about their case. They had two girls dead and two missing. The common denominator was a man named Gustavo Hernandez, or Gus as the girls called him.

At the mention of the name Gus, Beth's head jerked up from her western omelet to look at Carrie eye to eye. "Did you say Gus?"

Carrie felt her skin prickle. This was it. They were about to learn something key to help them in this case. "Yes. What do you know?"

Beth sat her eating utensils down before beginning. "One of the girls we now have lived with Gus. The other girl that lived with her there is one of the murdered girls," said Beth.

"Who do you have there?" asked Carrie.

"Lisa."

Carrie and Randy looked at each other, both about to shout, but didn't want to make a scene in the diner.

"We have been looking for Lisa," said Carrie. "We need to talk to her."

Beth had suspected they would ask to do that. She wanted to help in whatever way was necessary, to help find who was murdering those girls, while still protecting them.

"I know you need to, but we have to do it in a way to keep her and the others safe. These men, as you well know, will stop at nothing to take back these girls or kill them."

Randy and Carrie were nodding. "We well know," said Randy.

"I can't have you come to the safe house, but I can arrange for Lisa and I to meet you somewhere." Beth looked at her watch. "It's still early. What about meeting back here in a few hours at nine?"

Just then Beth's Safe At Last cell phone rang. She never wanted to miss a call on that line because to her it was a potential lifeline to a victim.

Mumbling her excuses she answered the call. "This is Safe At Last…" Before she could finish she heard Pride's voice on the line.

"We need to get Jenny to you now. When we came home last night, our door was busted in. I know it was Gus looking for Jenny. She went out and worked last night but avoided being where Gus would find her. We have to get her out of here now."

"Okay," said Beth. "Let me call you right back with a plan."

"Problem?" Randy asked, seeing the interaction between Beth and the caller.

Beth took a deep breath and looked intently at Randy and Carrie. She explained the situation behind the call.

"We know Jenny and Pride," said Carrie.

"Come with us. We will go get her right now," said Randy. He tossed some bills on the table and all three of them hurried out the door and to their SUV.

They knew the way and in fifteen minutes were pulling up outside of Pride's house. When they approached her house, they saw the mangled front door and frame. Someone had done a poor patchwork job to repair the damage that Gus had done.

Randy knocked on the door, and it quickly flew open. Having gotten a quick return call from Beth while on their way, Jenny and Pride had been watching out the window waiting for them.

Jenny was standing in the middle of the room with an old bag at her feet. She was wringing her hands and shuffling from foot to foot.

Beth put her hands on Jenny's shoulders and looked her in the eye. "You remember what we talked about yesterday? If you come with me you are breaking all ties to the past."

Jenny looked up at Pride. Her grief was clearly evident on her face as she nodded. "Can Pride come too, please? Gus will kill her."

Beth looked at Randy and Carrie. What could they do to help Pride? They looked back at Beth. "We can have a patrol car periodically drive by, but we can't guarantee constant surveillance."

Beth made a quick decision. "Pride we have room for you now. Would you consider helping us at the safe house? You have experience with these girls. You might as well help us out."

Pride smiled at Beth, then looked at Jenny. "I need to stay here Jenny. There will be other girls like you. I will be more help to them if I help them here and then maybe I can get them to Beth."

"Pride is there somewhere else you can go for a while at least?" asked Carrie.

Once again Pride smiled at Carrie. "I'll be fine." There was an eery calm to Pride, thought Carrie. It was as if she was resigning herself to her fate, whatever it should be.

Beth nodded. "If you change your mind, you have my number. Promise me you will call if you need us," said Beth.

Randy and Carrie confirmed their readiness to help as well, assuring Pride that a patrol officer would be close at hand.

Carrie was already on the phone requesting a forty-eight hour watch outside before random patrols started.

Randy, Carrie, and Beth stepped outside to give Pride and Jenny a private goodbye.

Pride was summoning all her strength for this moment. She'd never loved another person the way she loved and cared for this young girl. She was willing to give her life for her. She also knew she needed to be strong right then. If Jenny saw her waver in the least, then Jenny would not go.

"Jenny this is your chance to have a new life, a good life. Please go and do all that Beth tells you to do. Know you are loved. I will always love you." Pride enveloped Jenny in her warm embrace and held her for as long as she dared; any longer and she would have never let her go.

Jenny looked up at Pride and nodded, unable to say a word. With tears in her eyes, Jenny walked out of Pride's house for the very last time.

Gus pulled down Pride's street just as the black SUV arrived. It was those stupid OSBI cops. But they had someone else with them.

He ordered his driver to pull around where they could see but be better hidden. It was that lady from yesterday he'd seen Pride and Jenny ride off with.

His driver had gotten separated in the downtown construction traffic and they hadn't been able to catch up with them. But now she was here with the cops.

Waiting was not Gus' strong suite. He squirmed in his seat wondering what was going on inside. Then the door opened, and the three walked out and soon Jenny followed. But Pride remained inside. Good, he thought. I'll get her.

His driver was ready to pull up to Pride's curb as soon as the black SUV left, but a second before it did, a black and white patrol car pulled up across the street at the vacant house and parked.

Gus slammed the dash again and cursed. He couldn't catch a break.

"Let's go!" Gus demanded. "We'll come back. That car can't sit out there forever."

Four girls. He'd lost four girls. Alex would kill him for sure. But what if he replaced them? If he found more girls, profitable girls, then what could Alex say? It was all about the money right?

Gus made a few calls to the men who had brought

Mandy and Lisa from Texas. They had a steady supply. It would cost him, but it would cost him his life if he didn't.

After a few hours of calls and back-and-forth negotiations, he'd bought two more girls. He resolved to keep them far away from Pride though. It didn't matter; he would kill her anyway.

He would keep both of the new girls at his house, under lock and key if need be. Then the thought occurred to him he could still get Jenny back too. He resolved to find that lady and Jenny. He would take back his, well Alex's property.

He would do whatever he could to make this right with Alex. His life depended on it.

Lenny's phone rang until Pride assumed he was still asleep. Hanging up the phone she felt the emptiness in her house after Jenny's departure. She'd called Lenny for solace, but he'd not answered.

She walked to the front room and pondered the door. It was not secure. She was no carpenter and had few tools. Something would need to be done.

As she was considering who to call to help her repair the door, her phone rang. It was Lenny.

His familiar gravely voice felt comforting to Pride as it came through the line. Once their greetings were past, Pride said, "Jenny's gone."

"Gone?" Lenny was startled. "Gone where?"

"She got out. I helped her get into a program that will help her get an education and a job. They're really nice people. It terrified her thinking Gus would kill her, and she was right, he would have. I think he's the one who's been killing all those girls."

Lenny thought for a moment. "That don't make sense Pride. Them's his bread and butter. And he answers to Alex. No one in his right mind crosses Alex."

Pride thought about that for a minute. Lenny was right. But Gus' behavior seemed erratic lately. "I think he's gone crazy Lenny. He busted in my door last night looking for Jenny."

"He did!" Lenny's voice held panic. He wanted to help Pride, but he was old and brittle. What could he do? "Come stay with me for a while."

"No, there is a cop outside for now. But I need to get someone to come put me a new door in. I tried to fix it, but I'm no carpenter. I got a little money put back. You know anyone I can call?"

Lenny thought for a minute. "Yeah, I know someone. Let me get him on over there."

"Thank you Lenny. I loved her you know." With Jenny gone Pride broke down and sobbed. "I don't think I can do this anymore Lenny."

"Hey there, girl. It'll be okay. I'll come over with Bruce. We'll sit while he fixes the door."

"Ok, Lenny," said Pride. "Thank you."

Pride hung up and once again the silent, empty house suffocated her heart.

RANDY AND CARRIE drove Jenny and Beth back to Penny's Place where Beth had left her car.

Tears had gently rolled down Jenny's cheeks during the entire ride. Beth allowed her the time to grieve and remained silent.

When they were back at Penny's Place, Beth got Jenny in her car and walked back to say goodbye to Randy and Carrie.

"Thank you for your help this morning," said Beth.

"We're glad we were here to help," said Carrie. "We still want to talk to Lisa. Let us know when and where and we will be there. We still have a killer to catch and even though a lot of signs point to Gus, it still makes little sense unless he has genuinely lost his mind."

Beth nodded. She wanted the killer caught too. "Lisa is very fragile, like Jenny. Would it help if I brought her into my office in private and asked her a few questions? I would relay everything to you and also let her know she should talk to you as well. Sort of prepare her ahead of time."

"It could work," said Randy. "But you might miss something in her demeanor or tone of voice we would easily catch."

"The first inquiry we initially make is usually very informative beyond the verbal answers," said Carrie.

"Okay, I'll plan a time and we'll get together soon. Let me go back and get Jenny settled in."

Beth opening the car door startled Jenny, who was lost in thought. She already missed Pride and was second guessing her decision to leave her.

The ride to Safe At Last was a circuitous route. Beth never drove straight anywhere anymore. The ride was also quiet. She didn't want Jenny to feel that she was under interrogation.

Back at the house, Beth helped Jenny with her bag and gave her a big smile. "It'll be okay, Jenny. I've done this for a long time and seen many success stories."

Jenny looked up at her, "Are some stories not a success?" Her brows were pinched together with concern.

"Some stories are not a success, Jenny. But that will depend on you and how much you want your story to be one."

Jenny thought about that for a moment. "I want my story to be a success for Pride."

"You should want your story to be a success for you. Pride would want that."

Jenny nodded. That was hard to think about now. She would just take it a moment at a time and do what Beth said.

Once back at Safe At Last, Beth showed Jenny to the room she would share with three other girls when fully occupied. Right now it would be just Jenny and Lisa together. She then showed Jenny the layout of the house winding up in Beth's office. Beth shut the door behind them and gestured for Jenny to sit.

"This is my office Jenny. In here we can talk in private, so anytime you need to talk with no one else hearing, we can talk in here." Beth waited for Jenny to respond. Jenny nodded and Beth continued.

"This home is meant to be a sanctuary to help you and others heal and develop skills to move forward in your lives. While you are now free from the bondage of being forced to sell yourself, there are still rules of order we must maintain for your safety and ours. But I don't want you to see those rules as another form of bondage."

Jenny once again nodded. "It may seem at first as if you are swapping out one freedom for another, but if you feel restricted, it is for you protection. Do you understand?"

Beth handed a sheet to Jenny. "This is a list of our routine and basic rules here at the house. We have a set time for our meals, and then group time. You do not have to take part in group time, but I urge you to do so. Even if you don't want to talk, please be there to support the other girls.

"I'm assuming that you didn't graduate high school. Is that correct?" Jenny nodded. "We have volunteers that can tutor you so you can take your GED. That will give you a certificate of high-school equivalency. During that process we will explore career options. What are you good at, what you enjoy, that kind of thing. We want you to gain skills to work at something you will enjoy."

Jenny sat wide eyed. She had dreamed when she was

younger of what she had wanted her life to be, but not in a long time. "I don't know what I can do," said Jenny.

"We'll explore that. I think you'll be surprised." Beth smiled at Jenny, and Jenny smiled back for the first time that morning. Beth loved seeing these girls blossom from the pitiful life they had been forced into, and into something fresh and joyful, although it was usually a long and painful process.

"We have tight security here for obvious reasons. We want you to feel safe and able to sleep at night and live here in peace. With the current situation we are sending volunteers to go with the girls who leave for school and work. You are not in prison, but it may seem like it for a while until things settle down."

Jenny's eyes got big, and she huffed out, "Fine by me!"

Beth suspected that Jenny hadn't felt safe in a long time.

"Jenny I also have to ask you about drug use. Many of our girls come in here addicted to one or several drugs. We need to know so we can help you come off of them safely."

Jenny ducked her head. "I use meth from time to time. Pride got me clean, but sometimes I would get some when I couldn't take it anymore." Jenny looked up at Beth waiting for her reprimand.

"Are you on something now?" Beth asked.

Jenny shook her head. "No."

"When was the last time you used?" asked Beth.

Jenny thought back. She wanted to answer truthfully. "About a week ago."

"Ok. That's good. You've not had anything for a week. That is good Jenny."

Jenny's face beamed.

"Will you promise me something? If you get to feeling like you need to take something, will you come to me? You won't be in trouble. We will talk about why you want to use and hopefully we can get you past the urge."

Jenny nodded. She always had the urge, but Pride had helped in that way, too. She never wanted to let Pride down, and would resist the urge as long as she could.

"Do you have any questions?" asked Beth. Jenny shook her head no.

"Well, then let's get you out there meeting more of the girls. Would you like to help in the kitchen this morning getting lunch ready?"

"I can't cook." Jenny was instantly concerned. No one had ever taught her to cook, and she was afraid she would disappoint Miss Beth.

"You don't have to cook. But the cook's need help cleaning and with other chores. You can chop things, right?"

Jenny smiled and nodded.

"My goodness what a morning," said Carrie.

"I didn't expect that, did you?" asked Randy.

"Not at all."

Back at the office Carrie reworked the part of the board where Lisa was. She was now a known and was alive. Carrie erased the question mark above her square and wrote a note 'Safe At Last'.

"I like that name," said Carrie.

"What name, Lisa?" asked Randy.

"No, Safe At Last. I like that. Do you think these girls really are safe at last?"

"I hope so, but I suspect not all are," replied Randy.

Carrie sat down at the computer going through piles of emails. "Forensics got skin underneath both girl's fingernails. No hit in CODIS, but it was the same for both vic's. If we find the guy, we've got him."

"That lets Gus off the hook. We have his DNA," said Randy.

"He's still a killer," said Carrie. "I would like nothing better than to put him away too."

"I would like to take down the entire string of human traffickers," said Randy. "But that probably won't happen in my lifetime."

"So what if it was a client that both Cami and Mandy had? Something set him off, and he's killing the girls he was with. Maybe he couldn't perform. Killed Cami and then went with Mandy, and the same thing all over again." Carrie paused to let that sink in with Randy.

"Sounds plausible. Both girls worked the downtown area. Could be a guy that works down there or goes to events down there." Randy paused and leaned back in his chair. "Oh hell, there are thousands of men down there for thousands of reasons." Randy sat forward again feeling the frustration sink in.

"If it is a client, then the other girls may know him. We should ask them about clients who stand out to them in an odd way or who had trouble getting the job done," said Carrie.

Carrie turned back to look at the white board again. She'd written client on a list on the board. Gus was on that list but rather than erase his name she drew a line through it. The need to get him and see him rot in prison burned in her.

"Did Mike and Rick ever turn up anything further from Cami's family? Did they find any sign of where her sister went? We need to make sure the other agencies have her picture." Then almost to herself she said, "but it would be lost in a sea of others."

She turned around and rested both her fists on the edge of her desk and leaned in towards Randy. "Law enforcement gets a bad rap for not solving these types of murders. They accuse us of not caring or not working them hard enough. But the truth is, we have so little to go on. The people who can help us with information won't help us."

Randy nodded. "These trafficking rings scatter the girls world-wide, and there are so many of them I don't know what we are supposed to do. I have a daughter and it would kill me if she disappeared. I know the odds of finding her and getting her back."

Carrie stood upright and turned to look at the board again. "Does Sandy talk about Safe At Last?" Carrie asked.

Randy's face winced. "Yes, and no. I think she wants to gush about it, but is hesitant because she is so concerned about what I'll say."

"I thought you were finally on board with it?" Carrie asked.

"I am, or have tried to be."

Carrie turned back to look at Randy and grinned. "You make an effort to appear on board, but she can see right through it."

Randy sighed. "I know. But I just can't. I know it is important to her, but even though she's heard the stories and seen these girls this last week, I still don't think she gets just how dangerous this is."

"She has a good head on her shoulders. She'll be okay." Carrie smiled a reassuring smile at Randy.

"I hope so."

Just then Randy's phone rang. It was Beth. "Lisa has agreed to talk to you. She met Jenny this morning, and they talked. Jenny encouraged her to talk to you and she agreed."

"We got DNA from under the girl's fingernails. It wasn't Gus. Don't tell the girls. He's still a danger and we don't want them to get a false sense of security. He's not innocent and if we can get him on something, we will," said Randy. "Where shall we meet?"

"We can meet back at Penny's Place around one or one-thirty if that's ok with you," said Beth. "We'll get past lunch here, and then Lisa and I will head over there."

"We'll see you at one-thirty," said Randy as he hung up his phone.

CHAPTER 9

"Can Jenny go with me?" asked Lisa. It terrified her to do this. She was terrified to leave Safe At Last.

Beth pondered Lisa's request for a moment trying to decide if it would help or hinder what Randy and Beth needed to ask Lisa. Would she be more open and forthright, or more hesitant to answer their questions.

"I need to check with the agents first," replied Beth.

She dialed the phone and Randy answered on the first ring. "Lisa has asked me if Jenny can come along. She is terrified and hoped Jenny could come for moral support. I didn't know if it would hinder or hurt. What do you think?" asked Beth.

Randy looked at Carrie. She had heard Beth's question over the phone. Carrie nodded a silent yes and Randy responded to Beth, "We think that'll be fine. We know

Jenny, and who knows maybe it will help Jenny remember things as well."

"Okay. I just want to follow what will help this process, not work against it. We'll see you soon." Beth hung up and went to find Jenny.

"Jenny, I am taking Lisa to visit with Randy and Carrie back at Penny's Place. She's scared and wondered if you would come with us. The agents said it was fine if you came. What do you think?"

Jenny liked the agents. They hadn't seemed to judge her, and she felt comfortable with them. Maybe if she went, Lisa would feel comfortable. Jenny nodded and agreed to go.

Beth went to finish paperwork and take care of other things that needed her attention.

Jenny went to find Lisa. She was in their room. Beth had wisely put them together. Lisa sat on the edge of the bed hugging her pillow tightly to herself.

Jenny sat on the bed opposite of her. For a moment she said nothing. She understood the stress Lisa was feeling.

"They are good people, ya know?" Jenny's question wasn't really meant to be answered, but merely stated in order to comfort Lisa.

Lisa looked up at Jenny. "I'm so scared. I'm terrified Gus will find me."

"I know, but I feel safer here, don't you?" Jenny asked.

Lisa nodded and looked back at the floor. "We're kind of in the same boat you know. We are both Gus' girls and we both had our friend killed."

Once again Lisa nodded. "I keep wondering why Mandy and not me," said Lisa.

It was Jenny's turn to nod. "I know," was all Jenny could say. They sat for the next twenty minutes in silence before Beth came to get them.

The ride to the diner was quiet and somber. Beth reassured both girls that the agents only wanted to help them and to find the killer.

"You can help them do their job by telling them everything, no matter how small something seems. They have to have as much information as possible to do their jobs well."

"If Gus killed Mandy and Cami, and we say something that gets him arrested, will we have to go to court and see him?" Lisa trembled as she spoke.

"I don't know," Beth was honest. She didn't know how this would all turn out or what would be required of the girls in the future. "But if it gets him off the street and away from other girls he might hurt, won't it be worth it?" Beth asked.

Both girls nodded as they pulled into the lot at Penny's. Randy and Carrie were already there and were drinking coffee. Beth could see them laughing with Alice, the waitress who had served her parents for the last fifteen years.

The lunch hour rush was dwindling and several patrons were leaving the diner. Beth sat still in the car for a moment. She was always thoughtful of her surroundings and those around her. So as she sat she looked at those coming and going and at those she could see through the windows of the diner.

Everything looked normal and nothing seemed off, so she turned to look at the girls and smiled. "We're here."

As he adjusted the salt and pepper shakers on the table before him. he noticed that grains of salt had escaped their confines. His mind flitted about searching what to do.

He did not want his hands to touch the table. No doubt it contained bacteria. He could blow the salt to the floor, but then that would put the debris on the floor. There was no solution except having the waitress get a clean rag and wipe the table down fully.

A few booths away a tired waitress noticed his hand slightly in the air. It was as though he were a student not sure if he had the answer to a question the teacher had just asked, but who wanted to try it anyway. What on earth could he want now, she wondered.

She nodded his way as if to show she had seen him and would be there soon. She then finished pouring the black coffee into the old ceramic cup that sat in front of the handsome OSBI agent. It was the second time that day he had been in, both times with the with lady OSBI agent.

Just then Beth came in the door with two girls and sat down with the agents. Alice knew Beth well and what she did. Beth's grandparents had opened Penny's Place when they were young, naming the diner after Beth's grandmother Penny. Then Beth's father had taken the diner over. The entire staff was protective of Beth and those she helped.

As Alice approached the man's table, she noticed that he seemed like a relic from the 1950s. His short-sleeved white shirt and boring brown stripped tie stood out among the colorful attire of those in the booths surrounding him.

But the pocket protector, thick black-rimmed glasses, and the Brillcremed hair forced her to exercise restraint from her urge to belt out a laugh. *But that would be rude now, wouldn't it,* she thought?

"Yes, what can I do for you?" She asked as she walked up to his booth.

He swallowed as if almost afraid to talk, then pointed to the few tiny grains of salt on the table. "There. The table needs cleaned."

Alice looked at the table and frowned. She wasn't sure what he was referring to. Could it be those two or three grains of salt? She looked at him with a wrinkled brow. "Are you talking about the salt on the table?"

"Yes ma'am! I need you to clean this table, it's dirty."

Too tired for his games, Alice sat the coffee carafe down on the table, lifted the salt shaker and with her free hand swiped away the salt grains. She then plunked the salt shaker back down on the table.

He jumped with a start, and sat rigid in his seat, mouth hanging open. His gaze went back and forth between the salt shaker and the waitress.

"Anything else?" Alice asked picking up the coffee carafe.

He shook his head, quite intimidated by her, and asked for a menu.

She reached into the next booth, picked up a derelict menu and tossed it in front of him. He came in here often to Alice's dismay. He didn't set right with her but she could not say why.

Randy and Carrie had purposely gotten the large round booth in the corner so that there would be room for all five to sit. Randy and Carrie sat on opposite edges so they could easily exit if need be. When Beth and the girls arrived, Randy got up and let them slide in.

One girl sat on each side of Beth, with Jenny sitting next to Randy.

Randy smiled at Lisa. "Thank you Lisa for being willing to come and talk to us. I'm Randy and this is Carrie. We are OSBI agents and have been working on finding who killed Cami and Mandy." He stopped for a moment to gauge her reaction.

When she didn't respond he continued. "You lived with Gus and Mandy, correct?"

Lisa nodded.

"Were you and Mandy close?"

Again, Lisa nodded. Randy needed to get a dialog

going, so he asked, "Lisa can you tell me about you and Mandy's life living there with Gus?"

Lisa's eyes darted around as if searching for the answers Randy needed.

"What were your living arrangements? Did you come and go as you pleased?" Carrie asked.

"Not at first. Then he trusted us a little more. He always had people watching us though, so we were careful where we went and what we did," Lisa finally said.

"Was Gus pleased with you and Mandy?" Carrie asked. It seemed Lisa felt more comfortable with Carrie.

"I think so." Lisa's brow was wrinkled as if she wasn't sure.

"Did he punish either of you?"

Lisa looked down at her hands and rubbed them together. Jenny reached over and laid her hand in front of Lisa on the table. "Lisa, it's okay. They know what we did for Gus. We have to tell them so they can help find who killed our friends." Jenny pleaded with Lisa, and Lisa nodded in response.

Lisa took a big breath and looked at Carrie. "We had rules. We went out around nine or ten at night. We were to work our area and then when we came home, we gave him our money. He would give us a little back, but he said because we lived with him we had to pay him for rent and food. As long as we kept doing that, things seemed to go okay."

"Did anything at all change in the last few weeks? Did Mandy do something that upset Gus?"

Lisa sat thinking for a moment. "Well, she didn't like Gus at all. She got to where when he was saying something to us she would challenge him. I kept telling her to stop. I was sore afraid of him, but it seemed that Mandy just got bold."

"What would Gus do when Mandy would challenge him?"

"He would grab her arms and shake her. He threw her on the bed one time and took his belt off and beat her with it."

"Did he ever beat you?"

"Sometimes."

"What made him want to beat you?" asked Carrie.

Lisa snorted. "What didn't make him want to beat us? We tried so hard to stay out of his way. We would wait to go to the kitchen to eat until we knew he was out of the house or asleep. We were as quiet around there as little mice."

"But that didn't always work, did it?" asked Carrie.

Lisa shook her head. "Sometimes he would just come home in a bad mood and find us and take his anger out on us." Then as if she remembered something… "And sometimes he would say we didn't make him enough money."

"Lisa how did you and Mandy come to be with Gus?" Carrie asked.

Lisa told the story she had told to the others as Safe At

Last about living in south Texas, running away, and then being taken. "Living with Gus was better than living in that house."

The conversation lulled as Alice came to fill cups and ask if there was anything else she could do for them. Randy felt a need to break the somber mood for a moment and asked the girls if they liked pie. He knew a diner like this had to have good pie.

The girls nodded, and they all ordered a piece of pie. The agents were content to let the conversation take a break while they ate. Then just as Jenny ate her last bite, she looked at Carrie and asked, "Have you talked to Pride? Is she okay?" Her eyes were pleading with Carrie to give her good news of her friend.

"Jenny it was only this morning we left her," Carrie said as gently as she could.

Jenny nodded. *Had it only been this morning that she'd been ripped away from the only person who had ever loved her?* To her it already seemed like a lifetime.

Once they had devoured the pie, and Alice had cleared their table. Randy and Carrie got back down to the questions. Lisa had become comfortable enough with them by then that she easily answered them all, the best she could.

Randy jotted down in his notes the last time she'd seen Mandy, details as far as she knew when Gus arrived home that evening, and what beef if any he had specifically with Mandy lately.

Their answers revealed nothing earth shattering. Gus was highly irritated with Mandy and yes, knocked her around some when she mouthed off, but it didn't seem like enough to kill her over. But then, they were unsure of Gus' role in the girls' deaths at this point anyway.

According to Lisa, Mandy had left at nine when they had both gone to the Deep Deuce area northeast of Bricktown. They liked to hang around the bars there. Mandy went with a guy around nine-thirty. That was the last time Lisa had seen Mandy.

"I got home around three and went straight to bed. I didn't turn on the lights to our room and assumed she was probably not home yet, or asleep. I didn't want to wake her if she was, so I slipped in, undressed, and crawled in bed," Lisa was looking at Randy to make sure she was giving him what he wanted.

"Did you see Gus or could you tell if he was home?" asked Carrie.

"I didn't see him. The whole house was dark."

After asking a couple more questions Randy shut his pad and thanked the girls for being so open with him.

Carrie had noticed that while Lisa was answering questions, Jenny seemed distracted. Carrie had been watching her and it appeared she was inadvertently watching a guy about three booths down. Carrie thought he seemed disturbing to her.

"Jenny are you okay?" asked Carrie.

Jenny was mentally tugged back to the group at the table. She nodded at Carrie and said, "Yes, of course."

Carrie continued to watch the girl for a moment

longer. "You would tell me if you weren't, right?" Carrie asked.

Randy had not noticed Jenny's behaviour, but knew Carrie was sensing something was not quite right with Jenny. He sat watching both Carrie and Jenny.

Then finally satisfied, Carrie looked at Randy gave a shrug with her facial expression and moved to exit the booth.

Once out of the diner, hugs were distributed and Beth left with the girls while Randy and Carrie waited until they were out of sight making sure they were not followed.

"What was up with that last little bit with you and Jenny?" asked Randy.

Carrie took a breath and exhaled. "I don't know. Jenny sat watching that guy there while you were questioning Lisa. I didn't notice until you were almost done, but she seemed disturbed by him. She was fidgety and rubbing her hands together under the table. You saw her reaction when I asked about it."

Randy could see the man through the front windows of the diner. He was a funny little guy, almost like he was in a time warp from the 50s.

He looked over at Carrie. "Do you think he was someone who has paid for her services?"

Carrie looked at Randy and grinned, "Really? Not likely." She turned to look back at the man as Randy turned the key to start the engine.

"Where's my journal?" Jenny demanded from another resident of Safe At Last. They had just returned with Beth. When Jenny entered her room, she could tell that someone had been going through her things.

The other resident just stood with a smirk on her face grinning at Jenny. "I don't know what you're talking about."

Jenny had dealt with girls like this her whole life. She bowed up and marched over to the girl and looked her straight in the eye. Jenny knew she may look timid, but she was far from it.

"I want my journal and I want it now," Jenny demanded through gritted teeth.

The smiled faded from the girl's face and she fidgeted, unsure of whether to continue this confrontation, or give in. She decided to challenge Jenny's bravado.

The girl named Becky pushed Jenny back out of her face and snarled at her. "I don't have your stupid journal."

It was either from the stress of the day, or the fact that Becky had taken her one precious possession, that caused Jenny to snap.

She gritted her teeth and charged at Becky knocking her to the ground. The sudden move startled Becky who quickly found herself on the ground with Jenny straddling her.

They were still in the doorway of Jenny's room,

wedged between the open door and the end of the bunk beds, against the wall. There was little room and Jenny had Becky at a disadvantage.

Had Jenny been in a calm and calculating frame of mind she would have recognized her advantage, but she was operating under the influence of blind fury.

Becky represented every person in her life that had taken over and forced her into a life of heartbreak and despair. She wasn't thinking or even aware of her actions. Therefore, the shouts and screams of those who had gathered were only a distant hum.

Then hands, strong hands, were pulling her away from the floor. It was as if Jenny were coming out of a dream where she was suddenly noticing her surroundings.

Becky lay on the floor with big round eyes, holding her neck. The strong hands that had pulled Jenny up were Beth and another volunteer. It had taken them both to pull her away.

The room spun, and Jenny felt dizzy. As her body went limp Beth and the other lady guided her to sit on the bed. Nothing but empty uncertainty pulsed through her mind. She felt as though something had detached her body from her heart and mind. Then suddenly she slumped onto the bed and curled up in a ball.

Beth stood and went to Becky. "Are you all right?"

Becky nodded. She hadn't expected her actions to release the rage it had. Now that she was recovering from the attack, she cursed Jenny issuing vile threats.

Beth grabbed her arm and shoved her out of the room and down the hall to her office.

Fifteen minutes later, they emerged and headed to Becky's room. She retrieved Jenny's journal and handed it to Beth.

"This is a warning Becky," said Beth. "This kind of thing cannot happen here or you will have to move out." Beth's eyes met Becky's, and she held her gaze until she received a confirming nod from Becky.

Beth walked into Jenny's room with the journal and laid it on the small table beside the bed.

"Here's your journal." Beth sat on the edge of the bed next to where Jenny was still curled into the fetal position.

"We need to talk about what happened," said Beth.

Jenny's eyes had been open staring into nothingness, but at Beth's words she shut them tightly as if to shut out her request.

"Jenny I know this has been a tough day for you. I know that your emotions are teetering on the edge. That's the main reason we need to talk."

"Becky was wrong to take your journal, but your reaction was excessive."

Jenny couldn't talk. She couldn't find the words to say, and had she been able to, she didn't have the energy to say them. She felt as though exhaustion of the past several days had exploded down on her, and she was suffocating from the weight of it all.

Finally, she nodded.

"I see you're struggling, so I'll talk… Before Beth could finish her sentence Jenny interrupted.

"I want to go home. I want to go home to Pride." Jenny was sobbing now. A torrent of emotions were pouring out. Beth sat quietly and just patted her.

When the worst of the sobbing had subsided, Beth began again. "Jenny I haven't been through what you've been through, but I know it hurts and I know it's painful. Often whenever any of us are confronted with painful events our first instinct is to run, run back to a previous place in our life. Even if that place was a painful one, at least it is a painful place we know, and it feels safe.

"But you came here for a reason. Pride helped you to get to this place for a reason." Beth stopped for a moment to let her words soak into Jenny's heart and mind.

"Jenny I want you to sit up." Beth reached out for Jenny to take her hand. Reluctantly Jenny took Beth's hand and used it for leverage to pull herself upright.

They sat on the edge of the bed side by side. "Talk to me Jenny. Just say anything, anything at all."

Jenny took a deep breath attempting to gather the effort to speak. "I feel so lost. I came here to escape Gus and the threat of him hurting me and I get here and I hurt so bad needing to be with Pride and then this girl, Becky, she hurts me too." Jenny turned her head to look at Beth.

"Is there a place where no one will ever hurt me again?"

Beth hadn't thought it was possible for two eyes to contain the amount of pain that Jenny's eyes held. They reached deep into a wounded soul that was on the verge of collapse. She had to say or do something to bring that girl back, or she would lose her forever.

Beth reached out and pulled Jenny close and just sat gently rocking her. "Jenny this side of heaven there will always be pain of some sort or another, but I can promise you this, if you don't give up now, it will get better. There's so much more to life than what you've known so far.

"Someday you will be past this, and your wounds will heal. One day you will realize you are not noticing the bad so much, but the good too. Someday you will laugh without trying to. But to get to that someday, you have to keep moving forward a day at a time to get there."

"I can't imagine that kind of someday. I'm not sure it's even worth the effort," said Jenny.

In a wave of compassion, Beth said, "Hey, would you like to go to my office and call Pride? I think I can make an exception for today."

Jenny looked up into Beth's smiling face, almost unsure of whether or not to believe her. Then she nodded heartily. "Yes, please."

BRACKET CALLED both Carrie and Randy into his office as soon as he saw them return.

"I've been on the phone with the head of the human trafficking task force in our area. We had a good conversation. Have a seat and I'll go over everything we discussed."

Randy and Carrie sat hoping that Bracket would give them something to nudge their case further along.

"John Marshall is the FBI agent and liaison to the other agencies. As you can guess Gustavo Hernandez is not the top of this food chain.

Bracket shuffled through his notes then read, "Alexander Volkov is Russian. His crime family has a global operation. He has five brothers and they are all close. Could be because they have a common goal, and that their father saw fit to spread them out to different countries. That way, they have dominion over their territory and won't have to butt heads with each other.

"Their common goal is to dominate the black markets of the world. Now they haven't done that as of yet. There is stiff competition from the Mexican and Columbian cartels and the established human trafficking organizations in Europe.

"But that hasn't stopped them. They don't want to have a niche market, they want it all. The father, Sergei Volkov, was thrilled to have six sons he could trust. Their family bond is tight, as I said.

"Alexander Volkov is in charge of the US. He has several residences across the county so he can travel and keep on top of his organization.

"Gus is only one pawn in his game. And according to Marshall, Alexander was in Oklahoma this past week." Bracket paused to gauge Randy and Carrie's response.

What he saw was his two agents on the edges of their seats absorbing every word, so he continued.

"Apparently the way their trafficking organization works is that they will abduct young girls from everywhere, like Mexico, and large cities where there are run-a-ways. It doesn't matter, they will take them from just anywhere, really. They drug them and load them up on trucks and transport them as far away from their abduction site as possible.

"So for instance, those abducted in the northeast are transported to the southwest, and so forth. Here in Oklahoma there are a half dozen low levels like Gus that run things and girls wind up here from everywhere.

"There was a central house of prostitution that was raided a while back and several girls were rescued, but others were not. From what you've told me, Lisa and Mandy were two that Gus pulled out of the house at the last minute.

"Knowing the house was a bust, Gus let the two girls live with him. He has other girls that were not abducted and trafficked who just ran away and became prostitutes. He provides them protection." Bracket made air quotes when saying protection because they all knew the kind of protection that Gus provided.

"The girls all live with individuals who Gus can either control or has a finger on."

Carrie interrupted. "But what about Pride?"

"Pride is a little different. Since Cami and Jenny were not part of the trafficked girls, they were already living with Pride when Gus took them under his control. Pride has a reputation. She was a prostitute for most of her life and she doesn't want to interfere. But she provides a place for girls to live."

Randy and Carrie took this information in. Much of it they already knew, and some they suspected. They'd felt that Gus was not the top of this food chain but they didn't have a name to put on the next level.

"If Gus was killing these girls, he would answer to this Alexander and I can't imagine he would want to suffer his wrath. We have discussed the possibility that Gus just went crazy and lost his mind, but if that were the case he would be dead by now," said Randy. "And we have pretty much marked him off the list of suspects since his DNA didn't match what was underneath the girls fingernails. It could though, belong to one of his men who aren't in our database."

Bracket was nodding. "True. The task force has under cover operations in place as well. We need to be careful where we tread. We can't disrupt what they're doing while we're investigating, so be mindful of that. Know that at any time you could be interviewing an undercover agent."

"It seems to me that these drownings are not syndicate related. If the girls had crossed them, or violated some code, their bodies would have never been found or they would have been killed with a professional hit and zero clues. It's true we have almost no clues here, but drownings are not tidy like a bullet from an untraceable gun or a knife to the throat," said Carrie.

"These killings are personal. I can see a hothead like Gus being the perpetrator, but I am not sure even he would risk angering Alexander.

"We have to look further. We have to find another person who wants these girls dead." As Carrie concluded, she looked at Randy. "Any ideas?"

Randy was thinking and analyzing all that they had discussed. "We need to go back to the drawing board and comb every inch of these girls' lives. I keep feeling like we've missed something vital that will tell us what's going on," he said.

"And both killings were drownings. If it were a hothead, then the method would be whatever was convenient at the moment. It took thought and at least some planning to murder the same way both times," Randy concluded.

"Here's the contact information for Marshall. Keep him in the loop so you can work in tandem with their investigation." Bracket handed a note to Carrie as they stood to leave.

"And whatever you do, stop this before we have another dead girl on our hands."

CHAPTER 10

Carrie called Safe At Last early the next morning and asked to speak with Jenny.

"Jenny, yesterday when we were at the diner, someone you saw disturbed you. Please don't deny it. I saw that you were visibly upset."

"Yes, I was," replied Jenny.

"It was that guy who looked like a throwback from the 50s, right?"

Jenny's mind raced to remember the man Carrie was talking about. "No." Her reply held surprise.

"It wasn't? Who were you looking at?"

"There was a man in a suit sitting at a table in the middle of the room. I… I've been with him."

"Why were you anxious when you saw him? Did he hurt you or act strange with you?"

Jenny worked to remember the details of their time

together. She always tried to wipe each time as far out of her mind as possible. "I'm trying to remember," said Jenny. "He was bossy."

"Bossy?" Carrie asked. Bossy could mean a lot of things to many people, especially where sex was concerned.

"Maybe demanding is a better word. I think he's someone important."

Carrie searched her mind to recall the face of the man that Jenny was referring to. The diner had been full of people taking a later lunch.

"Was he sitting alone or with someone else?" Carrie asked.

"He was alone. He was reading a tablet of some sort and then he looked up over the top of it and saw me."

"What did he do then?"

"He just stared at me. He looked at you guys, then back at me and just stared a hole through me."

Carrie mumbled trying to put it together. "He saw that we were law enforcement and that you and another prostitute were with us. He may have been afraid that you would tell us about him."

"I'm sure. He won't want anyone knowing what we did."

"Okay, do you think if I found a picture of him you would recognize him?"

Jenny snorted. "Yeah, sure. Show me one of him stripped naked and I'll point out the mole on his left hip."

The reality of what they were truly discussing hit

Carrie like a brick. This poor girl had been violated time and time again on a daily basis for years.

"Jenny, you will get past this," Carrie said.

"Everyone keeps saying that. It's hard to believe though."

"Hang in there. Beth seems like a good lady and cares what happens to you girls. Follow her lead and it'll be ok."

"Carrie I don't know if I will ever be ok, even if I get an education, a fancy job, and money. There's a huge rock inside my heart and there is nothing I can think of that could ever make that go away. "What no one seems to get is how dirty we all feel. We've seen and done things that are horrible. There isn't anything, no amount of water or soap that can clean me where I'm dirty."

As Carrie listened to Jenny, she knew exactly what she was saying. She felt just as dirty as Jenny, and she had the education, fancy job, and money. It couldn't make her feel clean. And the sad part was that Carrie had chosen to live a life that defiled herself. Jenny had been forced into it unwillingly.

"I know you may not believe me Jenny, but I do know how you feel."

It was the last full day before Sandy's kindergarten class started and she wanted to spend it at Safe At Last.

So instead of driving to school, she drove straight to

Safe At Last after confirming with Beth that she could volunteer for the day. Once school started, her time would be very limited.

Sandy followed the protocol of parking and then entering the safe house. The house seemed quiet. She stopped by the kitchen to see if they needed any help, but the breakfast cleanup was almost over and lunch prep hadn't yet started.

Walking on into the main living area, she saw three girls, the young one who had complemented her hair and two others.

She walked over to young Emma and sat down next to her on the sofa. Emma's face lit up when she saw Sandy.

"Miss Sandy!" exclaimed Emma, and gave her a big hug. "I was hoping you would come today. They found my parents and I'll be going home later today. I wanted to see you before then."

A pang of sadness barely touched the joy of Emma's news about her going home. Sandy was genuinely thrilled for Emma but she had already gotten attached to her over the last few days.

Sandy beamed at Emma. "I'm so happy for you Emma. Where is home?"

"Phoenix. Mom and Dad are on their way to get me. They should be here this afternoon." A look of concern passed over Emma's face. "I'm a little worried. I haven't seen them since… since… Her voice trailed off. She removed her gaze from Sandy as if suddenly ashamed.

"Emma, I'm a mom, so I can say without a doubt, that

the only thing they will care about is getting you home safe. In their eyes, you are no different. But they will feel bad they let this happen to you."

Emma's eyes brightened. "But it isn't their fault."

"And they won't think it is your fault," said Sandy.

Emma was nodding, understanding. Sandy thought Emma was blessed to have good parents. So many other girls didn't.

They sat for a while and watched the tv. The feel of Emma's small hand inside Sandy's tugged at her heart. She made a firm resolve to try to not get so attached to these girls. This type of pain would not permit her to endure as a volunteer.

"Sandy, can I see you for a moment?" It was Beth beckoning her to her office. Sandy patted Emma's hand and gave her a smile as she stood to go.

Beth shut the door behind Sandy and motioned for her to sit. "We had a little incident here yesterday after you left. Becky took Jenny's journal while we were out yesterday and when Jenny discovered it, she attacked Becky.

"I think all her pent up rage for everything that has been happening unleashed all at once, and because Becky had taken her journal she was the recipient of it all."

Sandy sat and listened. Her entire body tensed as Beth began to tell her what had happened. "Are they okay now?" She had met Jenny and was surprised. She seemed so meek and timid. Becky on the other hand clearly had a chip on her shoulder.

"Yes, they're fine. Jenny and I had a long talk and I let her call Pride. They talked and Jenny felt entirely different afterwards. It's important for them to leave the old life and those in it behind, but Jenny needed to talk to Pride to know she was fine."

Sandy was absorbing all that Beth was saying. "Emma is leaving today," said Beth. She watched Sandy's face for signs of emotion. "You've gotten close to her in the last few days, and she with you."

"Yes, but I'm excited for her. Really excited. That's what we hope to achieve here if at all possible, right?" asked Sandy.

Beth smiled. "Yes. Unfortunately, many of these girls have very little to go home to once they leave. Often the traffickers watch for girls that don't have a solid support system at home. They bank on the parents or guardians just assuming the girls ran away and won't even bother to look for them.

"Emma was stolen in a mall in Phoenix. She had gone there with her older sister and when the sister came out of a dressing room, Emma was gone."

Fear gripped Sandy's heart. She needed to watch over her kids better. Beth read the look on Sandy's face.

"Sandy we can't live in fear that this will happen to our kids. We have to trust that we are doing the best we can and trust God to watch over them."

"Was God watching over Emma?" Sandy responded.

"He's bringing her home to her parents isn't He?" Beth asked. "I don't have all the answers Sandy. But I know that Emma's abduction was not God's doing. When bad things do happen here in this corrupt world, He is there for us when we need Him."

Sandy nodded trying to reconcile what Beth had just said. She had never felt she could just trust the safety of her children to an unseen entity. They were her children, and it was up to her and Randy to keep them safe.

"Ok, we have four new girls coming in to us today. Let's go over what I know about them and the procedure of orientation. I've also set up a schedule for you, now that you will be starting back to school."

Sandy took the schedule from Beth's hands and looked it over. Smiling, she looked at Beth. "Thank you Beth."

Gus sat with his crew watching the safe house. They had put enough pieces together through surveillance and a little investigation on their own part to find the house.

He'd bought two new girls out of his own pocket to add to Alex's trough, but he was furious at Jenny, Lisa, and Pride.

He would take care of Pride once the cops had tired of watching her house. They couldn't stay there forever, so he would bide his time and wait.

For now, he would be content to take care of Jenny and Lisa. He had replaced the two dead ones, so he was trying to decide if he would just add them back to the mix or just kill them for their betrayal, then buy two more.

He hated to have to buy two more, but he wasn't sure if Jenny and Lisa were worth the trouble.

Gus and his crew had been sitting watching the house since early morning. The only person he had seen come to the house, was a lady with straight, almost white blonde shoulder length hair.

"What, they go in and never leave?" asked Vince, Gus' driver. Gus knew they were all tired of sitting, but he didn't dare leave for fear of missing an opportunity.

"I don't know what they do," grumbled Gus. He thought to himself that at least he knew where the house was now. He could rotate his guys to watch for a few days then when they had established a pattern of behavior he would come up with a plan.

The last lady that had walked in, had caught his eye. She reminded him of Cami. That lady cop had been right, he had loved her. But the dirty little whore hadn't wanted him.

The lady at the house was older than Cami, but just as beautiful. He could imagine touching her silky smooth blonde hair. She had big blue eyes like Cami's too. He shifted in his seat and yanked the leg of his pants down to relieve his growing uncomfortableness.

"Okay, let's roll. I want you guys to rotate watching this house and make a list of everyone and everything that happens here. Then I'll decide what to do. I may just blow the whole thing up with them all inside."

"That would fix it," said Vince.

"Yeah, but I want to look those two in the eyes when the light fades from them. A bomb is only a last resort."

As the SUV rolled away from the house, Gus was plotting his revenge, still trying to decide if he would make them suffer before putting them back to work, or just killing them. He smiled at that last thought."

"It's Rick." Rick Morris's voice came through Carrie's cell phone.

"What have you got?" Carrie responded.

"We've been trying to track down the sister, Samantha. We were able to get a description of the man who took her. No name yet, but the description we got says he is somewhere in his fifties, dark hair balding on top, not fat that they could tell, but a jowly face." Rick paused.

"Where did you get the description from?" asked Carrie.

"From a neighbor."

Carrie's face wrinkled in concentration. "A neighbor? How would a neighbor know?"

"At the end of the street there was a little convenience store. Seems the neighborhood kids would hang out there a lot. They didn't sell gas, just a walk-up type little store to run in and get the necessities, and of course beer and cigarettes," said Rick.

"The shop owner lives on the same street as Cami and Samantha. It seems the day they went missing, they had been hanging out in front of the store, which they did a lot. He noticed late that afternoon that a man drove up in an old black Chevy Bonneville. The girls went to the passenger side and leaned in to talk through the open window.

"The man said that after a while, Sam got in the car and Cami sat back down in front of the store. He went out and asked Cami about Sam leaving with the man. He hadn't seen him in the neighborhood before and was concerned.

"He said Cami assured him it was all right. That was the last day he saw Cami too. When she left later that day, she never came back," Rick concluded.

Carrie was trying to wrap her head around all the facts they had. How did this work into the case, and with Gus and the human trafficking? Instead of things falling into place it just seemed like they were gathering a bunch of loose ends they couldn't connect.

But there was a connection, and they had to keep chipping away looking for more. Sometimes cases took a long time to solve. Carrie hoped that wasn't the case this time, because the longer they took, the more girls could die.

"Did he report this to the police?" Carrie asked.

"No, he had no idea the girls were actually missing.

Carrie thought about all that Rick and Mike had said. Her mind was miles away at the front of a little run down neighborhood store where two girls had left and never returned.

She didn't remember saying goodbye or ending the

call, but she must have, because the screen on her phone was blank. Then suddenly thinking of something she dialed Rick back.

"Did you talk to the girl's parents to see if they knew of a man with that description or a car like that?" Carrie asked.

"Not yet," said Rick. "We're trying to get over to them. Their work schedules are difficult to navigate. We called you as soon as we talked to the store owner."

"I want to go with you when you talk to the parents," said Carrie.

"Ok. As soon as I reach one, I will let you know," said Rick.

Carrie got up from her desk and went looking for Randy who wasn't at his desk. She found him in Bracket's office and rapped lightly on the door frame.

"Come on in Carrie," Bracket stood and welcomed her into the room.

"I didn't mean to interrupt. I talked to Rick Morris, and he has news."

"Sit down. I'd like to hear it too," Bracket motioned to the vacant chair next to Randy and sat back down. His eagerness led him to lean forward with his arms on his desk.

Carrie relayed what Rick had told her and then answered questions from both Bracket and Randy.

"I told Rick that when he locates the parents, I want to go with him to talk to them," Carrie said.

"Do you think you can get something out of them that will help solve your current case? Cami didn't go with that man and we have no idea where Samantha is. Sam's disappearance may have nothing to do with Cami's death. Why not let Rick and Mike do the interview?" Bracket asked.

"They're very capable, but I have this feeling it's all connected somehow. I believe the girls knew the man in the black car or Sam wouldn't have gone willingly with him and Cami wouldn't have been so unconcerned.

"What if it somehow involves the parents?" Carrie asked.

Bracket frowned and Randy shifted in his seat to better engage in their conversation.

"Why do you think it may involve the parents?" Randy asked.

Carrie was shaking her head as she answered, "I don't know for sure. Maybe this guy was a family member or a friend of their parents. What if he told them something like their parents were hurt or asking for him to take them to where they were?"

"But only Sam went, not Cami. If their parents were hurt or something like that, then wouldn't both girls have gone?" asked Randy.

Carrie sat thinking for a minute looking down at the floor. The sun shone through the large windows in Bracket's office and the dust motes danced their familiar rhythm. Carrie sat transfixed for a moment watching them.

"He could have said they were asking for Sam, not Cami." Carrie looked up at Bracket and Randy.

Bracket leaned back in his chair unconvinced. "I think that's a stretch. But I do believe you are right about the girls knowing the man. Go ahead and follow up with the parents when Rick calls and let us know."

Carrie sat and nodded looking at the men who sat quiet. She had the strange sensation she had interrupted a conversation, and that they didn't want to continue until she had gone. Uneasiness touched her and told her they were talking about her.

Suddenly self-conscious, Carrie stood to leave. From sheer nervousness she brushed the palms of her hands down her pant legs and then shoved them in her pockets.

She nodded awkwardly and turned to go. At the door, she turned back to look at them.

"Well… Ok, I'll just go now… Carrie thought how awkward that sounded and mentally berated herself for it.

She closed the door behind her and walked back to her desk. Her mind raced, jumping from one topic to another that they could be discussing.

Was Randy talking to Bracket about her continued drinking, she wondered. She was trying to stop. She was doing better, wasn't she? The sheer anxiety of the situation just made her want to drink even more. She slammed her palm on the desk, then rested her head in her hands. Would it ever end?

BETH HAD SPENT a full hour with Sandy going over what she knew about the incoming girls and the orientation process. They went over the forms to fill out, and also signs to look for in the girls.

It was important to make sure the girls felt welcome, and free to talk if they felt the need to do so. Also, there may be nightmares and trauma associated with their experiences. There could also be possible drug withdrawals.

Then there were those who might try to leave. This wasn't a prison, but if the girls left, then they would be right back in the same danger they had been in. Beth taught Sandy signs to look for in the girls that might indicate that they were thinking of running.

It's a lot to take in, thought Sandy as she left Beth's office. The smell of fresh-baked bread reached out to her in the hallway, and she knew it must be time for lunch. She followed the sounds of giggles and laughter to the dining room.

When Sandy entered the room, Emma patted the chair next to her and said, "Miss Sandy come sit by me."

"Lunch smells good. Is that fresh-baked bread?" asked Sandy as she reached for a hot roll.

"Yes. The cooks here are good. We don't always get fresh baked stuff, but today we did," said Emma.

On the table sat a large ham, and there were also green beans and corn. It was a home-cooked meal and Sandy filled her plate. She wasn't sure she'd eaten this well since she last ate at her mother's table.

The thought of her own mother caused gratitude to well up inside her. She had been fortunate to have grown up in a good home. Her mother and father had been good parents and her home had been one that Sandy always wanted to come home too, unlike many of these girls.

About the time that Sandy finished her meal, she heard voices and movement near the back of the home. She picked up her plate and utensils and took them to the kitchen where she rinsed them and placed them in the dishwasher.

She heard Beth call her name, and she turned to follow her voice. Coming from the back entrance were Beth and four teenage girls. They had varied expressions, some timid and others defiant, but all looked leery of their new surroundings.

"This is Abigail, Brianna, Ella, and Mia. If you will show Abby and Bri where their room is and help them get settled, I will take Ella and Mia." Beth handed Sandy two white trash bags and a few plastic shopping bags which held the girls' things.

Sandy smiled at the girls and led the way. As she led them up the stairs and to a new room that was not being used, she pointed out the bathrooms and other rooms of interest.

Neither of the girls spoke. Sandy didn't know if that was because they were scared, or just had nothing to say. She was curious and wanted to ask questions about the girls, but Beth had cautioned her not to. Especially on the first day, they didn't want to do anything to push the girls. Her goal was to help them relax in their new surroundings.

She entered a room with two bunk beds and sat the bags in the room's center. It was sparsely furnished, but welcoming. The beds had unmatched quilts done in the same color scheme of primary colors. Unique, but coordinated.

Between their beds, was a short chest that served as a nightstand for both bunk beds. In the center was a large rug. Across the room was a larger chest of drawers and a closet.

Sandy looked at the girls and asked, "Right now you'll be the only two in this room. You may have whichever bed you wish."

The girls looked at the beds and Abby shrugged. "I don't care, really."

"I don't want up on a top one. Can I have one on the bottom?" asked Bri.

"Yes, you may. Just choose whichever bed you want. There are two small drawers in this chest so you can each have one, but this chest here is good to put your clothes in. There are hangers in the closet so you can hang up clothes as well."

The girls just stood there, unsure of what to do. Sandy felt a little awkward, not knowing how to help them feel at home. She stood for a moment rubbing the palms of her hands together and then sat on one of the lower bunks.

"I don't know which bag belongs to who. Abby which are yours and which are Bri's?" Sandy said as she bent over to separate the bags.

It seemed to move the girls into action, and Bri sat on the bed next to Sandy while Abby sat on the opposite bottom bunk.

Soon they had the bags with their meager goods sorted, and with Sandy's direction, they had picked out drawers in the chest and folded and placed their items inside. They each filled their drawer less than half-way. They had also each hung up only a couple of items.

Abby stood at the closet door looking at one of her dresses. She held the hem in her hand. She then turned and looked at Sandy. Her eyes were sad, and she spoke as if she wasn't sure how Sandy would respond to what she had to say.

"I don't have normal clothes anymore," said Abby.

"What do you mean?" asked Sandy.

Abby looked back at the dress she held the hem of. "I don't want to wear these clothes here. I wore them to make men want me." She looked back at Sandy. "I don't want men to want me anymore."

Sandy stood rigid with compassion in the center of the room. Then moved toward Abby. She reached out her hand for Abby to take it. "They will help you get new clothes." Then she smiled.

Abby dropped the hem of the dress and walked to Sandy. She stood facing her and looked her square in the eyes. "I know they say I will get past this, but I don't know how."

"I know it sounds trite and cliche, but it will just take one day at a time. Think about today, this day, and what you can and need to do to get better. Then tomorrow will be another day."

CHAPTER 11

Jenny was trying to get used to Safe At Last. Everyone was nice to her there, but she severely missed Pride. She couldn't imagine a life without her and each time she thought of it, her heart broke all over again.

Beth had met with her and they went through a questionnaire about the things that Jenny thought she might like to do, careers or jobs she thought she might be good at.

After some discussion they had decided that she might like to be a beautician at a hair salon. She would work with the tutor to get her GED and then attend a trade school. That sounded good to Jenny.

At that moment though, there was nothing to do but sit and watch television. Jenny sat on the sofa and felt as though her skin was crawling with bugs, so she rubbed her hands up and down her arms. She had had nothing for several days, but the anxiety of missing Pride triggered familiar urges in her.

She sprang up off of the sofa and paced the room. Her nails were down to the quick, but she gnawed on one anyway, trying to slide her tooth under the slightest sliver of remaining fingernail. The sting of raw skin caused her to pull her hand away where she saw a thin line of blood. Aggravated, she dropped her hand and continued her pacing.

Just then, the four new girls walked into the room with Beth. She got the attention of Jenny and the other two girls in the room and made introductions all around.

Jenny remembered yesterday when she had first arrived. They looked as lost and scared as she had… still did. She walked over to the one nearest her and reached out her hand, "Hi, I'm Jenny."

The girl was Ella. She had short black hair that was spikey on top. Ella looked at Jenny's hand and took it. "I'm Ella."

Jenny noticed that Ella had stunning bright green eyes that stood out against her black hair and white complexion. I was watching tv. You want to watch with me?

Ella nodded in response and followed Jenny to the sofa. The other girls were quickly welcomed into the group and soon found themselves around the room watching the television. No one spoke. No one knew what to say. They all had basically the same story, and no one wanted to relive any of it, so they sat in silence.

Beth spent the afternoon having one new girl at a time come to her office so they could talk about themselves in private. She would spend at least an hour with each girl. It was a good time to get to know them and hopefully help them feel more welcome and at home.

After two hours of sitting on the sofa, Jenny thought she would go mad. Lisa had been out with another volunteer that day and Jenny was hoping she would be home soon. At the thought of the word home, she snorted. This wasn't home. Home was with Pride.

At the thought of Pride, a tear slid down Jenny's cheek. She didn't want anyone to see her sitting there crying, so she mumbled an excuse and got up to go to her room.

The bedroom she shared with Lisa was calm and quiet. As the door clicked shut, she felt as though she were shutting the world out. She'd made her bed that morning, since it was one of the rules, so she laid on top of the spread and curled up in a ball.

Then she let the tears come. She dozed in and out as the crying exhausted her. Then at about three that afternoon, Lisa came into the room. She wasn't used to the door being closed, so she opened it quietly, and then promptly shut it behind her.

She hurried over to the bottom bunk opposite of where Jenny laid and leaned over speaking to Jenny in a hushed but urgent voice. "I saw Gus!" Lisa let the words sink in.

When they did, Jenny's eye flew open wide, and she

swung her legs over the edge of the bed and sat upright. Her mind was still foggy from her crying jag, so she had a little trouble comprehending what Lisa had said.

"You saw Gus? Where?" Jenny asked with confusion on her face.

"He's watching this house." Lisa spoke slow and deliberate. She wanted the impact of her words to hit Jenny the way Lisa felt them.

And they did. Panic flashed through Jenny and she jumped up wildly searching around the room wondering where to go and what to do.

Lisa stood up and grabbed Jenny by the shoulders. "I saw him when we left, and his crew was still there when we came back. He knows we're here."

Jenny felt sick to her stomach and doubled over. "I'm going to be sick." She bolted from the room and pounded on the closed bathroom door.

Quickly the door opened, and she shoved herself past the girl standing in the doorway. She made it to the toilet in time to lose the wonderful lunch she'd enjoyed.

Her mind was pounding. Gus is here. Gus is watching us. *What am I going to do?*

Lisa had been right behind her and was now reaching down with a wet cloth for Jenny to wipe her face with. Jenny sat on the floor and leaned against the wall, wiping her face with the cloth.

Once again the sobs started. She didn't know how she had any tears left to cry, but she did. Maybe she'd been holding them back for so long they couldn't stay locked up any longer.

Lisa sat on the floor cross-legged facing Jenny. "We have to get out of here."

Jenny removed the cloth from her face and looked at Lisa. "Get out of here?"

"We have to run away from here and go somewhere he can't find us. If we don't, we will wind up dead like Mandy and Cami," said Lisa.

Jenny's hands plopped into her lap. The damp rag was soaking her jeans, but she didn't even notice, as she stared off into the distance.

Maybe Lisa was right. Soon they would go to class and out to part-time jobs and then Beth couldn't protect them from Gus. He would get them one way or another. As that reality soaked in, Jenny slowly nodded in agreement.

She looked up at Lisa. "You're right. They can't protect us. If we go, we have to go get Pride and take her with us. I can't stop grieving for her, and she's in danger from Gus too."

Lisa really didn't want the baggage of caring for a fat old woman like Pride, but she knew Jenny wouldn't go without her, so she nodded in agreement.

"Are you okay? Let's go back to our room and make a plan," said Lisa as she stood and reached out to help Jenny up.

Once back in their room, they shut the door and sat on their beds facing each other.

"We can't just walk out that door. They have security,

and alarms will go off. We don't have the code. We won't get to the end of the walk," said Jenny.

Lisa nodded thinking. "But we could get the code. If we stand to the side when Beth or one of the other volunteers goes out, we can watch what code they punch in to release the lock.

"But what about the monitors? Someone is always watching a monitor," replied Jenny.

"I went down in the middle of the night the other night to get something to drink and no one was watching them. They don't expect anyone to come to the door in the middle of the night, and no one can get in without someone from in here releasing the lock, so they don't worry so much.

"During the day they pay more attention. If we can get the code, we can slip out in the middle of the night and no one will even know we're gone until morning. We have to go at night anyway to sneak past Gus," said Lisa.

Jenny sat and thought for a moment. "We don't have much money. What are we going to do?"

"How much do you have?" Lisa asked Jenny.

Before Jenny could answer a knock sounded on their door and Sandy stuck her head in. "Is everything all right in here? One girl said Jenny had been sick."

Jenny and Lisa looked at Sandy with innocent eyes and guilty hearts. They both hoped they could pull off the innocent act.

"I was," Jenny stammered. "But I'm fine now."

Sandy wasn't buying it. She had taught school way too

long, as well as being a mother, to know when kids weren't telling the truth. She opened the door all the way up and walked on in.

She sat on the edge of the bed next to Jenny and attempted to look her in the eye. She reached her hand to Jenny's forehead to feel. "You don't have a fever."

Jenny ducked her head and pulled it away from Sandy's hand. "I promise I'm fine. I guess lunch just didn't set well with me."

Sandy looked over at Lisa, but she wouldn't make eye contact either. She wasn't sure what to say, not wanting to make false accusations.

Beth was now gone for the day and would not be back until tomorrow afternoon. She had told Sandy that she had pressing family matters to attend to, so basically while Sandy was here, she was in charge.

Concern creased Sandy's brow. "You know you can talk to me if you need to, right?"

Both girls nodded. They would not tell Sandy what they were planning. If they told anyone about Gus, it would not make any difference. There was nothing anyone could do to help them, so they had to help themselves.

Finally Sandy nodded, smiled, and rose from the bed. She stopped at the door knowing something was up, but feeling at a lost at what to do. She wanted to prove to Beth that she could handle this without her. She would just keep an eye on the girls while she was here.

With that thought, she closed the door behind her.

CARRIE MET Rick and Mike outside the Anderson's home. They agreed that it would be too much for all three to go in together, so Mike stayed out by the car while Rick and Carrie spoke with the parents.

On the way up the walk, Carrie asked, "Did you ask the store owner if he could instruct a sketch artist to draw a rendering of the man?"

"I did, but he said it was too long ago and that he only saw him through the dirty glass on the front door. Apparently he wasn't out there long before Sam got in and he drove off."

"What about a year on the car or a tag number?" Carrie knew Rick did his job well, but it was her nature to ask.

"He wasn't much of a car guy and couldn't decide on a year. He was guessing, but thought maybe late eighties or early nineties. He couldn't get a tag because the guy left turning the corner behind the store where there were no windows. Since he didn't go out to look, he didn't see it."

"He probably didn't realize at the time how important it would be now," Carrie said.

As they reached the porch, Carrie noticed the patches of dead grass and the unkept yard. On the porch was an old aluminum lawn chair with webbing that had seen better days. She could smell the stale stench of old cigarette butts and knew the old coffee can beside the chair had to be full.

At the sound of Rick tapping on the screen door, Carrie turned back waiting for someone to answer. Rick tapped again, louder this time, announcing that they were law enforcement.

Carrie looked at Rick's face for silent communication. When he shrugged, she looked back at the door. Then she opened the screen door and banged on the wooden door.

"This is Carrie Border with the OSBI. We had an appointment to talk with you. Please answer this door."

She stepped back a pace and waited. Finally, the door cracked slightly, and a lady peered out.

"Are you Mrs. Anderson?" Rick asked. He couldn't see enough of her to know if it was the lady he had spoken with before, or not.

Soon the door opened wider, and Mrs. Anderson pushed aside the screen door to welcome them in.

Rick had been here before in their initial inquiry, but this was Carrie's first visit to see where Cami had grown up. It was a mess. There were beer cans clustered on the coffee table among other stuff. Carrie couldn't even decipher exactly what.

The TV was on low, and the lady walked over and turned it off. "You can sit there." She motioned toward the sofa behind the beer cans. The mess didn't seem to bother her. Often when going into a home, the residents apologized profusely, embarrassed by the mess. This lady didn't seem to care.

"I'm Carrie Border with the OSBI. We haven't met, but I wanted to come with Rick today to ask a few more questions."

The lady sat in a chair angled to the side of the sofa and nodded. Rick began, since he had met the lady before. Carrie would let him interview her while she watched. Then she would jump in for further clarification should she feel the need for it.

"Ma'am I talked to a...," Rick paused to look down at his notes, "Ralph Nunez. He owns the store on the corner." Rick looked up to gauge her reaction. When there was none, he continued.

"Mr. Nunez said the day Cami and Sam went missing, they were at the store hanging out outside the front of the store. Apparently, they did this often." It was not a question, but Rick's tone rose at the end as if it were one.

Still the lady just sat looking at them, saying nothing. Carrie wondered if she was on some kind of medication. Her eyes didn't seem like they were glossy or glazed over, but sometimes you didn't know. But then, she had just been told about her daughter's death four days ago.

Finally, after a period of silence, Sue, Mrs. Anderson, filled the void. "Yes, they used to hang out at the store. All the girls did. Ralph didn't mind. He seemed to like the girls."

"On the day they went missing, Mr. Nunez said an old black Bonneville pulled up with a man driving. Then the girls, Cami and Sam walked up to the passenger side and leaned in to talk with the man. After a few minutes, Cami sat back down in front of the store and Sam got in the car with the man.

"Mr. Nunez went out and asked Cami about Sam going with the man. He was conerned, since he hadn't seen the man before and didn't know who he was. He said Cami assured him it was okay.

After Cami left that day, she never returned to the store. It seems that is the day that both girls went missing." Rick stopped once again to see if what he had said would draw out an emotional response from Mrs. Anderson.

She sat numbly listening to Rick's words. Finally, her eye dipped to the old shag carpeting, and she sat staring at it for what seemed to Carrie, like an eternity. About the time she was certain it had locked the lady into a catatonic state, she saw tears flow down both of her cheeks.

"Mrs. Anderson, are you okay?" asked Carrie.

She looked up at Carrie and shook her head no. "I may never be okay. I've not been a good mom to these girls." The tears had stopped but her voice was still thick with emotion.

"Buster works a lot, but he doesn't make much money. Most of what he does make goes to the bar or liquor store. I had to go to work when the girls were real young to pay the bills and for food.

"They were good girls too. I trusted that. I trusted that they were okay since there were so good. They learned to cook and take care of themselves when they were real young." Sue stopped, lost in her memories. She had that faraway look that was evidence of an escape to another place and time.

"I don't know cars very well. It would be two years ago. Do you have a picture of that kind of car?" Sue asked.

Carrie quickly searched the internet for that age of Bonneville. Finding one, she held the phone up where Sue could see it. Carrie wasn't sure if that was recognition she saw in her eyes or something else. Finally, Sue handed the phone back to Carrie.

Her face was pinched in thought. "I'm not sure. No one I know comes to mind. You said Cami wasn't alarmed that Sam had gotten in the car with the man?" Sue's voice was taught like a wire. Her face held fear and concern that was two years too late.

"No ma'am, apparently she wasn't," said Rick. "Do you think the other two girls might know the man or who he was?"

Sue slowly nodded, "Maybe."

"Where are they? Could we speak with them?" asked Carrie.

Sue's gaze swiveled from Rick to Carrie, then absently around the room, "I'm not sure where they are."

SANDY HAD AGREED to spend the night at the safe house since Beth would be gone. It was Friday and school didn't start until Monday. She would go home early the next day, which was Saturday, and get her kids ready for their school and her house in order.

Randy was furious, once again, when she had said she wanted to spend the night. She knew she was pushing her limit with him. But hoped that in time, he would see everything running smoothly and would relax.

She knew Lisa and Jenny were up to something, or so she thought. Keeping an eye on them without their realizing it was Sandy's goal for the evening. This was her chance to prove herself to Beth, and she didn't want to fail.

Dinner time went by without a hitch. The cooks had done a great job of preparing a salad with grilled chicken. The salad was full of several chopped veggies and even pecans.

The new girls were still timid and unsure of what to do and when to do it. Some picked at their food, others devoured it. All were thin and needed to eat as much healthy food as they could to regain their health, both mental and physical.

Emma's parent had picked her up around three. The warm greeting thrilled Sandy. That truly was what it was all about and why she was here. What would these girls success stories look like, and how could she make them happen, she wondered as she looked around the room at the remaining girls?

After dinner, they had played board games. It was a good way for the girls to interact casually and get to know each other. Sandy watched Jenny and Lisa. Something was off. Earlier she had wondered if it had all been her imagination, but by bedtime she was convinced that it wasn't.

During the games they were quiet and rarely interacted with anyone but each other, and that communication was usually in whispers. Not a good sign.

Some girls trickled off to their rooms around nine and others stayed up until eleven when it was all lights off in the main part of the house. They did not want to restrict their bedtime once in their private rooms, but felt that turning off the television and the lights in the main part of the house would help them establish a more normal nighttime routine.

These girls were used to sleeping late into the day and staying up most of the night. Changing their routine would need to be done gradually. They could stay up as late as they wanted in their own rooms where there were no electronics to busy themselves and keep them awake.

They could read or visit with each other. It rarely took long for them to get bored enough to go to sleep. Beth had told Sandy that after about a week of this routine, the girls were pretty much on a new sleep pattern.

Jenny and Lisa had both stayed up in the TV room until eleven, then went to their room together. Sandy had tried to engage them both in casual conversation, but neither one took her bait.

Sandy was exhausted from the full day, but knew she couldn't go to sleep in the room provided for house moms and other volunteers. If she did, she knew she would not be able to keep track of the girls and then learn what they might be up to.

Once all the girls were in their rooms, Sandy visited each one wishing them a good night's sleep and reaffirming that she was there if needed. She took two quilts out of the cabinet and the pillow off the bed and went to the sofa.

If she slept there, she could hear if someone came down the stairs and through the hallway to either door. She felt confident that the security system would alert her should they try to leave.

The doors had keypads with specific codes in order to leave without an alarm sounding. The windows also had alarms. They stayed locked for safety reasons, but if someone unlocked and opened one while the keypad by the door was engaged, an alarm would alert the entire house.

Sandy fought sleep for the next hour and then without realizing it, she drifted and was soon sound asleep.

Jenny and Lisa had been there earlier when Emma's parents picked her up. It was an exciting time and there were many people in and around greeting the parents and issuing hugs to Emma.

When it was time for them to leave, Sandy punched in her door code. Standing with her in the back hallway was only Emma and her parents. They would not be back, so it was irrelevant whether they saw the code, thought Sandy.

But what she hadn't known was that both Jenny and Lisa were watching from around the corner. Each one stood in an adjacent room and were peering around the door facing, watching from different angles. They had thought this through. If someone moved and blocked the keypad, then they would have two perspectives to view from.

Maybe it was the excitement, or maybe it was because Sandy was so new, but she hadn't taken extra precautions to hide the keypad when entering her own personal code.

As soon as Jenny and Lisa had seen the code, they ducked back, and then quietly retreated to their room. Their plan was coming together. Then all they had to do was wait for Sandy and the others to go to sleep.

They wanted to make it late enough at night so hopefully everyone would be asleep. They had taken turns sleeping so they would not be tired, but that didn't work. They were both so full of anxiety that the minutes seemed to tick by like hours.

At two in the morning, they tiptoed down the hallway to see if they could hear if any of the other girls were awake. They were too eager to get underway to wait any longer. If they found anyone still up though, they would go back to their room and wait.

Luckily they were all asleep. They had few items to take with them, so each girl could carry what they had in a small bag.

When they reached the bottom of the stairs, they stopped dead in their tracks. They hadn't expected to see Sandy asleep on the sofa in the television room. The house was old and didn't have an open floor plan like newer homes, so they didn't have to walk through the room Sandy was in. But, the old wooden floors creaked from time to time and in the quiet could be heard throughout the house.

From the bottom step, Jenny carefully touched the hallway floor with her foot. First the toe of her shoe, and then she eased her heal down. She'd held her breath the entire time, as if holding her breath would deaden the sound her footfall would make.

She exhaled when she'd been able to step without a sound. Each sequential step was made with the same deliberate care as both girls made their way down the hall to the back door.

They had made it to the backdoor when they heard Sandy move on the sofa. They both froze in fear of being discovered. After a few minutes, they realized that she had only moved in her sleep and was not awake. They could hear her steady breathing and relaxed.

Lisa was standing at the backdoor and dropped the small cover to reveal a lighted keypad. Suddenly she stopped and looked at Jenny.

"Does the keypad make a noise when the numbers are pressed?" she asked Jenny.

Jenny was trying to remember earlier in the day when Sandy had pressed the numbers. There had been so much talking and laughter it was hard to remember a specific sound the keypad had made.

"I don't remember," Jenny whispered.

"Me either." Lisa's face was pinched in concern. What

if they got caught? They might get kicked out, anyway. They wouldn't be wanted here if they broke the rules. But they wanted to get away not make a big production of leaving where Gus would see.

Finally, Lisa pressed the first number on the pad. Only a slight, quiet beep emerged. Relieved, she gently pressed the other numbers into the pad and heard metal shift in the door. They were free.

Now they had to turn the knob quietly so it wouldn't rattle. The outer doors were not the old original doors for safety reasons. Someone had replaced them with steel security doors. They were solid and tight.

The door handle turned with almost no sound. Then they slipped through the sliver of an opening they had created, and just like that, they were enveloped by the dark night.

IT WAS that last click as the back door settled back into place that woke Sandy. It was so low she wasn't even sure she had heard it. But something had woke her, and she knew she had to get up and check out the girls and the house.

She had fallen into such a deep sleep she had only registered that a sound had woken her, not what the sound had been or where it had come from.

Stepping into the hall from the television room, she looked to her left towards the front door and entryway, and then to her right towards the back entrance. The back door was not visible from where she stood so she stepped quietly towards it.

When she came to the back entry, nothing looked amiss. The cover was closed over the keypad. And the door was closed. She peered out the window but couldn't see anyone or any movement outside.

Letting the curtain fall back, she decided she needed to check on the girls. Walking quietly from room to room so she wouldn't wake them, she gently opened each room and peered in.

Most rooms were dimly lit by street lights outside their windows and it was enough light to see that they were in place. Jenny's and Lisa's room faced the backyard and there was no light shining in their window. At first glance, Sandy could see nothing amiss, but she stood looking into the room long enough that her eyes adjusted to the dark.

Soon, she realized that the lumpy forms on the beds were lumps of quilts and pillows. It took another minute for reality to sink in; the reality was that Jenny and Lisa were gone!

She sucked in a deep breath trying to not panic. Thinking clearly was her most important asset, and panic would prevent that.

First, she thought to call Beth, but she wanted so desperately to prove to her she could be trusted to take care of the girls. Then she thought of Randy, but if she called him, he would never let her come back.

She walked back down the hall and down the stairs.

She stood in the hallway with her hand over her mouth, desperately trying to determine what to do. The girls' lives were more important than what Beth or Randy thought about her. Maybe she didn't belong here anyway if she couldn't stop something like this from happening.

Tears slid over her face and hand. Then she had a thought. *What if she called Carrie? Would she come help and not tell Randy? Maybe they could get the girls back, and neither Randy nor Beth would ever know.*

Carrie had been working the case and would know where the girls might go. She also cared about the girls and what would happen to them. In a split second, her decision was made. Sandy hurried to her locker and retrieved her cell phone from her purse.

She dialed Carrie's number and waited. *What was she doing? Was she doing the right thing?* She was about to hang up when Carrie's voice came over the phone. It sounded like she'd been awake, which relieved Sandy.

"Hello. Sandy?" Carrie asked. She'd just come home from playing pool and was proud of herself for having had only a few beers earlier in the evening. She'd been stone cold sober by the time she had driven home.

"Carrie, I need your help." Sandy was trying not to break down over the phone, but the full reality of the situation had hit her, and it was tearing her apart inside.

"What's going on?" Carrie was instantly concerned. *Why had Sandy called her and not Randy?* "Where are you?"

"I... I'm at Safe At Last." She then blurted out what had happened midst sobs and tears.

"I can't call Randy. He will not let me come back. I can't call Beth. She won't let me volunteer anymore either. Please help me Carrie. Please." At her final plea Sandy broke down into sobs.

Carries mind raced. *Did she dare not call Randy? He was her partner. They didn't keep secrets from each other, or did they? He hadn't been forthcoming about his little tête-à-tête with Bracket earlier in the day.*

"Okay, but is there someone to stay there with the girls?" Carrie was gathering her things and rushing out the door.

"There's another lady who cooks breakfast. I'll leave her a note. I don't want to wake her. I'm hoping we can get the girls and be back before anyone knows they left."

"I'm not too sure about this." Carrie had a knot in her stomach. Everything within her told her this was the wrong thing to do, but if she hurried, maybe they could get Jenny and Lisa back before they came to any harm. Time was of the essence.

"I know," Sandy said as she paced the floor. "But we have to hurry. Text me as soon as you get here and I'll come out. I have to enter a code in the keypad to open the door. I'll write a note while I wait for you."

Carrie hung up the phone and was soon pulling into the driveway of the safe house. Sandy walked out and got into the passenger side door.

As Sandy slid down into the soft leather seat of Carrie's new sports car, a modest Dodge Charger this time rather than a Porche, the two women looked at each other.

They both knew there was no turning back now. Sandy could not re-enter the house without someone from inside opening the door. So with one final nod, Carrie shoved the car in reverse and sped out of the drive and down the street.

CHAPTER 12

It was a moonless night, but in the city fraught with streetlamps, one would hardly notice. Vince was tiring of sitting watching this silly house all because Gus had something to prove. But Gus was his boss and so he complied.

It was a boring job on a boring street watching a boring house. Little happened and few people came and went, especially at night when no one at all came or went. He knew the security was tight at the house and was convinced that they locked everything down for the night so no one could come or go.

The one perk was that he had convinced Gus he needed an iPad with unlimited data service so he would have some way to pass the time. Gus had unwillingly obliged.

Because Vince had settled in for the night to watch a

series non-stop on Netflix, he almost missed the movement next to the house. He shut off the screen of the iPad and watched carefully to see if he had been wrong.

Out of the corner of his eye, he once again saw movement and leaned in closer to the windshield and squinted. Then, with a huff of air, he leaned back in his seat. It was a silly cat.

He flicked the screen back on and resumed his series. Then he heard a noise, stopped the iPad once again and listened. Was it that silly cat again, he wondered. For what seemed like ten minutes he sat alert and listening. All he could hear was the sound of the nearby interstate and the middle of the night traffic. It was light but still noticeable.

When he was about to turn the show back on, he heard the roar of an engine approach from behind him. It was a Hemi; he was sure. That fact was confirmed when the sleek all black Dodge Charger passed his vehicle and pulled into the drive-way of the safe house.

He set the iPad aside, now glad that the light had been off when the car passed by him. He leaned in to see who would get out of the car. He pulled out his phone and tapped the camera app.

As he was clicking photos of the car sitting in the driveway a flash of white blonde hair caught the light. It was that lady Gus was so enamoured with. She was leaving the house and getting into the passenger side of the car.

Vince documented every step and sent them to Gus. *Who was in the driver seat,* he wondered? Since he was here to watch out for Jenny and Lisa, not the blonde lady, he once again leaned back in his seat.

As the car pulled out of the drive-way it headed back towards him. He had his camera ready and snapped several shots showing the driver. It was that lady cop!

He quickly sent those to Gus as well. *What could she possibly be doing here?*

The ding of the phone was loud in the quiet, and when Vince looked down, he saw Gus' response. "Follow them."

He replied that Jenny and Lisa were not with them, to which Gus replied, "I don't care. Follow them."

Vince started the engine and did a u-turn in the middle of the street. With few cars out at this time of night, he had to be careful or they would spot him following them.

As he drove along, his eye once again caught movement. It was the two girls. They each had a trash bag and were walking in the shadows of a street that ran perpendicular to the street he was driving on.

Torn between following the lady cop and getting the girls, he hesitated. Suddenly he whirled the SUV around once again and headed to where he had seen the girls.

Just as he was getting closer, a car pulled to the curb in front of them from the other direction, and they both got in. They had flagged down a taxi. He slammed his steering wheel, only slightly disappointed. He vowed that this guy would not see him following though, and he would get these girls back. The reward from Gus would be sweet.

JENNY GAVE the taxi driver Pride's address, which was only two miles away. Their plan was to get Pride and then get on a bus out of Oklahoma. She knew Pride would resist, but Jenny felt confident she could persuade her.

It was a little past two-thirty in the morning, but there was a light on in the front room. It was the glow of the television set.

Jenny paid the man, and she and Lisa walked up to Pride's front door and knocked. It took several seconds, but finally sounds of movement filtered through the door.

Pride called out, "Yes, who is it?"

"It's me Pride, It's Jenny."

The door whipped open. Pride glanced at Jenny and Lisa then quickly looked away to survey the street. She lived on a poor street and the closest streetlamp was busted out. It was pitch black out.

The door swung fully open, and Pride ushered the girls quickly inside. She engulfed Jenny in one of her all-consuming hugs and stood rocking her gently.

Then almost as suddenly, Pride released her hold and said, "Why are you here?"

"Gus was watching the house. He knows we were there." Jenny knew Pride would understand. "Lisa saw him outside watching the house. We knew we had to leave. We have a plan." Jenny's words rushed out in an effort to convince Pride before she could offer a rebuttal.

"We have enough money for three bus tickets out of here. You are coming with us." Jenny concluded.

"No Jenny." Pride's words were soft and her face was sad. "I'm not leaving."

"But you have to leave now. With us gone from the safe house, Gus will find you and kill you." Jenny was desperate to convince Pride to come with them. She needed Pride. The last couple of days at Safe At Last had proven that to her.

"Sit down, sweet girl." Pride had her hands on each of Jenny's arms and gently guided her to the sofa. Sitting there, Pride looked with love upon Jenny's face.

"I can't go." Her voice was calm in a way that frightened Jenny. "I understand that you feel you need to get out of here, but I cannot go with you. I'm too old and too feeble to run away and start a new life.

"You were safe at Safe At Last. Gus couldn't get you there. Why did you run?"

"We were safe, but soon we would go out like Lisa did earlier today with less and less supervision. Then Gus would get us. We would never feel safe."

"They have ways to keep you safe. That lady cop, she would help you."

Jenny was already shaking her head at Pride's words. "Not forever. You know Gus."

Just then all three of their heads swiveled to the front

door. The slow rumble of an engine was growing outside as a vehicle drove down the street.

Lisa ran to the front door and slammed the locks shut. Then the sound of the engine silenced as the motor shut off. Someone was outside close to Pride's house.

"Are the cops still watching your house?" asked Jenny.

"No. They left earlier this evening with plans to do frequent drive-bye's." This realization resonated through all three like a death sentence.

Just then Pride's phone rang, and she jerked her head to look in that direction, then back at Jenny.

Pride pushed herself up and walked to the phone. "Hello."

"Pride this is Carrie Border with the OSBI. I am sitting just down the street from your house. Jenny and Lisa have run away from the safe house and I believe they are coming to you." Carrie paused to see what Pride's response would be. When there was none, she continued.

"I'm going to come to your door now. Do not be alarmed. It's me."

Finally Pride said, "Okay."

She laid the phone back down and turned to look at Jenny and Lisa. Before she could decide what to say there was a slight knock at the door.

Pride went to the door and opened it enough for Carrie and another lady to slip through before she shut and locked the door.

Jenny jumped up from the sofa and Lisa scurried around the corner.

"Wait!" Carrie called out. "We only want to talk to you. Don't run. We won't force you to do anything you don't want to do."

Jenny felt penned in. She stood in front of the sofa, but Pride stood in front of her to her left and the other two ladies in front of her to her right. She had nowhere to run where they couldn't stop her.

In defeat, Jenny dropped back onto the sofa and laid her forehead on her knees and cried. Sandy had stepped around the corner and was attempting to stop Lisa, just as she was opening the back door.

"Lisa, wait," Sandy called out. But Lisa slipped out the door and ran with Sandy behind her.

Lisa had never been to Pride's house and with the dark night pressing in on her, she was literally stumbling to find her way off the porch and through the backyard.

The clatter of an old metal trash can told Sandy the direction to go, and she ran towards it. Lisa fumbled with the gate to the rickety chain-link fence and finally found the flip-up latch and disengaged it. She shoved the gate hard, but overgrown grass grabbed the gate from below, proving a formidable foe.

Shoving with all her might, she pushed the gate just enough to slip through. Somewhere along the way she had dropped her trash bag of clothes, but she didn't care. Once free of the gate, she ran with a fury knowing Sandy was right behind her.

The faster an object is moving, the greater the impact when forced to stop by an unmoveable object. The impact

Lisa felt caused her to nearly loose consciousness. Bright dots of light danced behind her eyelids as she lay dazed on the hard ground.

Hearing the impact and a grunt from Lisa, Sandy slowed her pace a bit. Her eyes still had not adjusted to the blackness and she could make out very little.

Then suddenly there was no ground beneath Sandy's feet. They were whirling in the air trying to find leverage. Strong, log like arms locked her tightly. She opened her mouth to scream, then more than the night went black.

As soon as Vince had seen that the taxi was taking the girls to Pride's house, he slowed and called Gus. Pulling onto the street he realized the cop car that had been watching Pride's house was no longer there.

He pulled over to the curb about four houses down from Pride's and sat waiting for Gus' instructions. He was sitting there on the phone when Carrie's black Charger crept down the street and parked in front of the house next door to Pride. He had hit the jackpot!

As soon as Carrie and the blonde lady had gone inside, Vince stepped out of his vehicle and walked toward Pride's. When he'd almost reached her front yard, he heard a voice call out from inside and then a clatter from the back.

He was standing alert and ready when Lisa ran solidly into him. In an instinctual response Vince resisted the impact with the full force. The result left Lisa sprawled on the ground. The impact against Vince, then the hard slam to the ground had rendered her immobile.

Then he saw a slight flash of blonde hair and grabbed the blonde lady around her middle raising her off the ground. As she screamed, he released his grip enough to punch her solidly in the face.

Now both ladies lay out cold on the ground. Gus was not close by, and it would take him time to get there. Making a quick decision, Vince decided he would take the two, tie them up and put them in his vehicle.

He picked up Lisa like a sack of potatoes and slung her over his shoulder. It took only a minute to heave her into the back of the SUV and tie her arms and legs. Soon he had done the same to the blonde lady, and both were secure.

He got back into the driver's seat and called Gus again, explaining the situation, and waiting for further instruction.

"So the lady cop and Jenny are still inside with Pride?" Gus asked for confirmation.

"Yes," Vince answered. "Wait. The lady cop just came outside. She's looking around. I'm sure she is looking for Lisa and the blonde. I can't stay here, boss."

"Yeah, right. Okay… Go on over to the house on Ivan Street. I'll meet you there.

Vince shut off the phone and hesitated. He was hoping the lady cop would go back inside and he could slip away unnoticed. *There she goes,* he thought, as Carrie turned to go back inside.

As she stepped back into the house and out of sight, Vince turned on the SUV. Hearing the car roar to life, Carrie bolted back out the front door and into the front yard.

Realizing that both Sandy and Lisa were missing, the car roaring to life brought her to rapt attention. She flung her car door open and was quickly inside, moving hard and fast after the SUV.

It had to be Gus or one of his men, didn't it? Her instincts from her OKCPD days compelled her to call her pursuit in and ask for backup, but this was abnormal. Her own partner didn't even know she was here. Should she call him even though she had promised Sandy?

Sandy was in that car! Sickness threatened her. Her partner's wife had just been abducted in a situation that Carrie had been talked into against her own better judgement.

She pressed even harder on the gas pedal. The SUV was no match for the Charger and she would catch up to him soon. They were in a part of the city, close to downtown, where the original grid layout of streets had since been adapted to a winding intercept of curved interstate highways, one-way streets, and boulevards.

Carrie was surprised that the SUV had so much power. She had caught up to it, but staying on its tail was a challenge. She realized they weren't heading to Gus' house, this was the wrong way. But of course he wouldn't want to lead her straight there.

A sudden curve came up, and the SUV skidded around it with two wheels almost leaving the pavement. Carrie responded with a quick whip of the wheel. Her car wobbled back and forth trying to regain forward momentum.

Vince was driving erratically trying to throw the cop off. She had a souped-up engine, and he knew his heavy SUV was no match. He would have to think through this to get her off his tail.

He attempted to navigate the one-way streets downtown, thinking he could throw her off by going the wrong way, but after she followed him relentlessly two blocks the wrong way down a one-way street, he realized that wouldn't work.

He had to get out of downtown. There was too much construction and torn-up streets. Just then proving that point, he accidentally hit a wooden barricade that went flying to the right and back.

Carrie dodged and ducked out of instinct as the barricade hurtled toward her car. She swerved just in time to miss it, but lost precious ground.

The engine roared as she pressed it harder, sitting forward in her seat from anxiety. Even if she wanted to call Randy now, she couldn't. She would lose them.

The SUV turned again and headed south. The stoplight was red, but that hadn't stopped it. Carrie looked quickly and then sped up to follow. She had not seen a car approaching and had to swerve to miss it as she careened into its lane. The other car screeched to a halt perpendicular to the street.

Again, she had to gain control of her car in order to press it in a solid, forward motion. The near collision had afforded the SUV some ground. Carrie was about five or six car lengths behind when she heard the dinging bells and saw the flashing red lights.

A train. A split second decision. The SUV flew across the tracks just ahead of the train as Carrie slammed on her brakes and spun the car sideways. Her car rocked hard to a stop with dust and debris flying all around her.

The rush of the train traveling inches away from her car door created terror like none she had ever known. She had missed death by a split second. Her life had flashed before her eyes and was now vivid in her mind.

What she saw blanketed her with a deep sorrow. Her body shook convulsively, and she laid her head and hands on the steering wheel and wept, with one thought ringing through her. If the train had hit her, would it have even mattered?

THE CHAOS of Sandy pursuing Lisa out the door, then Carrie tearing off in her car, left Jenny and Pride standing stunned in the middle of the living room.

Pride reached out and drew Jenny in close. They had once again shut and bolted both the front and back doors.

They did not understand what was going on and were both terrified.

Jenny pulled away slightly from Pride and looked up at her. "Pride we have to go." She watched Pride's face, hoping that she would understand that they couldn't stay where they were.

"Please Pride," begged Jenny.

Pride stood thinking. The anxiety was preventing her from clear thought and her emotions were tugging against her common sense.

After a few minutes of Jenny begging, Pride took hold of Jenny and looked her firmly in the eye.

"Jenny take my car and go. I can't go. I told you, I can't. But you should." Pride let go of Jenny and walked to her purse. She dug around, then pulled out her car keys and cash from her wallet. It wasn't much, but would help the poor girl a little.

The entire time Jenny was still begging, now pleading, for Pride to please go with her. Threats of not leaving without her fell on deaf ears.

Pride turned and pressed the keys and money into Jenny's hand. "Go. When this is all over and they have caught Gus, you can come back."

Jenny was furiously shaking her head and tears fell mixed with hot water running from her nose.

Suddenly, Pride slapped Jenny across the face, then in panic pulled her to her, hugging her tightly, then pushing her away again.

"Jenny you have to go! Now!" Pride shoved Jenny

towards the front door, unlocked it, and pushed her outside. She shut and locked the door quickly before Jenny could force her way back in.

Jenny sat down on the cold concrete step and sobbed. She wanted to die. It was all too much to bear.

In the dark quiet of the early morning Jenny finally realized that Pride could not be made to come with her and that she had to leave. She rose from the step as though her body were made of lead and walked to the car.

Jenny pulled out of the driveway and was three blocks away when Gus pulled up in front of Pride's house.

He and two of his men sat outside surveying the neighborhood. There was no cop car as there had been for the last couple of days, just as Vince had said. There was no sign of any cars for that matter, even Pride's car was gone. There was however, the faint glow of a TV on inside the house.

Gus opened his door and motioned for the other two to follow him. He walked with measured steps toward the front door looking all around, but it was still too dark to see anything.

He stepped up to the door and rapped with a single knuckle, then waited.

Inside, Pride wondered if Jenny had come back. She wouldn't answer the door. The girl had to know to leave, so Pride sat in her chair, silent.

Gus once again rapped on the door, this time harder.

He was eerily calm because he was about to feel the ecstasy of revenge, and he wanted to savor this moment.

When Pride still did not answer, Gus motioned for one of his guys to step forward. He was a master at picking locks and he had his picks at the ready.

Pride heard the picks in the lock and knew it was not Jenny. She hurried to push herself out of her chair and across the floor to the back of the house. She couldn't run at her weight, but tried to hurry the best she could. If she could just make it to the back door.

Suddenly the front door burst open and Gus was upon her in a flash. She felt the cold steel of his knife up under her chin. Her breath halted, and she stood stone cold still.

"Where are they?" Gus asked with a lilt to his voice. It was the voice of a madman. Pride knew that no matter what, he would slit her throat. Whether she told or whether she didn't, she would die here and now. In that case she would protect the young girl she loved as her own daughter.

Pride closed her eyes and stood silent. "I said, where are they?" He pressed the knife tighter to her skin and a thin red line emerged.

When the threat didn't elicit a response, Gus shoved her away slamming her against the kitchen cabinet. He had spun her around as he pushed, and her back had hit hard against the sharp edge.

Then he stepped right up to her, his nose nearly touching hers. "I said, where are they?" When he saw that she would rather die than talk, he backed down and motioned for the guys to take her.

He had them sit her into a kitchen chair and tie her down. She would talk. He would make sure of that.

Gus paced the room as a man who was in no hurry. He liked, no, loved the feeling of control, and whether Pride knew it, he was in control. Pacing quietly would add tension to the air and the more anxiety he could create in her, the quicker she would talk.

But he only had so much patience. After a few minutes he stopped in front of her and once again pulled out his knife. He grabbed the top of her thin cotton nightgown and ripped it downward with all the force he had.

The white cotton cloth gave way and left Pride sitting bare and humiliated. But she would not let it persuade her. She held her head high and sat stoic.

Gus sneered and added slurring insults to her already diminished pride. Then in a burst of aggression Gus flew forward and wrapped his free hand around Pride's throat. He squeezed and her eyes bulged.

"Where are they?" He screamed into her face. His spittle flew across her panic rippled face, but she did not speak.

Then Gus felt her body shudder, and confusion flooded his mind. He didn't want to kill her… yet. The grip he had on her throat was not enough to choke her, only hurt her and scare her so she would talk.

Her body was in some type of convulsion. Gus' eyes

grew round, and he stumbled backwards away from Pride. Her eyes closed and her head dropped to her chest.

Panic seized Gus. She was dead. How dare she! A moment of indecision gripped him and he stood in the middle of the kitchen floor.

"Let's go." He finally barked at the others and out the door they ran, leaving Pride all alone.

Carrie wasn't sure how long she had sat there in her car shaking, but she finally realized the train was gone and she needed to regroup.

She had lost the SUV which held Lisa and Sandy captive. She had almost died in pursuit, and no one would have even known if she had died because she had thought she could handle this herself. If she had died, no one would even know what had happened or where to look.

She leaned back, took a deep breath, and searched for her phone. It had been propelled into the passenger floorboard. She retrieved it and opened her phone app. Her car was still sitting perpendicular in the street, but she didn't have the energy to move it. Thankfully, it was still early morning on a rarely traveled street.

Her choice was to call Randy or Bracket. She couldn't call Randy. There was no way she could deal with telling him what had happened and her role in it all.

She clicked the button to call SAC Bracket. It was still

early, and she knew her call would wake him from sleep. After only a few rings he answered with a groggy voice.

"Yeah?"

"It's Carrie. I have a situation and I need your help." That sounded dumb, but she wasn't sure what else to say. How could she explain this whole mess in a sentence or two? She couldn't.

Suddenly alert, Bracket sat up. "What situation?"

"It's a long story, but Gus' man has abducted Randy's wife Sandy and he doesn't know." That would get his attention, and not in a good way.

Bracket sat for a brief moment, trying to comprehend what she had just said. It just sounded strange and too foreign to imagine.

"Okay, start from the beginning."

Carrie started her car and told Bracket in as concise as possible a manner, the story of the last few hours. Once done she wasn't sure where to go except back to Pride's in order to check on her and Jenny.

She pulled up in front of Pride's as a faint hint of light and color rose in the eastern sky. The call with Bracket finally ended as she sat there watching the sunrise.

The beauty midst the trauma of the early morning seemed in dire contrast. But as she sat and watched the glorious display of color, she felt a sense of peace wash over her.

She needed to exit the car and check on Pride and Jenny, but something held her to this moment. Something that seemed to want to comfort her. She felt so strange, so transfixed to the moment.

When she could finally open her door and step into the dim early morning, she carried that peace with her. Since her parents' death, she had not felt one moment of peace, until now.

The neighborhood was calm as most neighborhoods were this early in the morning. She didn't hurry to Pride's front door, but took the short walk to wallow a little longer in this new peaceful feeling that had eluded her for so long.

Then it ended almost as abruptly as it had begun. When Carrie approached Pride's front door, it stood slightly ajar. She knew Pride had been hyper-vigilant lately, and she would have never left her door open. It was then that Carrie noticed that Pride's car was gone.

She pulled her gun from its holster and gripped it, ready to shoot. She gently pushed the door open with the toe of her shoe. The television was still on, the volume low, but there was no one watching it.

She walked quietly through the door towards the kitchen and called out, "Pride. Jenny."

But as she turned the corner into the kitchen, she knew Pride would not be responding to her call. Carrie dropped her gun to her side and rushed over to Pride.

She touched the side of her neck and confirmed what she already knew, there was no pulse. She called Bracket and reported what she had found. There was no rush for an ambulance, it was too late for that. Bracket would send a crime lab and the medical examiner.

She wanted to cover Pride, but couldn't hinder evidence collection. Emotion welled up in her as she felt deep compassion for this lady. Then tearing herself away, she walked out to the front porch and sat on the step.

Carrie sat thinking. Jenny was not here, but since Pride's car was gone, she suspected that Pride had forced Jenny to take it and run. Or, Jenny had witnessed the murder of Pride and had ran on her own accord. Either way, Carrie didn't think Gus had Jenny. Had the car been here, then she would have thought otherwise.

The morning light had grown and the sounds of the city were escalating. Carrie pondered that peaceful feeling that had comforted her in the car moments ago. It was as if something other worldly was wrapping its arms around her and giving her a hug. It would be all right, it had seemed to say.

Soon Bracket pulled to a stop with uniformed OKC cops quickly in tow. They would secure the scene, another murder to solve. But Carrie knew who had killed Pride. She knew with certainty it had been Gus.

Carrie stood and met Bracket mid-way in Pride's front yard. "Did you call Randy?" Carrie asked.

Bracket perched his hands on his hips and wrinkled his face before dropping his gaze to the ground. He looked back up at Carrie and nodded an affirmative.

"I want to view this crime scene and then you and I

will go back to the office and you *will*, give me every detail of what happened. It was Carrie's turn to nod.

The investigation techs arrived, suited up, and headed towards the house that was already adorned with yellow crime scene tape.

She explained to Bracket that she had touched nothing except Pride's neck to check for a pulse. He gave a few explicit orders to the crime scene techs before turning and ushering Carrie out the front door.

Carrie had spent hours in this little house over the course of the last few days. She had come to know a sweet girl named Jenny and her surrogate mother, Pride. An abnormal family, but that is just exactly what it was. A little family of two.

Carrie's family had been wrenched from her years ago and she had built a wall up so thick and so high that no one could penetrate it. *But what if she could feel like a family again, like Pride and Jenny?* They weren't blood, but their bond was stronger than a good deal of blood-related families she had seen.

She got back in her car and followed behind Bracket heading to the office. He had said agents had gone to Gus' house and that no one was there, not even his thugs. He had also sent agents to the Safe At Last's safe house. The cook had called Beth immediately, and an agent had met her there and explained what had happened.

When Carrie pulled into the parking lot of the OSBI headquarters, she saw Randy's car. Her body tensed, and she dreaded the next few hours. There would be hours of interrogation and deliberation and Randy would be distraught and angry through it all. Angry at her. Angry at Sandy. Angry at the world.

She drew in a long breath, and stepped out of her car and into the building, ready to face the music.

CHAPTER 13

Vince had taken his female cargo to an old house that Gus kept for *projects*. In short, it was where he could take care of delicate and illegal matters without drawing law enforcement to his residence.

It was on the south side of Oklahoma City, but several miles to the west of where he lived. They took care of the house, with its mowed lawn, and tended flower beds. It was a house that appeared well taken care of by a loving family.

Gus took more care of this home than his own home. The last thing he wanted was a disgruntled or nosey neighbor complaining about the upkeep of the house.

It was still pitch-dark when Vince had arrived at the house, and with the garage door opener he could enter the house unnoticed. The large SUV barely fit, but he pulled as far up as he could to allow enough room to open the back of the SUV with the garage door closed.

He wasn't surprised to see two wide eyed, terrified women when he opened it up. "Good morning, ladies. Have a nice nap?" Vince grinned and reached for Sandy who was piled on top of Lisa.

She jerked back and tried to move backwards, but there was nowhere to go. Vice laughed and stood looking at her for a moment. "What? Where do you think you're going to go?"

Vince was like a huge brick wall. He was six foot four inches and weighed in around 365 pounds. These two little women had no chance against him.

Tired of messing around, he plunged in and grabbed Sandy around her waist and drug her out. He carried her under his arm into the house, flipped on a light, and plopped her in the closest kitchen chair.

Without removing his hand, which held her down, he leaned in close and stared into her eyes. "You move, I will kill you. Got it?"

Sandy understood and nodded.

Vince pulled some heavy duty zip ties out of a cabinet drawer and locked Sandy down tight to the chair. He left the rag in her mouth he'd used earlier when throwing her in the back of the SUV.

In less than five minutes, he had both ladies confined securely in the kitchen and went to use the toilet. Gus had sent him a message that he was at Pride's. It would be awhile before Gus could meet him here.

Once back in the kitchen, he flipped the light off and went to lie down on the sofa. He'd had a long night. He would rest while he could.

But his rest didn't last long. He was just about to doze off when his phone rang. It was Gus, and he was on his way.

Vince jumped up and went to pull his SUV out of the garage so that Gus could pull in. Gus' SUV flew into the open garage door and he was out of it before the door was halfway down.

Standing by, Vince watched as Gus slung the contents of the garage and threw them at him. *What had set him in such a rage? They had the blonde and Lisa.*

Finally, Gus's energy spent with one final kick at the wall, he went inside. The three goons followed, waiting for further instruction.

Seeing the two women strapped to the kitchen chairs soothed Gus somewhat. But he was still furious that Jenny and Pride had betrayed him. No one ever got away with betraying him. And now Pride was dead and they would hunt for him.

He wanted to play with his two new toys, but he had to figure out what to do. As he walked past Sandy on his way towards the living room, he stopped and brushed his hand down her soft cheek and held her chin. He tilted her head up, removed the rag from her mouth, and leaned down giving her a long slow kiss.

He didn't even mind that her face was wet and salty from her tears. In some warped way, her fear excited him even more.

Randy was pacing in a panic when Carrie walked into the room. As soon as she did, he flew around the desk and rushed at her in a desperate rage.

Bracket immediately reached out, protecting Carrie from the onslaught that Randy was about to deliver. But it didn't stop his screams. His vile, accusatory screams. And each one seemed true to Carrie, so she stood and allowed him to deliver them repeatedly.

Finally, when he was spent, he turned to walk into the conference room. Carrie's mind searched for something to say, but nothing seemed right. She could say 'I'm sorry, or we'll get them back' but nothing, not one thing at all, even came close to what the situation required. So, she quietly followed him into the conference room with Bracket at her side.

She pulled out a chair and sat quietly while Randy paced and rubbed his hand through his dark hair. Bracket sat at the end of the table and requested that Randy sit.

Watching his agony, Carrie could feel her blood pressure pounding against the top of her skull. She felt dizzy and thought she might pass out, but forced herself to endure this horrific moment.

When Randy finally sat, Bracket looked at Carrie,

started the video camera they left in the room for just such an occasion, and nodded for her to begin.

After an hour, it was all down on video. Carrie could have given the events much quicker, but was stopped periodically to answer clarifying questions from both Bracket and Randy.

She was glad it was over. She had rubbed her sweaty hands together from sheer nervousness until they felt chapped and raw. Randy couldn't make solid eye contact with her. She would catch him glaring at her, but when she would attempt to meet his gaze, he would turn his head.

He was her best friend, and she had destroyed that relationship. Could it be repaired? She hoped so, but only if they found Sandy alive and well.

One of their agents, Gerald, was searching for properties that Gus may own. He was diving deep to see if there were shell corporations or an alias he could have used to purchase them.

The techs were still going over Pride's home with a fine-tooth comb and the medical examiner had her body ready for autopsy. Someone had put a BOLO out on Pride's car. Jenny would only be detained for inquiry and for her own safety. As far as they knew, she hadn't committed a crime.

As soon as they shut the video camera off, Randy jumped up and left the room. Carrie looked over at Bracket with pleading eyes. He had a big heart and cared for all his agents, especially Carrie. He had seen the trauma her parents' death had dealt her.

Bracket reached out and laid his hand on hers. Let's go into my office and we'll talk. He patted her hand and rose to leave.

Carrie suddenly felt exhausted. The long night of adrenaline and anxiety weighted her body down. It took great effort just to rise from the chair and take a step toward Bracket's office.

Another agent was already taking the camera to offload her statement so it could be transcribed and placed in the file. Carrie couldn't look at her. They would all know the poor decisions she had made that put Sandy in danger, and which may also result in her death.

Walking out of the conference room to Bracket's office, Carrie couldn't look around the room. She felt the eyes on her, first glancing her way, then quickly darting away. She could read their thoughts. They were the same as her own.

Bracket's door clicked behind her and the blinds made a swoosh as he pulled them closed. That was a clear sign they were not to be disturbed.

The heaviness Carrie felt in her soul pushed her body deep into the chair in front of Bracket's desk. She slouched so low she could rest her head on the back of the chair. One ankle lay resting on the other thigh and her hands hung straight down on each side.

She shut her eyes for a moment and then heard

Bracket say, "Carrie this is just us in here now. What were you thinking?"

The only sound in the room was the ticking of the old school clock behind her on the wall, and the deep sigh she rendered. Pulling strength from somewhere, she pushed herself up and rested her elbows on the arms of the chair.

She looked down at her hands as she picked at a wrinkle in her jeans. Shame riddled her. It was yet one more bad decision in a long line of bad decisions.

"I thought if I hurried I could get them back. Sandy was panicked. She didn't want Beth or Randy to know. It was important to her that she get the girls back quickly before anyone found out. At that time we had no reason to believe they had done anything but run away back to Pride's house.

"It seemed to be just a matter of going and picking up two girls who had run away." She paused for a moment to gauge Bracket's reaction. When he continued to sit waiting, she continued.

"Before we knew it, things were out of hand and I was reacting. I didn't have any reason to expect that Gus or his men were watching Jenny or Pride. There is nothing you can say to make me feel any worse."

Bracket nodded and leaned back in his chair. Carrie was a good agent no, a great agent. She was one of the sharpest and best agents he had ever worked with. But she had issues she needed to resolve. *Was this latest episode driven by some internal need that drove her to make the same bad choices in her personal life or had she genuinely thought she was doing the right thing?*

"I understand that you responded to Sandy's call out of compassion, that you wanted to help her. Did you not see where this could end up?"

"I honestly thought we could get them quick and get them back to the safe house safely." She was honest. Yes, there was that little niggling feeling she had had that was attempting to caution her, but she had over road it.

"You think you can do anything, Carrie. You don't think you need anyone else. This job, this agency is a team effort. We work together here and with other law enforcement agencies. If we don't work together, things don't get done right and people get hurt."

Carrie nodded. She knew she had issues about asking for help, in anything. She was still struggling with her drinking because she was convinced that she could handle it herself and refused to ask anyone for help.

"I'm going to put you on administrative leave…

"Carrie jumped up before Bracket could finish his sentence. "You can't! I know too much. I can help. You need me on this case and the drownings." She moved closer to the front of his desk and rested both hands on it and leaned in.

"Please don't take me off of this case." Carrie hadn't pleaded like this… well, ever. *"Please."*

Bracket sat and thought, then leaned his chair forward. "Forty-eight hours." I do not want to see you around here for forty-eight hours.

"I also want you to report to the agency counselor and continue regular weekly meetings with her for the next three months or... Brackets' hand went up to stop her from protesting. "Or... until she says they are no longer necessary."

"Can I at least work here in the office?"

"No. I want you to go home, and I want you to get some sleep. You don't sleep enough, or eat enough by the looks of it."

Carrie knew there was no use protesting any longer. Bracket was compassionate, and she didn't want to test the limits of that compassion. She was truly exhausted, so she agreed.

"Can I ask one thing?" Carrie asked. "Will you please keep me in the loop? I've grown fond of Jenny. Pride too."

"No. I want you home and work free."

Carrie once again nodded and turned to go. The looks from co-orkers were still there but this time she looked back and could even return a bit of a smile. Were they wondering if she had been fired? her She probably should have been.

She walked back to her desk. Randy was not at his, and she wondered where he was. Should she wait to talk to him or search him out before she left?

Deciding to wait until she was rested and had a clear head before talking to Randy, she looked down and noticed an envelope on her desk. It was a plain white long envelope. On top was written, 'Please give to OSBI Agent Carrie Border'.

She picked it up and turned it over. On the bottom was a sticky note that read, 'Found this at the crime scene this morning. It was lying on top of the table next to the recliner.'

Carrie stood and looked at the sealed envelope. It felt thick as though it contained several pages. It couldn't pertain to this morning's events. It would have to be something that Pride had done since the last time she had seen her. If it was evidence in the case, she felt certain that Pride would have given it to her earlier.

Carrie folded the envelope in half the best she could, shoved it in her back pocket, and headed towards the door. She couldn't read it now. She couldn't think about Pride right now, or Jenny, or Sandy, or Lisa. The list was long of people she couldn't think about right then.

She would go home and try not to drink.

Randy was beside himself with worry. He hadn't been able to look at Carrie and made sure he was not around when she left. He was gripping the rail that ran along the top floor hallway that looked out into the lower entrance.

As he stood watching for Carrie to leave, his knuckles were white and taught. He was using the rail to anchor him in one place. He didn't trust himself right then to say or do anything, so he had come to the top floor and stood where he could watch for her to leave.

When he saw Carrie come out of their office on the

floor below and walk down the stairs to the lobby, his teeth ground together. They had worked together for years and she was his closest friend. He had loved having her for a partner, but that was all over now.

Just as Carrie reached the front door, she turned and looked up to where Randy stood. She must have felt his presence. Their eyes locked and several seconds passed as they both stood there. Randy with rage in his eyes and Carrie with tears in hers.

Finally, Carrie's upper body shuddered in a motion of defeat that disengaged her eyes with his. She turned and left the building.

Randy continued to stand for a while longer. Rage filled the cavernous space within him. Sandy's abduction and Carrie's betrayal had left him feeling empty, alone, and fearful.

"Randy." Bracket's voice jarred him out of his mental focus. He stood and turned to see SAC Bracket coming toward him.

Bracket rested his hand on Randy's shoulder and said, "I will tell you to go home, but I know you won't. I will also tell you that if you can't push past what you are feeling, I will take you off of this case completely. There is a conflict of interest. This is your wife. I'm concerned that you will do more harm than good." Bracket stopped to gauge Randy's reaction. When there was none he continued.

"You are temporarily confined to office duty. You can do good here, and I can't have you back in the field yet."

Randy nodded. He knew what Bracket was saying was right, but he had to be searching for Sandy and out there actively helping. He also knew Bracket wanted him here in the office so he could keep an eye on him to make sure he wasn't out there. If Bracket sent him home, he would still look for her outside of Brackets purview and Bracket knew this.

Bracket gave Randy's shoulder a double-pat and turned to go. "Come on, we need your help if we are to find Sandy."

The office was a flurry with all hands on deck. Agents had dropped everything and were busy on the phones, computers, and discussing possible options. Sandy was important to them because she was important to him.

He forced his body to move towards his desk. It seemed as though he were moving solid blocks of stone rather than his normally nimble legs. Once there, he stood staring before him at Carrie's desk. Her cheery face floated before him. He'd grown used to seeing her there, and it usually brought a sense of solidarity and comfort. But not today.

He sat down and tried to regain control of his thoughts. Thinking strategically was what he needed now, not wallowing in emotions.

One or two of their agents were searching for properties Gus could own. They'd found Sandy's phone, so they didn't have that to trace. They were searching for Jenny in Pride's car. Would she have insight that could help them?

The DMV would have Gus' license plates. They could

also put out BOLO's for those. He logged into the system and saw that another agent had already thought to do that as well.

Just then, commotion from the other side of the room stirred him back to life. As he turned, he saw Bracket motion for him to follow him into the conference room. Several other agents were also heading that way.

The clatter of chairs and rustle of arms and legs brushing against furniture halted when Bracket raised his hand from the front of the room.

"Good work so far. You have pushed hard. I wanted to get everyone in here together to go over what and where we should go from here.

"First off, the car we assume that Jenny Mason drove from this morning's crime scene where Diane Smith's, a.k.a. Pride's, body was found this morning. It was at the Petro Truck Stop off of Martin Luther King Ave. and Reno Ave. We also found that a Greyhound bus left for Dallas, Texas just thirty minutes afterwards.

"It would be safe to assume that Jenny, Jennifer Mason, parked the car at the truck stop then walked to the bus station just a block away." Bracket stopped for a minute, looked down and shuffled through the stack of papers he had before him on the table.

"No sign of the two vehicles which are registered to Gustavo Hernandez have been seen. I think we can assume that he knows that is one of the first things we would look for and has hidden them. There is no one at his primary residence either. On another note, the medical examiner said his preliminary exam shows that Diane Smith, Pride, died from heart failure. Her health was poor, and the possibility of a heart attack was imminent, but the trauma forced upon her by Gus instigated it.

"However, there is a bright spot, Gerald found a link between another property and Gus. I am confident that is where he is. I want a team of our agents to go down there with SWAT."

The room rustled to life and several agents stood to leave. Everyone was ready to go. "Randy, I want to see you in my office." Bracket said.

Randy was still seated. He knew he couldn't go to the house. Why did he feel as though he was already grieving? She wasn't dead. They would find her. He stood to walk to Bracket's office.

Bracket followed him in after giving further directions to the lead agent on this op and closed the door behind him.

"You know why you aren't going with them, right?" Bracket asked.

Randy nodded. To be honest, he felt so defeated that he suspected the worst and wasn't sure he wanted to see what they would find.

"Randy we will find her and find her alive. I can see it written all over your face you're expecting the worse case scenario. You can't do that." Bracket stopped for a moment.

"I want you on the comm system with me so you will hear what is going on even though you aren't there. As soon as we know anything, you will head there."

"Or the morgue," said Randy as he sat there. He knew he needed to have hope, but from the moment Sandy brought up working at Safe At Last, he'd had a dreadful foreboding in the pit of his stomach. He was now convinced that this was why.

Bracket was not in Randy's shoes and couldn't disregard how he felt, but that kind of self pity wouldn't serve anyone. "Get up. Come with me."

Bracket led Randy out to the tac gear room where the agents were gearing up. He handed an earpiece to Randy and placed one in his own ear.

Bracket's last-minute instructions to the team were lost on Randy. He stood numbly by, staring off at nothing, Bracket's voice sounding like white noise.

THE STAGING AREA was one city block from the house where Gus held Sandy and Lisa captive. There was an old commercial business, now defunct, that had a large parking lot. It sat diagonally behind the house, with heavy tree foliage and vegetation between them and the house, there was no way that someone from inside the house could see them.

Once all personnel were there, OKCPD, SWAT, and

OSBI, Bracket gave the go ahead. They had seen no one coming or going. SWAT was approved to lead the raid.

Gus was sitting on the sofa fuming. The women were still where Vince had planted them in the kitchen. He'd replaced blondie's rag after the kiss, and he hadn't taken their binds off or pulled the rags out since.

Two of his men sat at the kitchen table playing cards, keeping an eye on the women, as if they could go anywhere. Vince was in the living room with Gus.

Suddenly, with no warning, SWAT busted down the front door. Gus and Vince were immediately on their feet with their weapons pulled.

Before Gus could realize that he was out manned and out gunned, he fired, with Vince doing the same. As his finger was pulling the trigger, Gus realized that he was a dead man.

With bullets flying in the living room, Gus' other two men ran through the back door where more OKCPD waited for them. They raised their hands in surrender and the cuffs were slapped on.

OSBI Special Agent Gerald Walker rushed in and was by the women's side as soon as the gunfire ceased. Kneeling down by Sandy's side to cut loose the zip ties which held her, he felt her tears like raindrops falling on his balding head. It was a good feeling.

Both women felt weak as the reality of their rescue sank in. The men had locked the ties down so tight it had almost completely cut off circulation, which made it difficult to stand and walk. The needles flowed through their hands like rivers of glass. Even rubbing their wrists and hands to sooth them didn't seem to help.

Sandy looked around for Randy and Carrie but neither one were there. *Why,* she wondered? A new wave of panic surged through her. Were they dead? What had happened after she and Lisa had been captured?

Gerald felt a solid jerk as someone grabbed and pulled the front of his vest downward. Standing there was Sandy looking up at him with pleading eyes.

"Where's Randy?" Her panic chilled him even though he knew Randy was safe.

"Randy is at the office. He will be here soon. SAC Bracket prevented him from coming since it would be a conflict of interest."

Relief like a wave of nausea threated to drop Sandy to the floor. Reaching behind her she felt the cold of the old aluminum kitchen chair. She'd grown up with that same type of old 50s style kitchen chair and its old familiarity comforted her.

Her strength evaporated then, and just like a rag doll, she leaned forward laying her forehead on her legs. She wept with relief, not from fear. "Thank you God. Thank you so much!"

As she sat there doubled over, warmth filled her and she felt familiar arms wrap themselves around her. Without even looking to see who it was, she leaned into them and sobbed.

CHAPTER 13 | 233

Sharp pains ripped through Randy as he sat holding the love of his life. He was trying not to sob himself. The thickness in his throat prevented him from speaking, but words were not enough for this moment, anyway.

A female OSBI agent had tended to Lisa and stood by her now as emergency personnel tended to her wounds and checked her vital signs. Heartsickness and despair threatened to take her under as she stood by and watched Randy and Sandy.

Lisa wondered if it would even matter if she left this way of life, the way Safe At Last was working hard to do. *Would anyone ever want her the way Randy wanted Sandy? No*, she thought, *not after the things she had done. The filth she had laid in and with while allowing herself to be defiled for a little bit of money.*

Suddenly she lurched forward and was sick on the floor of the kitchen. The stench of vomit caused both Randy and Sandy to sit up alert.

Sandy jumped up and ran to Lisa. She brushed her hair back from her face. "Oh sweetie, are you okay?"

The medics quickly provided clean cloths to wipe her face and bottled water to rinse. Sandy pulled Lisa to her breast and held her as she had often held her own children. As she patted Lisa's hair and rubbed her hand along the windblown locks, she cooed, "It's going to be okay. I promise, it's going to be okay."

Randy watched as Sandy exited her own trauma in order to comfort this girl. The pain that had consumed him since Sandy's abduction, the pain that had driven him to rage was now melting like snow on a warm day.

Watching Sandy, and her ability to move beyond herself, made Randy stop and think he too needed to correct himself and forge past his anger and fear, but was it possible?

Randy stood and left to go find Bracket. What he found was Gus laying sprawled in a pool of blood on the old carpet. Vince was draped backwards over a stuffed chair.

Randy was standing silent and numb as Bracket walked up beside him. "Does this solve the drowning cases?" Randy asked.

"I don't know, but I doubt it. Are we certain that Gus was the perpetrator on those since his DNA didn't match?" Bracket asked.

Randy shrugged with both hands still in his pockets. "Both girls were Gus'. We haven't had a new murder in a couple of days. I'm fairly certain he was our guy, but not one-hundred percent."

"We need more proof. We'll have the tech crew go over both properties with a fine-tooth comb. Maybe there will be something there that will lead to the drownings. I'll send two of our guys over to his primary residence and have a couple stay here with the tech. You go home and be with Sandy."

Randy just nodded. Words still seemed elusive to him. He had been fueled by high octane adrenaline for several hours now and fatigue threatened to bring him down rapidly.

He walked back into the kitchen to find Sandy. The paramedics had finished with both ladies, but strongly suggested that they be checked out further by a doctor.

Sandy was standing holding Lisa and gently talking to her as she brushed her hand down the length of her hair. Walking up, he could hear her say, "Lisa you are loved and there are people who do care about you. Nothing you have done matters. Not to them. Not to me."

Her comforting words were cut short when Randy walked up. Sandy looked up at Randy and gave him a big smile. Then remembering where she was and why she was there, the smile faded. Suddenly conscientious about a possible onslaught of reprimands from Randy, she ducked her head and looked around the room suddenly unsure of what to say or do.

"Are you ready to go?" Randy asked Sandy.

Sandy walked up to Randy and ushered him into the next room. "What about Lisa?" Her eyes searched Randy's face. She didn't want to just leave Lisa.

"What about her?" Randy didn't have it in him to put forth care and concern for anyone other than his wife right then.

Sandy tilted her head in irritation. "Has anyone talked to Beth at Safe At Last? Can we take Lisa back there?"

Randy once again shrugged his shoulders. It was too much effort to think enough to derive a conversation.

"How should I know? I've had enough to think about

and to do to find both of you. Pardon me if I missed a detail."

"Can I have your phone?" Sandy asked as she reached her hand out.

As Randy laid his phone in her palm, the marks where the zip ties had been were vivid red and blue. It was a painful reminder he needed to muster up some patience.

Beth scrolled through Randy's previous calls to find the one she knew to have been Safe At Last's number. Finding the right one, she pressed the phone to dial.

As she heard Beth's voice on the other end of the line, Sandy drummed up all the courage she could and said, "Beth, it's Sandy."

"Are you all right? Thank God they found you! Is Lisa there with you?"

A sigh of relief escaped Sandy, and she answered affirmatively to all Beth's questions.

"Beth, Lisa has been through so much and is feeling so ashamed and afraid. Can she please come back to Safe At Last? Gus is dead, and he is no longer a threat to her. Please..." Sandy pleaded.

A moment of silent air filled the space between them. "Yes, she can come back, on a trial basis that is. Bring her here."

"Thank you so much Beth!"

As soon as Sandy ended the call with Beth, she handed the phone back to Randy and smiled before rushing back into the kitchen to tell Lisa the good news.

"Are you sure she wants me back?" asked Lisa.

"Yes, she does. She cares about you Lisa. We all do." Sandy pulled Lisa into a big bear hug.

"You are worth something Lisa. Never forget that. Promise me you will never forget that you are worth something."

Sandy could feel Lisa's head nod and she smiled.

CHAPTER 14

Sunday had been a quiet day. After the chaos of the previous two days, everyone was ready for some peace and calm.

Randy had nothing but love in his heart for Sandy. The topic of Safe At Last had finally demanded attention, but was quickly resolved with a loving nod from Randy.

He got it. He understood. When he had seen Sandy, so fresh from the horrific ordeal that both women had gone through, reach out without a second thought to Lisa, he had understood.

Randy also understood why Sandy had called Carrie instead of him. A wound like a hot rock rested in his chest. He had wanted to be the husband Sandy would call, but he hadn't been, but that would change.

Sunday morning Sandy pleaded with Randy to go with her and the kids to church. Finally, he gave in. It wasn't the dusty old type of religious ceremony he had remembered from the few times he had been in his younger days. It was actually very pleasant.

Bracket had only gone into the office for a few hours on Sunday. It was quiet there, and he was able to get caught up on the enormous piles of paperwork an operation like the one the previous day generated.

He thought of Carrie and Randy and wondered how they would be able to work together after this. But he had seen them go through tough times before and they had come through it even stronger. He felt confident this time would be no different.

Beth spent extra time with Lisa at Safe At Last. She had spent time listening to the girl's reasoning behind why they felt compelled to run away. She knew it had made sense to them at the time. They were not used to trusting anyone and were convinced that they had to fend for themselves once again.

There had been other discussions throughout the house about the reason for the house security and affirmations about coming to Beth with any concern no matter how large or small.

Carrie had spent the day home alone in her sweatpants. She'd picked up her phone repeatedly to call Bracket or Randy to find out what was happening, but would always put it back down.

She was concerned for Sandy, Lisa, and Jenny and she wondered how she would repair things with Randy. She also wondered how Bracket would resolve her actions, with discipline or expulsion. She wondered if they had caught Gus and if he was the killer of the girls.

In all her wondering though, she had stayed sober. A remarkable feat in and of itself, but with the windfall of events over the last couple of days, she would have normally fled straight to a bottle of whiskey.

But she wanted to be completely clear-headed when she went to work on Monday morning.

AND SO SHE WAS. Carrie walked into the office slightly early Monday morning with her head held high. She navigated her way to Bracket's office where he sat behind his desk still doing paperwork.

At the tap on the door facing, he looked up and smiled. "Good morning Carrie. Sit." He stood and motioned for her to sit, then moved around the desk, shut the door, and pulled his blinds.

"I'm surprised that I haven't heard from you since you left," said Bracket.

Carrie looked at her lap where her legs were crossed. She plucked at the ripple her pants made and thought through her words carefully. "Well, you requested that I stay away and not come back or call."

She looked up then just in time to see Bracket bellow out a full throttle laugh. "That never stopped you before!"

Carrie grinned. "No, it hasn't, but I did a lot of thinking, not drinking, thinking. I took a long look at myself and how I do things. I have to do things differently and I have to change. There is no other option.

"I rationalized that I was helping Sandy and helping to keep the girls safe, but it quickly spiraled out of control before I could even reach out for help.

"I betrayed Randy, and that regret is as sour as vinegar. He has been my best friend for years and with me, no matter what. I don't even dare to hope that he could ever forgive me."

"But maybe he can." Randy's voice came from over her shoulder. He had slipped quietly in Bracket's door while she and Bracket had been talking and had heard Carrie's painful words.

Carrie jumped up and whirled around. Tears washed her eyes, and she fought to push them back from where they had come. "I'm so sorry, so very sorry." But she lost the battle, and the tears escaped their boundaries and washed down her cheeks.

"I can't say I understand. Saturday I hated you with a passion. But after seeing Sandy alive and then seeing her ability to move forward, love, and forgive, I felt challenged to do the same.

"Yesterday she and I talked a lot. She is incredibly grateful you came to her aid. You were her champion and I need to see that you were acting to, hopefully, resolve the issue quickly, and for no other reason." Randy looked down as if his words had suddenly escaped him and were dancing around on the floor somewhere.

"Let's sit down and talk," said Bracket, and they all sat back down.

"I have to admit that I don't even know what went down after I left Saturday. I disengaged on purpose to reset myself. Pride's death, Jenny's escape, and Sandy and Lisa's abduction hit me hard, very hard," said Carrie.

Bracket and Randy filled Carrie in on all the details of the case and how things had happened. Had Gus lived, he would have been charged with kidnapping Lisa and Sandy, and manslaughter for Pride. Even though she had died of a heart attack, it was Gus' actions that had brought it about.

"What about the drownings? Do we have any evidence that Gus was the murderer?" Carrie looked back and forth from Randy to Bracket.

Bracket shook his head and took a deep breath. "No. Agents and techs have been over both of his residences and we can't find anything. If they were spur-of-the-moment killings, then there would have been nothing premeditated at home to link him to them."

"We have to get back into the war room to see what we have and what we no longer have," said Randy.

Carrie looked over at Randy and studied his face. "Are we still partners? Can you… will you forgive me?" Carrie asked.

Randy's jaw clenched and released a few times as he stared straight ahead. "I want to forgive you. Is that good enough for now?"

Carrie nodded her head. "That's more than I could have hoped for."

∼

BACK IN THE WAR ROOM, Randy and Carrie stood before two large whiteboards. They had filled one before the weekend's events. Today they had pulled another one in and were moving things around.

Gus was dead and neither one thought he was the killer. They moved his photo to the new whiteboard and wrote deceased over the top.

They moved Pride's photo over with Gus'. She was never a suspect, but the fact that Cami had lived with her gave her a strong link to the case.

Remaining on the whiteboard were Cami's photo and Mandy's photo. They had a photo of Sam with a question mark near the bottom of the board. They weren't sure where she played in to all of this if she did at all.

"What about Sam? In my gut it somehow connects her, but I can't imagine how or where. We need to see if we can find someone who saw or knows that man and get a photo or a sketch," said Carrie.

They stood quietly for a moment and looked at the pitiful amount of remaining pieces of evidence. Forensics had found no leads in the debris around the sites. The few footprints found were not distinct enough to get a print from. Most of the area surrounding the crime scenes had grass of some sort, mostly tall and unmowed.

Both girls were prostitutes, girls of Gus'. Previously they had thought that link meant something.

"I don't believe that Gus was the killer, but these were both Gus' girls. What if that fact is a trigger to the murder? What if a competitor wanted to remove Gus' girls for some type of revenge?" Carrie looked at Randy to see how he would respond.

Randy stood staring at the board. His hands were shoved deep in his pants and wrinkles of indecision creased his face. Finally, he turned to Carrie.

"That could be a link. Do we have a list of Gus' competitors?" asked Randy.

Carrie shuffled through some files and found one name, "Rudy Vargus," Carrie looked up from the file to Randy. "He can't be the only one though."

"Get on the computer and check out known associates. I'll get in touch with OKCPD Vice and see what they have." Carrie was already plunking the keyboard before Randy finished his sentence.

Carrie was still digging and searching a few minutes later when Randy came back into the war room.

"Vice gave me info on three different men. One we have a name on - Rudy Vargas. The other two are Gene, a.k.a. Tiny Simmons, and Herman Merrell.

"According to Vice these are the main players in this area. However, they have heard no talk on the street that there was contention between them. Yes, they were competitors and therefore enemies, but they each had their own territory so to speak and kept to that.

"Also, they are *all* under Alexander Volkov and knew better than to raise a stink with each other for fear of death." Randy finally stopped and looked up at Carrie.

"Did you find anything besides what I found?" asked Randy.

Carrie breathed out a heavy sharp sigh, "No."

She stood next to Randy as he put photos of the three new suspects on the board and wrote in pertinent notes.

The board still looked sparse when Randy finished and stepped back.

"It doesn't feel right to me. Does it to you?" Carrie asked Randy.

Randy shook his head, "No, it doesn't. But at the very least, we should talk to them and see if they know anything. We got so entangled with Gus that we dropped our focus on gathering info from other sources."

"Maybe Mike and Rick can help us. Have you checked in with the Human Trafficking Task Force lately to see if there is anything they could add?" asked Carrie.

"No. I'll go do that now. Why don't you call Mike and Rick to see if they can come over and go over some things with us? Then we can divvy up some of these interviews."

"On it," said Carrie.

She pulled out her phone and clicked Rick's name.

"Yep. How's it going?" Rick had seen Carrie's name pop up and got right to the point.

"Not so good. Randy and I were wondering if you and Mike could come over and go over some of this with us and then help us with some new interviews we want to do."

Carrie heard muffled voices as she waited for Rick to consult with Mike. "When?"

"You let us know. We are here at the office now, but not sure what your schedule is."

More muffled voices. "How about in an hour or an hour and a half?"

"Yeah, that'll work. We'll be here," said Carrie.

She hung up the phone, sent Randy a text, and then combed through each line of each file word by word. She felt there had to be something they had missed.

What if the killer was focusing on the human trafficking angle or on someone connected to prostitution? What if it was just someone else and completely unrelated?

Carrie searched the files for someone independent of the prostitution ring. No one. Not one witness statement mentioned anyone, except the man the girls went with.

Was there overlap there, she wondered. Had the girls all gone with the same man? Could this be the link, and how would they find out? The girls were dead, and they couldn't tell us who they had gone with.

Then Carrie remembered Jenny talking about the man at the Cox Center underground garage. They knew him and would spend time talking to him while waiting for events to let out. She needed to talk to him.

Frantically thumbing through her files, she finally

found a note Randy had written right after their first interview with Jenny. The man's name was Gary Bright.

She jotted details down to take with her and suddenly realized that Randy had been gone for almost an hour.

Frowning, she stood up and pushed her chair back. It screeched across the floor reflective of her own nerves. She was insecure from recent events, and she had a knot in her stomach as she walked to the door of the war room.

Once in the main area, she searched for any sign of Randy, but there was none. Continuing to walk to their desks she looked about. Then just as she reached her desk she saw that Randy was back in Bracket's office.

Her hand shook as she reached for the back of her desk chair. They were lying to her, keeping something from her still. Even if he had only been in there part of the time, it would still have been a long time.

She tried to focus on her computer monitor as she searched the database for Gary Bright. He was not in the system so she searched the internet.

A Facebook page popped up, and it wasn't private. Carrie almost forgot about Randy and Bracket as she scrolled through Gary's page. You could almost find more out about a person here than on any government database.

Gary was twenty-nine, had dark hair, and was reasonably fit. He was attractive, Carrie thought. His status said he was single, but several of the pictures showed him with his arms around a girl. Maybe he wasn't one of those who changed his relationship status every time he dated someone new.

He worked two jobs. She saw he had a part-time day job at one bank in the area. The name of the bank was there. It was right downtown.

What if he was the one, the killer? She scrolled through his Facebook page again eyeing him as if he were. *Did he fit the profile,* Carrie wondered.

He seemed happy and well adjusted, but then no one hardly ever put anything on Facebook but their very best. He could secretly be lonely and depressed off camera. She jotted down notes on the paper she'd started with Gary's details. Only meeting him and talking to him face to face would determine the truth.

"Sorry I took so long to get back to you. Bracket needed my help on something in his office." Randy said. He was chipper and happy, very uncharacteristic for him.

Carrie sat in her chair and just barely looked up at him from her monitor. She didn't smile. Her face was quizzical as she watched him.

"What did he need you for?" She asked.

"Oh, just some paperwork stuff." Randy glazed over the answer with a brush of his hand as he searched his desk for something.

The knot in Carrie's stomach grew. They were hiding something from her. If she broached the subject, she would sound paranoid. She swallowed it all and stood up.

"Do you remember that guy that Jenny mentioned in

her first interview? The one she said her and Cami would often chat with at the garage waiting for events to let out?" Carrie waited for Randy to remember.

"Yeah, I do." Remembrance lit Randy's face.

"I thought we should take another tack at this. I looked him up and I have two places of work. One is the garage, but another is a downtown bank. He works both jobs part-time."

Randy nodded. He knew Carrie so well he knew where she was going with this. She was right; they needed to find him and interview him.

"Great thinking, but Mike and Randy should be here any minute. As soon as they leave, we will head down there."

Carrie nodded and as she turned she saw Bracket in his office standing and looking around at it as if he was just seeing it for the first time. How odd, she thought.

Apologies for being late, led the way, as Mike and Rick entered the room.

"Sorry, we got tied up, but we're ready to get going now," said Rick.

Mike grinned at Carrie, but he knew that their time together had passed. She didn't even engage in mindless flirtation any more. She was changing. He wasn't sure how or why, but he could tell that she was. She seemed more settled, more focused, and mature.

Randy led the group as he went through their thoughts on the three competitors of Gus. He ticked off reasons both why they might be and why they might not be the killer.

Carrie then followed up with her thoughts on the garage attendant. She really wanted to do his interview and hoped that Mike and Rick would do the others. Soon they agreed.

The next item to discuss was Sam.

"I just feel in my gut that she's connected to this somehow. She could be dead, drowned and we just haven't found her body yet. The guy who took her, or rather who she willingly went with, could be the killer," said Carrie.

"Or, it might not be related at all," Randy concluded.

"True, but doesn't it seem strange to you guys that a young girl would go with this man that her parents don't seem to know, willingly? Cami didn't even think it was strange," said Carrie.

"We've been hard on that thread. We did get a maybe and had a sketch artist do a rendering." Mike pulled out his phone and sent it to both Randy and Carrie.

"The problem is," Mike continued, "is, that the sketch is iffy. We went back to the guy at the store and he said it could be him, but the sketch didn't help him connect it to anyone he knew."

"Did any of the neighbors or girls' friends act as though they knew who he was or why the girls were going with him?" Carrie asked.

"One girl said she thought, and I emphasize thought,

that he was the caretaker of the old amusement park," Rick said.

"Really?" Carrie was growing excited. After days of feeling lost on this case she suddenly felt hope rising from various sources.

"We can't find him though. The park was cleaned up and sold, then in less than a year the owner died," said Mike.

Just when she thought they were about to catch a break, it vanished. But they still had good leads. They would find out who did this.

"What about the two remaining sisters? The mom didn't know where they were when we were there. Have you talked to them since?" Carrie asked Rick.

"Yeah, we found them. The thing is, the two older girls, Cami and Sam hung to themselves. The two younger girls did the same. They had no idea what Cami and Sam were up to. I tend to believe them," said Rick.

"What about the picture of them all at the old amusement park? There were all there then. What did they say about that?" Randy asked.

"They remembered that day, but it was not normal for them to all be together. That is one reason they took the photo. Adelaide or Addy as they call her had a picture of all four of them at the park." Rick stopped for impact and raised his eyebrows. *Carrie was sharp. How long would it take her to get it?*

"All four? Who took the picture?" Carrie asked almost immediately.

"You don't miss a beat, do you?" Rick laughed. "Yep, all four of them. Addy couldn't remember. Maybe a guy who worked there." Rick was smiling big.

Carrie paced the room. She was deep in thought and trying to form random threads into a revealing tapestry.

"What if that guy in the car was the caretaker, and they tasked him with cleaning up the old park and getting it ready for sale? The girls knew him from the park, from going there, so he didn't really seem like a stranger to them."

Carrie looked up at the three guys. "Then what if on the day Sam went with the man, he said he needed more help so she went with him to help him?" Carrie paused looking for comment.

Their faces were all deep in thought. They were weaving their own tapestries in their minds.

"What about Cami not going with them? If he needed help, then wouldn't they have both gone?" asked Mike.

"Maybe, unless he said he only needed one of them that day. Or, if Cami had something else she had to do later, and couldn't go."

They had ideas that made sense, but they were only theories. What they needed was some kind of proof. But they were getting closer, Carrie thought.

The meeting had been fruitful, and Mike and Rick left with additional assignments.

Carrie was avoiding looking at Randy and busied herself straightening files and organizing them back into their boxes.

Randy stood watching her. Something was wrong, and he didn't know what. She'd been fine when he left her earlier, but when he had met up with her after being in Bracket's office she seemed nervous.

"Carrie what's wrong?" Randy asked.

She only missed a beat in her organizing when hearing Randy's question. "Nothing, why do you ask?" She was suddenly putting her full effort into acting as though there was nothing at all wrong.

"You've been weird towards me ever since I left you in here and came back from Bracket's office."

Carrie shrugged, still straightening. A hand on her shoulder stopped her nervous busyness. She still hadn't looked at him.

"Do you think we were in there talking about you or something pertaining to you?" Randy asked.

Carrie turned towards Randy but didn't raise her head to look him in the eye. Instead, she looked to the side past him.

"Were you?" Carrie asked.

Randy snorted a laugh and dropped his hand from her shoulder. "No. Look at me Carrie." Randy waited until Carrie held his gaze.

"We have not been talking about you." His words were slow and deliberate.

"So what were you talking about?"

"I can't tell you."

Anger gripped Carrie, and she pressed her mouth in a firm line. "Fine." She turned and walked out of the room.

CHAPTER 15

Traffic downtown was as relentless as ever with all the continued construction. Making their way to the bank was a challenge.

As Randy drove, Carrie was lost in the thought of her dangerous pursuit through downtown. Barricades flying, near collisions with a car, and the train. The thought of the train still made Carrie sick to her stomach.

She had told no one how close she had come, only that the SUV had gotten across the tracks before her, and that she had had to stop because of the train.

No one knew how close to death she had come. She wouldn't tell them either. They would bench her for sure. The antics they knew had put her on an unspoken watch. She would not tell the agency psychotherapist either when she met with her later in the day. She had to hold that secret close to her chest.

They parked in the Kerr Parking Garage just across from the bank and catty-corner from Kerr Park. Carrie had always loved that little park tucked into the hustle and bustle of downtown.

Once inside the bank, they showed their credentials and were escorted to Gary Bright's supervisor's office on the second floor.

"Gary has left for the day. He works mornings here and then I believe he checks in at the Cox garage to work the evening shift at around three. I'm sorry. You just missed him."

Carrie looked at Randy and neither said anything for a moment. Then the supervisor said, "Would you like me to call him?"

"No, we would like to just meet with him face to face without him expecting us. But we would like his phone number," said Randy.

"Well… I'm not sure if I should give that out. You don't have a warrant do you?" The supervisor was standing now and clasping her hands together in front of her as if she wasn't sure what to do with them.

"True, we don't have a warrant but all we are asking for is his phone number. You yourself offered to call him for us. We can jump through hoops to get a warrant, but then we would probably make its scope very broad so it wouldn't be wasted. You know… where we would search any and everything here in the bank that Gary ever came in contact with…" Carrie was so calm, but her stare was quite pointed.

"Okay, okay. I know what you are trying to do. You want to intimidate me into doing something I shouldn't." She was visibly disturbed.

"No worries. We'll get it on our own. But we will remember your lack of cooperation," said Randy as they both turned to go.

"Is he in serious trouble?" The supervisor called after them. She bore a deeply concerned look on her face and her posture was tense.

"Not right now. We only want to talk with him," said Randy.

The supervisor nodded. Her head bobbed up and down in a broken, jerky movement. "Okay, here it is," she said as she bent down to scribble out Gary's number.

Carrie smiled a crooked smile and nodded her head. "Thank you."

Once out the door Randy said, "Well, we have three whole hours before Gary is at the garage. I'm hungry. Let's get lunch."

"Sure, sounds good. I would like to spend a little time down here, anyway. After we eat, let's sit over in Kerr Park and watch. This is the killers world. Everything draws us back to downtown. The drowning sites, the girls, Pride's, the Safe At Last house, Gary, it all points back here."

Randy nodded. "What do you want? We've got Park Avenue Grill at the Skirvin, Coolgreens just past Kerr Park, and Kitchen 324 close by."

"I would love to go to the Skirvin and eat at the Park

Avenue Grill," said Carrie. "I'm in the mood for someplace nice, but they don't open until five."

They finally decided on Kitchen 324, and both ordered the Fried Chicken Pot Pie. While waiting, Randy brought up the change in Carrie's mood again.

"I don't know what happened this morning, but I would like to discuss it," said Randy.

Looking straight at Randy, Carrie said, "I think you and Bracket are hiding something from me. I've seen both of you in Bracket's office together several times pow-wowing. When I walk into the room, you both hush and wait until I leave to finish your conversation."

Randy let out a deep sigh and sat back in his chair. He wasn't supposed to tell her, not yet anyway. "I can't discuss it. I know you are my partner, but I promised that I wouldn't. I can assure you that it has absolutely nothing to do with you. You have nothing to be worried about."

"Why can't you tell me then what it is about? You do understand after all that has gone on with me why it concerns me, right?" Carrie was leaning into the table towards Randy. She was speaking adamantly, but quietly so those at the other tables couldn't hear.

Randy smiled at his partner. "You are the best partner I've ever had. You're my friend too. I get so angry at you sometimes…," Randy shook his head and continued, "but I can't stay mad at you. We've been through too much together. Carrie you are an amazing agent and an amazing person, even if you have trouble believing that."

Carrie sat looking skeptically at Randy. Was he merely flattering her to appease her, she wondered.

"You have one of the sharpest minds I know. You don't miss a beat. You can come up with theories out of nowhere that are often right on target. It's been an honor being your partner." *Oops,* thought Randy.

Carrie frowned and studied his face. She wasn't sure she bought all that sharp mind stuff, but she was sure of one thing, she was sharp enough to catch that last slip up.

"Has been?" Carrie asked. "It *has been* an honor being my partner?"

Randy just waved his hand as if it was just a silly slip of the tongue and nothing more, but he had succeeded in turning his stomach into waves of nausea.

"It *is* an honor being your partner. Don't go reading anything into it."

Just then their food was ready. The fried chicken pot pie was wonderful as always. The lunch crowd was at its peak, and the room was noisy, so Randy and Carrie ate quietly enjoying each bite.

When neither one had a morsel of food left on the plate, they sat back in their chairs and just stared at each other. Carrie suddenly burst out laughing.

"Good grief, it's awful that after all these years we can just look at each other and know what the other one is thinking," said Carrie.

Randy grinned and nodded his head. "Well, let's get out of here." Randy threw a generous tip on the table and they headed out the door.

The August sun bore straight down on them. Carrie straightened her cap and sat her sunglasses on her nose. "It was my idea to sit out in Kerr Park and watch, but I don't know how long I can stand the heat," said Carrie.

"There's a bench over there in the shade. Let's give it some time and see," replied Randy.

They sat down on a vacant bench underneath a tree and watched. There were people walking across the park from building to building going about their daily business. Most were dressed in business clothes.

Carrie sat back on the bench with her legs crossed and one arm slung across the back of the bench. A couple on a bench diagonally to her right caught her attention.

They weren't together, she could tell, but they were having a casual conversation. She wasn't sure what it was about them that had caught her eye, so she continued to watch.

"Randy, do you see those two on the bench to my right?" Carrie asked.

Randy barely swiveled his head to look without making it apparent. "Yep."

"Does that man look familiar to you?"

Randy repositioned himself and turned to look directly at Carrie. This would give him another nonobvious viewpoint. "Yeah. Wasn't he the man from the diner we thought Jenny had referred to the other day?"

Recognition flooded Carrie. That was it. He was the man in the diner. "How odd," Carrie said.

"Yeah, but he isn't the one that Jenny was referring to

when she was talking about being uncomfortable. It was that man in the suit."

They both sat for several more minutes watching the man and woman on the bench. Partially from lack of anyone else to watch, and partly from the couple's odd interaction.

"She's really young," commented Carrie.

"I wonder what he's saying to her," said Randy. "She has a strange look on her face. I can't tell if she is bothered by him or if it's something else."

"He's strangely odd. First, he looks like he fell out of the 1950s, but of course we talked about that last time. His behaviour is also odd too. Did you see him squish his sandwich?" Carrie looked over at Randy to see his reaction.

Randy was no longer trying to hide that he was watching them. In fact, he was looking at them openly with his mouth hanging open.

He looked over at Carrie and then back at the couple. Then after a few more minutes of interaction, the girl got up and walked away. The man sat watching her leave.

WORK WAS FRUSTRATING to Anthony Simmons. He had long prided himself on his perfection. His work was always correct. Lately though, with younger and younger supervisors being hired and lording it over him, he had found less satisfaction, and less praise from those who didn't appreciate him.

"Tony where is your report?" asked Brett, Anthony's immediate supervisor.

Anthony sat up to his full sitting height and wobbled his head ever so slightly. Through tight lips he replied, "You know my work is excellent, and it is excellent because I take the time to make sure it is. I will have it to you within the hour. And please don't call me Tony. My name is Anthony as I've mentioned many times."

Brett looked down at Anthony, disgusted. What was it about him that was so off-putting? "You better," Brett said as he walked away.

Anthony was getting older, and he didn't fit in any longer. There once was a time when the way he looked and talked was not so far off from his other coworkers, but that was a good twenty years ago, or more.

Since Mother's death he had struggled to find purpose. Memories of her life pounded him each night in his dreams and shamed him in his days. Sometimes the torment was more than he could stand. His head would pound and he would shake.

In those times, when he could no longer control the emotions, he felt compelled to do something, to help someone, someone like his mother. He was beginning to see his real purpose in life, and his desire to be at this lifeless human-grind of a job, dwindled each day.

He had always looked forward to his lunch break. Getting out of that stifling place refreshed him. He didn't understand the ways of the younger people, the millennials he had heard them called. They weren't rigid and structured the way he was, the way he felt the need to be.

It was another hot August day, but he found a bench in downtown Kerr Park where there was shade. He always stayed away from the Air Force Monument Statue. Its nudity troubled Anthony greatly, and he felt it vulgar. Yes, the man was draped with a small cloth over his lower abdomen, but that was just not enough.

The zipper baggie tore at the top as Anthony tried to open it to retrieve his sandwich. Frustrated, he vowed to buy the more expensive brand, but who was he kidding, he had to pinch every penny he had.

There would be no more promotions for Anthony, not since he had become an antiquated fixture at work. They couldn't fire him, he had been there for twenty-five years and his work was exemplary. But, they had passed him over many times for promotions; he knew now it would never happen.

The ham and cheese sandwich with exact equal amounts of mayonnaise and mustard tasted good. Eating the same thing everyday felt good. It was constant, and the sameness comforted Anthony.

Just as he was about to feel soothed and normal again, a young girl walked by and caught his attention. He tried to not look at her. He turned his head and yet still felt a stirring in his loins.

Determined to not give up his spot on the bench in the shade, he sat, forcing himself to enjoy his lunch. But his head throbbed and his ears rang. He struggled not to give in to the dizziness that threatened him.

As he was struggling to maintain control, forcing himself to keep his eyes off of the girl, suddenly she plopped right down beside him on the bench.

His heart gripped, and he thought he might have a heart attack. He sat rigid, staring straight ahead.

"Are you okay?" the young girl asked.

Anthony tried to push her voice out of his mind, but she had asked him a direct question. It would be rude not to respond. "Yes, I'm fine. Why do you ask?"

"Because you have squished your sandwich in your hand. I thought you might be having a spasm or something. Do I need to call someone for help?"

Anthony looked down at his lap where he had balled his hands into fists, the remains of the sandwich became mangled in the process. His beloved sandwich, a symbol of continuity was unedible now. It was her fault.

The girl was young and sweet and beautiful, and she was confused at Anthony's behaviour. *Should I help him? Should I call someone? He could be having a stroke and here I sit,* she thought.

Anthony recovered, somewhat, and pulled the squished remains from his palm. His lips were pursed together in disdain. That girl didn't belong here. How dare she talk to him?

He could tell she was a whore who seduced men in the night, just as his mother had done. *Why was she here in the daytime*, he wondered?

He cleaned his hand with a paper towel he'd carried with his lunch. He refused to give up his bench to this trollop. He would defend his right to sit there on his lunch break just as he did every day.

He sat up taller, smoothed down his short-sleeved white dress shirt and straightened his pocket protector. Three pens, red, blue, and black, and a mechanical pencil. All were fine.

The girl sat casually on the bench seeing that the man appeared to be fine. She had a wispy short skirt on, and the gentle breeze brushed it along the outside of her thigh. She had crossed her legs causing the skirt to hike up higher.

Anthony gulped. Did this whore know she was showing off most of her leg, almost up to her panties? Yet in his indignation, the stirring in his loins continued to grow. He would have to relinquish the bench after all.

But he couldn't stand up. She would know. Her power over him would be complete. He would have to get himself under control and then leave.

"Do you work around here?" she asked.

Anthony's eyes darted around. "Yes, I work in that bank over there. I work in the accounting department."

"I work at the gift shop in the Skirvin Plaza."

It confused Anthony. She had a real job? His mind tried to fight its way through the confusion. If she had a real job, she must work both at night and during the day. He was certain.

"How do you work all night and all day too?" Anthony wanted an answer.

"What do you mean? I only work at the gift shop." Her forehead was pinched in confusion and she was feeling concerned. "I have to get back now. Have a good day." The girl stood to leave, the gentle breeze still raising and lowering her short soft skirt around her firm thighs.

Anthony nodded and watched the girl walk away. She was a whore. He knew she was. Anger boiled inside of him. How dare she lie? She needed to be clean.

Suddenly he brightened. He could help her with that, he could help her become clean.

"It's too hot to keep sitting here," said Carrie.

The interaction between the man and woman had ended when the girl had walked away. The man remained for a few minutes then got up and walked away also, both going in opposite directions.

"So, we still have an hour and a half before Gary Bright is due at the garage. Got any ideas or should we fight traffic back to the office only to drive right back?" Randy asked.

Carrie looked at Randy. She knew he was hiding something from her, but she couldn't be mad at him. He had made a promise to someone to keep quiet about what he and Bracket were discussing and she had to honor that.

"Let's walk," said Carrie. She got up and walked towards The Skirvin.

"Okay, where're we going?" asked Randy.

"I want to talk to the girl who was on the bench if we can find her."

Randy snorted and gave Carrie a sideways glance. "If she is staying at the Skirvin, we'll likely never find her."

"We're not far behind her. Maybe she's still in the lobby or something."

The rush of cool refrigerated air welcomed Randy and Carrie to the luxury of the Skirvin Hotel. It had been the height of luxury in its early days, then through the years found decay and neglect it's only friend. But not any longer. It had been faithfully restored and stood grand and elegant once again. The soaring high ceilings and the rich dark wood caused one to feel like they were stepping back in time.

Carrie stood, as she always did once she entered, and took it all in. "I never tire of this place and its beauty."

Randy was looking up and down the hallways and around the spacious lobby area. There were so many places where the woman could be. She could even be in the same room as them, tucked casually into a deep tufted tall backed sofa, and they would never see her.

"Where do you suggest we start?" asked Randy.

"Let's walk." Carrie turned and walked through the lobby and towards the back wall of windows. Once there, she casually turned to view the room from that angle.

Randy just followed her lead as they roamed through

the halls. They passed doors to luxury conference centers, the business center, the lounge, the fitness center, and much more.

After about thirty minutes of walking, Carrie halted. "Look," she said and nodded her head in the direction she wished Randy to look.

There behind the counter of the gift shop stood the woman from the bench. Carrie turned to Randy and grinned. "Looks like we found our needle in a haystack."

They casually walked into the gift shop and walked up to the counter. The shop was empty except for the three.

Carrie flipped out her credentials as did Randy. "I'm Carrie Border with the OSBI and this is Randy Jeffries." The woman's eyes grew round. "We just have a question or two to ask. You aren't in any trouble."

The woman's eyes went from round to slightly suspicious. "What could you possibly want to ask me?"

"What's your name?" asked Carrie.

"Carissa. Carissa Stephens."

"Carissa we happened to be out in Kerr Park awhile ago and saw you sitting on a bench with a man. Do you know him?" asked Randy.

The woman rolled her eyes. "No, thank goodness! He was eight shades of weird."

"We saw you talking with him. Would you mind telling us how your conversation went?" asked Carrie.

"Not much of a conversation. I sat down because it was in the shade. I like to try to walk outside on my break even though it's horribly hot. That was the only bench in the shade with an open spot to sit.

"I sat down and was just casual, said hi or something. He got all rigid and acted like I had just sat on his very own private bench without asking. He got so rigid that his fists balled up and he squished his sandwich. I thought he had had a stroke or something.

"I asked him what was wrong. It concerned me, but he didn't even seem to realize what he had done. He kind of came out of his fit, or whatever it was, and said he was fine.

"Then he asked me about my job and how could I work both nights and days. That gave me the creeps! I don't work anywhere but here, but it was as if he was certain I worked nights. I got up and left after that."

Carissa's brows were furrowed and her pleasant smile was gone. "Should I be afraid of him?" Carissa asked.

"Have you seen him around here before?" asked Randy.

Carissa gave a tight shake of her head still frowning.

"We know nothing about him, but we were watching your interaction with him and thought it was odd. We wanted to make sure you were okay since you left so abruptly," Carrie smiled at the young woman. She wanted to put her at ease.

"I'm fine. But he's weird. Kind of makes me afraid to go back out in the park or on the street."

"Please don't feel like that. We have no reason to believe you are in danger. But as you know, a young woman like you should always be cautious when out walking alone. Just be aware of your surroundings," said Randy.

"Here's my card. If you feel threatened by him again, or if you think of anything else to add that you didn't think of, please call me," Carrie said as Carissa took the card from her outstretched hand.

Carissa read the card and pulled out a small blue purse from under the counter and tucked the card safely inside. "I will."

Both Carrie and Randy gave Carissa reassuring smiles and walked out of the gift shop. They walked back to the lobby and Carrie found a plush chair and sat down. Randy sat in the matching chair beside her.

"What are you thinking?" asked Randy. He could tell she was thinking and thinking hard.

"I can't pull it together. I can feel something, sense something, but can't seem to pull it into focus."

"The man is creepy. That's certain, but Carissa is not a prostitute and we have no reason to think that man has anything to do with our case," said Randy.

Carrie looked Randy's face over while she was thinking. His eyes were listening to her, not just his ears. His unruly dark hair was falling on his forehead and his laugh lines were relaxed and barely noticeable. *He said I was his favorite partner.*

"Carrie?" asked Randy. "What are you thinking?"

Carrie shook her head to refocus on Randy's question. "Remember the part where Carissa said the man was certain she worked nights? What if he thinks she works night as a prostitute? What if he has just put a target on Carissa's back as his next victim?"

Randy sat thinking. That was odd. Had they missed part of the conversation between the man and Carissa? Had she left something out? "Why do you think he assumed she worked nights?"

Carrie had turned and was tracing the pattern of the area rug in her mind as she thought. She was picturing the young woman. "She is young and beautiful. Did you notice what she was wearing?" Carrie turned towards Randy.

"Just some kind of sundress. Normal for this heat."

"It was, and she looked very enticing in it. It was very short and was made from a wispy fabric that fluttered around her legs in the breeze. The top only had tiny spaghetti straps. I would think it would be quite enticing to a man." Carrie left her meaning hanging in the air to see if Randy would take it and run with it.

"You think the man thought Carrissa was a prostitute because she was wearing that skimpy little dress?"

Carrie's eyebrow cocked upwards as did one side of her mouth. She waited for Randy to chew on it awhile longer. It was certainly a stretch, and the odds were long they had just stumbled onto this man, a person of interest, by accident.

Randy was shaking his head. "I can't stretch that far. I think we are so desperate to get this guy we are trying to shove square pegs into round holes."

CHAPTER 15

Carrie breathed deep and nodded. Randy was right. At the first sign of something weird she had tried to force it into a lead. "You're right. We can't waste time on a long shot like this. What time is it?"

Randy looked at his watch. "By the time we go get the car and drive back to the garage it will be close to time. We can park in the garage, and it will at least be cooler in there than waiting for him outside.

In just fifteen minutes Randy was pulling their SUV into the Cox Center underground parking. The window to their side of the booth was closed, but Randy stopped and held up his credentials.

The lady in the booth opened the window. "Yes?" she asked.

"I'm Randy Jeffries with the OSBI. We want to speak with Gary Bright. He comes on shift at three, correct?"

"Yes, he does."

"We want to drive in and wait," said Randy.

The lady nodded and indicated they would have to take a ticket from the machine.

Since they had a few minutes, they drove the vast underground parking garage and discussed conversations they had had with Jenny about the times she and Cami had met men there after events.

At five minutes until three they drove back to the east entrance and parked as close as possible. They watched as the shift changed in the booth.

Gary was about five feet ten inches tall, relatively fit, and average looking. "He looks like a nerd," said Carrie.

Randy chuckled. "You would know." And then ducked as Carrie's hand shot out at him from across the front seat of the car.

They gave Gary a few minutes to settle in and let the previous person leave, then walked over to the booth.

Flashing his credentials and smiling, Randy gave his name and that he was from the OSBI. "We would like to talk to you about Cami Anderson." Randy showed Cami's picture to Gary.

Gary looked at the picture and a gentle smile crossed his face. He looked at Randy in the eye as he said, "I knew her. She and Jenny would come around here often. They were sweet girls. I know that girls like that have a reputation of being hard and crude, but they weren't. I felt sorry for them. Sorry they had to make their money that way."

The initial surprise response that Randy and Carrie had hoped to see was one of compassion. Gary wasn't their killer, but maybe he had seen who was.

"Gary, can you think of who might have done this? I know you probably watched over them here in the garage, so you would have noticed anyone that might have gotten rough with them or someone who might have seemed off to you," said Carrie.

Gary was nodding. "I've thought about it a lot, ever since it happened." His eyes drifted off somewhere then back. "But, there isn't anyone. I'm sorry."

Carrie reached out and handed Gary her card with the same directions as always to call her.

Once back in the car, they buckled their seat belts in an

air of silent discouragement. The drive back to the office was quiet, but most of Carrie's thoughts were not on Gary and the murders, but of her pending appointment with the agency shrink. She would rather be out sitting on that hot bench in Kerr park again rather than in the hot seat of Dr. Lee's office.

CHAPTER 16

"Carrie, it's Randy. Bracket's in the hospital." Randy's voice jolted Carrie out of her middle-of-the-night slumber. She tried to snap her mind to attention so she could dive into action.

"I'm up," she said as she scurried out of bed and into the clothes she had left lying on the floor from earlier in the night.

"What happened? What hospital?" Carrie asked as she continued dressing.

"They aren't exactly sure what happened, but they think it's a heart attack. I guess his wife woke up when he got up in the middle of the night not feeling well. She recognized what she thought were heart attack signs and rushed him to the hospital, against his will of course."

"I'm on my way," said Carrie as she rushed out her front door.

It was three in the morning and still over eighty degrees. She remembered the panic she had felt over eight years prior, when she had jumped into her car to rush to the hospital, when her parents had their car wreck. *There is no panic like this panic,* she thought.

She rushed into the emergency room and saw Randy sitting with Diane, Bracket's wife. She realized they were deep in conversation so approached quietly with no fanfare.

They both recognized her and stood to greet her. "Tell me everything and if there is any news." Carrie's heart was beating so hard that she was sure they could hear it above her words.

The three settled into the cold waiting room chairs and Diane told the story. He had gotten up in the middle of the night unable to sleep. When she noticed he had been up for a while, she got up to look for him. He was in the kitchen scrounging in the fridge for something to eat.

That is when Diane saw him massaging his left arm. Ignoring his protests, she forced him into the car and drove to the hospital. She only slid clothes on as quickly as she could.

"He's in surgery. They were going to only put stints in to correct the problem, but realized that the extent of the damage was so severe they felt surgery was the best option," Diane concluded.

Carrie reached out and patted Diane's hand. She would have liked to say it would be all right, but what if it wasn't? It didn't always turn out okay. It hadn't for Carrie and her parents.

"We're here for you," was all Carrie could say, but she knew it wouldn't be enough.

Their conversation had quickly receded to silence. No one knew what to say once the adrenaline of fight or flight had begun to wain. They sat for what seemed like an eternity, and finally their eyes greeted the sun as it came through the windows, illuminating the day.

Carrie was struggling with exhaustion. She had only crawled into bed two hours before receiving Randy's call. She'd once again been out at the bar. She was proud of herself though; she had only had three or four whiskey's before stopping at midnight so she could sober up to drive home. She was making progress, or so she thought.

It was six-thirty when Randy's phone buzzed. He looked at the screen and frowned. "Hello, Randy Jeffries."

Carrie watched his face as he talked. She knew the gist of what he heard through his phone and was ready to bolt as soon as he hung up.

He looked at her and said, "That was Mike. There's another body."

Bracket was not out of surgery yet and they hated to leave Diane, but they had to go. They issued hugs and words of assurance, requesting she call as soon as she knew anything, then left.

"Where are we headed?" Carrie asked as she climbed into Randy's SUV.

"The body was found, drowned at the southern point

of the Bricktown canal. It is almost under I-40 and only about a half mile west of the first drowning."

Carrie's mind was working hard. It had already pushed out the fog of fatigue and hangover and was now fully engaged in the case. She wondered, *what if it's Carissa? What if we could have done something to have saved her yesterday?*

"What if it is Carissa?" Carrie finally voiced out loud.

"Huh? Carissa?" asked Randy thoroughly distracted.

"From yesterday."

Randy remembered and glanced at Carrie. "No. It won't be her."

Carrie nodded and rode the rest of the way in silence.

The usual cars and personnel were at the scene. When Carrie walked up, Mike said, "Rough night?"

"Bracket is in the hospital. As soon as I heard, I grabbed what was on the floor and put it on. It will work until I can do better."

"I'm sorry. I didn't know," said Mike.

They exchanged conversation to update Mike and Rick on the situation with Bracket. He was a good supervisory agent and a good man. Often those were rarely found together.

They found the body of the recent victim as the others, lying face down with her head in the water. The cut and color of the hair was the same as Carissa's and Carrie prepared herself to see her face as well when they rolled her over.

But it wasn't. Carrie didn't recognize this face. "Did we find any id or a purse?" Carrie asked.

"Yes," said Rick. "There was no id, only five twenty-dollar bills, three condoms, and a lip gloss."

"We've submitted the fingerprints too, no hit," said Mike.

Futility overwhelmed Carrie. Maybe it was the fatigue of sitting up all night or seeing yet one more unknown girl laying before her dead.

Uncharacteristically, she began to silently cry. She couldn't stop the tears from escaping onto her cheeks. She turned abruptly and swiped harshly at the tears as if they were an enemy that had violated her. She walked back to the car with heavy footfalls on the soft green manicured grass of the Bricktown Landing Park.

The car was hot inside, but Carrie didn't care. It was all too much. This case was getting the best of her. Never had she not been able to keep her emotions in check when working a case until now.

She laid her head back against the SUV's headrest and closed her eyes. Visions of Pride, Jenny, Lisa, Cami, Mandy, and the lost Sam floated past. Even Carissa. Why Carissa? She wasn't a prostitute, but there was something…

Carrie had dozed off and was startled awake when Randy opened his car door. She jerked and tried to regain awareness of where she was and what she was doing. In only the few minutes spent in the hot car, her cheeks had burned hot and her hair was limp with sweat.

Once in the car Randy took time to study her. "You look like shit." But his words were soft and kind, not accusatory as they had often been in the past.

He started the car and cranked up the AC. Carrie laughed. Then Randy laughed. "You know that will only blow out hot air until the engine cools…" said Carrie.

"I know," said Randy. The old familiar dialog, only in reverse, brought them back to their own center, that place where they knew each other and were comfortable in their daily routines.

The AC finally cooled the car as they sat. Randy was in no hurry to go anywhere and he knew Carrie wasn't either. He could ask her what was wrong, but he knew. This case had been hard on both of them.

"I have something to tell you," said Randy.

Carrie shut her eyes again, her head still resting on the headrest. "I can't bear to hear it right now," said Carrie. She knew he was leaving. She'd put it all together. The secret visits with Bracket and keeping her in the dark until the *right* moment. And then there was his little slip of the tongue yesterday at lunch.

Randy said nothing for a few moments. He watched as more tears rolled from the corner of Carrie's closed eyes.

"I have to tell you now."

Carrie's head shook gently back and forth. "Don't tell me you're leaving. I can't deal with that right now." She sat forward and wiped her face.

"Leaving? I'm not leaving."

Carrie's head jerked around and stared at Randy. Her

mind raced to understand what she had just heard in context with what she had thought she had realized.

"Here's the thing, Bracket is retiring. Or anyway he was before the heart attack, which I assume will accelerate things considerably. That is why I need to tell you now."

"Go ahead," said Carrie.

"I'll be taking his position. I'm going to be the new SAC."

Readjusting her emotions, Carrie was both relieved and sad at the same time. Randy wouldn't be leaving, but he would no longer be her partner. She couldn't find the words to express her jumbled thoughts, so she said nothing.

As they sat, the only sound they heard was the AC fan cranked up to high.

RANDY HAD TAKEN Carrie back to the hospital to get her car. He requested she go home, take a shower, and get some rest. He would check in on Bracket and then go back to the office.

He would have preferred that the changing of the guard could have taken place amidst quieter circumstances. It would have been nice if they had this case solved and out of the way where Bracket could have handed over the reigns healthy, and with an active retirement to look forward to.

"How's Bracket?" Randy asked Diane when he saw her in the hallway.

Her face looked tired, but there was no concern there. "He came through great, the doctor said. He woke up briefly, and I spoke to him, then he went back to sleep. I'm trying to let him rest. I was just going to go get me a cup of coffee would you like some?"

Randy agreed and walked with Diane to the hospital cafeteria. "Have you eaten today, Diane?" asked Randy.

"No, but I'm not sure I can."

"Let me buy you breakfast." Randy smiled at Diane and ushered her over to the food line where they were serving breakfast. "I'll have breakfast with you. I'm hungry." He would eat whether or not he was just so Diane would feel more comfortable about eating.

"Well, okay."

Once they had their plates and trays, Randy found an out of the way booth close to a window with a view of an atrium. There was lush vegetation and a waterfall which issued a soothing flow of sound. The entire effect was as calming as it was meant to be.

"John has talked to me about you taking over for him when he retires," said Diane.

Randy nodded as he cut his sausage into bite-size pieces. "I assumed the two of you have been talking and planning long before I knew anything about it." He looked up at Diane and smiled.

"Yes, we have. We've looked forward to it. We made a lot of plans." Diane's voice trailed off.

"Hey, nothing has changed. They fix him up and will be as good as new. You will be able to keep those plans."

Diane tried to smile. She genuinely hoped Randy was right.

"His retirement date will occur when he is still at home recovering. I haven't spoken to him yet, but I assume that I will need to step in for him. I was planning on doing that temporarily anyway while he recovered, then it occurred to me that he won't be approved for duty by then."

"Yes, well, that is all department stuff. I'm sure the commission will notify you."

"I got a message from the commission chair this morning I was to move forward in a temporary capacity until it was official. I wanted you to know."

Diane nodded once again. She was picking at her small bowl of oatmeal with blueberries on top. "Randy you have been such a wonderful agent for the OSBI and I know that John is truly appreciative of all that you've done.

"I also know that he was so proud to have someone of your caliber to hand the reins too. It was making a hard thing just a little easier."

Randy reached out and patted Diane's hand. "Thank you. Now eat that oatmeal so you will have the strength to keep John in line."

Bracket was awake and grumpy when Randy and Diane returned from breakfast, but as soon as he saw Diane he softened. "Where were you?" he asked.

"Randy forced me to go get breakfast. I complied," said Diane.

"Good man. Thank you, Randy for watching out for her."

They talked for only a few minutes about urgent issues back at the office which Bracket was working on so that Randy could jump right in. Soon, though, Bracket's eyes were beginning to droop and Randy took that as his cue to leave.

The ride back to the office for Randy, was filled with anxious thoughts. He had thought he would have more time to prepare. He had thought he would have more time with Bracket to help him transition. He had thought he would have more time to get over his fear of taking over this new responsibility.

The moment he walked into the room, all the agents confronted him. They all loved Bracket and were eager to hear news of his surgery. For efficiency's sake, Randy gathered everyone to attention in the conference room and took the podium.

"First let me say I just came from the hospital and Bracket came through surgery very well. I spoke with him for a few moments and I have no reason to suspect that he won't make a full recovery.

"He will be off duty until he makes a full recovery. That brings us to another topic, his approaching retirement. He was set to retire in two weeks which will be well within his recovery time.

"I have been notified from the commission I am to assume his full duties in the meantime."

The room filled with one-on-one conversations between the agents and personnel.

"Jeffries, will you be taking Bracket's place permanently?"

"It has not been announced officially by the commission, but yes, I believe so. Bracket has been working with me for the last few weeks to keep me abreast of what our agency is working on and how his office runs. This unforeseen event just shortened our timeline. But keep in mind that the commission has not issued a formal status change for me yet. That's all for now."

The room buzzed with activity as they went back to their work. Several agents came to shake Randy's hand and congratulate him on the pending promotion. He had their full support.

When Randy walked into Bracket's office it felt hollow. Pictures of Diane and his family were still in their rightful places. Commendations and pictures shaking hands with dignitaries still lined the walls. It didn't feel right to Randy.

He had a job to do though, so he forced himself to be thankful that Bracket would recover. At least he was not walking into this office from what could have been the worst-case scenario. Bracket could have died last night, but he didn't. For that Randy was thankful. It would be tough to fill this man's shoes though.

He sat down in Bracket's chair. Even the chair felt too

large for Randy, but then Bracket was about four inches taller and about thirty pounds heavier than Randy was.

The files were neat and tidy which was unusual. Had Bracket known unconsciously that he wouldn't be coming back today?

Randy pulled out the checklist he and Bracket had been working on. Top on the list for today was hiring the new agent.

He could pair Carrie with a seasoned agent, and had she been younger, he would have. But she was an outstanding agent, despite her personal demons. She would make a great mentor to a new agent.

Bracket and Randy had gone over several files. There were dozens of submissions to the OSBI every month. They had narrowed it down to three.

Randy picked up the phone and called to set up final interviews for them. He wanted to meet them personally, on his own, to get his take.

He arranged to have them each come in later that afternoon. It was a difficult thing to ask as they would have to rearrange their day on short notice, but doing this would speak volumes about them.

There were two men and one woman. All had come through the police academy with honors. All had high commendations from their superior officers. None of the three had any warnings or reprimands in their files. It would come down to who Randy thought would be the best fit for their agency.

He pondered, who would be the best fit with Carrie.

His stomach turned into a knot as he thought about the current personal mess she was navigating through. If he paired her up with a male agent would that complicate things? Was he being gender biased if he didn't?

He and Carrie had worked well for over eight years together. The fact that he was male had never seemed to be a problem at all. In fact, he had not had a closer friend other than his wife during that time.

A sudden rush of shame hit Randy. He knew too much about Carrie and her personal life and was allowing it to cloud his judgement. He had to look at her as if he knew nothing at all about her personal life and decide accordingly.

If that were the case, he could pair her with any agent at any time and they would do well for it. Okay then, he would hire the best agent and that would be that.

It felt good to get home and get a shower. The teeth of the comb massaged Carrie's scalp as she pulled it through her hair, and she didn't rush it.

She should be out working the case, but in her current exhausted state, that was impossible. Her bed felt good as she laid herself down. Her body submitted to the smooth sheets and the soft mattress as it enveloped her.

But her mind was another story. She had no energy to organize her thoughts as she usually did, so only fragments came and went. *Where was Cami's sister? Who was that strange man in the park? How would it be with Randy in charge? Who would be her new partner?* And then only dreams…

Four hours later, Carrie woke as the trash truck in her neighborhood roared and clunked about collecting garbage. She rolled over onto her back and stared at the ceiling. She needed to get up and go to the bathroom, but her body refused, choosing rather to hold it, rather than exert the energy to move from the bed.

As the sleep induced fog subsided, Carrie's thoughts reengaged. Her life was changing. It was changing permanently in a profound way.

The day before, she had kept her appointment with Dr. Lee at four p.m. She couldn't have avoided it; Bracket had insisted.

She went, with the mindset to cooperate. Not for her emotional and mental benefit, but because she knew the more cooperation she exerted, the quicker she would be released from the requirement to attend.

Skirting around issues was something that counselors and psychiatrists were used to, so when Carrie started in, it was no use. The best way through this, was through this all the way. And what could it hurt?

So she did her best. But it hurt. It touched places she had walled off and had refused to go many years ago. She knew it had all started with her parents' death eight years before so that is where she started.

Dr. Lee was kind and Carrie endured the hour. But once over, she had to medicate from the trauma of the session, so she had gone to the bar. And she forgot, for a time. But it never failed, once home and lying in her bed, the memories and the pain scorched through her mental fog.

It seemed she had barely gotten to sleep when she had received the call from Randy about Bracket. Dizziness engulfed her even though she was lying still in her bed. It was all too much.

She draped her arm over her face and hid her eyes in the crook of her elbow to shut out the daylight. Was hollowness an emotion? If so, then that would be her current and ongoing emotion. But what could fill that void?

Buzz - buzz - buzz, her phone danced around on her nightstand begging for attention. "Yeah?"

"How are you?" asked Randy.

Carrie sat and pulled herself up to rest against her headboard. "I got some sleep."

"Bracket is doing well. The doctors were very optimistic about the outcome of the surgery. He should be enjoying retirement very soon."

Silence filled the void between the receivers. "Look Carrie, I know it was a lot to dump on you this morning, but I had to tell you and tell you first. I knew as soon as I got back to the office I would be in charge."

"I know. That movie, The Perfect Storm, when a cluster of horrible things all came together at once… Well, that is how I feel. I feel like this is a perfect storm and I am trying my best to handle it."

"I know," said Randy.

"So, can you tell me a little about what is planned for the office? Have you decided who will be my new partner?"

"I'm navigating through that now. I've thought a lot about it since Bracket first told me they would offer me his position. I want to do the right thing, by both you and the agency.

"I'm doing three interviews this afternoon for a new agent. You are, in my opinion, the best agent we have, so I don't believe that putting you with another seasoned agent would be the best use of your abilities.

"So I will hire a new agent and partner them with you. You have a lot to give someone, Carrie." Randy stopped to see how she would receive what he had just said.

Again, tears rolled down Carrie's cheeks. What on earth was up with this weak show of emotions she had experienced today? Fatigue, that was all it was, sheer exhaustion. But his words… Randy thought highly enough of her, in the middle of her messy life, to entrust her with a new agent. He was either crazy or delusional.

"Are you there?" Randy asked.

"Yeah, I'm here." Her voice was husky and it surprised her. She cleared her throat and sat up straighter in bed.

"Speak to me."

Once again only silence filtered through.

"Carrie..."

"I'm afraid." Pain and fear hit her like a bomb. She doubled over onto her bed and a flood of emotions poured out. She let go of the phone and sobs wracked her body. She sobbed until she lay in a puddle of snot and tears on her soft quilt. When she could cry no more, she reached for the phone. Randy was still there, silently waiting by her side while she had cried.

He could hear as she once again picked up the phone. "Are you there? Are you okay?" Randy asked.

Carrie used her nightshirt sleeve to blow her nose, and it's tail to wipe her face. "I'm here."

"Talk to me," said Randy.

"We've been together so long that I could just be me and no matter what bullshit I was going through it didn't matter. We, you and me, were fine. I can't let a new agent be damaged by my mess and I don't know how to fix it. I don't know how to help someone else when I can't even help myself."

"Carrie, do you trust me? Really trust me?"

Carrie shut her eyes and searched for the strength to answer. "Yes. What else can I say, but yes?"

"Then really trust me on this. This isn't just for them. It's for you too."

"I want you to take the entire day off. Sleep and rest. That's a lot of what's wrong with you right now. You're exhausted. I don't want you back in here until tomorrow morning. And stay home tonight!" Randy was laughing when he delivered his last sentence.

"Okay. You're right. I need rest. I'm going to stay in bed until I can't any longer, then order a big pizza and pig out." Randy always had a way of making her feel better. At least he wasn't leaving. At least she could still go to him when she needed him. And they would fight, and she would feel better.

Carrie did as she promised and spent the rest of the day sleeping as much as possible. But by four that afternoon, she had to get up. She was starving and ordered a pizza, her favorite food. Her fridge was stocked with a six-pack of Michelobe Light so she was good to go for the evening.

Rested, she decided she would do a little laundry and clean-up around the house. As she picked and sorted through a pile she had thrown in the corner of her bedroom, she heard paper crunch in a pocket.

When she pulled out the folded up envelope from the rear pocket of a pair of work pants, she remembered having folded it and shoved it in her back pocket. It was the envelope they had found at Pride's house and brought to her.

It had remained sealed. Once in her pocket, she had forgotten all about it. Hesitant to open it still, she turned it over and then over again in her hands. She couldn't. Not now. She'd cried too many tears already today. The letter would have to wait.

She opened her top dresser drawer and put it inside and slightly to the back. *Someday Pride, someday*, she thought.

The rest of the evening was uneventful and even pleasant. She did laundry, picked up her house, stuffed herself on pizza and finished the Michelobe.

By bedtime she was rested and looked forward to a restful night, and not one forced on her from exhaustion.

CHAPTER 17

"Mike, look at this," said Rick as he held up a list of evidence collected from the most recent crime scene.

Mike took the sheet from Rick and read over it. The previous two crime scenes had been in areas where trash and debris was easily accumulated, but this was a small park at the end of the canal that the city kept mowed and cleaned. They had collected far less garbage this time.

Mike finished reading and looked up and Rick. "What are you wanting me to see?"

"I would understand if we found one ink pen or pencil at a scene, but did you see that there were three ink pens, a red, a blue, and a black one, and a mechanical pencil?"

Mike looked back down at the paper. "Yeah, so what? You think it means something?"

"Who knows, but I will call the lab and see if they can do the fingerprinting and swabs on those first."

Rick made the call and hung up with a promise to rush the testing on those items.

"Shame about Bracket, huh?" asked Mike.

"Yeah. What a way to retire!"

"Let's see where we are on all this," said Mike.

For the next hour they looked over the list of interviews they had finally gotten through. It had taken them awhile to find the competitors of Gus, but they pushed on until they found them under every grimy rock.

"These greasy slugs didn't do this. Honor among thieves, and such," said Rick. "They had no reason to."

"Has anything turned up on Sam that we know of?" asked Mike.

"Let me look. I really want to find that girl."

Rick fingered his copy of the photo of the girls. He wished it were not so faded and yellowed.

"Have we talked to their classmates yet?" asked Rick.

"No, only a few neighborhood girls. Their classmates have all graduated and are scattered to the wind by now. I'll get started digging. I can't think of anything else," said Mike.

By five they'd tracked down fifteen of Sam's classmates and had actually spoken to six on the phone. None knew who they could be talking about but were willing to look at the sketch.

"What if we are showing this sketch to the wrong

people? What if we took it around and asked in the vice section?" asked Mike.

Rick looked up at Mike and nodded thoughtfully. "Yeah, that might work. He may be connected there somehow. I hate it when I get tunnel vision."

They retraced the steps from the few days prior when they had hunted down Tiny Simmons, Rudy Vargus, and Herman Merrell.

Pulling up to Tiny Simmons' house, they thought no one would be home. There was no sign of a vehicle or persons about. Not wanting to just assume no one was home though, Mike went to go knock on the door.

No one had been home, or had answered. They knocked on two more doors before realizing they were making no headway. Rick pulled out his cell phone and called the lieutenant in charge of the Human Trafficking Task Force.

"Hey Bill, this is Rick Morris. We're trying to track down those three yahoos, Tiny Simmons, Rudy Vargus, and Herman Merrell we asked you about the other day. Where do they hang out? I want to get into the heart of where they do their dirty work."

Bill laughed. "No, you don't! But, I get ya. I'll send you a list of hangouts and haunts. Be ready to get dirty, or maybe just feel dirty."

"Thanks Bill." Rick hung up the phone. "He's sending us a list of places to go. I know some of these aren't just into prostitution, but bars and clubs. I want to do some sniffing around and see what we can dig up."

Rick's phone pinged, and he saw the file Bill had sent over. "First stop, Lawdie's on northwest tenth street." Rick shoved the car in gear and headed that way.

RANDY DIDN'T FEEL like he had time to do these interviews, but they were a man down and the drowning cases weren't the only heavy cases at the moment. He needed to finish this process and get them in the field.

"Sean, thank you for coming in today," Randy began.

The young man sitting in front of him was fit and attractive. He had sandy blonde hair and brown eyes. And he was extremely nervous. Randy watched as Sean's eyes flitted around the room and back at him several times.

After letting him sweat for a few minutes, Randy said, "You seem very nervous Sean. There is no need to be."

Sean nodded, or bobbed his head, up and down. "I know, sir. Sorry. I'm nervous."

"There is no need to be. I see high commendations here in your file. Can you tell me what was the most challenging thing about being on the OKCPD?"

Sean cleared his throat and sat up straight. Almost as if rehearsed, he succinctly described a robbery and how he and his partner found and took down the assailants.

Randy wanted to ask Sean if he had memorized that response, but didn't want to put the poor fellow in any more distress than he was already in.

After about twenty minutes of questions, and having received rote answers which Sean had clearly memorized, Randy concluded the interview. He had tried to trip Sean up a few times, but didn't feel it was worth the effort. He wasn't a good fit for their office.

Next was Gabriel Lane. A quick review of the file reminded Randy that, he too had high commendations.

Gabriel, Gabe as he liked to be called, was quite the opposite of Sean. He was easygoing to the point of being too familiar with Randy as if they were equals and buddies. He was braggadocios and proud when he answered the interview questions.

Randy closed that interview. *He wouldn't do at all*, thought Randy.

Lainey Tate was next. Her file was full of recommendations from not only superiors at the police force, but from non-profit organizations where she had volunteered. There were various teachers, supervisors, and others who had taken the time to write glowing letters of recommendation for this lady.

When Lainey entered the room, Randy immediately knew without asking a single question she was right for the job. She stood tall and assured, but not arrogant or proud. Her smile lit the room, and she seemed… happy.

After a full hour with Lainey, Randy had long since asked every question he had intended to ask and continued to chat with this young woman. She had energy and loved to engage in conversation, but she was humble about all the achievements she had earned and accomplished. She was a genuine pleasure.

Randy knew he wanted to offer her the position, but as of that moment he was still officially serving as SAC in a temporary capacity. He would need to get the final approval from the commission to extend Lainey an offer.

It briefly crossed his mind to bring Carrie in for a meet and greet with Lainey, but he was the supervisor now, and needed to wean himself away from their partnership.

The moment Lainey had left his office, he dialed the number to the chairman of the commission. Before hanging up the receiver, he had the approval to make the offer.

LAWDIE'S on northwest tenth street was filling up. It was almost five p.m. and there was a steady stream of those who came straight from work to get a beer.

"What a dumb name," said Mike. "Where on earth did the owner come up with that one?"

Rick chuckled and shook his head. He took a deep breath and grabbed the folder he had brought. He wasn't ready for this, going into a place he knew they weren't wanted.

As they approached the door, two men who were about to go inside opened the door for them to enter, then turned and went back to their car. "I guess they weren't in the mood to share a strip joint with a couple of detectives," said Mike.

They stood for a few seconds just inside the door, to let their eyes adjust to the dim light. It was a very large room with the bar on the far west side.

The north side was nearly taken up with the stage. It expanded the width of the room with a large finger shaped extension protruding into the center of the room. In the garment district in NYC it might have been mistaken for a larger version of a fashion runway.

Various tables were scattered across the open space of the floor, and several men had both beer and ladies sitting on their tables, getting equal attention.

A lonely thin figure with long dark hair and sad eyes, dominated the stage. She was numb from drugs and alcohol and made her moves in a trancelike state.

Rick and Mike walked over to the south end of the bar where it curved back to meet the wall. Standing there, they could see the bar and talk to the bartender without having to turn their backs to the crowd.

The bartender threw down his towel and walked over to the two men. "What can I do for you fine gentlemen?" His tone was sarcastic. He wanted them to know they were not welcomed there.

Rick pulled out the sketch of the man who had picked up Sam. "Will you look at this sketch and see if you recognize him?"

The bartender barely glanced at it before saying, "Don't know him." He stood staring straight into Rick's eyes with his fists firmly on the bar spread apart by locked arms.

"Look, we don't want to cause any trouble. We're just trying to find a missing girl and this guy is the last one someone saw her with. It isn't a great sketch, but will you please just look at it?"

The man shrugged and took the sketch from Rick's hand. He looked for a few seconds as Rick and Mike watched for recognition on the man's face.

Handing it back, the man shook his head. "I honestly don't know. You know how many men come and go in this place. He isn't someone I have come in contact with enough times to remember."

Rick nodded his head and put the sketch back in the file. Then he pulled out an enlarged photo of the three girls. "What about these girls? Do you know any of them or have you seen any of them?"

He didn't want to let on that one girl was already dead. For a brief second, he thought he saw a flash in the bartender's eyes. Did he recognize them or was he simply attracted to them? That picture held the image of three beautiful light blonde haired girls, the one of Cami, Sam, and Addy. Rick couldn't imagine any man not being attracted and interested.

The bartender fiddled with the pic in his fingers then shoved it back at Rick. "No."

Rick didn't immediately take the picture from his hands. "Are you sure? No crime if you have. Surely you would remember beauties like those."

The bartender was getting visibly rattled. "Look, I don't know them."

"Okay, okay," said Rick as he placed the photo back in the folder. "Now can you point us to Tiny Simmons?"

"He ain't here."

"We'll wait," said Rick. Then to Mike, "Let's take a look around. Find ourselves a good front-row seat."

The bartender took a deep breath and turned to go back to his tending. His body was as taught as a piano string. He didn't need these cops patrolling the club and Rick knew it.

They took a seat front and center so that everyone looking at the stage would have to look at them too.

Soon, a scantily clad waitress came to take their order. Mike wanted a bourbon so bad he hurt, but they both ordered soft drinks. Soon an older lady, well, older for that place, came over and attempted to sit on Rick's lap.

"No, you don't!" Rick sputtered. "Go sit on his lap," he said as he pointed at Mike, who was already shaking his head.

Not to be deterred, the lady pulled up a chair to their table and scooted in close, her nearly bare breasts purposely on display.

"What can I do for you fella's?" When she smiled, the creases around her lips from years of smoking, briefly melted away.

What the hell, Rick thought and turned his chair towards her. He pulled out the sketch and the picture of the girls. "We need to find this man and these girls. Can you help us?"

The lady straightened in her chair and moved the pictures around on the table, placing them side by side. She studied them for what seemed like an eternity. *Is she merely playing us,* wondered Rick.

Then she picked up the picture of the girls and brought it closer to her face. Her nails had been professionally done at one time, but now had a few chips. She tapped the photo with one.

"This girl here. She seems a little familiar."

With that comment, Mike turned from watching the dancer on the stage to the table. "Which one?" he asked.

"This one here." She had tapped Sam.

Neither of the seasoned detectives wanted to frighten her away, and they didn't want to be played either, but she *had* tapped Sam's photo and not either of the other two girls.

"Yes, I'm certain. But I'm trying to place exactly where it was."

The lady continued to stare at the photo. Then she laid it back on the table and picked up the sketch. Creases furrowed their way through her forehead as she thought.

Laying the sketch back on the table, she then took both hands and laid them on each side of the man's face hiding the long dark hair. Slowly at first, then more aggressively, she nodded. "I know him too. Not with this long hair. He keeps it short now." She looked up at Rick with hope in her eyes that she had pleased him.

In return Rick studied her face. He didn't like wild goose chases. "Where do you know him from?" Mike asked.

She turned to look at Mike and said, "He used to be my guy, you know…" She ducked her head to look back at the photos.

"You mean your pimp?" Mike didn't care if he was blunt.

The lady nodded.

Rick was pulling out his notebook and pen. "We need to get some information from you."

Just then Rick felt an abrupt shove from the back of his chair. He whirled around to see who had done it. The bartender stood there. "You've got to leave."

Rick stood and looked the man firmly in the eye. "I don't *got* to do nothing." Mike had also risen from his seat and now stood next to Rick as a show of solidarity.

"You can't be here messing with the ladies and taking up a table if you aren't drinking and playing."

Rick casually motioned towards their soft drinks. "We're drinking." The corner of his mouth turned up as he spoke.

The bartender's face was not just red, but deep crimson. His jaw was clenched tight and his eyes were dangerously round. "The boss said you have to go."

"The boss, huh?" asked Mike.

"Let him come tell us," said Rick.

"Suit yourself. He's through that door there." He indicated a closed door at the north end of the bar. Two large muscle in jackets, despite the August heat, stood on either side.

Rick turned to address the lady at their table one more time to get her name and contact info, but she was gone. She had slipped away the moment the bartender had approached. He quickly scanned the room looking for her. "Damn."

He scooped up the pics and slid them back into the folder. Both he and Mike headed for the door. As they approached, the muscle stood even taller and filled the space they were in with greater force.

"Okay, let us in." Rick didn't have time to play with these goons. The man on the side where the doorknob was reached over, and without taking his eyes off of the detectives, turned it. Once open, he gently pushed so the door swung open into the room. He kept his post.

Rick and Mike entered the room. It was an office like any other office. It had a desk and some file cabinets, and there was no one in there. But there was an open door on the far side of the room that led to another office.

As they entered that room, they were ready to pull their weapons. In the center of the far side of the large room, sat a large dark mahogany desk filled with stacks of cash. A money counter was on one corner.

Behind the desk sat Tiny Simmons and on each side were two more goons. The room was bathed in more light than the bar area, but only slightly more. There were stacks of crap everywhere. Rick guessed the maid must have taken the day off.

Tiny was exactly what his name implied. He was about five feet tall exact. On his best day he would weigh in at around one hundred twenty pounds. He could have been a jockey, but he hated horses.

His artificially blonde hair was cropped short and stood up in tufts on top of his head. The white blonde hair was in sharp contrast to his fake tan. He sat without looking at the detectives, stacking coins on his desk. The diamond rings, one on each finger glinted in the dim light.

He wore an expensive suit and tie. Rick thought he might puke. Here this man sat surrounded by money made by using and abusing women. What he wouldn't give to set them all free and on the right track to a better life.

Tired of being ignored, Mike marched up to the desk and slammed his fist down hard. The stacks of coins shifted and toppled as did a few of the bills. Hardly rattled, mostly amused, Tiny finally looked up at Mike.

Tiny sat back in his tufted leather chair and folded his hands in his lap. "What can I do for you gentlemen today?"

Rick walked up next to Mike and opened the folder. He pulled out the sketch and laid it on the only empty area of the desk in front of Tiny. "We need you to tell us where we can find this man." It wasn't an ask and assumed that Tiny knew the man.

Tiny picked up the sketch and glanced at it, then

tossed it back down on the desk. "What makes you think I know this man?"

Mike placed his hands on the desk and leaned forward. "A man of power knows everyone in this line of work. Are you saying you are no longer on the top of your game?"

He knew he was being goaded, but Tiny couldn't resist showing his power. "So what if I do know him?"

"We want to talk to him," said Mike.

Tiny shrugged his shoulder and glanced around the room. "I don't know where he is or how to find him."

"Let's start with a name," said Rick. He pulled out his notepad and pen.

"Hmm. Well let me see if I can remember." Tiny tapped his lip with his index finger. He was purposely toying with them. He really didn't want to give them a name. It could very easily topple things and all hell could break loose.

"We're not leaving. Your goons can throw us out and then be arrested for an assault on an officer. We *know* you know who this is," said Rick.

With a sharp inhale and Tiny complied. "His name is Hugh Bennett."

"Hugh Bennett," Rick mumbled as he wrote. "Where can we find this Hugh Bennett?"

Again, Tiny shrugged. "I don't keep tabs on him." He looked up at the detectives with round innocent eyes.

"If you wanted to reach out to Mr. Bennett, where would you start?"

Suddenly the door to the outer room swung open and in rushed a young girl with so little clothing on that Rick couldn't look at her. She didn't look like she was over fifteen or sixteen.

Right behind her was another man, younger than Tiny. This man was obviously trying to mimic Tiny in every way, but on a budget.

Tiny stood and glared at the man. "Get her out of here."

"Wait just a minute," Rick bellowed. He reached out and grabbed the man behind the girl and pulled him on into the room. Mike, in sync with Rick, shut the door.

He firmly held the man by the back of his collar, but looked back at Tiny. "How old is this girl?" Rick asked.

A smile spread across Tiny's face and he clasp his hands together in front as if he were a choirboy. "She's of age."

Rick turned to look the girl in the eyes. His voice softer. "Don't be afraid. How old are you?"

Her eyes darted from man to man around the room. There was no doubt it terrified her. Rick finally released the man. Mike stood guarding the door, so he wouldn't be escaping.

Once again Rick addressed the girl, "What is your name?" His eyes looked at her as a caring father and she found comfort there.

"I… I… Uh…" Her gaze darted over to Tiny and the two brutes on either side of him.

"Ma'am, what is your name? I'm a detective with the

Oklahoma City Police Department and you need to answer me."

"Maggie."

"Maggie what?"

"Maggie Jenks." She was trembling and her eyes continued to dart from Tiny to Rick.

"Maggie I need to see some id, please."

Once again her eyes darted to Tiny. She didn't have any id. She hadn't had any id for a very long time.

"I... I... don't have any."

Rick seeing her trembling, either from terror or the frigid AC, turned to survey the room. An old throw of some type was lying on the sofa to the side of the room.

Even though Rick thought it was probably infested with all types of dried fluids he'd rather not think about, he grabbed it and draped it around Maggie.

Rick looked at Mike. They knew they had a dilemma. In order to find out more about the man in the sketch and Sam, they would need to stay here and get more information. But this girl needed out of here, and getting her out might be a valuable resource. The question, *should they stay or should they go*, passed as a look between Rick and Mike.

Maggie, I'm taking you in for questioning. You can't produce id and you are working under age. Maggie's eyes grew round with fear and she trembled even harder. The thought that she was being rescued never crossed her mind.

"You can't do that," bellowed Tiny.

"I can and I will." Rick gently turned Maggie around to make it look official, and put his cuffs on her thin wrists, making sure they were loose enough to not hurt her.

"But don't worry, Tiny. You aren't off the hook either." Rick radioed in a message for backup. The last thing he wanted was for Tiny and his men to flee and hide. He also didn't want Tiny having time to hide any other girls that might be on the premises.

Soon sirens were heard, and Mike looked at Tiny. "Awww there's your babysitters now!"

"Tiny we will be back," said Mike as they left the office.

MIKE PURPOSELY LEFT the throw draped across the girl's shoulders. It was a long shot, but maybe, just maybe if the lab tested it for DNA, they would find a familial match for Sam.

Would it hold up in court since he took it without a warrant? Under the circumstances, maybe. There had been no objection from Tiny as they walked out of the office, which Rick could stress was uncontested consent.

Once in the car and headed back to the station, Maggie cried. Large black rivers streaked her cheeks as her mascara bled from torrents of tears.

"Maggie, it's okay. We aren't arresting you. We just wanted to get you out of there, for your own sake," Mike tried to reassure her, but all he got in response was a nod of her head.

"Are you all right?" Rick asked. Again another nod of her head.

Once at the station, Mike went in and got a female officer and some generic scrubs in the smallest adult size they kept on hand for just such occaisons, and brought them back out to the car.

Maggie was nearly naked in a bra type top that completely bared her breasts and a slim g-string panty. They wanted to spare her any more humiliation, and Rick wanted to preserve as much evidence on that throw as possible.

The female officer slid into the backseat with Maggie, uncuffed her, and handed her the scrubs with instructions to slip them on over her current clothing. Being barefoot, the officer had also gotten a pair of flip-flops for her to wear.

With gloved hands, the officer slipped the throw out of the car and into a large paper evidence sack Rick held waiting.

Rick and Mike led Maggie into an interrogation room as the other officer took the evidence to process.

Maggie sat in the steel chair cold to the touch from the blasting AC. She slumped over with her arms between her knees. It reminded the detectives of a defensive position meant to shield herself from an attack.

Rick left to go get a bottle of water for them all, and Mike took the chair across from Maggie.

"Maggie, my name is Detective Mike Brown. I don't want you to be afraid."

Maggie looked up at him. Her sweet tired face was wracked with sorrow, which was accentuated by the hideous black streaks on her face. But she said nothing.

The door opened, and Rick presented a cold bottle of water to Maggie, then one to Mike. He had already downed half of his.

"Here you go Maggie. You can use these wipes to clean your face if you want. I thought it might feel good." Rick placed a container of wipes on the table next to her water.

Maggie just sat and stared at both without saying a word.

"Are you hungry? How long has it been since you've eaten?" asked Mike.

Maggie just looked up at him and then away. They all three sat there for a few moments. Finally, Maggie sat up and reached for the wipes. She popped one out and began to clean her face.

"I am a little hungry," she said as she wiped.

"What would you like? It's up to you. We'll send someone out to get whatever you want."

Maggie reached for another wipe and replied, "I like Taco Bell."

"Okay, great! We like Taco Bell too. What do you like from there?" Rick was thrilled she was talking.

"Tacos. I like their tacos and nachos."

Instantly Rick was up and out in the hall giving

instructions. When he had reentered the room, Maggie looked much better. Not only had the wipes taken off the streaks of black, but all the heavy makeup she had worn.

With her face fresh and clean before them, Rick and Mike both realized just how young this girl really was.

"Maggie, how old are you?" asked Mike.

She dipped her head and said, "Thirteen."

Rick jumped up and was once again out of the room and in the hallway giving instructions. They would bring Tiny and his entire brood of merry men in. Then he would get the answers he wanted.

He tried to calm himself down before reentering the room. He did not want Maggie to see him so enraged and think she was the reason for it.

With the heavy makeup that Maggie had worn, she could have passed for legal age, they weren't sure then. Had they been, they would have never left Lawdie's without Tiny in cuffs.

They had gotten a warrant en route to the station for the patrolmen they'd left behind to execute. He gave further instructions to bring Tiny and his men in.

"Maggie can you tell us who your parents are and how we can contact them?" asked Mike.

Maggie sobbed. She dropped her face into her hands and gave into her grief. They let her cry. They knew she had had to get tough or numb to endure what she had been through, so now they wanted her to have time to let it out.

Soon, her sobs subsided, and she looked up, grabbed

the wipes again and blew her nose. By now her pretty little face was red and swollen.

They didn't want to push her, so they resisted the urge to ask more questions. Their need to know couldn't override this young girl's vulnerability.

"I don't have anyone anymore," Maggie finally whispered.

"What do you mean, Maggie?" asked Mike.

She shook her head and just looked at her hands in her lap. "I used to live somewhere cold. I think maybe Michigan. Yeah, that sounds right. But I haven't been there for a long time."

"Maggie, can you please tell us how you came to be at Lawdie's? Tell us why you aren't with your parents now?" asked Rick.

Maggie nodded, but continued to look at her lap. "I barely remember my parents. They took me when I was about six, I think. I honestly don't remember much about it. My memories are just flashes of this and that."

A knock on the door announced the food was there. They had ordered Maggie several items so she could choose what she wanted and eat as much of it as she wanted.

As soon as the smell of the food hit Maggie, her stomach growled. She dove in as if she hadn't eaten in days and devoured almost everything.

They hadn't pushed her to talk while she was eating, but the moment she stopped, they asked her again to tell them her story.

"I just remember a man, actually a man and a woman who took me from the park across the street from my house. It terrified me. I screamed and cried for my mommy, but she never came.

"I knew she wouldn't, because she couldn't hear me in the van. I don't know how long we drove. There were a bunch of other girls in the van with me. Some were a little older than me and some were about my age.

"We were all scared, but when we cried, the lady would reach back and slap a strap at whoever was crying. It hurt bad, so we didn't cry.

"That was a long time ago. We traveled for a long time and then they took us to a house somewhere and shoved us all in a room. There was a man there with a gun who made sure we stayed in the room and stayed quiet.

"The next thing we knew, we were being herded off in a truck. There were even more girls and women in there. Somehow I wound up here in Oklahoma. Tiny said he bought me and that I was his."

She stopped for a moment. Her memories had trapped her once again, and a tear slid from her eye.

"What did you do for Tiny?" asked Mike.

"Well, I guess I was too young to go out on the stage where someone might report me being underage. So, he charged big money for me to dance in the private back room. There are a lot of men who will pay big money for young girls."

"Is that all you did, was dance?" asked Rick.

"No, he made me have sex with men too. The first

time, since I was a virgin, the man was very wealthy. I could tell. He wanted to buy me from Tiny, but Tiny knew how much money I could make him, so he wouldn't sell me. But the man paid $50,000 to have sex with me as a virgin. I was seven."

Rick thought someone had just punched him in the gut. He made an excuse and slipped out of the room. His head was spinning, and he knew he would be sick.

Afterwards in the men's room, all he could see were his daughters and their innocent faces. They were teenagers now, much older than Maggie, but what if it had been them? It couldn't have been them.

Rick washed his face and stared blankly at the chipped mirror in front of him. When he suddenly snapped out of his trance, he called his oldest daughter from inside the men's room. His call went to voicemail, and he told her he loved her and wanted to get together with her whenever she could.

Since she had just graduated and left home to go to college, he'd seen very little of her. Her younger sister was still at home and a senior. He couldn't wait to get home to hold her tight. But right now he had a job to do, so he went back to Maggie.

"Maggie do you remember your parents's names or where in Michigan you lived?" Maggie shook her head. "I'm not real sure my name is Maggie Jenks. That's just the name they gave me after I got here."

"Maggie I'm so glad we found you. Why did you come bursting into Tiny's office today?" asked Mike.

"Wally was beating on one of the new girls and I'd just had enough. I didn't care what they did to me."

"Does Tiny have other young girls there?" asked Rick.

Maggie nodded. "He has about five or six. He says they are too high maintenance, so he only keeps that many."

"So how old are they?" asked Rick.

She sighed deeply before answering, "They are really young like I was, six, seven, something like that. There is one really small even though she is older, she's eight. But she isn't cut out for this and cries all night long. Then, Wally beats her. I couldn't stand it any longer."

Mike and Rick weren't sure they heard her correctly. Her words, *'weren't really cut out for this'*, assumed that she had taken it for granted that some young girls, even herself, were cut out for this type of cruel behaviour.

Rick once again left and radioed into the Sergeant in charge of the raid on Lawdie's. He explained that there may be other very young girls and minors on the premises.

The Sergeant radioed back that they had shut the place down for the night at least, and were working their way through the building searching for anything that would lead them to another location where they could find more girls.

Once again back in the room, Rick asked Maggie, "Maggie, did you and the girls stay there at Lawdie's all the time or did he keep you somewhere else?"

"No, not all the time. In fact, we were rarely there. He

kept us in an old house close to there. I guess when someone wanted to be with us, they would bring us over."

"Do you know where that was? Could you help us find it?" asked Rick.

Maggie sat thinking for a moment. "I don't think so. I can try, but I can't promise."

"Why were you at Lawdie's today?" asked Rick.

"There was a little party in the back room that Tiny wanted me to dance at. He had brought me and two other girl's over. Then when eight-year-old Kiley, cried and didn't want to dance, Wally beat her. That's when I went running into Tiny's office."

"Okay, thank you Maggie. Mike we have some work to do," then looking back at Maggie. "Stay here just a minute and we'll get back to you. Are you okay for now?" Maggie nodded.

"What's going to happen to me now? Where will I go?"

Mike and Rick didn't know, but they were in agreement she wouldn't be going back to that life if they had anything at all to do with it.

CHAPTER 18

For Carrie, Wednesday morning began with a call from Rick regarding the discovery of Maggie the previous evening. Files were waiting in her in-box and details came over the phone.

As she burst through the door, she headed to her desk with a purpose; her phone still to her ear. She could feel the adrenalin surging through her body.

The desk chair skittered as her body dropped awkwardly into it. Focused on seeing the file, and hearing the update Rick was giving her, dominated her mind. Entirely engrossed in the influx of new information, she was unaware that Randy was motioning for her to come to Bracket's office.

By the time Carrie had ended the call, Randy was standing in front of her next to his desk.

"Was that Rick?" asked Randy.

Carrie stood. Randy noticed the color back in her cheeks and felt the energy she had gained from physical rest and new leads. This was the Carrie he had missed.

"I guess you're up to speed..." Randy said.

Carrie nodded. Her eyes twinkled, and she appeared to Randy as a racehorse waiting for the gate to open.

"I know you are ready to get out there, but I need you to come into my office first."

Carrie's mind shifted. *Oh, that's right. It's not Bracket's office anymore, it's Randy's,* Carrie thought.

"Carrie..." Randy had noticed her mind space out for a moment.

She shook her mind back into focus, and said, "Right, sure. I'm just getting used to you being SAC and now in Bracket's office."

The corner of Randy's mouth turned up. "So am I. It feels like I will get caught any moment playing boss in my dad's chair."

They both chuckled. Bracket's office still looked the same. Randy knew he was still interim and couldn't bear to touch one thing, one picture, one cute family memento, nothing.

Once there, Randy shut the blinds and Carrie shut the door. It felt odd to Carrie seeing Randy behind the desk rather than next to her in the chair beside her.

"Well, what else happened while I was out yesterday?" Carrie asked.

Randy looked down at the desk and opened the file before him. He knew it would be hard telling Carrie that he had hired another agent who would be her partner. He took a deep breath and mustered all the courage he had.

But before he could say a word, there was a tap on his door. "Yes?" asked Randy.

The door opened slightly and Gerald's head poked through. He could see Carrie sitting in there with Randy and was unsure what to do, so he just jerked his head at Randy in a motion indicating that he should come out.

Sensing he knew what it was about, Randy stood and left the room. In just a few seconds, the door reopened.

"Carrie, I'd like you to meet your new partner, Lainey Tate," Randy said as he ushered Lainey into the room. Lainey stood tall and proud, even a little stiff from nerves, Randy surmised. She smiled broadly and reached her hand out to greet Carrie.

Carrie knew she should shut her mouth, but her chin felt frozen. *That was what Randy wanted to talk about this morning*, she thought.

At first glance she saw a late twenty-something attractive lady with very dark, almost black hair, done up on top of her head in a random messy bun that made her look incredibly stylish in an unassuming casual way.

As Carrie stood and shook Lainey's hand, she noticed that her eyes were bright and expectant. Almost like a puppy wanting to engage a new friend. Her smile was broad and… *genuine*, thought Carrie. She stood respectfully though, waiting for Carrie to take the lead.

Carrie liked what she saw, but she wouldn't officially form an opinion, just yet. Trust and respect wasn't something that Carrie could just offer to someone. It was hard enough to have trust and respect for those who had proven themselves over time, much less those she had just met.

They all sat in their respective chairs. Lainey sat straight and slightly forward in her chair. Carrie sat casually back in her chair with her legs crossed while Randy sat forward with his forearms resting on the desk.

He looked straight at Lainey. "I had hoped that there would be time to get you acclimated gently to our office, but we don't have the luxury of time right now. I gave you the obligatory paperwork to fill out when you came back to the office yesterday evening. I trust you've filled that out."

"Yes, sir." Lainey handed Randy the thick manilla envelope of paperwork she had been carrying with her.

"Wonderful. I'll look at this and make sure everything is in order. In the meantime I will have you go with Carrie so she can fill you in on everything that's going on with this current case. Do you have any questions for me?"

Lainey shook her head. Randy stood, and Lainey and Carrie followed his lead. "Carrie can you hang back a minute? Lainey if you will wait just outside, this will be quick," said Randy.

As soon as Lainey stepped outside the door and it clicked shut, Randy and Carrie stood looking at each other. "So this is it," said Carrie.

Randy nodded. Words hung in the air unspoken. They knew them by heart without uttering a one. Carrie reached out to shake Randy's hand. They shook, and for a brief moment their hands held suspended between them.

Then Carrie let go and turned to leave.

LAINEY WAS STANDING DUTIFULLY OUTSIDE the office door waiting for Carrie. She was nervous, but it barely showed. Carrie was a legend in the local law enforcement community and it thrilled Lainey to be partnered with her.

She was also somewhat apprehensive too. She had not just heard the accomplishments, but the rumors too. She wanted to learn from Carrie, and be a partner who served her well. But she also wanted to learn to navigate her moods and emotions well, too.

As Carrie walked out of the office, she smiled at Lainey. She wanted this to be a new start. She wanted to go into this new partnership on a positive note. She wanted to learn to work in a new role with a new partner. But there was a knot of apprehension in her stomach.

"I hope you can catch up while we run. We need to get down to the police precinct as soon as possible. I'll do my best to fill you in while we drive. Ask questions if you need to."

Lainey nodded and followed Carrie out of the office. The drive from the office to the precinct needed to be three times longer than it was, in order to fill Lainey in on everything, but Carrie had hit the highlights.

Inside, Carrie found Rick and Mike and introduced

them to Lainey. "These are the two you need to watch out for Lainey," Carrie said with a smile. There were dozens of good detectives in the city, but these were the two she enjoyed working with the most.

Rick smiled, but wasn't in the mood to socialize. He hadn't slept a wink last night. Thoughts of these young girls and his own daughters, haunted him.

Not getting home until one in the morning, he was exhausted and assumed he would fall right to sleep, but he hadn't.

Rick summarized what had happened the day before, the visit to Lawdie's, bringing Maggie in, then interrogating Tiny and his men.

Maggie had gone with a social worker from DHS until they determined further how to help her. She would sleep the night in their custody. Tiny and his crew were in holding.

"So, here's what we know. Tiny has a house near Lawdie's where he keeps young girls. Maggie looked at a map for us to see if she could remember where it was. We also looked at tax records. We think we have the house and have patrolmen watching it in case Tiny's men try to run with the girls.

"There is a waitress slash dancer at Lawdie's that recognized the man in the sketch. She also thought she recognized Sam from the picture. We were about to get details when we were so rudely interrupted by one of Tiny's men.

"When we turned back around, she was gone. We

have to find her and we have to get into that house and see what girls are there. Lawdie's is shut down and we have a warrant to search. We should have the warrant for the house by now as well.

Carrie's mind was swimming. All this activity was wonderful and felt like they were making solid ground forward, but was this going to move them forward on the drownings?

"What are you thinking," asked Mike. He could tell by the look on Carrie's face she was overexerting mental energy.

"I'm thrilled at what you guys have uncovered. I just have a sinking feeling in my gut, that although this is wonderful, it may not help me find my killer."

Mike was thinking and nodding. "Well, do you have any other leads you feel you should work?"

"No, so we will work these with you and see what pans out. I want to find that man in the sketch and Sam. Those are the closest links to my case."

"Then we need to find that waitress. You two come to Lawdie's with us and we'll search for any information at all on her and I'll send another team to the house."

Fifteen minutes later, Carrie and Lainey were pulling up to Lawdie's. The exterior reminded Carrie of an old frontier store front, only on a much larger scale. The word Lawdie's was plastered in four foot high neon letters that spanned a broad arch over the front doors.

An officer in uniform guarded the door and Carrie

nodded to him as the four of them entered. It was quiet and empty.

"The office is back this way. I don't hold much hope that he carried W-4 forms on all his employee's, but you never know. Sometimes they surprise me," said Rick.

The office in front of where Tiny's lair was, looked more like a working office than his did. There were file cabinets and a desk with a computer. They divided up the area and dove in with their gloved hands. Carrie had quickly volunteered to take the first filing cabinet.

After an hour of searching, Carrie finally found what she'd hoped for. "Found it!"

They all stopped and came together in the center of the room. "They did have W-4's on the employees. At least some of them." Carrie laid the folder on the desk and the other three huddled around. She flipped the papers a page at a time.

They were a little in awe that the file was so thorough. They even had copies of drivers' licenses attached. Drivers' licenses meant photos.

Carrie turned the pages much slower than she probably needed to, which created an atmosphere of suspense, but she didn't want to rush this. She didn't want to hurry past and fail to find the person they needed.

"Her!" exclaimed Rick. Before them was a license photo of a forty-six-year-old woman named Jennifer Jenson. The woman looked much older than she should have looked at her age.

Carrie lifted out the page and walked over to the copier and made two copies of the page, giving one to Rick and the other to Lainey. She then continued to look through the folder. No one else stood out to them, but they bagged the file to take back to the precinct just in case.

"I know you guys built rapport with her and I feel she will open up to you guys because of it, but I need to get to this woman. How do you suggest we handle this? If we all four roll up on her, she'll either panic and babble out everything, or she'll clam up and scream lawyer."

The four of them stood thinking and playing out scenarios in their minds for just a moment before Rick said, "Let Mike and I go see if we can get her and bring her in. We'll emphasize that it is only for questioning and that she is not under suspicion for breaking the law. Once at the precinct we can take turns visiting with her."

Carrie liked that idea. "Okay. Sounds good. Have we finished here? Get the tech guys to take that computer in and finish combing over things and we will take off."

Back in the hot car, Carrie cranked the engine and the AC, and smiled. Lainey watched and felt like she was on the outside of an inside joke.

As they drove back to their office, Carrie asked, "Lainey I know you have been dumped into the middle of this case rather late in the game, but just from what you know so far, what are your thoughts?" Carrie was hoping her fresh eyes would show her the forest instead of the trees.

Lainey swallowed and thought. Her mind was darting

like fire sparks from the anxiety of being put on the spot. Then she took a deep breath and looked at Carrie.

"You said someone drowned three young women. They murdered all three the exact same way. All three were prostitutes. Have you in your experience seen thugs like Tiny get rid of people that way?" She stopped for only a brief second before resuming.

"From where I stand, it looks like a serial killer with a psychopathy and an agenda. I am thrilled that all these girls are being found and helped, and that Tiny and his crew may be taken down, but the only thing I can think of that will come out of this for our case is if we get a lead, back to where our girls might have come in contact with their killer."

Lainey stopped to see how Carrie would react. Carrie drove in silence as she navigated the early morning traffic. Lainey was right and confirmed exactly what she had been thinking all along. As wonderful as this bust was, it was a rabbit trail that was taking them off course.

"I agree. That's what I've been thinking. Let's get back to the office and go over things again. I want to get you all the details and see if there is something we've seen so many times it doesn't stand out to us any longer."

Lainey felt relief at Carrie's words. She wanted more than anything to do a good job and have Carrie's approval.

BACK AT THE office Carrie took Lainey to her desk, Randy's old desk and helped her get settled in. Randy had laid a file on the desk for Lainey with a list of login credentials, and password codes. Carrie took a few minutes to get Lainey up to speed on their system.

Lainey had worked in law enforcement for several years now and it was an easy transformation from one type of system to another. They were all basically the same, just small variances in operation.

Once acclimated with those few housekeeping issues, Carrie showed Lainey the war room where they were working on the drownings.

Lainey strolled up to the first board with wide eyes, soaking it all in. Carrie stood back and watched, assessing Lainey. *She's sharp*, thought Carrie. The way she studied certain things and moved quickly over others; and the way Carrie could see in her eyes that her internal wheels were turning, thinking, calculating.

Finally, Lainey stopped at a huge map with pushpins they had up. The red pins were murder sites. The blue pins were other points of interest such as Pride's house, Gus's two houses, and the SAL house.

Lainey tapped the location of Lawdie's, "See, this is several miles away from all this other activity. It doesn't fit." She turned to look at Carrie.

Carrie studied the map. Oklahoma City is a large city in area. With so much land, it has spread like an uncontained water leak through the years. The area where all the current pins were could be contained in less than a three-mile radius, small for this city. Lawdie's was at least nine miles to the west.

"I see what you're saying." Carrie knew Lainey was right, but she still couldn't pull it together. She suddenly turned and went to retrieve a file which was lying on the table.

"The new victim. I don't see here in the file if we have an id yet." Carrie shut the file and sat down at the computer in the war room. She typed furiously as Lainey stood by and waited.

Tapping the screen to show Lainey, she said, "Here is the list of evidence found at the scene. Let's print this out and go over it line by line." Carrie clicked to print two copies and gave one to Lainey.

"Let's sit here and look at this evidence list. If anything looks odd to you or stands out to you, circle it and make a note." Lainey nodded.

About half way down the list Carrie came to the items, *red ink pen, blue ink pen, black ink pen, mechanical pencil…* She sat looking at those items. Her mind was firing synapsis, but not connecting with anything. She knew those items, but from where?

She shut her eyes and retraced their steps over the last week. *Had it only been a week and a day*, thought Carrie? She mentally went over each person they had interviewed, each person they had come in contact with. Then it hit her. The funny little man at the diner and the park.

"I've got it!" Lainey looked up with eyes as big as

saucers. She was alert and ready to charge in whatever direction was deemed necessary.

"There was this funny little man. I know he was younger than he looked, but he looked like an eighty-year-old man that had been dropped here from the 1950s.

"We first saw him at Penny's diner when we went to meet Beth, Lisa, and Jenny. He was there eating. Nothing unusual, except I noticed him because he seemed so out of place.

"Then when Randy and I were at the park on Monday, he was sitting on a bench and acting strange. He had a pocket protector with pens in it. No one does that anymore." Carrie's voice was escalating with excitement. She tapped the paper, "These pens could be his!"

"How do we find him?" asked Lainey.

"There may be DNA, but if he isn't in the system, then that won't help until we catch him. He was at Penny's which is close to downtown. He may be a regular there. We need to talk to the waitress, then we can go back and talk to Carissa, the girl he was talking to on the bench."

Carrie grabbed the file, and she and Lainey flew out the door. She wanted to rush in and grab Randy to go with them, but knew she couldn't.

The drive to Penny's was uneventful. Carrie and Lainey were excitedly throwing out thoughts and suppositions regarding new theories.

It was ten a.m. when they pulled up to the diner. Once inside, they looked around. It was mid-morning on a workday. Alice, their previous waitress waved at them and asked them to take a seat.

They did, and ordered coffee when she came to take their order. "Alice," began Carrie, "we are actually here to ask you about a man who may be a regular customer here."

When Alice stopped pouring the black liquid she looked at Carrie, just a tad weary. "Okay."

"The last time we were here with Beth and the girls, there was a man sitting in that booth there." Carrie pointed to the third booth from the corner booth. "He looked like he had dropped out of the 1950s."

As soon as Alice heard that, she relaxed. That man gave her the creeps and she wouldn't mind saying so. "Yes, he comes in here from time to time. Not real often, and there doesn't seem to be a regular pattern, but he has been here before."

"Do you know anything about him? Does he pay with a credit card?" Carrie was holding her breath in anticipation.

"No, sorry. He is always a cash only kind of guy."

"Do you know his name?" Alice was shaking her head before Carrie had even gotten to the end of the question.

"Is there anything at all that you can think of to tell us about him?"

Alice stood and looked off into nowhere, thinking hard. She had detested the man so much that she spent as little time as possible waiting on him when he was here.

"I think he drives an old Plymouth. I remember that

because I thought how fitting it was that he would drive that kind of car. Let me see... Alice was tapping her chin trying to remember more. "It was a faded blue, and I think the name was a Retalent, or something."

Lainey jumped in. "Reliant?"

"Yes! Reliant."

"My grandpa had one years ago." Lainey shrugged at why she should know such a thing and smiled.

Suddenly Carrie remembered that Randy used to always take notes profusely, and so she had never had to. Now they were sitting there, and no one was taking notes.

"Lainey, you got a notepad?" Carrie's face was twisted in a hopeful question mark.

Lainey winked and pulled a small notepad out of her back pocket. "Even got a pen."

Carrie huffed a sigh of relief. "Take notes please?"

There was little else that Alice could tell them. Lainey wrote down everything necessary for further reference.

Back in the hot car, Carrie looked at Lainey. "Thank you for taking notes. Randy always did that, so I never did. I got caught off guard."

"Well rest easy boss, I'll be your note-taker."

"Lainey, I'm not your boss. We are both OSBI agents and I appreciate your experienced and fresh eyes on this case." Carrie paused then added, "But I would love it if you would be our official note-taker."

"Ok, now let's go talk to Carissa again." Carrie shoved the SUV into gear and they headed the mile and a half to downtown.

They pulled into the drive of the Skirvin and Carrie showed her ID to the attendants at the front entrance. She parked for easy access, but also so that others could easily come and go around her.

At first, the gift shop looked empty, then from the back storeroom, out walked Carissa with a box. When she saw Carrie a flash of concern crossed her face.

Carrie smiled and stepped over to help her with the box, which was obviously heavy.

"Thanks," said Carissa. She was very concerned about this revisit from the cops.

"I don't know if you remember me," began Carrie.

Carissa nodded. "I remember you and that other guy, the one with the black hair. You were here to talk about that man."

"Yes. That was Randy Jeffries. This is Lainey Tate. We've come to talk with you about him again." Carrie watched to see what Carrissa's reaction would be.

With a pinched forehead and concern in her eyes, Carissa said, "That creepy man that was on the bench with me?"

"Yes. I would like to locate him. Can you remember anything else about him that might help us locate him?"

Carissa shook her head way too quickly. "No. I told you everything I knew."

"I know you did. You were very helpful, but sometimes there are things you don't realize you know at first. Can I just take a few minutes and ask you a few more questions?"

Carissa nodded. Not sure if it was the chill of the AC or the thought of that creepy man, but Carissa rubbed her bare arms and felt chill bumps.

"Do you remember anything in his shirt pocket?"

Carissa nodded. "He had one of those funny plastic pocket things in there. It had some pens in it."

"Do you remember what kind of pens; what colors they were?"

Carissa shook her head. "Wait, yes, there was one of each color, and a mechanical pencil." Her face brightened, proud that she had remembered.

"That's great Carissa! Now did he say anything at all about why he was at the park? Where he worked? Anything you can remember?"

Carrie gave Carissa a moment to think. "He said he worked at the bank across the street from the park. The one on the north side of the street on the corner. He said he works in the accounting department there."

"Carissa, thank you so much. You have been a wonderful help." Carrie felt momentum again. "I know I gave you a card last time, but take this again and if you see him again or if you need anything, will you please call me?"

Carissa nodded. "Should I be worried?"

"No. I don't think so. But please keep an eye out and be responsible when your are coming to work and leaving. If possible, have a security guard walk with you after dark to your car."

Back out in front of the Skirvin, Carrie paused. From

the back circle drive, they had a full view of Kerr Park and the 1st United Public Bank on the north side.

"What are you thinking?" asked Lainey.

"The pens could be his. Circumstantially it is probable they are his, but we need something more concrete to tie this to him. If we go in guns blazing, we could jar him loose enough to talk to us, or…"

"Or, he could jump off the deep end and run, or the stressor could cause him to kill again." Lainey knew exactly what could happen.

Carrie looked at Lainey and nodded her head. "What would you do?"

It was a test. Lainey wanted to get it right, so she quickly weighed possible scenarios in her mind. "I think I would wait. I'm as eager as you to charge in there and confront him. But I think it would serve us better to try and find out more about him before we do."

"I agree. You know, he stands out. It shouldn't be too hard to find out who he is and then do a background check on him. Let's go back to the office and do some research."

On the drive back, Lainey said, "He's a weird duck. Stuck in the 1950s. So there was a trauma of some sort that stuck him in a time warp. That doesn't just happen on its own. Something critical has happened in his life to fix him in that way."

Carrie nodded. "Yes. There is someone in his life he emulates dressed that way. That time period is seventy years ago. It couldn't be a father. He's too young."

"A grandfather, maybe?" asked Lainey.

"Maybe," said Carrie.

"Then someone has done something horrific to traumatize him to kill prostitutes. Maybe his mother was one, and he is ashamed of it."

"Could be. Then maybe her death triggered it?" said Carrie. "You know this is all supposition at this stage. But its strong supposition."

"Now, all we have to do is take it from there to reality," said Lainey, as she watched the city fly by outside her passenger window.

A serial killer. My first case at the OSBI and it's a madman, thought Lainey. *I don't know whether to be excited, or terrified.*

CHAPTER 19

Back at the office, Randy rushed up to Carrie as soon as she and Lainey came through the door.

"Rick called. They found ten underage girls at the house. Their ages were from seven to twelve."

"Did they find the man, or that waitress Jennifer Jensen?" asked Carrie.

"Not sure. Give Rick a call." Randy gave her shoulder a pat and turned to go back in his office. He felt a strong pull to go with Carrie and get involved deep into the case again. After all, it had been his case too, but he had to pull back and let them do their jobs.

As they entered the war room, Carrie was listening to her phone ring. "Yep." Came across the line.

"Rick, It's me, Carrie." She flipped her phone on speaker so Lainey could also hear.

"Got the girls out of the house. There were ten of them. Man, I want to break some necks."

"Did you find Sam?"

"No, she wasn't in there. These girls were all really young. Sam would be eighteen or so by now, right?" asked Rick.

Carrie nodded. "Yes. She would be. Did you find that man or the waitress, Jennifer?"

"No. Just got back here with all the girls. That is our next stop, to find her."

"Did you have a chance to ask the girls if any of them recognized Sam?"

"No, haven't had time yet, Carrie." Rick's voice was tired. "You just don't know what we walked into over there. I keep thinking about my own daughters and how all of those girls were someone's daughters, sisters, babies!"

Carrie's stomach lurched. This was hard on everyone, but especially Rick because he had daughters of his own. "I can't imagine how you are handling this, Rick."

"It's been hard. I just want to catch them, but we've had to bring in the Human Trafficking Task Force to take over on this one. We'll be helping them, but this is their area of expertise and they've been working on some of this for a long time.

"I'll go look for that waitress and see if I can find anything out about who that man is. I'll call you when I know something."

The phone went silent and Carrie looked at Lainey.

"Okay, Lainey, let's put our heads together and figure this thing out." They were in the war room and looking at the whiteboards.

Carrie put up a silhouette of a man and put it on the board. Underneath she wrote 1950s man. She moved all leads associated with human trafficking to the second white board. The clean slate felt fresh and ready for action.

"Thoughts?" Carrie asked Lainey.

"From what you said, and hearing from Carissa today, I'm concerned for her. If he is our killer, and we think he is, I think he may have her in his sites."

Carrie was nodding in agreement as Lainey spoke. "We could put a tail on Carissa."

"I may be out of line here, but what if we drew his attention away from Carissa?"

Carrie turned to look at Lainey straight on. Her wheels were already churning and was wondering if Lainey was on the same page as she. "Go on."

"What if, I were to dress up like a prostitute, go downtown and draw him out? I've done some undercover work before. I think if we can draw him away from Carissa and to us, then we can snare him."

"I don't know that I like that. This is your first case with the OSBI. We don't normally do undercover jobs. It's awfully risky."

"Do you have a better idea?"

Carrie hated to admit it, but it might work. "No."

"Let's get Randy and see what he thinks. I know he'll

say no, but after recent events, I don't dare move forward without his approval."

Carrie sent Randy a quick text asking him to come to the war room. She didn't have to ask twice since he was just waiting for an excuse to get involved.

"Yep. Whatcha' got?" asked Randy as he came through the door.

"Lainey this is your idea, you tell him," said Carrie.

Lainey went through the scenario she had in her mind of going downtown as an undercover prostitute. She had an idea of whom to target and would like to hang out around the underground parking garage of the bank.

They knew he drove an old Plymouth Reliant in blue. They could scout out the garage and see if they could find the car. Lainey would hang out around the car and approach the man and see what would happen.

Randy had a frown on his face. He was still temporary SAC and hated the idea of an operation this risky going on so quickly after he was in charge. So much could go wrong so quickly. And it was incredibly risky for Lainey.

"I don't like it," said Randy.

Carrie had been standing to the side and behind Lainey out of the way to let Lainey present her idea to Randy. She now moved around to face both Lainey and Randy.

Carrie only stood saying nothing when finally Randy looked at her. She knew what he was asking her with his eyes. "I think she can do it."

Randy huffed and shook his head. He rubbed his forehead and turned around. "I say we wait," said Randy.

"If we wait, something could happen to Carissa," said Carrie.

"We can tail Carissa."

Again Carrie stood quietly. Randy needed to come to this decision on his own.

"Tell me more and give me plausible scenarios and outs," said Randy.

The three of them sat at the table for the next hour and came up with a plan, options for various scenarios, and escape plans for emergencies.

They would go back down to the garage now and try to scout out the car. Then later in the day, Lainey would go down to hang out. Carrie would be in the SUV watching. They would have under cover patrolmen stationed around at various exits and routes.

As soon as Lainey had anything that could absolutely link him to the killings, she was to give the safe word and Carrie and the others would move in.

Once they had a plan, they went over it two more times and gave it their best shot to poke holes in it and come up with solutions. Finally, they felt they had covered all their bases and were ready to give it a go.

Carrie and Lainey made another trip back downtown and parked in the Kerr parking garage across the street from the bank.

"What if he doesn't park in the bank garage?" asked Lainey.

"We didn't think of that. Let's drive around this garage and see if we can see his car."

They spent the next half hour driving slowly looking carefully for any car that might resemble that man's car. They found nothing in the Kerr parking garage.

They finally parked and got out of the SUV. Behind the Kerr garage to the north was an outside parking lot. "Well crap, we didn't check that one," said Carrie.

Having already parked, they walked the outside parking area on foot. The sun was hot and high and they were soon ready to get back in the shade. A quick walk-through showed no sign of the Plymouth.

They crossed the street to the bank, and walked along the east side, which was now in the shade. Then they turned to the north side where the garage entrance was.

Carrie showed her badge to the garage attendant, and they walked on in. The garage was much larger than they had expected. It was actually three floors of parking, all underground.

It took over an hour for them to walk the garage. When they were done, they realized they had not found his car.

"Okay, so maybe he didn't come to work today?" asked Lainey.

"Maybe," replied Carrie. "What if we went into the bank to see if we can see him?"

"If he is there, he'll spot us and that will change everything," said Lainey.

They walked back out to the street and turned to go

back south along the side of the bank. Just then a metro bus pulled up at the bus stop and Carrie stopped walking.

"The bus. Maybe he rode the bus today," said Carrie.

"Maybe."

"So we can wait for him and follow the bus and find his house," said Carrie. "You can get on the bus and I'll follow behind in the SUV."

"Okay, sounds good. Let's go back and get ready," said Lainey.

Anthony Simmons was still in shock that the bank had just fired him. *After all I've done for them, how dare they?*

His supervisor had taken him into his office and had tried to explain that Anthony just wasn't meeting department expectations. Cited reasons were, his slow work pace, lack of technology experience, lack of willingness to learn, and poor interaction with co-workers.

They had asked him if he understood that the previous attempts to warn him had gone in his file as disciplinary warnings and that this was his final one, which would result in termination?

Anthony had just sat there numbly staring at him, attempting to comprehend what was really going on. How could they be firing him?

The shock had still not worn off yet as he drove down the street. The normal sights and sounds of downtown were blurry and surreal. His reactions were robotic as he stopped at red lights and moved through traffic.

Suddenly, he was jolted out of his stupor when he saw that whore cross the street in front of his car. Sheets of anger slicing through him displaced the stupor.

A horn honked behind him and startled, he raised his foot off of the brake. His mind was careening out of control, and he surrendered to it. Then he knew. He knew why he had been fired. His true mission in life was to cleanse those in need, the dirty ones.

Relief rushed over him as he welcomed a renewed sense of purpose. They had released him from the bank so he could pursue his mission full-time.

He was certain that divine providence had caused that particular woman to walk in front of him at that precise moment. It was an awakening.

He entered the small home he had shared with his mother. The proximity to downtown had made it perfect for working at the bank. He had never seen a reason to move.

During the rest of the drive home, he knew that he must develop a new system to increase his effect. He would need a way to cleanse more than one at a time. Efficiency. He needed to be more efficient to be more productive.

His heavy footfalls echoed sharply on the basement stairs. *Yes, this will do nicely*, he thought as he stopped just as the basement came into full view.

There was little in the basement. Anthony prided

himself in living simply with few possessions, but the truth was that he rarely had money to buy anything with.

While his mother was alive, he had given every penny over to her. She had needed his money when she could no longer walk the streets as a dirty whore.

He puffed his chest out at the memory. That tragic life, he now realized, was the very thing that had groomed him and brought him to his destiny. Now, he knew. Now, it was time.

The basement floor was cold, not damp, but cold. They had done the concrete floor in an era when quality mattered, so it was solid and flat with only one slight crack in the corner.

The walls were concrete blocks stacked solidly, one on of top of the other. The only light in the room other than the single bulb hanging from the center of the room, was a tiny window near the ceiling.

Back upstairs, Anthony made a list of all that he would need. He had to be quick so he could start immediately.

He had gained some carpentry and construction skills from their next-door neighbor when he was in high school and college. Another smile spread across his face as he realized that had been destiny as well.

He finished the list and headed to get what he needed. By early evening, he was done. Energy and strength flowed through him as he had worked in the basement, unlike at the bank. But then this was his purpose in life.

Now, it was time.

Carrie and Lainey were back downtown by four p.m. Not being sure what time Anthony got off work, they wanted to be early. They were positioned in the outside parking area to the east of the bank.

They had received a call from Rick and he could not find the waitress from Lawdie's. Also, there had been no fingerprints or other evidence on the ink pens. The only findings were a type of gelled hand sanitizer.

Lainey was dressed provocatively. They had both agreed that if the sundress that Carissa had worn spooked the man into believing her to be a prostitute, then Lainey only needed to dress the same.

Their goal wasn't for her to be pegged as a prostitute outright, but enough to make sure to catch his attention and set him on edge.

Lainey wasn't comfortable dressing in clothes that were so revealing. As they sat in the SUV, she pulled and tugged at them in an attempt to cover herself.

Carrie watched Lainey out of the corner of her eye. *Was it a nervous twitch or were the clothes uncomfortable,* Carrie wondered.

"Sitting here we can see if he catches the bus, or if by chance he did park in the garage, then we can see him pull out," said Carrie. "You can wait for the bus, and if he shows up, get on. Then I will follow. If he doesn't get on the bus, then we can move inside the garage."

"Good plan," said Lainey. She had a frown on her face and was focused on the bus stop, still tugging at her top.

Carrie watched for a moment and then asked, "Are you okay?"

Snapped out of her focus, Lainey looked back at Carrie and nodded. "Yes."

Carrie continued to look at Lainey. When she had answered her head had bobbed up and down unnaturally. "Are you nervous?" asked Carrie.

"Maybe a little. But I've done some undercover work before."

"You're fidgety and you're frowning. In the short day I've known you, I've never seen you frown."

Lainey let a short laugh burst forth. "Oh, I frown." Once again she was unconsciously back to tugging on the clothes.

"Are the clothes bothering you?" asked Carrie.

Looking down at her lap a minute before looking at Carrie and answering, Lainey took a deep breath.

"Yes. I'm very uncomfortable dressing like this." Her forehead was pinched as if she were afraid to tell Carrie.

Carrie studied Lainey's face for a bit. She sensed that she was about to get an answer to her next question she didn't expect, but felt compelled to ask it, anyway.

"Why do they make you so uncomfortable?"

"I don't think it's right to dress to temp men to look at you with lust. In my heart I know it's wrong."

Carrie rolled the words over in her mind. This was something very new to her. For the last eight years that is exactly how Carrie had dressed when she wasn't at work. She had wanted men to want her in a sexual way, and they had.

Lainey looked away back towards the bus stop. The silence in the SUV was loud. Lainey was thinking how she might have offended Carrie and Carrie was suddenly feeling shame about her sexual behavior.

Carrie knew Lainey had no way of knowing how Carrie lived. She did not understand that Carrie felt driven to entice men and sleep with them to fill a void deep inside. So, she knew Lainey was not directing her words at Carrie, but she still felt the weight of them.

When her parents had died, and she had pushed her fiancé, Billy, away. She still had the drive to be with a man, but without emotional entanglement. She had convinced herself she was getting the best part of a relationship, and on her terms.

She would meet up, have sex, and as soon as possible, leave. With her system, she didn't have to feel. No love, no hurt.

The problem with that plan was, she did hurt. Each year that had passed, she had entrenched herself deeper and deeper into herself, increasingly walling herself off from others. Except for her friendship with Randy, that was. She missed him now, and the thought of him brought pain.

"I hope you understand about the clothes. I don't want you to think I'm criticizing other women who do dress like this. I just don't feel comfortable about it for myself."

Carrie nodded and shot Lainey a quick smile. She liked Lainey, really liked her, who wouldn't? But she was a curiosity to Carrie. She was happy, but in a subdued sort of way that didn't push others to be happy. It was a quiet, gentle happiness, and it was pleasant to be around.

Carrie smiled back at Lainey. "No, I know you didn't."

Several more minutes passed by with no sign of the man. "Do you have a boyfriend?" Carrie asked.

"No. I don't date very much."

"Why is that?"

Carrie could see the Lainey was gauging her words and taking time to organize what she wanted to say. "I guess I have very high standards about who I see myself with forever. To me, dating a lot of different people who I know I don't want to be with gets complicated. I don't want to get someone else's hopes up and I don't want to wind up in sticky situations."

"How can you know if you want to be with someone without dating them?"

"Oh, I have tons of friends. We all do stuff together. I meet a lot of guys when I volunteer and do other things. So there hasn't been a shortage of guys around." Lainey stopped again to think.

"Don't you think that you just kind of know?" Lainey asked Carrie. Her eyes were searching Carrie's.

"You mean love at first sight kind of thing?"

Lainey shook her head. "No, not really like that. But you know how it is when you meet someone and in a few moments your gut tells you they aren't the one. I think when I meet the right one, I'll know that inside too."

Carrie reflected back to Billy. They had been young when they had met. They had both been popular in high school and had both dated quite a bit, but there was just something about Billy that stood out to Carrie. She had loved him pretty quickly and never looked back.

"I think I know what you mean," said Carrie.

"So you have met your forever love?" Lainey was suddenly excited for Carrie.

Carrie looked away out of her driver side window. Even after all this time, she still missed him; still loved him. "Yes. I guess I have."

Lainey sensed this was an uncomfortable moment for Carrie, so she sat quietly. There was a story there, but she knew it wasn't the time to ask. *Did he die, or did he leave her*, wondered Lainey.

Carrie's voice was thick when she answered. "I was engaged to be married once." She continued to look out the window with her face turned away from Lainey who was content to let her talk in her own time.

"My parents died almost nine years ago. Billy and I were planning our wedding. I was happier then than I ever remember being.

"Then one night I got the call that my parents had been in an accident. By the time I got to the hospital, they were both gone. I didn't handle it well.

"They had been my entire support system. My entire self was tied up into them, who they had encouraged me

Carrie nodded and shot Lainey a quick smile. She liked Lainey, really liked her, who wouldn't? But she was a curiosity to Carrie. She was happy, but in a subdued sort of way that didn't push others to be happy. It was a quiet, gentle happiness, and it was pleasant to be around.

Carrie smiled back at Lainey. "No, I know you didn't."

Several more minutes passed by with no sign of the man. "Do you have a boyfriend?" Carrie asked.

"No. I don't date very much."

"Why is that?"

Carrie could see the Lainey was gauging her words and taking time to organize what she wanted to say. "I guess I have very high standards about who I see myself with forever. To me, dating a lot of different people who I know I don't want to be with gets complicated. I don't want to get someone else's hopes up and I don't want to wind up in sticky situations."

"How can you know if you want to be with someone without dating them?"

"Oh, I have tons of friends. We all do stuff together. I meet a lot of guys when I volunteer and do other things. So there hasn't been a shortage of guys around." Lainey stopped again to think.

"Don't you think that you just kind of know?" Lainey asked Carrie. Her eyes were searching Carrie's.

"You mean love at first sight kind of thing?"

Lainey shook her head. "No, not really like that. But you know how it is when you meet someone and in a few moments your gut tells you they aren't the one. I think when I meet the right one, I'll know that inside too."

Carrie reflected back to Billy. They had been young when they had met. They had both been popular in high school and had both dated quite a bit, but there was just something about Billy that stood out to Carrie. She had loved him pretty quickly and never looked back.

"I think I know what you mean," said Carrie.

"So you have met your forever love?" Lainey was suddenly excited for Carrie.

Carrie looked away out of her driver side window. Even after all this time, she still missed him; still loved him. "Yes. I guess I have."

Lainey sensed this was an uncomfortable moment for Carrie, so she sat quietly. There was a story there, but she knew it wasn't the time to ask. *Did he die, or did he leave her*, wondered Lainey.

Carrie's voice was thick when she answered. "I was engaged to be married once." She continued to look out the window with her face turned away from Lainey who was content to let her talk in her own time.

"My parents died almost nine years ago. Billy and I were planning our wedding. I was happier then than I ever remember being.

"Then one night I got the call that my parents had been in an accident. By the time I got to the hospital, they were both gone. I didn't handle it well.

"They had been my entire support system. My entire self was tied up into them, who they had encouraged me to be; raised me to be. Without them I don't think I knew who I was anymore, or how to be."

"I'm so sorry Carrie." Lainey's voice was barely above a whisper.

Carrie wiped tears she couldn't prevent and shook her head to disengage from sad old memories. She turned to look at Lainey.

"That was a long time ago."

Lainey thought her heart would break. Carrie was wearing the pain in her heart like a mask on her face, for the world to see. *I want to reach out and help her pull off that mask*, thought Lainey. *I want to help her be free.*

"Carrie I don't want to pretend I know the pain you're feeling. But I do know one thing; you can recover, move on, and find happiness again. You want to know who you are? You are someone of worth.

"Your parents did a great job in raising you to be a strong woman of integrity and value. Don't dishonor the great job they did as parents by deciding you are nothing without them." Lainey stopped. It was always best to say less than more.

Lainey's words penetrated somewhere deep inside of Carrie. No one had ever spoken words that had attacked her emotional walls the way those words did.

She had worth. She mulled those words around. Her parents had thought she had worth. Why had she felt her worth had died with her parents? Not only her worth, but her will to live too.

They had fed into her life and she had relied on their

words, encouragement, and love. Without them, she felt she couldn't be worth anything anymore.

Was Lainey right? Did it dishonor the great job her parents had done by wallowing in self-pity? She knew it would break their hearts if they knew.

That thought, that one single thought, broke something inside of her. She came to realize at that moment she loved her parents enough to honor them by tearing down the walls she had built. She had to try anyway.

"Lainey."

"Yes?" Lainey looked over at Carrie unsure what was about to come.

"I need to break free of this emotional dungeon I've sentenced myself to these last eight years. Grief and anger dug the pit and then I willingly crawled down into it and slammed the top shut.

"I drink too much. I sleep around with men. I've convinced myself that if I kept my distance emotionally from people, then I wouldn't have to feel pain like that ever again. But it doesn't work, so I drink."

Lainey sat quietly and reached her hand out to cover the hand that Carrie rested on the center console. "It's okay. We all hurt. But we have to learn to navigate it.

"We can't park there and build a house there. We have to keep moving and put it in our rearview mirror as quickly as possible. The only way to do that is to acknowledge it, accept it, and move forward.

"We have to let God heal our wounds so we can move forward and heal and love again." When Lainey mentioned the word God, Carrie slid her hand out from under Lainey's.

God was a lofty concept that was a faint idea to Carrie. She had not gone to church growing up. Well, a couple of times for certain things with friends. But she didn't know anything about God.

With all the surrounding pain she questioned just how powerful this God really was.

Lainey pulled her hand back and sat quietly again watching the bus stop. "I was raped when I was only fourteen."

Carrie's head jerked around to look at Lainey. Thoughts like rockets shot through her head. *But, she's so happy. She doesn't act like someone who was raped. How can she be so happy?*

"I know what it is like to feel pain. I know what it is like to hurt deeply. I know what it is like to be filled with white hot rage and murderous anger. I know what it's like to want to crawl in a hole that self-pity dug. I know Carrie."

Lainey turned to look at Carrie. "It was only by talking to God about it. Yelling at God about it, then working my way through it with Him, that I was able to heal. It was His love that brought me out and helped me to love and be happy again.

"You're probably wondering if God is such a loving God, why is there so much pain in the world, why doesn't He protect us? I hear that all the time. Well, we can either have a free-will to choose, or we can be robots.

"Let me ask you Carrie, would you rather have a stuffed puppy who sits only on your shelf doing nothing bad, but never able to do anything good either? You can hug them and touch them, and they offer a small measure of comfort, but they're powerless to reciprocate your love.

"Or would you rather have a real puppy who bounces in exuberance when you walk through the door happy to see you, and licks your face until it's raw, even though they poop, pee, and chew up your favorite shoes?

"God wants us free. If we choose to use our freedom to do bad things, then He must allow that because you can't have it both ways. But there is so much He does stop. We just don't realize it because we can't see what He has prevented."

Then Lainey looked back at the bus stop. "He isn't coming. It's six o'clock, the bus has run, and there has been no sign of him out of the garage."

"What now?" asked Carrie.

"I guess it's time for me to walk the street." Lainey looked at Carrie and grinned.

LAINEY GOT out of the SUV and walked over to Kerr Park. She sat on a bench that faced North Broadway. She could see the Skirvin to the east and the bank to the north.

Carrie had also gotten out of the car. She had chosen to wear a tank top and shorts rather than her navy blue OSBI polo shirt. Today it was all about blending in.

CHAPTER 19 | 355

About ten minutes after Lainey took her seat on the bench, Carrie casually walked into the park with her iPad and sat on the other bench. She wore her cap and sunglasses which would allow her to look around with no one noticing.

She glanced out of the corner of her eye towards Lainey, who was playing the part. She had a tight tank top on with spaghetti straps. Its unique design had a v-neck that dipped low, then had three buttons at the point of the V which could be opened below that. All three were unbuttoned and with her arm stretched out across the back of the bench, the extent of Lainey's endowment was not in question.

She wore a short denim skirt that slid so far up when she sat down and crossed her legs, that Carrie realized Lainey must be wearing g-string underwear. She thought about just how uncomfortable Lainey must feel right then.

It was Thursday and past quitting time for most people downtown. People hurried through the park on their way to their cars or hotels.

Some small groups of two or three chatted and talked about getting a drink or going to dinner. No one wanted to stop in the park. The enduring August heat contributed to that.

Lainey and Carrie sat on their perspective benches, roasting in the sun for at least forty-five minutes. Lainey's fair skin, which normally looked lovely against her dark hair, was now bright red.

I've got to get her out of the sun, thought Carrie. She sent Lainey a text saying as much.

The phone Lainey had stashed in her small purse, produced a muffled ding. She casually pulled it out and read Carrie's text. Lainey recrossed her legs the other way and responded.

Carrie got up first and walked north towards the parking lot where they had left the SUV. Soon after, Lainey got up and walked south on Broadway. The shade of the building was a welcome relief.

At the corner of Park Avenue, she turned west and stood looking in the windows of BC Clark Jewelers, an Oklahoma icon since long before Lainey was born.

Out of the corner of her eye, she saw Carrie drive past on Broadway going south. After giving the beautiful jewelry in the window adequate review time, Lainey casually turned and walked east on Park towards the Santa Fe parking garage, just to the east of the Skirvin.

Another text from Carrie indicated that she was on the second floor of that garage, on the west side. Lainey found her and crawled into the SUV.

When Carrie saw Lainey she had to chuckle. "My goodness you look like something the cat drug up! Here, drink this water and cool off."

Lainey felt like something the cat had drug up. Walking in the heat after sitting in the hot sun for so long had drained her. She pulled out an old t-shirt from the backpack she had stowed in the SUV, and wiped her face, then reapplied sunscreen.

Once she had finished the bottle of water and combed her sweat laden hair, she felt like a new woman.

"What now?" asked Lainey.

Carrie shook her head thinking. "Are we spinning our wheels out here? Our plan was to get the guy coming from the bank. Without that I didn't have a plan. What do you think?"

"It's too early to be out walking the streets. If we wait until dark at least, then I can go out and strut my stuff some more." Lainey was grinning at Carrie.

"Well, I have to give it to you. You sure know how to strut it even if it makes you feel uncomfortable."

"Let's go get dinner and come back," said Carrie as she shoved the SUV into gear.

Lainey threw the t-shirt on over her tank top and replaced the skirt with a pair of shorts. With a heavy note of sarcasm Lainey said, "Lookin' forward to it."

CHAPTER 20

Anthony saw that woman was working late at the gift shop. He still didn't understand how she could work both jobs. And why would the Skirvin want to hire someone like her, anyway?

He had parked on the lower level of the Santa Fe garage as close to the Skirvin as possible. He had watched her the other day and saw the exit she liked to take and where she had parked then.

At precisely ten-fifteen, the girl left the Skirvin and headed towards the garage. Her head was down as she dug in her purse for her keys. When she stepped into the shadow, a hand came from behind and smothered her face with a damp rag.

The ether worked quickly, and soon she was a limp rag in Anthony's arms. She had another wispy thin dress on and he was trying to move her body to his car without touching her bare skin in those places.

Finally, he had her in the back seat and was headed to his house. Excitement surged through him. He had grown sweaty trying to get her into the car and sweat dripped from the curl on his forehead. The heat had dissolved the Brillcream and his hair was hanging limply now. Fortunately, the garage was only a few blocks away and in less than five minutes he was back home.

Carissa was coming to when Anthony opened the car door. Just as her eyes grew wide, his hand shot out to once again cover her mouth. She struggled this time, and he had to endure her flailing arms to push the rag over her mouth.

Quickly, she went limp again. Tired of this mission already, he scooped her up and carried her to the house. Feeling her smooth legs draped over his arms was causing him an erection which rather irritated him.

The instant he had her in the basement he dropped her on the concrete floor and began to beat his head against the block wall. He couldn't allow this! He couldn't be like all those men who had bought his mother.

The beating did the trick. Even though it left his head scraped and bruised, it had served its purpose. He was once again able to control his thoughts.

He grabbed Carissa's wrists and put each wrist in one end of a pair of handcuffs. He then took the other end and clamped it into the end of a chain he had hanging from the ceiling. Once both wrists were cuffed and attached to their individual chains, Anthony stepped back. The duct tape he had placed across her mouth would keep her quiet while he was gone.

Carrissa was hanging with her head slumped forward. *She won't be going anywhere while I go get more dirty whores,* thought Anthony. Once he had decided to make quick work of his new mission, he devised a plan to gather as many whores as he could, and contain them in the basement. Then he would cleanse them all at once.

He smiled as he drove the short trip back to the center of downtown. His plan was genius and living so close to the target area was perfect.

This time, he pulled into a parking spot alongside Sheridan Avenue just to the south of the Sheraton Hotel and parked. There were no events that night, and it was fortuitous that he had found street parking.

He was heady with elation. Soon, he spotted another. *Yes! I will help her. I will help her get clean too!*

CARRIE AND LAINEY had taken their time eating. Nothing nefarious would happen until after dark and with the summer days lasting until nine-thirty, they knew they had time.

They were becoming more comfortable with each other and after the revelation Carrie had experienced earlier in the day from Lainey's poignant words, she was eager to learn more about her and how she had overcome such a tragedy. Maybe it would work for her as well.

Their talk was light-hearted, and they chatted about the guys at the agency, and about the crazy things they had experienced in their law enforcement careers. Carrie wasn't sure, but she thought she felt a little lighter when they drove back downtown. The laughter and comaraderie had done her good.

"Where to?" asked Carrie.

"You said all three of the girls worked this downtown area, but it seems they worked mostly around the hotels and convention centers. What do you think about going to somewhere on Broadway where the Renaissance and the Sheraton are?"

"Sounds good," responded Carrie.

"I want to park somewhere that I can easily pull out should I need to follow you."

Carrie let Lainey out in front of the Cox Center and circled the downtown streets several times. Finally, thirty minutes later, she was able to find a parking spot on the street, just south of the Renaissance Hotel facing west.

Lainey had texted that she had walked up Broadway on the east side of the street and then back down on the west side. She had finally found a short brick retaining wall on the southeast corner of the Sheraton hotel and was sitting on it.

From there, Lainey was visible to anyone at either hotel and those coming out of the north entrance of the

Cox center. She had once again assumed a lurid pose and waited.

From where Carrie had parked, she could easily see Lainey. There were only four cars parallel parked in front of her along the curb. She wasn't as close as she would have liked, but then she didn't want to be seen either.

The AC felt cool and after the meal, she was having to resist feeling sleepy. She repositioned herself and even opened her window to hear the street noise, but then quickly closed it again because of the heat.

They had advised patrolmen of their operation. They couldn't devote additional manpower to focus solely on an operation that was as iffy as this one, but they knew to be on alert should Carrie radio in. And after the other day, she would radio in before she took a breath.

Lainey was getting stiff sitting so long in an unnatural position, so she stood and walked back and forth. She turned the corner and walked west along Sheridan still where Carrie could easily see her.

Suddenly, before Carrie could respond, her passenger door flew open and electric shock jolted her body convulsively. Two electrodes protruded from her chest.

Almost as quickly as she had felt the pain and her body went rigid, a large man with dark hair slid into the passenger seat next to her. He reached over, took her gun and tossed it into the backseat.

Then, just as suddenly, a girl jumped into the backseat, picked up her gun and pointed it on her. The man retrieved the electrodes, and the girl jabbed the gun into her ribs.

"Drive!" barked the man.

"Where to?" asked Carrie.

The girl jabbed the gun deeper into her ribs. "Just drive," he said.

Carrie put the SUV in gear and pulled out into the street. It was around midnight and with no events, there was little traffic. She turned to watch for Lainey as she passed the area where she had last seen her.

Panic seized her as she noticed the blue Plymouth and Lainey talking to the man. Engaged in conversation, Lainey never saw Carrie pass by in the SUV.

Lainey was expecting Carrie to be watching her, but with her own gun jammed into her ribs and her phone displaced into the passenger floorboard, what could she do?

Carrie could hold her own in a fight, but now it was two against one. The man had reset and readied the taser and had it once again pointed at her. The girl had her gun firmly on her. If she could take out one, the other would surely fire.

"Who are you and what do you want?" asked Carrie.

"Just drive."

About three blocks ahead, he instructed Carrie to pull over to the right, alongside the street. The girl gave the gun to the man, shoved a dark pillow case over Carrie's head, and jumped out.

She quickly jerked Carrie's door open and slapped a

handcuff on her left wrist. The man shoved Carrie forward against the steering wheel, and the girl swiftly pushed the cuff across Carrie's back. The man grabbed Carrie's right wrist and slapped on the cuff.

The man then came around, pulled Carrie out of the front and shoved her into the backseat face down. Then he seated himself in the driver's seat, and the girl got in the front passenger seat. It all happened so quickly and efficiently that Carrie was convinced this couple had made many abductions just like this one, or similar.

The area where she had stopped the car was a run down commercial district. Many business still operated in the area during the day, but at night there was no one around.

Carrie was trying to feel the movement of the car to determine the direction and distance between turns they were taking. But at one sharp right turn, she was slung to the floorboard. By the time she had recovered, she had lost track.

She knew however that they hadn't gotten far when the man pulled the car over and stopped. It was pitch dark out. It was a moonless night, and they were in an area with almost no lamps or artificial light.

It had all happened so fast that all Carrie could tell about the man was that he was large and had dark or black hair.

The girl was small and had stringy long blonde hair, but she could not determine exact facial features or eye color.

The man turned around and faced the backseat. "Now, what I want to know, is why you're looking for me?" he asked.

Carrie's mind accelerated to attempt to determine which man this could be. Suddenly she realized, the man had to be the man in the sketch. And the girl with long stringy blonde hair. *Could that be Sam?* Carrie wondered.

"I'm looking for a girl named Sam, Samantha Anderson. We thought you might know where she was and if you could help us find her." Carrie was hoping to elicit a response from the girl. With her head covered, she couldn't see the expressions on their faces.

In the front seat, the man and girl looked at each other for a long moment. "Why do you want to know?" he asked.

"We are concerned about her. Her parents miss her." Then Carrie realized that Sam had probably not heard about her sister Cami. *Should I tell her now? Would that be cruel*, wondered Carrie?

"No one ever seemed to care before. Why are you looking for her all of a sudden?"

"Her sister Cami is dead."

A huff of air and a freakish squeak as if someone had punched the girl squarely in the stomach, flew out. "No!" she screamed as she doubled over, gripping her hair with two fists and banging her head on the console. Wails of agony continued.

The man grabbed the back of her hair at the nape of her neck and jerked her head up. Once upright, he back-handed her face with the hand that held the taser. "Shut up!"

The girl's head snapped and then hung limply from the man's grip. Tears, mixed with snot ran in rivers down her red splotched face. Her eyes were dark and hollow. "You, don't speak again. You hear me, you dirty whore."

The girl remained silent. *What else can he do to me*, she wondered. Then the man slung her head backwards toward the passenger side window and let go. She hit the window with a thud, then slumped into the seat, wishing for death.

"You need to stop looking for me," he once again addressed Carrie.

Carrie's mind was searching for some way out of this. She had lost her gun. Being in shorts and a tank top for undercover work left few places to conceal a weapon, but she had a knife.

These particular shorts had an inside pocket at the waistband where she kept a small retractible knife. In her current position, though, it was of little use to her.

"I'm just looking for Sam. They told me you were the last person to see her. I just wanted to question you. We were looking for the man who killed Cami and thought that person might have Sam too."

In the front passenger seat, the despondency that had invaded and consumed Sam over the past two years, was rapidly turning into a rage.

This man had manipulated and controlled her. Had he killed Cami too? The more Sam thought about it, the angrier she became. The pain she felt just now, receded as splinters of light flashed in her mind. Her breathing was growing jagged and as if launched out of a rocket, she came off of the seat and aimed the gun she still held, squarely at the man.

Before the man had time to think, Sam was unloading the clip into the man's chest. She didn't stop until all that was heard was *click, click, click*.

Carrie was writhing in the backseat at the sound of the first gunshot, trying to turn over and right herself. Once awkwardly up on her knees, she scooted up onto the seat. She bent forward and grasp the top of the pillowcase between her knees and pulled it off.

There before her was Sam holding her empty gun, still pulling the trigger. The man was slumped back against her driver side door with blood dripping from the splatters on the ceiling of the SUV.

"Sam," said Carrie. "Sam."

Finally, Sam slowly turned her head toward Carrie. She held a blank stare as if looking, but not really seeing.

"Sam, I need to get these cuffs off. Can you give me the key?" asked Carrie. "Sam?"

Carrie knew Sam was in shock. She may be drugged too, but she needed to get the cuffs off. She needed to call this in and get back to Lainey.

Finally, Sam seemed to notice her surroundings and looked around as if for the first time. She reached over and dug in the man's pockets and found the key and unlocked the cuffs.

Sam didn't notice as Carrie reached over and gently removed the gun from her hand. Sam's face was turned down, focused on something unseen. She released the gun to Carrie.

As soon as Carrie had secured her weapon, she reached across the front seat and down into the floorboard. She grabbed her phone and dialed 911 to report her situation, then immediately afterward called Lainey.

The phone rang and rang. The hair on the back of Carrie's neck stood on end. *No, this can't happen. She has to be okay*, thought Carrie as she redialed Lainey's phone. Again, the only response was Lainey's voicemail.

Suddenly panicked, she had to respond. She got Sam out of the front seat and shut the doors. They stood next to the SUV waiting for OKCPD.

Sam was a skeleton and had aged considerably from the picture that Carrie had been carrying around. Her hair was long and stringy, and unkept. Her face was gaunt and her eyes were ringed with sunken dark circles.

She stood limp next to Carrie on the gravel lot, her head hanging down as she appeared too tired to hold it up. She had not spoken a word since she had screamed in rage at the man.

Carrie reached out and put her arm around Sam and pulled her close. Compassion for this young woman consumed her and broke her heart.

She felt sorrow, which gave her pause. She had been sad for Pride, and Jenny. She had felt a measure of pain and regret, but she realized now that formidable emotional wall she had surrounded herself with had suppressed it.

Earlier, when talking to Lainey, she had felt that wall begin to crumble. Now she could feel the raw emotion of sorrow and compassion for Sam, and it hurt so good.

Tears rained down Carrie's cheeks and she thought she might just be on the path to emotional recovery.

"Sam, it will be okay," Carrie said as she hugged Sam tighter while wiping her own eyes.

LAINEY HAD SEEN the man approach her as she stood on the south side of the Sheraton hotel along Sheridan avenue. He'd pulled the blue Plymouth up next to the curb and got out.

Confident that Carrie was watching, she engaged with the man. He stood rigid and jutted his chin up in a superior manner.

"Can I help you with something honey?" Lainey drawled. She reached up and brushed his cheek with her palm and felt the tension ripple through his body.

"Yes, I think you can." He stepped back and opened the door to the Plymouth. "Please come with me."

Hesitation gripped Lainey's heart as she began to get into the car, but with a quick glance back in the direction where Carrie had been parked, she got in.

"Where are we going?" Lainey asked.

"I have a special place," Anthony replied.

Lainey settled into the car, and in just a few brief turns, they were pulling into the dirt trodden drive of a ramshackle old house, a stone's throw from downtown.

As Lainey exited the car, she noticed the neighborhood consisted mostly of small boarded-up and abandoned houses. They had shot out the street lights and there was no light coming from the house where they were.

Before she knew it, his hand was over her nose and mouth and the darkness became even darker.

Soon, pain surged through Lainey's wrists and ejected her from her stupor. As she looked around, she realized she was in a basement with a concrete floor and block walls.

From the two by six first floor joists, were chains which had been bolted in and fixed with nuts. At the end of each chain were handcuffs.

To her left was a young woman, Carissa she realized, hanging from a set of chains. She had a large swath of silver duct tape firmly across her mouth as did Lainey.

To her right, was another young woman that Lainey didn't recognize. The man had the three of them anchored by chains in the basement. This realization shot adrenalin through Lainey.

Her mind began to frantically search for solutions. *Carrie had followed her, right? Carrie would be here soon. Soon? How long have I been down here?*

The man had blown up and was filling, a small swimming pool in the center of the room near the foot of the stairs. Across the room there was a set of shelves over the space where a washing machine had once been. There was a green garden hose snaking from the water valve.

"There now," the man said as the water reached the top. "That will do."

He walked to the other side of the basement to turn off the water. The valve was leaking and that end of the basement floor was covered in a thin layer of water.

As he turned around, Lainey saw the pleasure on his face. He looked up at her and smiled. "You're awake, I see." He stood about four feet away from Lainey with his hands resting on his hips, smiling up at her.

Lainey struggled against the chains, but her feet barely touched the floor and she had no way to extract herself from the grip of the handcuffs. So, the result of her struggle was only a meager wobble of her body at the end of the chains.

"There now. It will all be okay soon. We'll get you all nice and clean and everything will be all better. Now then, who wants to go first?"

Lainey thought someone had sucked the air out of her lungs by mechanical means. It was fierce and overwhelming. All three girls struggled against their chains to no avail.

"There now. There's no need to worry. You will feel so much better once you are good and clean. You must be washed, you know? You must become clean."

The man walked over to the girl on Lainey's right. "We'll start with you. I like to do things in an orderly fashion. You're first."

He turned to get a stepladder he had nearby, and once up high enough to reach the cuffs, the woman kicked with all her might and the ladder toppled to the concrete floor.

The man was thrown to the floor, tangled in the rungs. Stunned, he sat for a moment to regain his senses. Anger was visible on his face, but his voice belied what was clearly evident.

"Now then, that was unnecessary." He proceeded to untangle himself from the stepladder. When he had, he turned towards the back of the basement and retrieved a dark brown bottle and rag.

As he approached the woman, her eyes grew round, and she kicked and attempted to scream behind the duct tape. The man sat the bottle down just out of her kicking range and picked up a whip that had been lying to the side of the room.

He approached and whipped the woman's pumping legs, leaving deep red whelps. Her muffled screams soon turned to sobs, and she became still.

"Don't fight me. This is for your own good. You don't want to be dirty, do you?" he crooned.

When the woman's legs finally ceased their fight, he picked up the bottle and rag and continued to move towards the girl.

Lainey decided that she wouldn't let him hurt these women even if it meant suffering the whip. Just as the man reached them, Lainey twisted to the side and thrust both legs out with all her might towards the man, kicking him backwards.

Her force was on target and caused the man to stumble backwards and toss the bottle behind him. The moment of impact was announced with a loud shattering sound and liquid being dispersed throughout the room among slivers of glass.

As the bottle hit the floor on the far side of the basement, it burst temporarily into flames, the water on the floor quickly extinguishing it.

The man donned a gasmask that had also been sitting on the shelf and then grabbed the water hose. He flooded the area where the ether had ignited.

The man could no longer hide his anger, throwing down the water hose. He stormed towards Lainey who continued to kick with both legs. The success of her boldness empowered the other two with confidence to fight back. Soon the man was suffering an onslaught of kicking from every direction.

He ducked his head and raised his arms to shield himself, but the women were relentless. Backing away, he dropped his arms and glared up at the women.

"You don't want to be clean? You want to be dirty whores? Then so be it! You will suffer." His voice had changed, and it sent chills up Lainey's spine.

As he turned to leave the basement, Lainey felt the first effects of the shattered bottle as the fumes filled the room and wafted upwards. Soon, they were all once again asleep.

Anthony slung the gass mask off once upstairs. He was furious at the women and paced the floor. *How could they not see what he was doing for them? Why did they not want to become clean? He was trying to help them.*

Soon Anthony calmed down and returned to the basement. He was feeling disappointed. He had wanted to help these women, but they were just like Mother. She had left him alone every night to go sell herself to men.

When Anthony looked at her, he felt the shame of being her son. He had driven himself to attempt perfection, to be a model son and then grow to be what he thought was a model man.

They hadn't been able to afford cable TV, so Anthony had watched hours of reruns from a long-ago era. He remembered yearning to have the home life that Leave It To Beaver provided. A perfect home, a perfect mother, and good boys.

He would watch endless shows just the same, Father Knows Best, My Three Sons, and others. He couldn't bear to watch contemporary shows where the children were disrespectful, and the parents were flawed. That wasn't the life he wanted.

So, as Anthony had grown, he had done his best to emulate the men on those TV shows. He dressed like them, attempted to think and talk like them. But, he never fit in. He was meant for an era long past.

Now, all he felt was the disappointment. He had once again failed at his mission. He had had high hopes earlier in the day, but had failed again.

He didn't want to live anymore. No one appreciated his work. He stood looking at the three women now hanging limp and asleep. He would just dispose of them and then he would dispose of himself.

The ether fumes were not affecting him since he had put the gas mask back on before re-entering the basement. He went to the first woman and removed her cuffs. Her body slumped into his arms and he carried her to the waiting pool and laid her head into it.

As her head drifted to the bottom, bubbles rose and then, there were no more. He pulled her out, laid her aside, and turned to get the next one. The one with fire and courage would be next, and he reached up to undo the cuffs which held Lainey.

CARRIE WAS STANDING with Sam as she heard, then saw the blue Plymouth approach. It was traveling slowly on the side street next to the lot where they stood.

Indecision slammed Carrie. She needed to run after the car, but she couldn't leave Sam until a patrolmen came. Making a quick decision she said to Sam, "Sam, stay right here. I'll be right back." Carrie watched to see affirmation in Sam's eyes, then took off running towards the street where the car had passed.

She cursed the darkness, but finally the car passed under a streetlight and she was able to get the tag. She committed it to memory and ran back to Sam.

She had pressed Randy's name to quick dial on her phone, and soon he was on the line. At the risk of being incoherent, Carrie babbled out as quickly as possible her situation.

They needed to run a scan on the license plate and try to find that man as quickly as possible. Just as she was hanging up the phone, red and blue lights bathed the darkness.

Sam stood still just as Carrie had left her, not moving an inch. *What had that man done to her*, Carrie wondered.

She gave the patrolmen a quick synopsis of what had happened and the dilemma she was in. Her SUV was now a crime scene, and she needed to find Lainey before it was too late.

Gerald had been the OSBI agent on call should Carrie and Lainey need him. He was there almost simultaneously with the first patrol car.

As soon as she had done all she could do, she and Gerald jumped into his SUV and were driving down the street where Carrie had seen the Plymouth.

"You know by now he could be anywhere," said Gerald.

"I know. But no one would be on this street if they didn't live here. No one who doesn't have to, drives on these streets in the daytime, much less at night."

Gerald nodded. Carrie was right. No one wanted to be around here, ever. For the next several minutes they methodically worked their way back and forth combing each street within a half mile of where she had seen him.

Carrie looked down at her phone to see Randy calling. "Yes?"

"I've got an address!" exclaimed Randy. "I'm texting it over to you now." I'll send patrolmen as well.

They were only one block from the house. It relieved Carrie as they pulled up in front of the house. The house and surroundings were completely dark both inside and out.

Gerald snapped a full clip into his gun after handing Carrie his backup weapon. They stepped out of the car and shut the doors gently in order to keep from alerting the killer.

"Is anyone here?" asked Gerald.

"The car is here."

They tried the front door, and it was locked tight. They walked around and tried the backdoor which was also locked. Then Carrie noticed a faint glow on the lawn on the west side of the house. She walked around and saw the small window to the basement.

The window was about nine by twelve inches. She got down on the ground to peer into the window. It was grimy and difficult to see through.

Finally, her eyes were able to distinguish movement. She saw a woman hanging from the ceiling, limp and lifeless. Then she twisted around to see what was at the other end of the basement and what she saw caught her breath. The man was laying Lainey, limp and lifeless into a pool of water.

She took the butt of her gun and slammed it against the glass. But as it shattered, she realized she could not get through the small opening.

"Gerald go, now. Bust the door down." Carrie yelled. Gerald responded and as she was picking herself up off the ground she saw the man who was laying Lainey in the water, turn and simply look at the window.

Carrie was only two steps behind Gerald as he burst through the backdoor. They found the door to the basement which was locked with a deadbolt from the inside. This door was a thick solid wood door and would not be easy to break through.

Being a large man with a muscular build, Gerald rammed his body against the door four times before there was any sign of weakening.

He then stepped back and with one solid kick, punched a large enough hole through the door so they could crawl through.

As they rushed down the stairs, they saw Lainey laying with her head below water and the man smiling up at them. To the side of the pool lay another woman, limp and lifeless.

They ran to Lainey and pulled her from the water as the man reached down, picked up a large glass shard from the broken bottle and slid it across his throat.

As Carrie pumped Lainey's chest, Gerald called for an ambulance and worked on the other woman. He soon realized that she was gone, and worked to help Carrie with Lainey.

"No Lainey! Wake up. Don't do this to me!" Carrie was feeling intense fear of losing someone unlike any fear she had felt in a long time.

As she pumped Lainey's chest she cried, and she prayed. "God please don't let her die! Please stop this horrible thing. Please God!"

Suddenly, there was a cough and a sputter and water came gushing out from Lainey's lungs. They rolled her over and helped the water to pour out.

Carrie then sat back and wept for joy, relief flooded her. Gerald laid Lainey back on the concrete floor and moved to check on the man who now lay dead in a pool of his own blood.

Lainey's eyes were closed and her face was pale. Then, hearing Carrie's sobs, Lainey reached out and clasp Carrie's hand.

"God is good," said Lainey softly, and smiled.

He went to Carissa and quickly took her down, working to revive her. As she was coming to she looked into the face of a handsome man with dark golden skin.

"Am I dead?" she asked Gerald.

He smiled. "No, you're not dead. You are very much alive."

CHAPTER 21

Friday morning Carrie was once again exhausted. They had kept Lainey overnight at the hospital for observation. Carrie had stayed with her for a while, but then knew Lainey needed rest as much as she did, so she had come home.

After sleeping for several hours, she woke feeling peaceful for the first time in over eight years. She was feeling again. Yes, there was acute pain, terror at almost losing Lainey, but the joy she had felt at seeing Lainey take a breath was worth the pain.

She replayed the memory of finding Lainey, thinking she was dead and the sheer panic she had felt. Then how Lainey had smiled at her and said, "God is good."

Carrie laid there dwelling on that comment. She had never known God, so she couldn't really pass judgement on whether He was good or bad. But last night, when He had rescued Lainey, she knew He was good — very good.

Had He answered her cries out to Him, desperate to save Lainey, or had He just saved Lainey on His own? She didn't know. But she knew she wanted to experience the peace she knew Lainey felt. She had begun to, and she wanted it to continue.

She finally got up, stretched and decided to shower. As she passed her dresser mirror, she realized she had a smile on her face, and it caught her off guard. The reflection was foreign to her, and she laughed to herself.

Standing there, she remembered the envelope that was resting, waiting in the drawer in front of her.

She gently slid open the drawer and reached back for the letter. The weightiness suggested several pages. She had felt, maybe known, it was a letter to her from Pride. Even in her numbed state, it had hurt too much to think about, so she had shoved it to the back of the drawer, to the back of her mind.

But, now she wanted to read it. She took the envelope and made her way to the sofa and curled up under the soft quilt she had laid there.

The paper crinkled as she opened it, and she felt it ripple through her entire body. Three or more sheets of lined yellow paper from a notepad carried blue ink in a deliberate handwriting.

Dear Agent Border…

OVER AN HOUR LATER, Carrie carefully folded the yellow pages back into their original position. Her mind was calm. Peace seemed to have settled on her like a thick blanket.

She thought about how Pride had talked of her life and how she had almost died before realizing her desperate need for change.

She had gone to church growing up, but couldn't bear the thought of going back into a judgemental institution, only to be criticised for her lifestyle. Even though she had had a desire to change, she didn't think they would understand.

One day at her lowest point, she noticed her mother's bible on a shelf in her room, took it down, and began to read. She hadn't stopped reading it for the last forty years.

What Pride knew, had learned, was that change can't come from sheer force of will and determination, but from just resting in Father God. The more she had just trusted Him and rested in Him, the changes had just came.

Her desires had changed, so she had automatically changed her life because of those different desires. Some things had challenged her, but she felt an ability to make better choices than she had ever had before.

Finally, after many years, she had found a church that didn't care what her past or present situation was. They had loved her and welcomed her, so she had eventually gone back to church.

But, she had spent many years at home just reading her bible and praying. She knew that it wasn't about a building, or an institution, but about relationship. She had learned that God loved her and He just wanted her to let Him love her. *Carrie, He wants us to let Him love us.*

Carrie sat and pondered those words. *Let Him love us... Let Him... Let...* The thought of how she had built up walls to completely shut everything and everyone out, came to her mind.

She had shut Billy out when he had wanted to love her and she had shut out friendships and co-workers. She had only allowed people into her life she could easily toss aside once she was done with them.

Shame overwhelmed her. She felt like a despicable person. She felt dirty and mean.

Pride had felt dirty, too. Carrie thought about Pride sharing how dirty she had felt when she began to be disgusted by her lifestyle. She described how shame and guilt had overwhelmed her, often to the point where she had entertained the thought of taking her own life.

It was at those low points she would feel God wooing her and comforting her. Then she would pick up her bible and read how that yes, He did indeed love her.

Pride had written how the bible said even Jesus himself had a prostitute in His family lineage. Then, when the men of the city threw a woman caught in adultery in front of Jesus, and had demanded He charge her with sexual sin, He had just written, no one knows what, in the sand until they all left. He did not condemn her. He responded to her with love and compassion.

Carrie closed her eyes. "God, I have no idea how to

pray. I don't even know if You can make me clean. But Pride says you can; not only can, but want to.

"I can't stop doing the things I know I shouldn't do. Even though I don't want to do them anymore, I can't stop. So if you are going to demand I do things I can't do, then I'm going to tell you right now, I can't. I've tried.

"Pride says all I have to do is trust You. I haven't trusted anyone in so long I don't think I even know how. I don't know what to do except say, I want to try to trust you."

Suddenly Carrie's heart cracked wide open. She doubled over in body wracking sobs. Out poured years of pent up pain and emotion. Feelings and hurts she had stuffed so far down, she had forgotten they existed purged out through her tears.

Then, almost just as suddenly as it came, it was done. The tears stopped, the surge of rushing emotions subsided. It was all gone.

Carrie sat with her head on her knees completely still, totally at peace. *I feel… what? I feel… clean*! She raised her head and laughed out loud. *How could this be? This is nonsense. But I feel relief no, I feel joy!*

She sat very still for a moment as if afraid that making the wrong move would cause it to all dissipate as though it were a thin vapor. But it felt solid and substantial. It didn't feel fleeting and fragile.

I see you Carrie. I've always seen you. My love for you is real.

Carrie's eyes widened. *Did I imagine that,* she

wondered. Did she just hear God speak to her heart, her mind?

She sat still a while longer waiting to see if she would hear more. But there was only silence, and peace. She smiled, curled up under her quilt and snuggled in for a nap. She slept soundly for the first time since her youth.

CHAPTER 22

The following weeks after finding the killer, details continued to emerge. Anthony Simmons had been an only child who never knew his father.

His mother had been a prostitute, and he assumed that his biological father had been someone who had paid her to have sex with them.

He had lost himself in a world of the past, old television movies and shows where things were simpler, more innocent. At school, he had isolated himself from the other classmates. He didn't know how to explain what his mother did, so he avoided situations where he would be forced to do so.

Instead of social activities, he focussed on school work. He loved math and had gone to college on scholarships. His major had been accounting. The rigidness of the numbers had attracted Anthony. If everything was in its place, then the equation would be solved.

But being stuck in the past hadn't worked well for Anthony once he had entered the workforce. He still lived at home with his now aging mother.

Never having learned how to socialize, he only spent time at home with the mother he resented. The shame of who his mother was overwhelmed him. He saw her as dirty, and therefore he was dirty. He had hoped by helping clean the girls, it would help him to feel clean as well.

Lainey recovered quickly and was back at work in fine form. The day that both she and Carrie returned to work, Randy looked up from his desk to see two smiling faces before him. What, two?

He looked from one to the other in confusion. What's wrong with Carrie? Or maybe he should say, what's right with her?

He laughed. "I see you two are pleased this case is closed."

"We are," said Carrie.

"You did well. I know it was a close call there, but you were both professional and all's well that ends well, right?"

They nodded and sat down. Randy went on to explain that Sam was emotionally tapped. She would recover quickly physically, but it would take some time to recover emotionally.

Beth had taken her, Maggie, and a few of the other

girls from the raid on Tiny's house into Safe At Last. They were currently at capacity but another safe home in town was able to take the remainder.

Counselors had committed to volunteering additional time to these girls in order to help them deal with the trauma they had suffered. That life had become their normal, so it would be challenging to reverse and heal the damage.

Since Tiny had been more or less caught in the act, he was singing to the feds who were working with the human trafficking task force to build a case against Alexander Volkov. They would need many more pieces to the puzzle before they would have a solid case against him, but it encouraged them to have Tiny's testimony.

The man from the sketch, Hugh Bennett, had indeed been the caretaker of the amusement park, which is where he had met the girls. He had casually befriended them, recruiting their help to dismantle and clean up the park.

The day of Sam's disappearance, he had come by asking for help. Cami had plans with friends later in the day, so Sam had gone alone. He had kept Sam and through time, brainwashed her into thinking she deserved him and what he did to her.

Cami hadn't left that day, but when Sam didn't return and her parents had seemed so indifferent about it all, she had left home too.

With no high school education, she had wound up working on the street and was soon caught in Gus' web. The only fortunate thing was that she had wound up with

Pride who had cared for her and watched over her the best she could.

"I'm overwhelmed at the number of girls we came in contact with whom are caught up in this net of prostitution and human trafficking," said Carrie.

Randy nodded. "I know, and we have only uncovered a small portion. The sad thing is that the moment those girls were rescued, there were many more supplied to take their place. It's a battle that won't be won overnight or easily."

They all three sat for a moment lost in their own individual thoughts.

"Well, how are you two getting along? Is your partnership working out well?" asked Randy.

Both Carrie and Lainey smiled, then looked at each other.

"Yes, very well," they replied simultaneously, then laughed because they had.

Randy's eyebrow rose. "Well, okay then!"

Randy stood, and the women rose and went back to their desks. Carrie had had no time to really tell Lainey about Pride's letter and how she had responded. She felt shy about it and unsure of what to say. She would tell her — someday.

"This is Carrie," said Carrie as she answered the call on her cell phone.

"Carrie, this is Jenny." Her voice seemed tiny and distant.

Carrie's entire body tensed and went rigid, then she

stood up from the sheer need to move. "Jenny. Where are you?"

"I'm back here. I came to check on Pride. She wouldn't answer her phone. I can't find her Carrie."

"Where are you exactly Jenny and I'll come get you?"

"I'm sitting on Pride's front porch."

"Hold on. I'll be right there," said Carrie.

"Lainey I'll be right back. I have to go." Carrie grabbed her keys and ran out the door.

The need to get to Jenny quickly was born out of compassion. No one was out to hurt her now. She was safe. But Carrie acutely felt the pain that Jenny would quickly feel when she would soon break the news of Pride's death.

Carrie pulled up to the curb and as she was getting out of the car she whispered, "God please help me."

Jenny stood when she saw Carrie pull up. The closer Carrie got to Jenny, the deeper the frown grew on Jenny's face. Then Jenny suddenly gasped, "No!" Her trembling hands flew to her face, and the tears flowed.

Carrie reached out to take the young woman in her arms despite her tiny fists pounding on Carrie's chest. She would hold this girl until time ended if it would help her feel comfort.

Finally, Jenny went limp and Carrie had to react quickly to keep her from falling to the ground. She helped Jenny back to the porch step and sat beside her, holding her close.

"Jenny I am so sorry about Pride."

"Was it Gus? Did he kill her?"

Carrie thought briefly before answering. "She died of heart failure. Gus is dead, Vince too."

They sat there quietly for a long time just staring out at the street in front. The wind was picking up, and the trees rustled. An empty styrofoam cup tumbled down the street creating a hollow tune.

Has it only been a little over a week since I first stepped foot on this porch, Carrie thought?

Neither Carrie nor Jenny could seem to find words to say, but they took comfort in each other's presence.

Finally, Carrie said, "Pride wrote me a letter."

AUTHORS NOTE

My first novel, The Blood, was set in a completely factious town. With The Water I set the characters in downtown Oklahoma City. The landmarks, streets, businesses, are almost completely genuine. I have however taken creative license with certain aspects. I meant no disrespect to those places and I hope that they will view my creative license as neutral and having no bearing on them whatsoever.

If you would like to read Pride's letter to Carrie, go to The Water page and click the button 'Pride's Letter to Carrie'. You will need this password to access and read the letter. 7Pr89de1

The characters in this book are all completely fictional. The safe house, Safe At Last, is also completely fictional. There are however a few ministries who do offer this kind of service, this one was not patterned after any first hand knowledge of them. I created this from only my imagination of how it would be, were it would be, and how it would be run.

This is a heartbreaking and series problem worldwide. If you know of someone in need of rescue or a way out, please call one of the numbers below:

National Human Trafficking Hotline 888-373-7888

Beautiful Dream Society 405-717-1201

The Dragonfly Home Shelter 405-212-3378

Once again let me say that I have no operational knowledge of how the OKCPD or the OSBI are ran. I mean no disrespect to these outstanding agencies in my creative depiction of them and their officers. I hold law enforcement in the highest regard and I hope, should they read my books that they can laugh at my creative portrayal and not take it as disrespectful.

ABOUT THE AUTHOR

Nancy Jackson is a mother, grandmother, and great-grandmother, and lives in Edmond, Oklahoma.

When given various writing assignments in her seventh grade literature class, she discovered a love for writing. The praise of her teacher fueled her passion and she flourished.

Throughout her life, she worked in various positions where she was responsible for writing policy and procedure manuals, and a steady stream of corporate correspondence.

In 2003 she published Career Quest, a book on how to determine the best career for a person based on their true hearts desire, talents, and skills. Then, how to pursue that career from resume creation to offer acceptance. It also included how to establish a reputation of excellence from day one.

Her creative writing side was somewhat satisfied by writing at home. She later shared many of those various short stories on her blog. But she never stopped dreaming of the day when she would write her first novel.

Working in many different industries in a variety of

roles, she was exposed to a treasure trove of people, places, and things that would later serve her well as she wrote her first, and subsequent novels. She continues to write both non-fiction and short-story fiction which she posts on her two blogs.

Before publishing her first novel, she spent many years as a silver/metalsmith designing and making jewelry. As a metalsmith, she taught for several years where she developed teaching curriculums for each class.

She is also a licensed Realtor, in the state of Oklahoma. Her true passion though, is writing and she is thrilled that she is now able to pursue it with the passion she has always had.

Her first novel, The Blood is the first in The Redemption Series trilogy and is now available. The Water and The Fire are soon to follow.

If you would like to know more about Nancy's books, Nancy herself, and be the first to receive one of a kind short stories, and other musings, sign up for the Inside Track on her website www.NancyJacksonAuthor.com

If you enjoyed her book, please review on Goodreads.

You can also find her on Facebook, Instagram, and Twitter.

CPSIA information can be obtained
at www.ICGtesting.com
Printed in the USA
BVHW030613040419
544552BV00002B/2/P